SHANGHAI
STATION

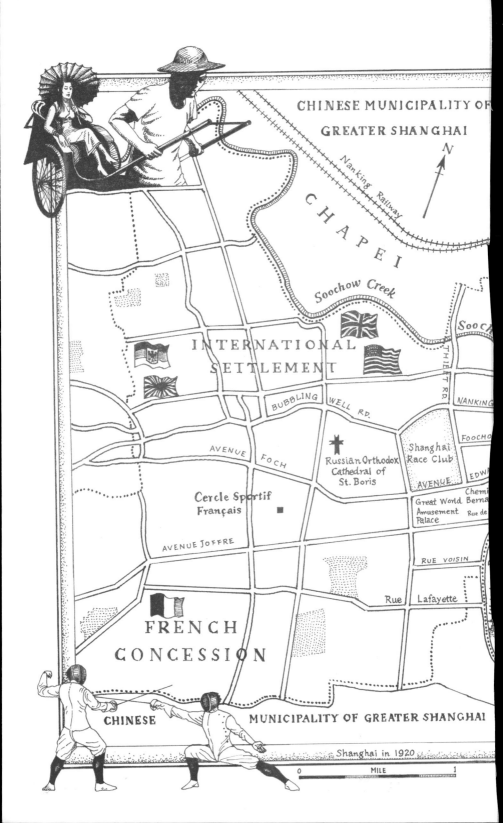

CHINESE MUNICIPALITY OF
GREATER SHANGHAI

N

CHAPEI

Nanking Railway

Soochow Creek

Soo...

INTERNATIONAL
SETTLEMENT

THIBET RD.

NANKING

BUBBLING WELL RD.

AVENUE FOCH

Russian Orthodox
Cathedral of
St. Boris

Shanghai
Race Club

FOOCHO

AVENUE

EDW

Cercle Sportif
Français

Great World
Amusement
Palace

Chemi
Berna
Rue de

AVENUE JOFFRE

RUE VOISIN

Rue Lafayette

FRENCH
CONCESSION

CHINESE   MUNICIPALITY OF GREATER SHANGHAI

Shanghai in 1920

0   MILE   1

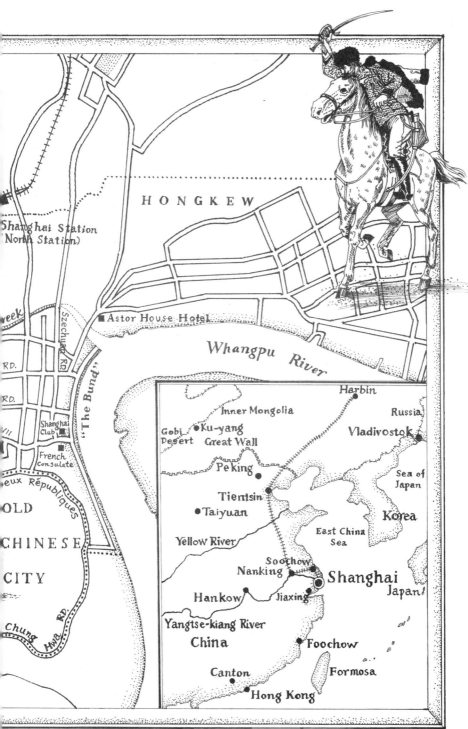

HONGKEW

Shanghai Station
(North Station)

Astor House Hotel

Szechuan Rd.

"The Bund"

Shanghai Club

French consulate

eux Républiques

OLD

CHINESE

CITY

Chung Hwa Rd.

Whangpu River

Harbin

Inner Mongolia

Russia

Gobi Desert   Ku-yang   Vladivostok
Great Wall

Peking   Sea of Japan

Tientsin

Taiyuan   Korea

Yellow River   East China Sea

Soochow

Nanking   Shanghai

Hankow   Jiaxing   Japan

Yangtse-kiang River

China   Foochow

Canton   Formosa

Hong Kong

Bartle Bull © 2003

ALSO BY BARTLE BULL

Safari: A Chronicle of Adventure
The White Rhino Hotel
A Café on the Nile
The Devil's Oasis

SHANGHAI STATION

BARTLE BULL

CARROLL & GRAF PUBLISHERS
NEW YORK

SHANGHAI STATION

Carroll & Graf Publishers
An Imprint of Avalon Publishing Group Inc.
245 West 17th Street, 11th Floor
New York, NY 10011

First Carroll & Graf edition 2004

Chapter illustrations and map by Pan Xing Lei

Library of Congress Cataloging-in-Publication Data is available.

ISBN: 0-7867-1314-3

Printed in the United States of America
Interior design by Jennifer Steffey
Distributed by Publishers Group West

For
Uncle Michael

Oxford University Fencing Club
1928

G. TOYNE
(Chorpus Christie)

MICHAEL BULL
(Magdalen)

J. W. OGILVIE *(Sec.)*
(Queen's)

H. R. H. PRINCE OLAV
(Balliol)

C. S. A. SIMEY
(Oriel)

—The Characters—

Mikhail Borodin *A Soviet agent, Lenin's man in China and the Russian adviser to Sun Yat-sen, the "father" of the Chinese Revolution of 1911.*

Billie Hudson *A young English businessman and horseman in Shanghai.*

Jessica James *The young daughter of United States missionaries resident in Shanghai.*

Chiang Kai-shek *The leader of the Kuomintang, the Nationalist Party of China.*

Alexander "Sasha" Karlov *A seventeen-year-old Russian military cadet in 1918, the son of Count Karlov.*

Count Dimitri Karlov *A horse breeder and a major in the 5th Hussars of the czar's army.*

Katerina "Katia" Karlov *The twin sister of Alexander Karlov.*

Pavel Krupotkin *The proprietor of the Casino Belle Aurore, a cousin of Countess Karlov.*

Hak Lee *Known as "Big Ear," the leader of the Green Gang, Shanghai's biggest tong or secret society.*

Lily *A sing-song girl from Madame Wong's brothel in Frenchtown, Shanghai.*

Vasily Petrov *A lieutenant in the 2nd Lancers of the czar's army.*

Viktor Polyak *A Russian commissar, a member of the Cheka (the Soviet secret police) and an agent of the Comintern (the Communist International).*

François Ricard *The eighteen-year-old son of Captain Ricard.*

Maurice Ricard *A police captain in Shanghai's French Concession.*

Ivan Semyonov *A Cossack hetman (chief) who flees to Shanghai when the Whites lose in Russia.*

Hideo Tanaka *The son of the Japanese Minister to Shanghai.*

Mei-lan Wong *The madam of an exclusive Shanghai bordello.*

Andrei Yeltsov *A Russian officer and rickshaw puller.*

-1-

Voskrenoye, Russia
September, 1918

"Don't look back." Alexander's mother gripped his shoulder with one hand. "It will never be the same."

But the boy could not resist. He turned around in the crowded open motorcar and gazed through the pale cloud of dispersed smoke that gusted across the cornfield along the rough dirt road. Somewhere out of sight, the farm buildings of the neighboring estate were on fire. The driver glanced at Alexander and shook his head and drove on.

Two dense columns of darker smoke rose far behind them. One must be their house, the flames spreading inwards from the porches and the summer room to consume the drawing rooms, the billiard room and the upper floors. The second plume must be rising from the stables that had been his home since infancy, where for five generations his family had bred black chargers for the Horse Guards of the czars.

Alexander feared that his own horse was trapped in a burning stall. He imagined Taiga sniffing and stamping as he smelled the smoke, then rearing and snorting and striking with his fore hooves at the wooden walls as flames flashed through the straw stacked inside the stable and his mane caught fire. Named for the dense wild forests that stretched across Russia from the Pacific to the Baltic, Taiga was one part Siberian mustang. Some mornings, when they were cantering across the new fields of the estate and the wind blew cold and ruffled Taiga's winter-thick mane and tail, Alexander could feel the steaming horse fill his chest and prepare to run without stopping until he reached the land of his sires.

Alexander was proud that his father often said he had an eye for horses. "Like your grandfather," the Count had remarked one afternoon when the two were studying the spring colts. "He could glance at one of these and see exactly how it would look as a two-year-old. He foresaw each new pound of bone and muscle."

"Misha!" Alexander screamed at the driver, horrified to imagine his horse being burned alive. "Stop. Please, *Maman*! Back to the stable!"

Alisa Karlov leaned forward and squeezed the shoulder of her seventeen-year-old son.

"We can't, Sasha," she said quietly, her green eyes large in her pale face. "It's too late. We escaped just in time."

His eyes filled. She was right.

Five days earlier, after a final drill on the parade ground and a last service in the chapel, his military academy near Kadnikov had closed its gates. The senior cadets and the training officers had already left to fight their countrymen, the Reds, after three years of preparing to fight the Germans and the Austrians. Wearing their czar's-green uniforms, they took with them all the school's flags and rifles and machine guns.

Though he was not Russian and was too old for war, Alexander's favorite instructor, the Italian fencing master Achille Angelo, had left with them. "I must see how well my boys have learned their lessons," he had said while Alexander helped the maestro pack his swords. Before leaving, Angelo had presented him with an old foil, a blade of the Italian school with a cross-bar behind the bell guard and a leather martingale to strap the weapon to the hand. "Please take my Pulotti," said the master. "You have earned it. Put it in this case." Thrilled, Alexander slipped the light weapon into a canvas bag with a leather handle. He wanted to go with the fencer but knew his father would expect him to rush home to look after Katerina and his mother.

Before leaving on service his father had always knelt on one knee and placed both hands on Alexander's shoulders and looked him hard in the eye. "Take care of your mother and Katia while I'm away," he would say. Alexander understood that when he was younger his father said this to make him feel like a big boy who should not cry at these departures, but this last time Alexander knew that he had meant it. Alexander was proud of the responsibility, but now he worried about his ability to honor it.

He had seen his father only three times in the last four years, on brief leaves between various wounds and battles and campaigns. The last time, leaning down from the saddle to embrace Alexander when he departed, his father had said, "Wherever I go, Sasha, you will be riding with me every day."

Over a year before, returning injured from the slaughter of the "meat-grinder" at Lublin in 1915, Dimitri Karlov had told his son how the Germans had massed artillery and machine guns to obliterate entire Russian divisions, regiment by regiment. Wounded early in the action, Count Karlov had watched his men and friends disappear into the exploding fields. Thousands of unarmed Slav peasants had waited in the rear to collect the boots and weapons of the fallen and to dig fresh graves and trenches. When their turn came, they had joined the Russian "chain," the formation of men who marched two yards apart into the chattering machine guns and charged with the bayonet if they made it within fifty yards from the enemy lines.

"The Germans use up metal the way we use up human life," his father had told him as he drank one night, recovering slowly from the horror. "What must our men think when we lead them into this?" In the end he had been sent four thousand miles east to Vladivostok just before the October Revolution in 1917. Alexander had not seen his father in the year since.

Only a pair of decorative cannon, captured from Bonaparte at Borodino, were left to guard the gates of the Academy. The younger boys and a few masters had scattered on their own and made for home as best they could. The old French teacher held open the dormitory door as the boys left. "*Bon courage, mes jeunes*," he had said with some affection. "*Sauve qui peut*," he whispered to their backs.

Alexander had been lucky. He had travelled home with little difficulty. He bought a mare from the stable master, passed one night at an inn and spent several sleeping in farm fields. He avoided other travellers and camped far from the dirt roads. Back home, nearly two hundred and fifty miles north of Moscow, at first it seemed that nothing had changed.

"Young master!" Misha had greeted him at the bottom of the front steps with a smile of relief. He was working on the oil gauge tubes on the dashboard of Count Karlov's favorite motorcar, a 1912 Panhard et Lavassor. The maroon coachwork shined like the feathers of a peacock.

"Is everyone all right?" said Alexander as he dropped his rucksack and sword case by the car.

"They have been waiting for you, sir," said Misha, adjusting a brass plunger on the dashboard.

"How is she running Misha?" Alexander asked as he ran up the steps.

"She should get us to the station."

Katerina, Alexander's twin, was in the studio packing up her paint box. He could hear his mother on her beloved Pleyel piano. Mozart, he thought. There was always music in the house. But as Katia ran to him across the entrance hall, Alexander noticed the packed bags, the shuttered windows, and his father's favorite English rifle leaning against the wall in its leather case. He stood near the broad hall stove and felt the warmth of the blue Dutch tiles. He hated to see the furniture in the reception rooms covered with sheets.

"Sasha!" cried his mother as she hugged him. "Thank God you are here. We are leaving on the Trans-Siberian to join your father." He heard the strain in her voice and flinched when she tousled his hair. "You must take off that filthy uniform." Then she stood back to look at him before continuing. "You've grown too tall for it anyway. Dress warmly and put on your winter boots. We must leave at once."

Alexander knew how his mother disliked leaving her house. Even in normal times, the season in St. Petersburg and summer weekends at elegant estates only made her long for her own comfortable household.

"Forgive me, Countess," Misha interrupted from the doorway. "Since the other motorcar was stolen last night, I must know what you wish to take. We cannot bring everything."

"I understand, Misha," his mother replied in her quiet tone, but with a crisp edge of urgency. "Just take my portmanteau and those two bags, please, and the icon and the gun case. We can pile things in the backseat and leave the top down."

Alexander saw his mother raise her chin and straighten her back as she looked around the hall, her eyes brimming. "Everything else we shall leave behind." Then she walked back and kissed the cook and a housemaid who stood crying by the pantry door.

"The new chamberlain and most of the staff have been slipping away one by one," she explained quickly to Alexander. He saw that the parquet floors no longer shone as they used to when several servants would pull felt pads on their feet and glide about like ice dancers as they buffed the patterned wood.

Katerina sobbed behind Alexander as they motored on. She sat close to her mother, both of them bundled in a wolf rug. "We'll never come back," Katia cried into the wind. "Will we?"

"*Golubka*," said her mother twice, taking her hand. "Little dove."

Alexander gripped the rifle case between his knees and stared ahead.

Misha used an old farm road to skirt the center of the first village. Their log walls patched with mud and moss, the two-room houses with their stone chimneys and single window were still the same. Inside, unwashed in their work clothes, with a dog and old sheepskins for added warmth, three generations slept together each night on and around the high brick stoves.

The remains of St. Vladimir's, the small Orthodox church, were still smoldering. It was the report of this fire that had induced Countess Karlov to prepare to flee at last. The bulbous cupola had collapsed, smashing its precious bright blue, green and red tiles, the gift of Alexander's grandfather. The illiterate old priest, with his long unclipped hair and tall felt hat, had disappeared one week earlier.

A knot of peasants stood in silence at the edge of the village and watched the big Panhard bump across the corrugated surface of the hardened mud. Alexander had known many of them for years. Often he had stopped to chat while on a ride, or had found one or two of the villagers in the overgrown abandoned orchard when he stood in his stirrups to pick a small tart apple from the saddle.

Today the village was unchanged, but the people were different.

For the first time in years, Alexander saw younger men among them, the *frontoviki*, back from the Austro-German war, hollow-eyed sullen survivors of the slaughter. The journey home, too, had made their faces old. Lying on the roofs of freight cars, crouching on the couplings, starving, they had struggled homeward in their *shineli*, their worn lice-filled greatcoats, and walked the last sixty miles back. Now they harbored more anger than respect. Round-shouldered and bearded, their tired lined faces impassive, the men leaned on wooden pitchforks and long-handled shovels and stared at the touring car. Their coarse padded jackets hung open in the autumn air. Several stocky women stood among them in thick dark robes, with long flowered head scarves knotted under their chins. One old man, standing behind the others, removed his cap as they passed. A large mongrel snarled and charged to the end of its chain.

Revolution, Alexander knew, was flashing here and there across the countryside. Some regions and estates still survived. Others had been taken by the Reds or had suffered peasant uprisings. The huge wall maps in the war room at the Academy, displaying the details of the bloody battles of Flanders and the Masurian Lakes, had been removed and rolled up and replaced. In recent months the maps had been of Mother Russia herself. One city after another had fallen to the Bolsheviks as fighting spread east from the Crimea across thousands of miles of the heartland, driving masses of refugees before it.

Suddenly a stone struck the top of the coachwork beside Alexander's mother. A tall gaunt youth shook his fist as the open car moved slowly past the village.

"Who did that?" yelled Alexander as the Countess wrapped her arm around Katerina. He drew the long-barrelled Holland from its case, turned swiftly to the side and raised the empty rifle to his shoulder.

Several villagers flinched and turned away. Two young men shouted curses as Misha hunched down and pressed the pedal. The Panhard rumbled past the ragged crowd.

Alexander returned the rifle to its case. He was filled with anger and loss, as if he were standing by an open grave, waiting for the body. He was certain that the life he knew was finished, that their country was no longer theirs, that never again would he find his way home.

Nestled in one corner of the sandbags that surrounded the machine gun, Alexander finally fell asleep to the clacking of the wheels of the Trans-Siberian. Three gunners sat nearby, their legs stretched out on the wooden floor of the open railroad car, their backs to the wind as they stared at the ever-narrowing tracks that disappeared to the West behind the train. They wore green service caps with a red band and loose *gimnastyorka*, the shirt-tunics that resembled pullover peasant blouses, closed at the top by small horn buttons set in a line off center. The men shared a smoke with cupped hands. Knapsacks and ammunition boxes and pistol belts were piled beside them. One soldier cut rough slices from a thick sausage and passed them to his mates on the tip of his bayonet.

At the back door of the next car, Alexander's sister pressed her nose against the small window. She knew how he liked to ride in the guard car with the soldiers.

Katerina's long dark hair, gathered in two pigtails, framed her face against the glass as she smiled and waved towards Alexander, but she was unable to see his head above the sandbags. Like Alexander's, Katia's right eye was a bit more blue, her left a shade more green. Her twin brother had always played at soldiering. She was certain he had their father's heavy English bear rifle straddled across his knees.

For days they had been running in an almost straight line through the endless taiga of Siberia. They were not travelling in the well-appointed blue cars of the Wagons-Lit, with a library and lounge, but their mother had made no complaint. She was content to have escaped with her children and to be hurrying east to rejoin her husband. It was not the first time a woman of her family had made this unpromising journey. A week had passed since the train had paused to take on coal and water at Zlatoust, the border village of the Boundary Post, the Monument of Tears that marked the entry to Siberia.

Descending from the train, Alexander had strolled along the track with Katerina and his mother. Misha followed with the lunch basket. Countess Karlov paused by the triangular marble monument and spoke in her quiet voice.

"Here the prisoners and exiles, hundreds of thousands of them, left European Russia behind." She rested one hand on a shoulder of each child. "It is here they finally lost all hope. Here they entered Siberia, a huge bleak prison, a place of Mongol tribes and snow and gold and murderers and bears." She hesitated, as if not wanting to say more. "Most never came home." Alexander knew she was thinking of her grandparents, Decembrists, members of an earlier aristocratic revolution, cruelly exiled in 1825 to a desolate frozen land three and a half thousand miles from their elegant life in St. Petersburg.

On one side of the dreaded tall white marker Alexander read the single word 'EUROPE.' On another, 'ASIA.'

His mother knelt beside the Monument of Tears and clasped her hands and closed her eyes. Katerina poked her brother and pointed at the cold rough ground. Both twins knelt behind their mother. Instead of praying, Alexander recalled how his mother shared her exiled grandparents' instinct for compassion and liberal advancement. Indulged by his father, the Countess had built a new schoolroom and a clinic for the peasants at Voskrenoye. Now, his knees aching, Alexander wondered what their own life would be like when the family joined his father in Vladivostok. Would it be a second exile?

After they rose, Katerina and Misha spread out the cloth by the edge of the forest. The four shared their last roast chicken and some hard cheese and wild currants. Still hungry, Alexander wished they had a few more *vareniki*, the sugared black-cherry dumplings they had eaten during the first two days on the train.

After lunch he strolled into the forest to relieve himself. He moved quietly through the hooded shadow of the birch and aspen as his father had taught him during their days of hunting. He remembered rising at dawn to shoot duck and Siberian geese, snipe and woodcock. He recalled the excitement of the weeklong hunting parties when his family's friends arrived in motorcars and coaches and sleighs to course bears and wolves with their borzois. Sometimes a young pig was tied to a stake to draw the wolves. Usually the guests' dogs and horses arrived several days earlier with their handlers and grooms. "Serf boys" would perch on the springs of the hunting carriages. Hares hung from the saddle of the whipper-in.

His father, oblivious to extravagance, always wished to live as Alexander's grandfather had half a century earlier, in the days before the czar freed the serfs, when the two thousand *dushi*, the two thousand souls, living in contained peace at Voskrenoye had been the measure of their family's wealth. In those days the long trip to St. Petersburg for the winter season was a cavalcade of carriages and wagons. Without proper roads, they would wait until the ice of the rivers thickened enough to support the coaches. Servants, pets, furniture, paintings, musical instruments, barrels of meats and vegetables, cases of fresh game and conserves would travel to the capital in a caravan that resembled a moving village. The children and their governess would be bundled into a *dormeuse*, their own six-horse sleeping coach. Months later, with the spring *déménagement*, the family would move back from town to country, the larder wagon heavy with fresh stores of tea, sugar, coffee, wine and candles, all the luxuries of St. Petersburg.

It was a costly life. One that even the estate and the stables could not support. Debt, too, was a part of the family history. A tradition that Alexander's father honored too well, the Countess often lamented. "You care more about your dogs than our debts, Dimitri," she had complained one evening. His father shrugged and doubled the backgammon cube. At least now, thought Alexander, their massive obligations would vanish with their privileges.

In the woods Alexander scrambled over the thick overlays of fallen trees that made the taiga virtually impenetrable. Standing in the deep absorbing silence of the forest, there seemed to be no other world. A wind rose and caught him among the trees. It felt almost solid, dense like a block of ice. He knew the Siberians feared the winter wind more than the snow or the cold. "When the last leaf is blown down," a gamekeeper once told him, "your father's forest belongs to the wolves."

Alexander raised his collar and turned back. As he picked his way through the deadfall, something pale drew his eye to the ground. He rested his hand against the trunk of a tall larch and peered down through the tangle of deciduous branches, some living, many dead.

He saw the bones of a human foot, and a leg, and more, doubtless frozen the previous winter and picked clean by the wolves and forest birds. Transfixed, staring down, he discerned more and more of the scattered remains. Retching violently, Alexander vomited and spat, then wiped his mouth before rushing from the forest. He hesitated before telling his mother what he had seen.

"Yes, Sasha," she had said gently, touching his white cheek with one hand, pausing, not wishing his sister to hear. "They call the bodies 'snowdrops.' The corpses of fleeing convicts, frozen in the winter. They appear in the spring when the snow melts, like the little yellow flowers they're named after."

That night Alexander thought about those bones as he stretched out on a bench near one end of the railcar. He listened to an elderly couple on the next seat whisper about their lost life and their dread of the flight and poverty that lay ahead. Finally the two pulled a topcoat over each other and huddled together in sleep like a single figure.

Alexander reached up to his jacket, which hung from a hook beside the window. He took out the German pocketknife that his father had given him the last Christmas he was home, three years ago. He opened and shut the knife again and again while he listened to the rattle of the train and wondered what his family's new life would be. Perhaps he would have a chance at last to serve at his father's side, to ride and fight like his older schoolmates, to draw his sword for the czar and Russia and their families. Katia had told him that his mother had already spoken of other families and friends fleeing to wait out the civil war, some to Paris and Warsaw and Stockholm, others journeying as far as Constantinople and Shanghai in China.

A different sound startled him. Someone was moving at the other end of the car. Alexander stared and made out a bundled figure that stood and stretched, then slowly moved down the aisle towards him. The man paused and leaned over a sleeping neighbor. He lifted a bottle and tilted back his head. He moved closer, bent for a time over another traveller, then did something Alexander could not see. In the middle of the car, he reached over to a coat that hung between two windows. He appeared to be searching the pockets. A thief? Watching, Alexander moved his eyes but not his head.

The man stopped in the aisle beside Alexander's seat.

For a long moment he stared down at the boy who lay in his shadow. Then he edged closer and slipped a hand into a pocket of Alexander's hanging jacket.

In one motion Alexander leaned forward and struck upward with his knife. The thin blade cut through the heavy cloth of the man's coat and pricked his side. As he had been taught in bayonet drill, Alexander immediately twisted the blade and pulled it out, then prepared for a second stab.

The thief jerked backward with a startled gasp, barely heard above the rattle of the train. Then he pressed one hand to his side. For a moment he stood and squinted silently at the boy.

A touch of light caught the edge of the blade when Alexander held it up between them. The man's grey hair stood out against the moonlight like a silver helmet.

"*Suka!*" the man hissed. "Bitch!"

The man swung the bottle and struck the hand that held the knife. Trained as a fencer never to lose his grip, Alexander accepted the pain and kept the small knife in hand. As the thief raised the bottle for a second blow, Alexander spoke in a louder voice.

"Shall I wake the others and tell them what you've been doing?"

Then Alexander stood up, the blade still between them. He did not want to have to alarm his mother and sister.

The man spat on the floor, turned and walked quietly down the car.

The next morning the train slowed as it approached one of the curves that wound around the mountains. Suddenly it scraped to a halt, so fast that Katerina, standing, fell onto her backside. A window shattered. She heard her mother cry out, "Katia!" Shots tore through the thin wooden sides of the passenger car.

In the guard car, Alexander rolled across the floor. Gunners cursed and returned the fire. He heard the slap of bullets punching into the sandbags. Gripping his father's Holland, he peered between two bags towards the front of the train. The long prow of the black locomotive was buried in a jumble of logs and tree trunks and brush that was strewn across the tracks. Steam clouded up around the tall driving wheels. Dark smoke from the locomotive blew back along the train.

"*Bolsheviki!* " shouted one of the gunners. "Red Guards!"

Alexander saw an engineer leap down from the coal car. The small man dropped his shovel and raised both arms in surrender. Alexander was just noticing the engineer's black hands when the man's head was nearly severed by the bullets that cut him down.

All along the six-car train Alexander saw glass shatter and splinters rip from the wooden cars as bullets struck. He looked toward the next car and prayed that his mother and Katia were safe. Alexander considered running to the passenger car but decided he could help more where he was. After all his training, he must be a soldier.

Passengers shot pistols through broken windows and soldiers returned fire from between the cars. Uneven lines of attackers swarmed from the woods on either side of the train. Several horsemen riding among them urged on the roughly dressed Reds. All the riders but one were wearing scraps of uniform. Alexander saw the commander of the train shoot a mounted Red with his revolver, then use his sword against another boarding the locomotive.

Alexander slapped the bolt forward and pressed a long .375 into the chamber of his father's rifle. He knew the heavy bullet would stop any man.

The soldier nearest to Alexander, a youth little older than himself, struggled forward on his knees with an ammunition box and prepared to feed the machine gun that was firing long bursts.

"Always shoot the officers first," Alexander's instructor had said. Alexander led one horseman with the open sight of the long-barrelled hunting rifle. He squeezed the trigger as the horse wheeled. The rifle punched into his shoulder. Shot in the head, the horse collapsed on its side. Its legs kicked and twitched.

Disappointed he had hit the animal, Alexander ejected and reloaded. He saw the rider free himself from the fallen horse. The burly man wore a heavy coat with a red band around one sleeve. It was the horseman with no uniform. For an instant Alexander thought he saw the man staring at him through the smoke. Holding his pistol before him, the big Red ran towards the train.

Suddenly the young soldier next to Alexander put both hands to his neck and collapsed onto his back. Blood gushed from his throat.

"Boy!" the two gunners yelled at Alexander. "Ammunition! Ammunition!" Instinctively, recalling his training in the machine-gun pits, Alexander used a bayonet to pry the wooden lid off the ammunition box. He fed the ammunition into the side of the trembling Mauser as the gunners fired through the smoke.

He looked back at the nearest passenger car. Red soldiers were climbing aboard at both ends. He must defend his mother and his sister. He recalled his father's favorite military advice: *Ura!* Attack! Charge! Alexander grabbed a pistol belt and, standing up, slipped in blood before he jumped down and ran along the track through the smoke.

The car was a chaos of fighting and gunfire. He saw Katerina struggling with a Red who had seized her by both arms. Alexander rushed towards her, but the narrow aisle was blocked with baggage and fighting men. He saw one passenger, a jeweller who had befriended them on the trip, empty a small pistol at a Bolshevik before another stabbed him in the back with a bayonet.

Alexander heard his mother scream.

Misha, defending her, was grappling with a big man in a ragged tweed coat with a red band around one sleeve: the horseman. The Red had thick wild brown hair and a square craggy bronzed face. The man's revolver misfired and he slammed the old servant across the side of the head with the heavy weapon. Alexander heard the crack of metal on bone. Misha collapsed. Blood ran from his ear and cheekbone. Alexander clambered over three benches in his desperation to reach his mother. "I'm coming, Maman!" he yelled. With shaking hands he began to unholster his pistol.

His mother's assailant, ignoring the appeal of the Red wounded twice by the jeweller, turned to face Alexander. Pink bubbles on his lips, lung-shot, the wounded Bolshevik fell against a window. "Help me, Commissar!" the man gargled. "Viktor! Comrade Polyak!" When he fell, his blood smeared the window in a rosy arc like sunset striking the glass.

As Alexander raised his pistol, the Commissar knocked him down with a single backhanded blow to his neck. Alexander felt he had been struck with an iron bar. In his fall his head banged against a bench. Dazed, his weapon lost, he came slowly to his feet. Fighting continued in the car behind him.

The burly man held Alexander's mother by her wrist while he tried to rip her rings from her fingers. "How dare you!" she cried, and then, seeing her son, "Alexander!" Her dress tore open as she resisted the Red. No longer hidden, her long pearl necklace hung between her pale breasts. Alexander had never seen his mother so revealed. He knew what his father would expect of him.

In a rage Alexander grabbed the Commissar from behind. He hooked his arm around the man's thick neck and fought to drag him back. They collapsed together in the small space between two benches, the man's back against the wall. Dimly Alexander was aware of a tobacco pipe falling from the Red's pocket and breaking as they fought.

Tall, the same height as Alexander but far stronger, the man rose, lifting Alexander with him while the boy hung on desperately. The man turned in his grasp and freed himself. Alexander's left leg became wedged between a bench and the corner wall of the train. The Commissar punched Alexander twice in the face. "*Svinya!* Little swine!" the man grunted. Groggy with pain, his face cut and his nose running blood, the boy heard his mother cry out once more.

"Help me!"

Alexander tried to grab the big man by the throat, but the Red swept his arms apart and seized Alexander's head between his hands. Helpless to stop him, Alexander felt his neck about to snap as the man twisted his head to one side, then, leaning over him, forced his body down and back into the aisle. His left leg remained jammed against the wall. He heard a bone crack in his leg as the big man fell on top of him in the struggle. Screaming with pain, Alexander drove his fingers into the Commissar's neck. The Red lifted his empty pistol from the floor and clubbed the boy violently across the temple.

Stunned, Alexander heard his mother cry his name.

"Sasha!"

Still dizzy from the blow, Alexander saw another man drag his sister down the aisle towards the door at the end of the car. Katerina reached out, her fingers bent like claws. She grabbed the edge of the bench beside Alexander with both hands. A bullet shattered the window by her side. Then a fusillade of heavy gunfire exploded outside the train.

For a moment Katerina held her grip while the Red pulled her around the waist. Alexander could not reach the man but managed to seize his sister's wrists. The Bolshevik jerked violently and Katerina lost her hold. Her hands slipped through Alexander's. Her clutching fingernails cut his palms. She screamed and disappeared from the car.

"Katia!" yelled Alexander.

He twisted his body to look behind him. Fierce pain tore through him from his leg. Through the shattered window he saw Katerina still resisting as she was thrown over the shoulders of a horse. The rider grabbed her collar and the animal plunged into the woods.

The Commissar was holding his mother by her hair with one hand and was grabbing for her pearl necklace with the other. Her face was scarlet. A vein pulsed in her forehead.

Furious with helplessness, Alexander struggled to release his broken leg. He sensed a bone coming apart in his limb as he wrenched himself free. When he tried to rise on his right leg, he realized the other limb was useless, suddenly more of a burden than a strength. He had never imagined such pain.

Alexander saw his mother draw a knife from her attacker's belt and with feeble blows attempt to stab him through his heavy coat. The Commissar cursed and wrenched back his mother's head with one rough motion.

Alexander heard her neck snap like a branch breaking in the forest. Suddenly she was still. Her body slumped and the Red dropped it to the floor facedown between two benches.

At first Alexander could not absorb or accept what had happened. His mother could not be dead. "Maman!" he cried.

He stretched out and grabbed the edge of the Commissar's coat and fought to pull the man towards him. Oblivious to Alexander, the Red stuffed the pearls into an inside pocket.

Then the Commissar turned and lifted Alexander by his lapels. He swung him violently from side to side while the boy yelled with fury and pain. Their cheeks slapped together for an instant when Alexander's head swung forward. He felt the scratch of the man's beard and smelled the stink of old tobacco. The man smashed Alexander's head against the wall between two windows and flung his unconscious body to the floor.

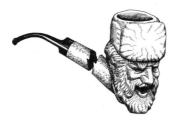

-3-

When Alexander woke up, he was lying on the floor of a freight or baggage car. The doors were open on both sides. He tried to move but his left leg was paralyzed by pain. Straw covered the boards beneath him. He smelled the familiar odor of horses and ordure over the cool sharpness of the forest air. Smoke gusted past the open doors. Bits of tethering rope hung from nails along one side of the car. Wounded men lay nearby, groaning, muttering and crying out with pain. He turned his head and saw others sitting up against the wall. They were bleeding and waiting for attention. One was a gunner from the guard car. Some wore the tunics and trousers of a Lancer regiment that earlier had not been on the train.

Misha sat motionless amidst them, his face white, both eyes staring. There was a large black patch of dried blood under the chauffeur's ear where the Commissar had struck him. Misha's boots were missing. Alexander was about to call out to him when he realized that Misha was dead. Then he felt several men seize him as he closed his eyes and tried not to scream.

"Hold him still, damn you." The voice cut through Alexander's haze of pain. He cried out when someone pulled his trousers down around the ankles of his boots. From the hip down, his left leg felt as if it were smoldering like coals at the edge of a fire. He tried to look at his leg but the men were in the way. He could see only his bunched-up filthy trousers gathered above his boots.

"It's bent, broken just above the knee," said the soldier who knelt on his shoulders. "You can see the sharp bone pointing there under the skin, like a tent pole. Are you going to have to pull it straight to set it?"

"Of course," said the other man with impatience. He gripped Alexander's left ankle and pressed down on the boy's hip with his free hand. "Get me two scabbards to use as splints, and be quick about it. He's not the only one."

Determined to ignore the cruel rocking of the train, Alexander bit his lower lip until it bled. He closed his eyes and wept. As if in a dream he saw Katia being thrown onto a horse and heard the sound of his mother's neck cracking. He could still feel the vise of the Commissar's hands squeezing his head as the Red sought to break Alexander's own neck.

"Open your mouth," said the man kneeling on his shoulders while he reached for Alexander's belt. He put the end of the worn leather between Alexander's teeth. "Bite this. You'll need it."

"Here's what he needs," said a man with an educated voice. Alexander opened his eyes as the young officer removed the belt. "Drink this, boy." He poured vodka into Alexander's mouth as the injured youth stared at him. "I'm Vasily Petrov, Second Lancers." Alexander gulped and spat and gasped. The lieutenant filled his mouth twice again. The raw rough spirit ran down his cheeks and chin. "Now be still."

Alexander nodded and wiped his face with one hand and put the belt back in his mouth. Lieutenant Petrov smiled at him, then knelt on Alexander's right arm and hip and pressed down hard on his left hip with both hands.

"Hold him!" said the man who seemed to be a doctor. He cut several lengths of rope from the wall. Petrov and two soldiers held Alexander firmly against the rocking floor. The doctor took Alexander's left knee in one hand and his boot in the other. Then, pulling hard, he extended his leg once, twice, and ended with a slight jiggling motion. Almost unconscious with pain, Alexander buried his teeth in the belt.

"Trick is to lock the bone edge to edge without breaking the skin. Gives him a better chance against infection. Just have to pray it's a clean break without any chips or fragments." The doctor grunted and gently set down the boot. "Hope that knee's not gone, too." He wrapped an old shirt about the injured limb. Then he bound two metal scabbards against the leg with the belt and bits of rope. "Best we can do for now," he said.

Two weeks later, Vladivostok welcomed them with an arctic wind that blasted along the crowded railroad platform.

"Don't expect your father at the station," said Lieutenant Petrov in a kindly voice when he saw Alexander peering out the window. "No one here knows when these trains will be arriving. We'll have to find out where his regiment is camped."

Alexander guessed his father had been fairly fortunate in the German war. Although he had seen too many men lost, he had missed the slaughters of the Masurian Lakes and the Kerensky summer offensive. And he had done what he would have wished: led his men in the last cavalry-on-cavalry battle of the war, charging boot-to-boot against the Austro-Hungarians. Alexander wondered how it had gone for him thereafter in the civil war so far. There seemed to be less honor in killing one's own countrymen, even for the czar.

A pair of old crutches leaned against the seat beside Alexander. Useful but too short, they had belonged to an elderly man found slouched dead on his bench after the attack. Alexander stood and leaned on the crutches. His canvas foil case hung from his shoulder on a cord. His knee and upper leg felt hot and tight inside the splints, as if they were growing inside the wrapping that bound them to the scabbards. The constant shaking of the train had sawed at his knee throughout the trip. Each spasm brought back the agony of his mother's death and his sister's abduction.

Alexander hobbled after Lieutenant Petrov toward the end of the car. The officer had befriended him during the long ride across Siberia. Each day he had seen that the boy received the best food and care available. During the trip, one Lancer told Alexander that Petrov's first regiment had been annihilated in the German war. Wounded himself, Vasily Petrov had carried his dying elder brother across a muddy field of fallen Russians, searching unsuccessfully for a medical wagon. Now the last son of a family of minor country aristocracy, he was known for taking unusually good care of his men, and for his balalaika.

Feeling shaky, Alexander leaned on his crutches and raised his collar while he watched Petrov's men assemble reasonably smartly on the platform. Each man had his shinel rolled up and wrapped around his left shoulder like a horseshoe, with his spare boots and cowl inside the greatcoat, and its ends tucked into the mess tin on his right hip. Petrov gave an order and the men eagerly unrolled their coats and pulled them on.

Alexander followed the Lancers slowly as they marched along the platform in loose double columns. Built to be the imperial terminus of the world's longest railroad, the station was unfinished. Part of the steel structure of a great enclosed hangar was framed overhead, still open to the sky. Unfinished walls of red brick rose unevenly along its sides.

Soldiers were everywhere, many in uniforms that Alexander had never seen, even in the regimental picture plates at the Academy. The only common marking was a stripe of white over green, sometimes on armbands, but most soldiers wore the colors as chevrons or patches on their fleece hats or caps. Some were Buryats, short dark-faced hunters from the taiga, with shabby astrakhan hats and bandoliers of five-bullet ammunition clips crossing their chests. Reminded of the burly Commissar on the train, Alexander wished these men would kill every Bolshevik in Russia.

"The New Siberian Army," commented Petrov. "Those colors represent snow over the forests. The chaps with the badge of a sword over a crown of thorns were on the Ice March to Lake Baikal last winter, poor devils. Most of them left their toes behind."

Porters with dark flat Mongol faces stepped back as Petrov's Lancers passed. Broad leather luggage straps hung from their shoulders. Women in wool kerchiefs held out baskets of hard-boiled eggs and small green apples and loaves of black bread. One woman was assisted by what looked to be her daughter. The girl wore bulky straw shoes with cloth wrappings. Her pigtails made Alexander think of Katia.

They paused near a group of soldiers who bore over their shoulders heavy knapsacks topped by rolled blankets. The men had khaki caps with white and red ribbons stitched diagonally across their visors.

"The Czech Legion," said the lieutenant. One officer carried a "German broomhandle," a Mauser pistol with a large wooden holster.

"Bohemians, captured in the West," added Petrov. "Then rearmed and brought out here to guard the railroad. Sixty thousand lost souls. Poor devils don't even know where they are. Strung out along the line all the way here from Lake Baikal."

Petrov stopped for a moment to let Alexander rest near a brass plate commemorating the start of work on the railroad. "Here's where the Czarevitch laid the first stone in 1891," he said.

"Master Alexander?" called a deep voice. "What has happened to your leg?"

Alexander turned to see Gregori, his father's orderly of many years. The old soldier smiled and shook his hand. "Your father's been sending me to the station every day to watch for you all."

Alexander had never seen the small trim man so thin and tired, nor imagined him in a uniform so torn and filthy. The lines in his narrow face were deep as the corrugations on the road at home. He recalled Gregori assisting at Voskrenoye, cheerfully waiting to lead away the horses of their guests. He would stand near Alexander's mother on the steps by the circular drive bordered with lilac bushes. Now Gregori seemed a different man.

"How is my father?" said Alexander.

"The Major is well, sir," said Gregori. "Where are the Countess and your sister?"

Alexander hesitated. A wave of fever and sadness overcame him, his manliness lost for the moment. And he still had to face his father.

"We had trouble on the train," said Petrov at once. He handed Gregori the Holland & Holland in its leather case. "I will explain things to Major Karlov."

"Yes, Lieutenant," Gregori said doubtfully. He clicked his boot heels and saluted. "If you'll wait outside, sir, I will fetch a horse cart."

Alexander and Petrov walked to the rough sidewalk in front of the station. To one side Alexander saw rows of one-story log buildings with small shuttered windows and steep roofs. To the other, at some distance, extended a street of three-story stone and brick structures. Coal and wood smoke rose everywhere, joining to form a dark shroud over the city beneath the low grey clouds. Could this be Vladivostok?

Glancing down the dirt-packed nearly-empty street before him, Alexander abandoned another of the schoolboy assumptions that had supported his belief that he and his family were secure and privileged parts of a powerful and noble empire. Schooled to consider Vladivostok as the czar's citadel in the East, as the city that made Russia a two-ocean empire with a great port on the Pacific looking towards Japan, Southeast Asia and the Americas, Alexander instead saw muddy destitution.

Nearby, groups of soldiers clustered around open fires. Some men had sacking wrapped around their feet instead of boots. Others stood stamping their feet and wore scraps of bags sewn together in place of uniforms. Many had shoes that seemed to be made from the bark of trees. As if feeling Alexander's inspection, one man looked up and squinted as he caught the boy's eye. After a moment, the soldier looked down and shuffled closer to a low fire, apparently deciding that begging from a young cripple would yield nothing.

Alexander moved away, leaning on his crutches, his back against the station wall. He knew he was not well. He felt thirstier than he had ever been, hot with fever. How, he had worried for the past week, would his father react to his wife's murder? To his daughter's kidnapping? To learning that his son was crippled?

Lieutenant Petrov interrupted Alexander's thoughts.

"I have been saving something for you that I believe belonged to your mother." Vasily Petrov wore a greatcoat gathered at the back with a half-belt and two metal buttons. He reached into a pocket, then opened his hand. "We found these under her seat. Lord knows what happened to the rest. I'll give her wedding ring to your father."

"Thank you." Alexander took the four pearls from the lieutenant's hand. He knew how his mother had loved her pearls. They had been in her family longer than anything else she owned. As he rubbed each one between his fingers, he remembered how she had enjoyed their luster. He tried to feel her warmth when he touched them. He would save them for Katia.

Alexander turned away from Petrov and swung on his crutches to the edge of the station wall. Standing with his back to the trains, he began to cry as he had not before. He thought first of his mother, then of Katerina. Their mother once had told them something he would never forget. It was the human condition to be alone, she said, but twins were the exception. Twins were never alone, even when separated. Alexander thought of the years when early every evening Katerina and he had sat naked at opposite ends of a copper tub of warm water in the sunroom and shared the soap and sail boats and wooden swans in the bath while their *nanya* warmed towels on the large stove in the corner. Sometimes Katia had sneaked across the hall at night and climbed into his bed.

He slipped the pearls into one jacket pocket, then, jolted by a dark thought, reached into the other. His fingers found the bowl of a pipe, then the broken stem. He remembered the pipe falling from the Commissar's pocket and breaking during the struggle. Afterwards he had found it as he lay stretched out on the bench in the train. He examined the pieces again. The bowl was carved from some pale wood, in the form of a face or head. He sniffed the pipe and noticed the stale smell of very sweet tobacco. Seeing Gregori arriving with the horse cart, Alexander put the fragments of the pipe back into his pocket .

His belly tightened when the cart approached the first of the long brick barracks on the edge of town. What was he going he tell his father? That their house and family were gone, that he had been helpless as a child to intervene? That he had done his best but failed?

The smells of woodsmoke and horses greeted them when Gregori led them into the busy courtyard of the barracks. A row of horse-drawn ambulances was lined up along one side. Pink waste flowed from one wagon that a soldier was flushing out with buckets of water. Other men forked hay to lines of shaggy horses picketed at two long rails. Firewood was stacked along the sides of every wall. Sheets of old newspapers covered the insides of the small windows. Winter was never far from Vladivostok. Alexander was astonished to see a flag of the United States of America flying in one corner of the yard. Beside it flew a blue pennant bearing the designation, "31ST REGIMENT, U.S.M.C."

Gregori opened a door near one corner of the courtyard. He stood aside as Petrov and Alexander approached.

The lieutenant entered first, clicked his heels and saluted. Eager to see his father but dreading what he must report, Alexander hung on his crutches in the doorway. The last weeks had never felt so real and terrible as now.

A tall lean man with broad shoulders and a high bridged nose turned from a chipped mirror. A vivid rope-like scar ran down the right side of his back. A black bear skin was nailed to the wall between the mirror and the curved horns of an ibex. The massive uneven antlers of an elk reached out from the opposing wall. Worn wolf rugs were scattered about the floor. A battered tin samovar stood steaming in the corner with a big teapot set on top of it. Large lumps of coarse tan sugar rested on a nearby plate.

The tall man's face was half covered in shaving soap. He held a towel in one hand and a straight razor in the other. His blue eyes, set deeply in dark circles above his knobby cheekbones, were sunken above the white lather like those of a snow owl caught in a winter storm. The Count wore the patched black breeches of the 5th Hussars. A once-white stripe ran down the outside of each leg. He seemed thinner than Alexander remembered, less substantial, though still perfectly erect and hard with muscle.

"Alexander!" Dimitri Karlov cried. He stared at his son as each of them examined the changes in the other. Then Karlov dropped his razor on a table beside two empty vodka bottles. He tossed the towel over one shoulder and strode to his son.

"Sasha!" He took Alexander's head in both hands and kissed the boy on each cheek. Careful of the crutches, he wrapped his arms around his son's shoulders and hugged him.

It was the warmest greeting Alexander could remember. But he was not able to speak in reply. He could not tell his father what had occurred.

"What has happened to you, boy? Are your mother and sister outside?" Count Karlov stepped towards the door, then drew back and looked at his son, one hand on each of his shoulders. "Where . . ."

Alexander's eyes filled. He was overwhelmed by the affection, and by the horror that he knew his father sensed. The image of his mother struggling in the railroad car, her breasts exposed, flashed in his mind like an illuminated nightmare. It was something that only his father should have seen. He tried to suppress the memory. He did not want to hear again the snapping of her neck, or to revisit the desolation of her sudden silence.

"Major," said Petrov, "allow me to explain." He stepped towards Karlov. "My regiment, or what's left of it, was on the train following closely after your family's. We found their train under attack. We drove off the Red Guards after a hard fight along the tracks. There was a Communist political officer with them, what the bastards call a *komissar*. He had the commanding officer of the train, half dead already, flung into the furnace of the locomotive."

"Do you know the name of this *chyort*, this devil?" asked Karlov with a strain, aware that terrible news must be coming.

"One of our prisoners told me the Commissar is called Polyak, Viktor Polyak. Says he's one of the devils charged with destroying all their enemies left behind the lines as the Reds advance. A real butcher."

The Count nodded impatiently. "Where are my wife and daughter?"

Alexander heard the desperate self-control in his father's voice. For a moment he did not feel the pain in his own leg.

"Polyak killed your wife, sir, broke her neck fighting for her jewelry." Vasily Petrov handed Karlov a gold ring. "I gave your son four of her pearls we found on the floor of the train."

Alexander reached into a pocket. "No, Sasha," said his father, holding up a hand. "Keep them for your sister."

Petrov continued in a quiet voice. He spoke slowly, giving the Major time. "And Polyak's men took your daughter when they fled."

Count Karlov turned away. He leaned both hands against the rough brick wall and lowered his head.

Believing it was his fault, not able to forgive himself, feeling guilty for surviving, Alexander stared at his father's trembling shoulders. He took a step forward on his crutches and placed one hand on his father's back.

After a moment Count Karlov wiped his face with the towel, then turned and faced Petrov. He gripped Alexander's shoulder with one hand before he spoke.

"Where did you bury my wife?"

"Near a peasant village by the tracks, sir. With a cross, well covered with stones. The others were not taken care of so well." He uncapped a pocket flask and held it out to Karlov. The Count shook his head. Petrov continued.

"We did our best, Major, but we were pressed." Petrov hesitated. "There was no time for coffins. My orders were to keep the track open, sir, and it became more difficult every day."

The Count nodded and squeezed Alexander's shoulder with hard fingers.

Alexander said nothing. He did not want his father to learn the rest. He remembered Petrov ordering his men to strip the bodies of their boots and coats, to bury them all, including his mother, wearing only their underclothes. "Otherwise the peasants will dig them up after we leave," the lieutenant had explained. "Then the village dogs will have them."

-4-

"You're next, Sasha," said his father the following morning. They stood with Gregori near the gangway on the deck of the *Sherman*, a four-masted American troop transport. Booms unloading cargo swung out from the masts. Despite his low spirits, Alexander was excited by the salty air and his first sight of the sea. He admired the heavy gun turrets of the cruiser *Carlisle* moored nearby. She was flying the British flag.

"These Americans have the finest doctors in Siberia," added his father, "and they tell me this ship is the best place to get looked after. We'll see they fix you up."

But Alexander doubted he would ever walk and run like other boys. He feared his father was too hopeful. Perhaps he should not have tried so hard to conceal the pain.

He stared down at an American machine-gun company reoutfitting on the wharf below. Mounted on wheels, each heavy water-cooled gun and each caisson was drawn by a mule and attended by a team of six soldiers in tight gaiters, well-cut uniforms, fur caps and gloves. Cases of what he guessed was ammunition were strapped on small flatcars on the railhead nearby. Other crates of supplies were stacked down the great quay as far as he could see, most of them under heavy canvas that flapped in the cold wind. Two-man patrols in blue French uniforms paced about the dock guarding the supplies.

"Bring in your son, Major Karlov," said an American medical officer as he stepped out on deck. He inspected his hands in the daylight, then dried them on an apron. "We've converted the wardroom to a surgery while we're here. With nine thousand Yanks ashore, there's always somebody who needs patching up."

The three Russians followed the American inside.

"We've brought a small present for your ship's officers from the people of Muscovy." The Count smiled and gestured towards Gregori. The orderly bowed, then unknotted and spread out a cloth containing jars of black caviar and six bottles of Abrau-Durso. "Hope you enjoy our Crimean champagne."

"Thank you, Major." The medical officer put the bottles into a cabinet. "The United States Navy forbids alcohol on board, but of course these belong in our medical stores."

The long dining table was covered in fresh white sheets. Alexander was directed to sit down on the edge of the table. He had forgotten things could be so clean. It reminded him of home, with the laundresses pegging up the linen sheets to dry flapping in the sun.

The men helped Alexander to raise his legs and recline. He tightened his lips while his father and Gregori removed his boots and cut away his trousers. He tried to avoid looking at the medical tools in the open cases on the side table. The doctor raised a needle while an assistant placed a chloroform pad over his mouth and nose. He had an alarming sense of losing control.

"This is not my specialty, Major, but we'll do our damned best to save it," was the last that Alexander heard until he awoke several hours later.

That evening, still groggy from the operation, Alexander sat with his left leg raised and set in a heavy plaster cast around his knee. The leg felt numb when he was still, painful when he moved. His father's room at the barracks was warm from the fire and thick with tobacco smoke. Alexander's crutches leaned against a rifle rack beside a balailaka and his father's violin case.

At first Alexander was not hungry, but as he watched a bald red-bearded Cossack officer fussing with a stewpot, the smell of simmering onions gave him appetite. "Impossible without bacon fat and sour cream," the big man grumbled. He wore breeches with the scarlet side stripe of the Kuban cavalry.

Spoiling him, Gregori handed Alexander a plate of the potatoes and onions and bits of some greasy tinned meat. Kidneys, Alexander guessed by the tubes in the sticky spongy pieces. A little sour cream would help, he thought.

Then Gregori went to the samovar to get the boy a glass of tea. Finding the water cool and the charcoal barely glowing, Gregori took a boot that leaned against the wall. He lowered the tall wrinkled boot upside down over the central heating chamber of the samovar and pumped it up and down like a bellows. The fire flared. "An old cavalry trick," Gregori explained to Alexander as he served the tea.

Alexander ate quickly while listening to the officers talk. He loved sharing the hunting-lodge feeling of the room, the animal pelts and antlers, the smoky soldierly conversation. He no longer felt apart. Every man in the crowded room appeared to have been wounded. His training and his injury made him one of them. He knew his father was proud that Alexander had helped serve the machine gun and had fired the Holland on the train. "You did well, Sasha. They tell me you shot like a Karlov." The previous week the Count himself, skirmishing with the Reds near Novitskaya, had been grazed by a bullet.

"Another month like this, and we won't know who to kill," said the big Cossack officer. Wearing only his baggy breeches and high soft leather boots, the red-bearded hetman was now bathing his scarred hairy torso with a sponge from a bucket. Ivan Semyonov's left arm looked powerful enough to Alexander, but his right arm and shoulder, after a lifetime of deadly sabre work and drill, seemed fit for a giant twice his size. The hetman's thick drooping mustache was stained tobacco yellow. He dropped the sponge into the bucket and splashed vodka into a cup before continuing.

"Seventy thousand Japanese here now, and Romanians, Poles, Royal Canadian Mounted Police, some kind of Italians, whatever they're worth. Most of them came to hold the ports and help stop the Reds. The Americans came to block the Japanese. Now they're all getting in the way. They won't let us take the damn supplies they promised even though they're stacked up in the harbor."

"Another month like this, Ivan," said Major Karlov, forgetting that his son was listening, "and we'll all be either dead or on the boats. Every time we butcher one of their regiments, Trotsky finds more Reds to fight us. You would think he'd be busy enough with the Don and fighting Denikin in the Crimea."

The door opened and banged against the wall. A blast of freezing air cleared the smoke and pulled ashes from the fire. Lieutenant Petrov entered.

"More bad news." He stamped the light snow from his boots and flung down his sheepskin-lined coat. "Denikin's been driven back." Petrov poured himself a glass of tea as the other men asked questions. "The British fleet may evacuate his men to Constantinople." Vasily put a big lump of sugar between his teeth before he drank.

Semyonov cursed and hurled his cup into the fireplace. "Even if we kill every Bolshevik bastard in Siberia, we'll be lost if they beat us back there."

"*Au lit*, Sasha," said Karlov, his face grim. "Time for bed. The doctor said you must get all the sleep you can. I'll take the cot."

Alexander wiped his plate with a bit of black bread. It was no use arguing with his father. He rose and hobbled to the small adjoining room. Petrov slapped his shoulder as he passed. Alexander closed the door and bundled himself in a blanket. He sat on the bed, then changed his mind and moved to the narrow cot that stood beside it.

More smoke than heat seemed to be coming from the other room. Before blowing out the lamp he reached up and lifted the only object that rested on his father's bedside table, a yellowed photograph of his mother and Katerina and himself on a midsummer-night's picnic by the lake at home. Alexander knew he was looking at a dream.

When he lay down, his leg ached less. "But don't expect it ever to be the same," the American doctor had warned his father after the operation. It was the report Alexander had expected.

His leg throbbed as he lay in the darkness and listened to the men talk about women and argue about the civil war.

"Admiral Kolchak is our last chance, and he's crazy," he heard Ivan Semyonov grumble in his deep Cossack voice. "Says he's the supreme ruler of all Russia, but he's already lost the Urals." A bottle smashed on the stones of the fireplace. "If the Bolsheviks take Omsk, the Allies will sail home and we're finished."

Alexander heard the strumming of a balailaka. The instrument stopped, then started again, as if searching for its mood. Vasily Petrov, he guessed. A man began to hum and tap his foot. A *domra* or mandolin joined in, then a violin, played with spirit, like a gypsy guitar rather than a string in a symphony. Deep voices rose and turned from argument to song, at the same time melancholy and robust. The "two hearts of Russia," Alexander thought he had read somewhere in Dostoevsky. He felt the walls shake as men roared and stamped to the music. Alexander began to cry when his father's favorite tune, "Aspens of the Volga," filled the two rooms.

"One last hunt," the Count told his son. He lifted Rizhka's left rear hoof between his legs. Squinting in the cold blue light of predawn, he brushed off the snow and picked out a stone with his pocketknife. "This could be the last time any of us ever rides in Russia."

Karlov's high-fronted Hussar boots gleamed. A white metal rosette was set at the top of each black boot. He wore a black leather jacket cut like a tunic, with a brown leather harness crossed behind his back and the two stars and two stripes of a major on his shoulder boards. Alexander had heard that the Reds had nailed the boards of some captured White officers to their shoulder blades, in order to remind the troops that in the new Soviet army all men were equals.

Earlier that morning, he had seen Lieutenant Petrov borrow a lance from one of his men, and then sit by a fire sharpening its tip with a steel and drops of pork fat.

"May I ride with you, Papa?" Alexander said. "They've taken off my cast." He could see his own breath as he spoke. "It's been five weeks."

Karlov checked his double-action Nagant revolvers without answering. Alexander knew it was his father's custom to ignore what he did not wish to hear. He was proud to see the orange-and-black ribbon on his father's tunic, the Order of St. George, the colors of fire and death. Most men did not survive the earning of it.

Alexander watched a dozen other officers mount up and tighten their reins. Their horses snorted clouds of steam and stamped in tight circles. Most of the men carried bolt-action carbines slung over their left shoulders. They were about to leave Russia altogether. He knew that they wanted to strike one final blow at their enemies. They would do it the old way, the way they had done it before they fought machine guns in the German war. Still gentlemen on horseback, they would charge their enemies one last time. This morning they were determined to avenge a party of wounded Whites murdered by Red partisans near Posolskaya. A Bolshevik prisoner had been tortured, Alexander had overheard, until he divulged the location of the valley where the partisans were camped.

"May I ride with you, Papa?" he said again as Gregori tightened the black mare's girth. The tall heavy hunter was the only horse that still survived of the six his father had brought east on the Trans-Siberian from their estate. Alexander recalled the morning he had helped his father choose them. "You're good at this horse business, Sasha," the Count had said. "But remember, today we're after hardiness, not looks."

Alexander decided to try once more. "I can ride now, Father. Please. Let me come with you." Alexander wanted his share of vengeance. "My leg's not so bad."

"Sorry, boy. Impossible. Not on this ride." He would not lose his son as well. Alexander was the family's only hope. "You don't know what we have to do." Karlov settled his pistols in their saddle holsters. "But I'll get one for you, Alexander." And several more Bolsheviks for your mother and sister, thought the Count, overwhelmed again by a rush of rage. Then he recovered himself. "Make certain you see all our kit is safely on the icebreaker." The major swung up and stood in his stirrups. The leathers creaked before he spoke.

"Tonight, Sasha, we sail for Shanghai."

By now Alexander understood that none of these officers expected to return home when the war was over. They had fought the Germans and the Reds from Poland to the Pacific, and every day they talked about how their world was ending. They came from different regiments, Lancers and Hussars, Guards and Dragoons. Without their men, Alexander thought they seemed more like a hunting party than a military command. He heard steel slide in scabbards and the clicking of chambers revolving as men rechecked their weapons. He saw Vasily Petrov pass around a bottle of vodka from the saddle. He watched his father examining each man and mount, straightening a bandolier here and tugging on a girth strap there. At last he was seeing how his father had lived the past few years.

Alexander noticed that only Vasily carried a lance. Its butt rested in the small leather holster hanging beside the lieutenant's right stirrup. Alexander wondered if Petrov would lead the attack in the traditional lancer way. He recalled the immense detailed painting that dominated the great hall at the Academy. A screen of lancers preceded Kutuzov's regiments in the fields near Borodino, where 25,000 men would die. In one corner the French cavalry skirmished with a troop of Cossacks. Behind the horsemen, the Portuguese, Germans, Poles and French of Bonaparte's *Grande Armée* waited to engage the army of the czar. It had been Russia against the world.

Ivan Semyonov carried two large Mauser holsters belted across his chest over his *burka*, the sleeveless black Cossack cloak made of felted goat hair. The left sleeve of Semyonov's tunic bore the triangular patch of a wolf's head with bared teeth. Long leather earflaps hung down from his tall grey wolfskin hat. A carbine and a curved sword in a black scabbard were suspended from his saddle. The hetman carried his *nagaika* in his left hand. The plaited hide of the heavy whip swung against the belly of his big pearl-grey gelding, Osetra. Alexander knew this was the weapon that had made the Cossacks hated by generations of rebellious demonstrators. The stiff-handled knout with the long lash had cleared the streets in a score of cities and kept order for the czar.

"*À cheval!*" ordered Major Karlov. He spurred Rizhka and left at a trot without looking back. As Alexander watched him ride away, he envied his father's effortless control and perfect oneness with the animal. The other horsemen followed.

Leaving the dirty narrow streets at the city's edge, the riders began an easy canter. They rode steadily through three forested valleys. They plowed through thin patches of snow in the clearings of the coniferous forest. They paused by an ox-bow stream while the horsemen let the horses drink and checked their girths.

Lieutenant Petrov whistled twice. An old bearded forester emerged from the woods. He was dressed in the thick long green felt jacket his profession had worn for generations. A hunting rifle with a battered stock hung barrel-down from his shoulder. "Mount up with us," said Major Karlov, handing the man two coins, "and show us the way."

The forester climbed up behind Petrov and their horse moved to the front of the line. The riders continued north without speaking. They followed the stream on their right until they came to the entrance of a narrow valley. The coursing water covered the sounds of the horses. After a time the forester held up one hand. The horsemen stopped and gathered. The woodsman jumped down, pointed to a path through the trees and disappeared into the sloping forest. Petrov lifted his lance from its holster and nodded at Major Karlov.

The Count clapped Petrov on the shoulder and gestured to the other riders. The Cossack drew his sabre. Other men pulled out their pistols. Karlov himself never drew his weapon until the last moment. The major's *shashka*, his heavy dragoon-style sabre, hung at his left side in the oriental style. He spurred his horse and they all rode forward along the narrow trail.

Soon the path broadened. A man jumped up at the edge of the woods and raised his rifle.

Semyonov was on the sentry before he could fire. Rising in his stirrups with his right shoulder forward, he slashed down with all his weight like an instructor splitting melons in sabre drill. The blow chopped through the man's right collarbone. His rifle fell to the ground, sleeve and severed arm dangling by the cloth of his coat. A second rider shot the sentry before he could scream.

The horsemen burst from the forest trail with blood in their eyes and the rising sun behind them.

"Ura!" yelled the Cossack. "Ura! Charge!"

At Semyonov's side, Petrov lowered his long weapon and spurred his horse.

The disorganized camp, larger than they had expected, spread directly in front of them where the valley widened. It was a chaos of blankets, low tents, stacked weapons and smoldering fires. Karlov saw the charred haunches of a horse at the edge of one of the cook fires. The animal's head lay nearby. The brown skin of its neck hung from it like a cape. Two human bodies, half naked, erect like scarecrows, were tied to the trunks of two poplars at the far end of the clearing. After months of civil war, Major Karlov was not surprised.

As the riders tore through the camp, the Reds jumped up and grabbed for their weapons. Several were cut down in the first charge. Gunfire and the screams of fighting and wounded men carried across the camp. Karlov saw Vasily's lance snap as it spitted a Red and drove the man stumbling backward into a fire.

The Major drew in his horse between the two largest tents, low brown canvas structures that were loosely pegged out. Count Karlov emptied his revolvers into the barefoot men who struggled from the tents one by one. Four fell. None fought like soldiers. He finished two others with his sabre, using careful measured strokes like an old farmer scything grain. Never had he killed so surely. Two of the Reds had pale bodies but their necks and faces and hands were permanently blackened and pitted by coal dust. Bolshevik miners recruited from the Siberian pits, he guessed.

Karlov pulled up his mount at the far end of the camp. While he reloaded, he saw his men fighting beside the tents. One Red at the edge of a camp fire raised both arms, probably surrendering, but Petrov shot him down.

Major Karlov rode to the two hanging bodies. Both were lifeless and marred with cuts and burns like Christian saints in an old icon. Dismounting, the major cut free the two corpses and gently laid them on the frosty leafy floor of the forest. Most of his men rode up and gathered nearby. Gasping and excited, further enraged by the signs of torture, they stared at the mutilated bodies. Panting like dogs, wild-eyed, they broke into groups of two and three. Galloping back through the camp, they charged into the growing clusters of Reds who this time received them with rifles and bayonets. The clamor of running horses and cursing men and gunfire and the cries of pain and death surrounded them.

A big man, bleeding heavily from a head wound, lifted a log from a camp fire and clubbed Petrov across the chest as the lieutenant rode past. Petrov wheezed and fell from his horse. He staggered to his feet with his pistol still in hand. Another rider fell beside him, shot by Red rifle fire. Petrov, on foot, defended himself with his pistol against a small man who swung at him with an entrenching shovel sharpened like a hatchet. The burly Cossack and the other horsemen were fighting all around him, exchanging shots and blows with the Communists. Two more Whites were shot from the saddle. Riderless horses stampeded about the camp.

Karlov, calmer, steadier than the others, rode up to Petrov with the reins of the lieutenant's mount in one hand. While Karlov waited with the horse, a Red lunged at his chest with a fixed bayonet. At the last second, the Major jerked back, but the tip of the bayonet stabbed his cheek. Enraged, Semyonov backhanded the Red with the reverse of his sabre. The hetman's horse reared when a gunshot struck its shoulder. The Cossack turned to search for the shooter. He cursed and sabred a wounded man who was trying to reload a pistol with one hand.

Petrov remounted as Karlov wheeled his horse in the middle of the camp and seized a red flag that was hanging from a tent post. The morning was growing brighter and the rifle fire heavier. Karlov sensed that in an instant the confusion of battle could turn the raid into a disaster. Vaguely he was aware of the blood flooding down his cheek and neck. A man grabbed his reins and missed him with a pistol shot as Rizhka pranced and spun. Karlov shot the assailant with the two bullets remaining in his second revolver. He drew his sabre and yelled for the outnumbered Whites to disengage. Petrov freed his right foot from its stirrup and gave the stirrup to a dismounted Hussar who flung one arm around his waist.

Karlov followed his men from the camp with the red flag stuffed in his belt. Several riderless horses came after them. The Hussar mounted one and led the others by their reins. The Count held the red flag to his bleeding cheek as they rode back to Vladivostok.

* * *

Alexander stood at the bottom of the gangway and watched Gregori direct the porters. Most of the officers and many of the men of his father's regiment would be boarding one of the two icebreakers commandeered by Admiral Kolchak before he had been captured by renegade Czechs and turned over to the Reds. Reports said the Communists had shot the admiral and stolen his boots and medals before dumping his body into a hole cut in the ice of the Angara River.

A double line of Petrov's Lancers guarded the entrance to the wharf. The regiment was assigned to keep order at the dock while the two old ships prepared to sail for the China Sea. With the Reds closing in around the city and thousands of Japanese troops waiting to intervene and seize the harbor, looters and crowds of hungry unpaid soldiers were taking over the frozen muddy streets of Vladivostok. Wild dogs loped here and there amongst them in the filthy snow. Hundreds of crates of English boots and blankets and heavy winter coats were waiting for the men on the docks.

The *Murmansk* was already overloaded. Groups of officers occupied every cabin. Rucksacks and weapons were piled in the narrow passages. The dining cabin and the captain's lounge were crowded with smoking, drinking men. Others lined the rails and stared at the grey city set on the bare hills above the harbor. Alexander heard the boom of artillery in the distance, echoing under the heavy dark clouds that hung low over the port. Pieces of filthy ice, washing down from the north, drifted across the oily waters of the harbor. In a few weeks ice would choke the docks.

Alexander went up the gangway to check that everything was in his father's cabin. He was embarrassed to be climbing so slowly, his short crutches in one hand and the rope rail in the other. Once on board, he heard the ship's captain arguing near the bridge with an officer of the Dragoons. The white-bearded seaman, hardened to the icy passage across the northern seas, appeared not to be accustomed to rearguard sailings under fire.

"We sail at once. I am not waiting for the Japanese." The captain looked down at his sailors who stood beside the four hawsers that secured the ship to the dock. Each sailor carried an axe. "And the Reds will have artillery at the mouth of the harbor by nightfall."

"No, Captain," said the cavalryman harshly. "My men are still boarding and we are waiting for several more officers. This vessel will not sail until every man is on board."

"My ship sails when I give the order." The captain stiffened and turned away. Alexander's attention shifted at the sound of clamor and hoofbeats on the quay. Suddenly anxious about his father, he descended the gangway.

Almost at once Alexander saw him. The Count looked tired and stern. Blood was on the hilt of his sword, and more on his cheek and right arm.

The line of Lancers pulled back around them as Major Karlov, Petrov and the Cossack and six others rode up the wharf through their ranks. The horses were lathered but shivering. A Hussar led two riderless animals by their reins. A crowd of restless would-be refugees first parted, then pressed slowly forward behind them. Alexander saw Petrov speaking to his line of men. The lieutenant seemed exhilerated, more vigorous and cheerful than Alexander had ever seen him.

The Major dismounted at the foot of the gangway. His face was lean and drawn. A long cut, still bleeding, crossed his right cheek just above the jawbone.

Alexander took the mare's head. "Are you all right, Father?"

"I'm fine." The Count looked down at his son. Karlov's eyes were still hard, his brow creased as if he never had been young. A torn red flag was tied with a thong to his cavalry saddle. Gregori quickly loosened the girth and carried the saddle up the gangway on his shoulder. Rizhka's back steamed where the saddle had rested.

"How was it, Father?"

"Messy." His face did not soften. "Close work. But at least we killed a few more Bolsheviks before they drove us into the sea."

Karlov glanced up at the light gangway and the crowded deck. Rows of White soldiers stared at them from the starboard rail. The ship's captain glared down, a leather megaphone in one hand. A knot of sailors in thick jackets stood beside him.

"We have to get some of these horses on board," yelled Karlov to the captain. Meanwhile Semyonov was leading Osetra to the bottom of the gangway.

"Impossible!" roared the captain through the megaphone. "There is no space and no fodder. We sail now."

"Go reason with him, Ivan." Karlov took the bridle of the hetman's horse. Bleeding from a bullet wound in the shoulder, the grey gelding resisted stepping onto the narrow shaky platform. Alexander raised one hand to the horse's wound. He was relieved it was not deep, but he wanted to clean and dress it as soon as possible.

The Cossack and the other returning officers grasped the rope railings and climbed the gangway. Carrying his heavy knout in one hand, Semyonov took the ship's captain by the left arm as if leading a mule. The man resisted but went with him. As the two disappeared in the direction of the vessel's short forward mast, the soldiers on the rail turned to watch.

In minutes, a boom with two canvas slings was lowered over the side, ready to lift the horses. The pair were quickly shipped on board. The sailors cast off even before the boom was secured to the mast. The remaining horses were already distributed among the men left on the wharf.

Alexander leaned on the railing of the afterdeck and watched Russia slide away in the gloom as they entered the Sea of Japan. He felt himself shudder at the sight of the thousands of desperate Whites abandoned on the docks. The last lights of Vladivostok rapidly receded to a dim glow in the distance. Horns moaned and sighed across the water.

It was not as bad as leaving his own home, but Alexander wondered if he would ever see his country again. Into his mind came images of his mother, and of the sister he and his father were abandoning. His mother's delicate sensibilities could never have endured this new life that seemed to grow harsher every day. She would have insisted on assisting others, and on sharing whatever she herself had left. The suffering of those around her, not her own, would have destroyed her innocence. Alexander wondered if he would ever meet another woman like her. Katia, he knew, was more like him. She could survive, he thought. He put a hand in his pocket and rolled the pearls between his fingers. He guessed his sister would find adventure even in most hardships. He wondered where the Commissar had taken her and prayed that she was being treated tolerably well. He recollected how Katerina shared his gift for languages and horses, and how she loved to ride bareback in the training ring. The memories made Alexander feel still more guilty for his own escape, and for how little he had done to help her and his mother. But the pain when he shifted his weight on the greasy deck reminded him that he had tried his best. How inadequate, he thought, his best had been.

Every soldier on board, several hundred, seemed to be massed on the deck behind him. Almost silent, sharing smokes and bottles, they gazed back at the dark shadow of Siberia. They ignored the freezing drizzle that settled over the *Murmansk* as she steamed south for Shanghai.

-5-

"Keep it clean, Major," said the medical orderly. He used a penknife to trim the ends of the black stitches that ran from Karlov's chin to his right ear. Except for tapping his heels, Karlov had made no sound while the orderly stitched the wound.

Alexander stood with his back to the narrow door, conscious that everything his family possessed had been reduced to what was in this tiny cabin: three heavy campaign cases of patched canvas and leather stacked beside the door; two photographs and his mother's favorite icon; and his father's bath kit with its straight razors, ivory-backed hairbrushes and metal military mirror. The single porthole, painted shut, was black with the cold night.

Dimitri Karlov sat on the edge of the narrow bunk. His tall worn black boots stood beside him like two tired sentries. The old leather case that held his sabre leaned against a corner with Alexander's foil inside it. The dark stains on the leather were blood. The hunting rifle rested in the opposite corner.

The Count drank from the bottle and passed the last of it to Gregori. He pulled a heavy leather purse from a pocket and gave a gold ten-ruble coin to the medical man. "See you look at my son's leg each morning, if you please."

After the man left, Karlov emptied the remainder of the gold coins into his hand. He handed most of them to Gregori, along with a thick fold of French francs. "Sew these into the top lining of my boots, and a few in the collar of my tunic. Where we're going, I've heard, nothing is safe." The Count turned to his son. "And of all the thieves in Shanghai, I'd wager that cousin of your mother's, that toad Krupotkin, is among the worst. He always had priest's eyes, able to spot a kopeck in the muddy snow at night."

Alexander recalled his mother's dismay, and his father's scorn, whenever she tried to reconcile her sense of family loyalty with her distaste for Pavel Krupotkin. He remembered the summer afternoon Krupotkin had arrived at Voskrenoye for a family party. Alexander had hurried to open the door of Krupotkin's brown Citroen. At first he had thought it was the odor of some rotting cheese, or perhaps an old picnic, that burst forth as the door swung open. But it was the scent of the man himself.

"Would you thread the needle for me, please, Master Alexander?" Gregori squinted in the dim light and handed the boy the thread and needle. "My eyes, you know." Alexander did as he was asked.

Afterwards, he mounted the metal companionway to the deck. Hungrier than he had ever been, he joined a line of men shuffling forward in the darkness for their evening ration. Some staggered with the rolling of the ship. Nothing had been served all day, neither to officers nor men, except a pinch of bread and a scrap of cheese at midmorning. Alexander glanced through a window of the dining cabin and saw Petrov and a group of officers playing what he supposed was baccarat. Bottles and currency and a large map rested on the table. As they had been doing last night, they probably were debating battles lost and the future of their country, now taken by the Reds.

Barrels of apples and loaves of bread were stacked on a forward hatch. Each man took two apples and cut a thick slice of bread. Alexander's stomach groaned when he saw the food.

"Three days to Shanghai," grumbled the soldier ahead of him, stamping his feet in the cold wind. "By that time we'll be eating the horses."

"I don't think so," said Alexander.

The soldier laughed harshly. "One day, boy, you'll learn that there are worse things than eating horseflesh."

Alexander took his bread and apples and limped to the rear deck. There the two horses were tethered to cargo rings behind the upper deck that housed the officers' quarters and the bridge. Alexander had cleaned Osetra's wound with seawater and Gregori had tied a canvas awning to the ship's cables to give the horses shelter.

Alexander cut an apple in two. "Here you are, old girl." He cupped Rizhka's soft muzzle before he fed her. "You, too, Osetra. This will make you better." He fed one piece to his father's mare and the other to the hetman's horse on the palm of his hand. He sat on a ventilator between the animals and took a big bite from the second apple. Then, after they nuzzled him and whinnied for more, he cut the rest in two and fed it to the horses.

He recalled riding once with Katia, their last ride before winter hardened around the estate. As the short afternoon darkened he suggested returning home but each time he spoke his sister waved at him and cantered on. When they returned in darkness, they found their mother standing at the stable door, her face shadowed in the deep hood of her cloak. Her hands trembled from cold and worry as she took their faces between her fingers and kissed them each without speaking a reproach. "It was my fault, Maman," Katia had said at once. But Alexander knew better. His father would have expected him to be responsible.

On deck the next morning, the day was the same, but colder. The salt air was inside him. He noticed the imperial flag of the Romanovs snapping at the sternmast.

Clouded with blowing spray from the wave tops, the sea was a skim of dark marbled green above a bottomless black depth. Alexander joined the men standing in line on deck. They stamped their feet and banged tin spoons against their mess plates while they waited for a ladle of oat porridge served from a row of buckets. Alexander found Gregori and the two sat on the narrow deck along the starboard side of the superstructure. They leaned against the cold metal wall with their collars up and gulped down their breakfast. While they ate, they watched Korea slip by to the west. Gregori had never heard of it. Alexander cleaned his spoon with tight lips, thinking of *piroshki* and *golubsty*, *baba* and duck stuffed with raisins and walnuts. When the men were finished eating, Alexander and Gregori scraped all the remains into two buckets and set them down before the horses.

A few moments later, Alexander looked up from the deck and saw his father and a group of officers from other regiments on the bridge with the captain. He listened to their raised voices as they argued about the cost of the voyage and the food and what to do when the *Murmansk* reached Shanghai.

"I want this vessel cleared for sailing the day after we anchor at Shanghai," said the ship's captain. "We'll be taking cargo for Manila."

"This ship belongs to the Imperial government," said Karlov, "and as the senior officer on board, I'll tell you when you're free to sail."

"How do we go ashore?" asked another officer. "As organized, uniformed remnants of our regiments?" He paused. No one answered. "Or as individual refugees running from the Reds, asking for asylum in the French Concession or the International Settlement?"

Alexander wondered if they would be welcomed or resented.

"The French will help the way they did in Vladivostok," a man snorted. "Selling blankets and winter coats the British sent as gifts."

"We'll go ashore the way they want us," said another in a tired voice. "If they want us. I've heard there've been too damn many like us landing in Shanghai already."

"The other Russians will help us," said Petrov.

Alexander thought he heard Semyonov's low Cossack laugh.

"How could they help?" said another officer. "The more of us who come, the harder it is for the men already there."

"We will manage it with the authorities when we make port," said Karlov. Alexander heard the drink in his father's voice. "We will go ashore like Russian gentlemen. Every officer will provide for the men of his regiment."

A party of men was sent down to search for food in the forward locker. Curious to see what was below deck, Alexander watched the hungry men lift the lid off the square hatch and climb down into the darkness near the thick bow of the icebreaker. A dense odor of something salty and rotten rose from the hold. He peered down, then looked over at his father. The Major was leaning against a nearby rail, smoking a cigar with Lieutenant Petrov. His hand was on Vasily's shoulder. When Alexander pointed down, requesting permission, his father shrugged.

More nimble now, more confident on his stiff leg, Alexander set aside his crutches. Careful to move slowly, he set both feet on each slippery rung and climbed down the narrow metal ladder.

He stepped down into two or three feet of melted ice and sea water. Piles of old fish, mostly cod and mackerel, were stacked in the corners. The deck beneath his feet was slick as a jellied eel. Lifeless fish floated in the sloshing water. He could hear the sea rushing past the sides of the ship.

Alexander shivered and looked up to see a net being lowered into the locker. A circle of faces bordered the open hatch against the dark grey sky above him. Two sailors and several soldiers holding small pitchforks waited near him in the icy water. The sailors wore tall rubber boots. Alexander's eyes had adjusted to the gloom enough for him to see two rats trotting along a ledge-like seam in the metal plating.

"Catch 'em, boy, and they're yours for dinner!" yelled a soldier. "Come on there, don't be idle. Hold the blasted net open."

Alexander released his hold on the bottom rung and advanced to the net. Suddenly he slipped. His right foot scooted forward and his weight fell onto his left leg. A white-hot blast of pain shot up his leg from knee to hip as he went under. He swallowed water and slid about the floor on his back with the movement of the sloshing pool. Desperately he reached up and grabbed the net. He was spitting filthy salty water when he surfaced. Laughter echoed off the walls.

"I said, hold it open, not climb in. Hurry up, you young idiot, the men are starving."

Numb, feeling only pain below the waist, his clothes like sheets of ice whenever his body moved against them, Alexander hooked one arm through a rung of the ladder. He gripped the net with both hands and spread his arms. Pitchforks rose and dropped icy dead fish into the net. Dripping water doused his face with every stroke. Fish slapped him in the chest and face. Alexander cursed himself for ever coming down here. Four times the net rose and the men on deck emptied the fish into waiting buckets. After the first time Alexander no longer looked up to receive the dripping spray in his eyes. Trembling with cold, he and the others stood waiting for the net to come back down.

When it was done, Alexander was the last to ascend, afraid he would climb too slowly for the others. Both his legs seemed heavy and frozen. Rung by rung, he hauled himself up by his arms.

His father waited by the hatch on deck. Alexander hoped he did not feel that his son had embarrassed them.

"*Bien fait*, Sasha." Karlov handed the boy his crutches. "Now get below and change into my clothes."

In the cabin, Alexander wiped himself dry and put on his father's oldest uniform. Although it was too broad in the hips and shoulders, he was astonished to find the length was perfect. His father had always seemed so tall and daunting. He remembered being overwhelmed by the weight of his father's greatcoat when he had helped him take it off on his homecomings. But soon he would be bigger and stronger than his father. Except for his damned leg.

The cabin door opened and the Count appeared. Karlov took a bottle of plum brandy from a pack. "Time you started on a bit of this," he said with tight lips.

The Major poured brandy into a tin cup and handed it to Alexander. He tapped the cup with the bottle. "To Shanghai," he said, and drank deeply.

Determined not to gasp or cough, Alexander emptied the half cup in one gulp. He opened his mouth wide and stared. He felt the fire run to his belly.

The two sat side by side on the bunk and drank again.

"You did a fine job down there, Sasha. You have never complained about your leg." The Count gripped his son's shoulder with one hand and looked him in the eye. "Your mother would be proud of you," he said. It was the first time he had spoken of her. The words filled Alexander's head with a thousand thoughts of family and home.

"What are we going to do about Katia, Papa?"

"What we can, Alexander, when we can. If they take her back to Moscow, Katerina will find some of our old friends, and when we can we will go for her, or pay someone to find her." He squeezed his son's arm. "But for now we can't do much. You know she and your mother would want me to take care of you. You are their future."

"Don't say that, Papa." Alexander thought of what had happened the last time he had been responsible for them. "We must do something."

"It was my fault, Sasha," said his father slowly. "Mine. Not yours. I should have been with you."

Shocked, his own guilt lifting, Alexander took a moment to reply. "No, Father. It was not your fault." He shook his head. "But what about that Commissar?"

Karlov's voice changed. The warmth of the cabin was replaced by the wind of Siberia.

"We will find Viktor Polyak. You have my word, Alexander. And when we do, this Commissar will enjoy a punishment from Dante."

The Count stared at his son with sunken blue eyes. "And if I don't do it, you will. You must do it for me if one day I cannot. Do you promise me, Sasha?"

"Yes, sir." Caught in his gaze, Alexander nodded.

Karlov released Alexander's shoulder and clapped him on the arm. "Now it's time you went on deck and ate some of that dinner you fetched up."

The Major filled the cup while Alexander put on an old Hussar jacket and lifted his crutches. For the first time Alexander felt that he and his father shared one world and one journey. The tunic made him feel like an old soldier, an old comrade in arms.

The main deck was crowded with hungry men devouring a briny stew of boiled fish and rotten potatoes. Alexander stepped in line beside one of his companions from the fish locker. Smiling at him, the sailor filled the boy's plate before he served himself.

"*Paren*," said the man, nodding as he gave him a bit more. "Tough guy."

Alexander ate the salty dish as quickly as he could. When he had finished, he rose and searched for the empty apple barrels. With his spoon he scraped out the pulpy sweet mess he found in the bottom of each container and divided it into two buckets for the horses. He should have served the horses before himself, Alexander thought as he walked aft.

Rizhka whinnied and strained against her rope when he approached. He stroked the nose of each animal before he fed them. Osetra's wound had closed. Alexander guessed the salt water had helped. Suddenly a nauseous wave of dizziness overcame him. He sat on the ventilator with his head between his hands. Plum brandy, old fish and the motion of the ship were too much for him. He stood and hobbled to the side. He gripped the rail and vomited until he thought he had lost his stomach. He spat and gulped the bitter cold air of the Sea of Japan. He was ashamed that he did not feel like a soldier now.

Alexander straightened slowly and walked back and stood for a time with his arms around Rizhka's neck. Leaning against the horse, his face in her coarse mane, he found comfort in her smell and touch. She reminded him of Taiga and the old stable and home. It was her smell even more than her warmth. He stood between the two horses with an arm resting on each. Their heat protected him from the wind and the cold. He felt strangely strong and clean. He could just discern the straight pale lines of the wake disappearing into the night, the opposite of the train tracks in Siberia, spreading apart instead of joining together.

He thought of Katerina and his mother, and felt that hollowness from missing them. Still, he was relieved they were not sharing all this loss and hardship. Or could it be worse where Katia was? Before going on to Kadnikov, Alexander had been a Page at the Corps of Pages, the czar's school for officers and courtiers in St. Petersburg. Now he was grateful for his training as a Page cadet, for the winter camps at the training base of a Guards regiment where his form would spend ten days, living in the snow in double tents, drilling on frozen lakes and, in the evenings, skating on a river by torchlight. The tradition of the Corps required that its cadets abjure ostentation when not at school, dressing simply and taking a public tram or one-horse sledge rather than a showy *izvozchik* drawn by several horses. The lessons of the Corps were serving him already.

Thinking of his mother, Alexander became conscious for the first time that there were no women on board, not one, and no children. It made a different world, one harder and simpler, less happy, not complete. Even at the Academy, there had been the nurse and maids, the cooks, the laundresses and the wives of the instructors and their children. He had not realized how much their presence softened and enhanced each day.

He saw a shadow pass on the port side of the afterdeck. A man was walking slowly, with his hand on the rail. Every few steps he hesitated and looked out to sea. A cavalryman, Alexander could tell by the tight breeches and short tunic. The soldier walked to the narrow fantail. He swung one leg over, then the other, and stood on the outer lip of the stern with both hands holding the rail behind him.

Realizing too late what he intended, Alexander jumped up, about to call out.

The man released the rail and straightened his shoulders. For an instant he stood alone above the dark ocean with his hands at his sides, as if on parade. Moving rapidly towards him, Alexander started to speak. "Please, sir, don't …"

The soldier dived into the night.

"Tsushima Straits." Major Karlov squinted as he glanced east into the rising sun. "Japan is on our left. Korea to the right. This is where the Japanese navy beat us fifteen years ago, Sasha, when we lost Manchuria and our only warm-water port. Admiral Togo began the war the year before with a surprise attack on our fleet at Port Arthur. Sank our battleships at their moorings."

Karlov pointed at the distant coast and glanced at Alexander to be sure that his son was listening. "That's where your mother's father was killed fighting for the redoubts. It was a new kind of war, ten years before we saw it in Europe." Karlov shook his head. "Rapid-fire artillery, machine guns, field telephones, firepower becoming more important than maneuver. We should have learned the lesson then."

Alexander nodded. He was sitting on a hatch with his crutches beside him. He had been brought up on his father's military lectures. He liked what he learned, but not the lecturing.

"After Port Arthur, our Baltic Fleet sailed around the world to fight them. Our ships were steaming north in line not far from here. But they couldn't sail faster than the oldest slowest vessels. The Japs came from the west and crossed the T, so six or seven of their ships could fire broadside at the bow of each of ours. The Russian warships came up to them one by one with only their forward guns in action. We never thought the little yellow devils could beat us. Now they're in Siberia."

"I know, Father."

Always alert to disrespect, the Count flicked his cigar into the sea.

"Suppose you think you learned everything as a young Page or a junior cadet at the Academy?"

"I didn't mean that, Father," said Alexander quickly, feigning deference. His father had already enjoyed a drink or two.

"How many ships did we lose?" asked the Major.

"All eight battleships, sir, and seven of eight cruisers. Ten thousand men."

Karlov nodded. As he stared at his son, his mood changed. He rubbed the red wound on his cheek with a thumb and looked at the boy in the cold sunlight. "Stay here, Sasha. I've something to give you." He paused and steadied himself when he stood.

The Count returned from the cabin carrying a cane made of some hard dark wood.

"Time you got rid of these sticks." His father lifted the crutches. "You don't want to get used to looking pathetic."

Before Alexander could react, Karlov hurled the crutches into the sea one after the other. "They were too damned short for you anyway."

Dismayed, Alexander jumped up. He watched the second one splash and get swallowed up in the immense dark ocean. How could his father do that to him?

"Now you can walk about like a Russian gentleman." The Count handed his son the cane, then continued. "This was my father's walking stick when he journeyed. I've always kept it in my sword case. I think you need it more than I do. With this, you'll be stronger instead of weaker."

Furious, slow to appreciate his father's thinking, Alexander reluctantly took the proffered present. Then he felt himself tingle when he turned the fine cane in his hands. He was thrilled to see a small silver plate set in the wood just below the curve of the handle. He glanced up and smiled. The Karlov crest was engraved on the plate: the double head of a bear, facing in both directions, like the double eagle of the Romanovs. "A reminder always to look behind you," his father once had told him. When they were younger, Katia used to sketch the double bears, one head being her own, the other her twin brother's.

"Press that button," said the Count, delighted with his son's reaction to the present.

Alexander pressed the silver button. Smooth as a snake sliding from a hole, a short sword came free in his right hand. Sunlight caught the slender blade when Alexander turned it left and right. He looked up at his father and grinned.

"Papa! Thank you, Papa."

"*De rien, mon petit.* Think of it as a present from your grandfather. I meant to give it to you when you won first prize for foil, but I was down at Tannenberg." Karlov's stern face broke. He smiled at his son. "Running from the Huns."

Alexander could not sleep, for dawn should find them at Shanghai. Shanghai! Where they would starve or prosper or maybe just erode away. The Orient. His father lay grinding his teeth and snoring like a locomotive. Alexander picked up the cane that rested beside him and fiddled with the silver button. The cabin was cold and stale from damp clothes and old cigars. Lying on the floor in his army blanket, Alexander stared up at the porthole, awaiting the first suggestion of blue light. He clasped both hands around the shin of his left leg and tried to bend his knee, as he did most mornings, in hope of finding even a tiny increment of flexibility. A brief exclamation escaped him. His father snorted and twitched on his bunk.

Alexander pulled on his boots before he rose. His head hurt. He remembered the brandy. He took his blanket and cane and opened the cabin door.

He stepped forward with the walking stick in his left hand and practiced shifting his weight from right foot to cane and back so as to avoid the pain that always seemed to be waiting just above his left knee. He tried to stand straight and walk more naturally, without the rocking motion of a man on crutches.

He sat on a coil of heavy rope just behind the bow with his chin resting on the handle of the cane. Curious like a child, proud of his new weapon and eager to examine it, he pressed the button and drew the silvery sword from the round wooden sheath.

The blade was almost two feet long. Triangular at its base, pointed at the tip, each of its three surfaces was slightly hollowed. Only the front portion of the weapon, the foible, was sharp on the three edges. The sword was rigid, nicely balanced, with none of the whip of a foil but with a similar lightness in the hand. It combined the cutting or swiping action of a sabre with the lunging and piercing action of a foil. Grandfather Karlov must have designed it himself. His grandfather, so he was told that afternoon, had carried the sword cane on his travels but had blooded it only once, when set upon by footpads early one morning in Padua.

From a pocket Alexander took the stone Gregori had given him, spat on it and began to sharpen the tip and forward edges of the blade. He recalled a lecture at the Academy on the history of personal weapons. In the fifteenth century, despite the resistance of the English, the thrusting rapier began to replace the cutting sword. Fights became linear rather than in-the-round, Maestro Angelo had explained. From the rapier came the short or "small sword," a favorite duelling weapon, much like this one, well suited to speed and handy for defense. Alexander wondered if he would need it in Shanghai. His father had called the place a jungle.

He was still hungry after the light supper of watery potato-and-beet soup. The ship plunged into a wave, bucking and sending up a wall of spray. Already more at home at sea, he licked the salty moisture from his lips. The coast of China, still only a jagged dark shadow separating the horizon from a blue-black sky, closed slowly to starboard. The sea calmed as they drew closer to the coast. The sky brightened over the East China Sea.

The first rays of the sun danced across the tips of the swells as the *Murmansk* turned more sharply west toward a break in the coastline. The ship slowed as they approached a belt of fog that clouded the broad mouth of a river. He made out the shapes of many ships moored along the south bank of the river entrance. The horn of the *Murmansk* sounded while she sailed slowly into the Yangtze delta.

As the fog thinned and parted, Alexander stood and gripped the edge of the tall steel bow. He heard men shuffling forward and exclaiming behind him. He knew they were waiting to see the Bund, Shanghai's celebrated harbor avenue. He wished Katerina were with him. She would have loved this new adventure. Often it was she who led him as they followed a new game trail in the forest or explored an abandoned building on the estate. He remembered stalking about the woods with her once when they were young. They had followed the prints of a wolf and her cubs along a muddy riverbank. They crept up near her sheltered rocky lair and found two furry grey cubs dozing, cuddled together on a bed of leaves, but no she wolf. Katia had taken his hand and led Alexander silently away, lest they disturb the family. "Twins," Katia whispered as they withdrew.

Alexander stared across the water. He stopped breathing.

The early light caught the tops of a row of buildings. Gilded like pyramids rising in a desert dawn, for a glittering moment the bright facade of Shanghai shone alone over the China coast. So this was to be his new home.

-6-

Alone at last, Jessica James waved at her mother and father as the old Humber drew away to take her parents to Shanghai Station. They were off again to begin their tour of Presbyterian missions. She, however, had a different sort of adventure in mind.

"You come inside, Miss James?" called the houseboy from the top step.

"No, Wu, I'm going for a bicycle ride." Like her mother, she had never felt comfortable reclining in a rickshaw while another human being slaved between the shafts like a draft animal, even though she knew it was the poor puller's rice bowl.

Jessica checked her watch and swung one leg over the man's bicycle. She pulled her cap down tightly over her tawny curls, trimmed short now in an "Eton crop." Her even features and slightly broad open face gave her an eager welcoming expression that was enhanced by lively brown eyes. Only her full lips gave a suggestion of something more sensual. Cycling clips held in the cuffs of her tan trousers. She wore a baggy blue cotton jacket cut like a coolie's coat, shapeless enough to conceal her figure. The size of her breasts sometimes embarrassed her, especially among the slender Chinese. Hoping to be taken for a boy today, she wore no makeup.

As she left, a horse-drawn wagon drew up outside her family house. SAM JOE, BROADWAY ROAD, proclaimed gilt letters on the back of the wagon, SHANGHAI'S LEADING GROCER. Jessica was not certain she liked the New York street name, like others chosen many years earlier, before Shanghai's American Concession was absorbed into the International Settlement.

She pedalled down the Rue de Saigon and made her way into the busier traffic of Thibet Road, enjoying the game of swerving and dodging to avoid the plodding carriers with poles over their shoulders and the honking lorries and trotting rickshaws. Jessica hoped that François Ricard would be waiting at the bridge as he had promised.

She came to Soochow Creek and stopped her bicycle by the entrance to the steep stone bridge. As usual, her handsome French schoolfriend was late. His words often seemed more flattering than his behavior, she thought with irritation. She herself was determined to be on time tonight. It was awkward enough being a "European" at these meetings, but to enter the yard once the speakers had begun would attract more attention than Jessica wanted.

The rallies were always held when the shifts changed, so both sets of workers could be present, between six and six-fifteen in the afternoon. Today's was of special importance: worker delegates were coming from Canton and Nanking. Two celebrated leaders would address the crowd. For their safety, the names of the two had not been revealed in advance.

Jessica bought a paper cone of chestnuts from a street vendor, then sat on her bicycle and watched the waiting porters compete to help overloaded barrows and carts climb and descend the bridge. Roasted chestnuts always smelled better than they tasted, but she liked the idea of eating street food. It made her feel more at home, as if she were not so removed from the Chinese proletariat.

A head shaver leaned against the parapet nearby. The barber's razors and ointments were displayed like jewelry on a cloth beside him. The man sharpened a razor against a leather strop that hung from his waist. A client sat on a stool before him while two others waited to one side.

Warm from the ride, Jessica took off her blue cap and shook out her tight wavy blond hair. She wondered how she would look, and what her mother and classmates would say, if she had the barber shave her head.

She watched a stream of household and office workers crossing in her direction, cheap labor for the European families and businesses of the International Settlement. Too cheap, Jessica thought. Why should their hungry children live on dirt floors when Shanghai's Europeans were spilling champagne at the Astor Grill and leaving their plates half eaten at the Majestic?

A tea vendor stopped beside her. A black kettle hung from one end of his bamboo pole, a round tray of blue-and-white cups from the other. They exchanged smiles and she bought a cup. While she drank the green tea, she stared across the creek into Chapei and the Chinese Municipality of Greater Shanghai. Even the air seemed different when one crossed the bridge: more dense and full of odors, the smells of food and industry, of slaughterhouses and boiling fat, of industrial fumes and smoke and night soil. It sometimes seemed to her that the vast multitudes of China were held back by this bridge before her, as if an ocean, restrained by a single slim dike, were waiting to pour through one narrow funnel. Or was it more like an angry dragon leashed on a chain, as one union organizer had told her?

She could not wait any longer. Jessica returned the empty cup, checked her watch and set out for the factory. She knew it would not be François's sort of evening anyway. Nearly nineteen, and very French, he seemed to have other things in mind than native politics.

As she rode, Jessica idly considered what it might be like to oblige François one day, or perhaps a different boy, possibly someone older and more experienced. Some modern women, she had been reading, and not just bohemians, were learning to take pleasure like men, to liberate both their bodies and their minds. Although many men objected, apparently others did not. Some men, it was said, preferred experience to innocence in their ladies. Jessica longed to be bold enough to try such an adventure. Reportedly it had all started in Paris, and here, after all, she was in the French Concession. She enjoyed the wind in her face as something like expectation lifted her spirits.

Feeling free on her bicycle, adventuring away from the European city towards the factory district along Yangtsepoo Road, Jessica passed crowds of Chinese, mostly women and children, emerging from warrens of narrow alleys and hurrying along towards the smoking mills. Each worker was carrying a small round basket containing, she knew, cold rice and bean curd, and perhaps a small scrap of salt fish. To keep the workers in place, the mills provided boiling water for making tea, and for pouring through their food baskets to heat the rice. The cotton spinning factories ran twenty-four hours a day without stopping. Most workers ate where they stood attending their spindles and reels. The babies of nursing women, Jessica thought grimly, lay all day on the floor at their mothers' feet. With fifty cotton mills and over a million spindles running night and day, Shanghai's factories consumed women and children like fuel.

The road grew rougher and narrower, the traffic slower, without motorcars or horses. Every man and vehicle was overloaded as if on a final desperate journey. Jessica sensed she was sharing the route with a column of exhausted trudging refugees rather than day workers. She saw wheelbarrows carrying seven or eight people on their way to the night shifts at the cotton mills. They sat sideways, with their feet hanging down over the edges of the carts. Each barrow coolie, the veins of his face and neck standing out like whipcords, steadied his load with a heavy woven rope that crossed his shoulders and was bound to the handles.

Though she was familiar with the conditions that awaited them, Jessica was disturbed to see children asleep in the wheelbarrows, preparing for their next twelve-hour shifts. The more fortunate ones worked in the silk filatures, where the weaving was done only by daylight. But even there each child stood for twelve hours before a shallow copper basin filled with boiling water, softening each cocoon by swishing it around with a fine reed brush. With nimble parboiled fingers the sweating girl would pick a thread from each cocoon and fasten it to a frame and treadle so it could be wound onto the reels. The steam pipes that provided the boiling water kept the long rooms Hades-hot, but the windows could not be opened lest a breeze break the delicate silken threads.

The children earned about fifteen cents a day, perhaps half as much as their mothers, and all at about half the value of American cents. The working children often supported their families. This generation of girls, thought Jessica, were being liberated from the horror of foot binding only to be enslaved by the mills and the brothels. Even poor families often bound their daughters' feet in order to make them more marketable as prostitutes and domestic servants.

Invigorated by indignation, Jessica walked her bicycle across the raised roadbed and the single track of the Nanking Railway. She could see the long shell of Shanghai Station in the distance to her right.

The route became even more dusty and uneven. It jarred Jessica's narrow tires when she bumped across the deep ruts of dried mud. She passed factories and warehouses. Finally she came to the brown brick buildings of the Hin-Sin Cotton Goods and Dye Company, home of seven thousand steam-driven spindles. She smelled the odor of some ghastly chemical. A line of dark flat-faced men with prominent cheekbones and sunken eyes loitered near the factory entrance. Some wore tall shabby felt boots. They were armed with bamboo staffs. Mongolians, hired to intimidate the workers. Several groups of burly Chinese loitered across the road from the factory. A lorry drew up and a score more leaped down and joined them. Toughs from the tongs, Jessica reckoned, probably members of the Green Gang, which had always organized the cotton workers until the coming of the union and the Communists.

She continued on to the far side of the mill, where a rough courtyard was formed between the factory wall and the adjacent Shing-So Match and Boxes plant. Rusting machinery and abandoned packaging were scattered on the ground. Jessica stopped. Careful with her tires on the uneven surface, she walked her bicycle towards the crowded yard.

Tight with anticipation herself, Jessica felt an excitement in the gathered workers that she had not sensed before. She looked about her and used her count-and-multiply formula to estimate the crowd. There were about four hundred, and perhaps a third were women. Fifty or sixty young children, eleven or twelve years old, were clustered in small groups among the other workers. Sweepers and thread collectors and spindle operators, the girls and boys rubbed their eyes, no doubt irritated by the fiber dust and the fumes of the dyes.

Two men at the back unfurled a long red banner and held it up between two poles: UNION OF COTTON AND SPINNING WORKERS. Four narrow vertical red flags were attached to long bamboo poles that leaned against a brick wall: STRIKE TO EAT, PEASANTS AND WORKERS UNITE, DEATH TO MONEY-LENDERS AND LANDLORDS, BROTHERHOOD WITH MOSCOW. She watched four men with red armbands lift the banners and wave them slowly in parallel unison.

Several Chinese, wearing flat blue caps like Jessica's, nodded towards her as she walked her bike to the rear of the crowd. It was her third meeting, and Jessica knew why she was welcome. Each time she contributed generously when baskets were passed through the crowd to raise money for the strike fund. She wondered what the Presbyterian congregations in California would think if they knew that their contributions for the Chinese missions, which paid for her allowance, were helping to finance the organization of the proletariat of China.

Each meeting was bigger and louder and better organized than the last. Soon the workers would take the streets, she thought, like their brothers and sisters had already done in St. Petersburg and Moscow.

A man climbed onto a broken loom set beneath the long horizontal flag. Jessica recognized him as the leader of the Cotton Union. The crowd hushed when he began to speak. Two other men stood behind him. A cordon of eight or ten workers arrayed themselves before the three and faced the crowd with folded arms. The union leader spoke with the sharp clipped accent of a Cantonese. Though her Shanghainese was improving, Jessica could not understand it all. Snatches came to her while she listened.

"Doctor Sun Yat-sen . . . Sun Yat-sen . . . land for the farmers . . . money for the workers . . . rice for the children . . . Shantung . . . Japanese dwarf pirates." The crowd laughed and clucked and cheered. "Kuomintang . . . Chen Tu-hsiu . . . strike."

Jessica felt someone lean against her bicycle. She looked down.

A thin girl, perhaps twelve, gripped the other handle and knocked against the bicycle every time she coughed. "Cotton lungs," Jessica knew. The child's chest would soon be filled like a pillow with the fibrous dust collected by the factory sweepers. Jessica smiled at the girl when she ceased coughing and looked up with narrow sunken eyes. The child's round bronze face looked painted like a harlequin's. Her chin and lips were covered with blue and red dye from the factory. The girl smiled and put two blue fingers in her mouth and tried to suck off the painful coloring. The ends of her fingers were raw and swollen and peeling like so many little snakes shedding their skins. The child seemed to have no fingernails.

Sickened, embarrassed that her own hands were smooth and perfect, Jessica handed the girl a coin. She was careful not to flinch when the girl's hand touched hers. Jessica was angry that the factories hired more young girls than boys because their fingers were more dexterous and because their families valued them less.

"Comrade Mao Tse-tung!" The union leader turned to extend both arms towards one of the two men behind him. "A leader of our youth movement and a delegate to the First National Congress to build the Communist Party of all China." The crowd pressed forward and began to still.

A thrill passed through her. She had heard so much whispered about this man. "He is our tomorrow," one organizer had told her.

A slender man stepped forward and climbed onto the loom. He was wearing a white gown, closed with a clasp at the right shoulder. She thought Christ must have worn something like it when he spoke to the disciples at Gethsemane. Mao Tse-tung's open, almost innocent pear-shaped face appeared to sit on the tall rounded collar of his gown. He had prominent black eyebrows and thick rising hair parted in the center. He waited for the first speaker to descend, then bowed slightly when the crowd acknowledged him.

The man spoke slowly in a quiet voice that Jessica could scarcely hear. The crowd pressed forward. Their straw sandals shuffled in the grimy yard. She could understand occasional words: "Youth . . . united masses . . . Workers and peasants . . . Russian revolution."

Then, more loudly, "Gradualism is death."

Jessica felt the crowd respond to the rhythm of Mao's words. As his audience grew more attentive, the young man raised his voice and spoke more rapidly.

"If we want reforms, we must have a revolution." He paused to let the point settle. Instead, Jessica heard the gang of toughs laughing and hollering from across the street. The speaker continued in a stronger voice.

"If we want our revolution to be successful, we must learn from Russia." He paused again. "But remember, a revolution is not a dinner party. It is an act of violence."

Mao Tse-tung turned and beckoned to the other man still standing behind the loom. "I introduce to you our comrade from Moscow, Mikhail Borodin of the Comintern, the Communist International."

A European in a rough blue tunic climbed the loom. He had long ears, a gaunt face with a deep vertical trench in each cheek and an uneven thick drooping mustache that covered all but the middle of his lower lip.

Jessica could not believe that it was he, Mikhail Borodin, Sun Yat-sen's Russian adviser. She felt herself tremble with the excitement of the crowd. She thought of the courage it had taken to bring revolution to Imperial Russia, and of the vision and concern that were required for a Russian to risk his life to bring revolution to China.

Borodin crossed his arms and glared over his audience. He clenched his hands into fists beside his elbows. He began to speak in a deep growling voice, almost barking when he spoke, pausing before every phrase. An interpreter stood on the ground before him and hollered out Borodin's words in loud Shanghainese.

"Comrades! I have worked with Vladimir Lenin in a cellar with ink on our hands and the printing press rolling beside us." He raised both hands and extended them palms first to the crowd. "I have been arrested by the secret police of the czar of Russia and exiled from my country. I have been arrested by the English Scotland Yard in London." Borodin hesitated, as if waiting for a reaction. "I have stood with the workers in Petrograd and Moscow and Istanbul in Turkey and Chicago in America. I have worked in ten countries for the workers' revolution. Now that revolution must come to China."

Sandalled feet began to stamp. The pennants waved faster.

Borodin was right, Jessica realized. The revolution of 1911 had ended the Manchu Dynasty, but it had not brought the transformation that China required. It was not enough to end footbinding for women and the pigtail for men. Oppression and cruelty and corruption must be destroyed in every village and enterprise in China.

Standing to one side, Mao Tse-tung nodded and applauded as Borodin repeated his words more loudly.

"Revolution must come to China!"

Borodin lifted his right arm and pointed at the assembled jeering toughs across the road. "There, there are the enemy dogs who work for the factory owners and the usurers and the landlords that make each of you a slave." He hesitated while many workers raised their fists. "In Moscow they used the Cossacks to keep us in our chains. In Shanghai they use those gangsters."

Jessica looked down at the little girl beside her. The child was sucking her blue fingers. Tears came to Jessica's eyes as she raised her own hands and clapped.

"Today, comrades, I come to Shanghai to help you organize the revolution in the biggest country in the world."

Voices cried out. Hands clapped. Jessica lost hold of her bicycle as the crowd pushed forward all around her. She realized why when she heard a roar behind her and the clacking together of sticks and batons.

The Mongolian guards and the mob of gangsters surged into the crowd of workers. Yelling oaths, they cracked heads and ribs, flailing and beating everyone who stood before them.

Jessica saw Borodin jump down from the loom and slip through a space between the brick walls of the two factories. The other two speakers and their protective cordon followed. Workers streamed after them. A few resisted their attackers.

In the struggle, Jessica was knocked down by a blow from behind. She cried out from the pain to her shoulder. As she rose, Jessica saw the young girl fall, trampled down by the panicking crowd. She struggled towards the screaming child but lost her in the press that swayed and roiled around her. She saw several workers overpower one Mongolian and seize his staff.

Jessica crouched against a wall and looked in vain for her bicycle and the young girl. Both had vanished. She pushed her way along the wall as men fought all around her. She had to escape. Stumbling onto an abandoned packing case, Jessica dragged the empty crate against the wall and climbed up and fell over the other side into a second smaller yard. She staggered to the road and looked back at the fighting mob. Everywhere were running blue-clad figures. Several lay on the ground, victims of the Green Gang violence. She prayed the little girl would manage.

Jessica turned her back on the factories. She had seen enough brutality. Jessica gathered herself and began to run towards the city. She paused once and looked back, furious at the persecution of the workers, but thrilled to have participated in their defiance.

-7-

"Welcome to the Republic of China." The Deputy Harbor Master bowed his head to the ship's captain and to each of the three Russian officers who sat across from him at the dining table. A short slight man in loose black trousers and polished European shoes, the Chinese wore a blue cotton jacket with a high round collar and one large knotted silk button at the throat and on each cuff.

Alexander leaned against the cabin window behind his father's chair. "You must learn how things work here," his father had told him. "It's all good training."

"No doubt you carry gold rubles?" said the port official. He looked without expression at the dark tea that had been placed before him, served in the Russian way, in a small glass set in a metal frame with a handle. "Captain, gentlemen?"

"Gold rubles?" said the captain. "The *Murmansk* is an icebreaker, not a bank. I have delivered my cargo to Shanghai, three hundred and forty men and two horses.

The rest is between you and them."

"You are anchored in the mouth of the Whangpu River, gentlemen. This is not some colonial wilderness. You are in China. You are visiting the fourth-largest city in the world. Here we have laws and harbor rules, fees and custom duties." He folded his thin hands on the table so that the tips of his fingers were just inside his wide sleeves. When no one replied, the Chinese continued.

"Is this not so in London and St. Petersburg?" He looked around the table with no challenge in his eyes. "There are things one must arrange before coming ashore in Shanghai."

"Are there not several Shanghais?" said the Major firmly but without disrespect. "Chinese and French and International? We will see what we must do." Dimitri Karlov was rarely driven by the pace of another man's interests or conversation.

Alexander glanced out the window and saw a second launch approaching the ship. The tricolor of France waved from her brass stern-mast as the trim vessel passed a line of warships moored nearby. The grey destroyers, cruisers and minesweepers flew the flags of the United States and Japan, Germany and France and Italy. The horn of a French destroyer saluted as the launch crossed her bow.

"Or perhaps you would prefer to sail to Manila, honorable gentlemen, like many of your countrymen who chose not to make arrangements here?" said the Chinese. "Other White Russian vessels, such as the *El Dorado* off Chinhai, have been interned in our ports, rusting in harbor for a year now. Their men are still on board, trying to sell their old weapons to the warlords." He stirred his tea without drinking. "Perhaps in the Philippines . . ."

"The *Murmansk* will sail where I decide," said the captain.

"Of course." The official nodded respectfully. "Once you are again at sea. After the completion of formalities. But first there are harbor fees to be paid. Also it is my duty to ask you if there are weapons or other contraband on board."

Losing interest in the formalities, Alexander looked back across the cabin and out the starboard window as the older men conversed. He raised a set of binoculars he had borrowed from a side table.

Seagoing steamships were moored between the *Murmansk* and the tall buildings that lined the harbor shore. He tried to count the different flags and lines and colors. The nearest ship was the *Empress of Australia* of the Canadian Pacific Line. Behind her lay the *Nippon Fushimi Maru* and the *Triestino*, then a mail steamer of the Peninsular and Oriental Line, and vessels of the Messageries Maritimes and the Hamburg-Amerika Line, the Dollar Line and Jardines. Plying between them all were junks and sampans, colliers and tugs and lighters. Huge dredgers were at work on the far shore, and behind them wharves and warehouses, loading cranes and jetties, smokestacks and landing ramps. He refocused and stared at the great harbor avenue that fronted Shanghai's waterfront. Alexander could not wait to get back on deck and find a boat and go ashore.

"We are not pressed for time. I will call again tomorrow or the next day, gentlemen. What are a few days to warriors who have come so far?" The Chinese rose. Hearing no reply, he continued.

"May I remind you that we were with you in your German war. One hundred thousand Chinese served in France, despised, used as laborers, digging trenches, dying in the mud. Now you come to China for refuge." He looked at each Russian as he spoke. "Soon I will bring with me the harbor agent to collect the fees. Please have ready a list of passengers and cargo, and all weapons and currencies on board. Then we can make arrangements for any visits to China. Until that time, of course, no man may go ashore." He bowed from the waist and waved vaguely towards the waters outside. "In the meantime, you may purchase your necessaries from the floating markets."

Alexander held open the door. The Chinese official stepped out and a heavyset European in uniform entered the cabin. He wore a sidearm and carried black leather gloves in his left hand. He was followed by a slender uniformed oriental with a fine dark face and high cheekbones.

"*Bienvenus à Shanghai!*" said the portly officer, saluting the sea captain. He wore the dark blue uniform and black leather harness of a French policeman. He put his gloves in his kepi and handed it to his escort. "Captain Ricard of *La Gendarmerie*, at your service. May we attend to a few formalities, Captain? Perhaps first you might offer me a cup of coffee?"

"I regret we have no more coffee," said the ship's captain, introducing the Russian officers. "Perhaps tea, vodka, a little apple brandy?"

"Things must be difficult in Vladivostok." The Frenchman pointed at the brandy. "*Après le déluge*, no doubt. We have so many White Russians with us now in Shanghai, you know. Perhaps twenty thousand in the French Concession alone." Alexander had the impression of a man who thought he was preparing others for his requests. But he doubted that this Frenchman was used to dealing with men like his father. Alexander prayed that the Major would not show his Russian temper.

"We are grateful, Captain Ricard, for the hospitality that France has offered to our compatriots, both here and in Paris." Count Karlov spoke with dignity, as if giving a *fonctionnaire* his due, and perhaps just a little more. He poured brandy for the gendarme and himself. "I believe a cousin of my wife's, of my late wife, has been here for two years. Pavel Krupotkin."

"Prince Krupotkin? Indeed, Major Karlov. The prince is said to own, or at any rate to manage, one of our finest gaming houses and cabarets, the Belle Aurore. Occasionally I pass there myself."

It was the first Alexander had heard that his mother's distant cousin might be a prince.

"May I inquire, sir. Are you a Cossack?" asked the Frenchman of Ivan Semyonov, eyeing the long slanting cartridge loops on the front of the hetman's jacket.

The Cossack chieftain hesitated, uncertain whether the query was offered with good humor or intended to offend.

"Down to my spurs, Captain," said the bearded horseman finally, with a smile. He slapped both palms on the table. "But not a steppe Cossack from the Don. I am a Kavka, from the Caucasus. And I've ninety men on board. For a hundred years our Caucasian sabres and whips kept order for the czar. If we can help you do that here . . ."

"For that duty we have Annamite gendarmes, such as my sergeant here from Phnom Penh." Ricard gestured over his shoulder at the man who stood behind him. "And for more serious troubles, with the Chinese, we can call on Shanghai's Volunteer Defense Corps of reserve companies from each of our European communities, and also the American and Japanese companies, of course, not to mention the Jews, and even a few Chinese."

"Would you prefer that we go ashore as individuals or as soldiers?" said the Count, a bit of stiffness in his voice. He did not wish to concede too much.

"Landing rights are no longer a simple matter." The Frenchman raised both eyebrows. "Permission is required to come ashore. Under treaty, we French have been trading here since 1844."

"*Monsieur*," said Karlov, annoyed that the French should attempt to regulate Russians in China, "a century earlier than that, one hundred years before French ships anchored in this harbor, when Shanghai was but a swamp, Russian caravans were trading in Peking, following a mission sent by Peter the Great in 1716."

Habituated to more brutal problems, Karlov realized that more subtle forms of conflict would now engage him.

"Forgive me, Count, but you would not be so proud of all the Russians in Shanghai today. A year or more ago the first arrived as honored guests after the beginning of your revolution. Their enemies were our enemies. Shanghai is a city of commerce, and we knew the Soviets despised business." The police officer's forefinger traced the rim of his empty glass. "The first White Russians came as gentlemen suffering temporary dislocation. For a time most paid their way. But they are still here. Now we have many times more Russians than Frenchmen in the French Concession.

Hundreds of your old soldiers sleep starving in the streets like coolies, able to find money to drink but not to eat, it seems. They make us all lose face. And some Russian girls are very naughty."

Ricard pursed his lips and glanced at the empty bottle. "Very naughty. Crime follows. They make themselves my concern. I will say nothing of the Cossacks. Even Shanghai can only tolerate so much."

"Shanghai will learn to live with us," said the Cossack with a hard smile.

"We will see." The Frenchman shrugged. "Even in retreat, soldiers must keep their discipline, monsieur."

"One hundred years ago," said the Count, almost amiably, "starving French soldiers stripped their own wounded and ate each other as Bonaparte abandoned his men shortly before Christmas while the Grande Armée fled from Moscow. Some Frenchmen were heated quickly over open fires by their comrades, like the horses of your cavalry. Others were devoured where they fell in the snow, too weak to prevent their countrymen from first stealing their boots and clothing."

This time Alexander smiled to himself as he listened to his father's military lecture.

Count Karlov paused, then added, "Perhaps you have seen the splendid colored engravings of your Major du Faur? He served in the long French retreat with Marshall Ney."

Without speaking Ricard rose and took his kepi from his aide. His face pale and thin-lipped, he slapped his gloves against his leg as he turned to the door. Seemingly relaxed, Karlov accompanied the Frenchman on deck. Once they were alone outside, he broached a different subject.

"How may you and I arrange things?" said the Count more smoothly, accommodation in his tone, as if recognizing that sophisticated gentlemen such as Ricard and himself could always find a way.

"If you wish to apply to enter the Concession of France," said Ricard slowly, drawing on his gloves, "you must prepare a manifest listing every man and beast and property that you wish to land. We will submit this to the Consul of France. I may do what I can. You understand, of course, that such things go slowly and are very costly." He descended the ladder to his launch. Karlov returned to the cabin.

"That policeman must know it was the Cossacks who hounded Napoleon's rear guard," said Semyonov. "Filthy little French whore."

Count Karlov nodded. "Every tart has a price."

-8-

I t was easier than Alexander had expected. An hour after Captain Ricard left, Alexander handed a Chinese boatman ten rubles and put a finger to his lips. He crouched down between the baskets of vegetables under the bamboo canopy covering the sampan. He rested his cane across his knees and waited for the flat-bottomed skiff to make for shore. The boatman squinted at the coin in the darkness. Then he nodded and raised a scull and pushed off against the rusting hull of the *Murmansk*. Standing at the stern, the man used the long single oar to work the boat forward in the water.

Alexander checked his jacket pocket for the thirty francs and for the note from his father to Pavel Krupotkin. "I will have to be on board if either of those thieves returns to the boat," his father had told him. "But the captain won't miss you, Sasha. I'll say you are below resting your leg."

The Russian vessel disappeared from sight when they passed under the square prow of a tall junk that towered over the sampan like a Spanish galleon. A large blue eye was painted on the side of her bow.

The street that fronted the harbor was a wall of light in the early evening. Alexander had never seen such illumination. Some buildings resembled the minor columned palaces and government buildings of St. Petersburg. Others reminded him of the merchants' grand villas in Odessa. The crowds on the boulevard before the buildings were so thick that Alexander could not see the doorways.

As the sampan drew closer to shore, the water itself seemed to be alive. Driven by sweeps and oars and poles, some by motors and sails, so densely arranged that they appeared to cover the entire surface of the water, the boats swarmed about with the wild darting instinct of starlings or minnows, pursuing their own courses without ever quite touching one another.

Many small vessels were tied in place, to the ramps and short quays, to iron rings and ropes and buoys. Sometimes they were tethered one to another, lashed side to side so that a line of sampans floated together like a village or a many-legged water insect. Duckboards led from one sampan to the next. Laundry and fish and paper lanterns painted with Chinese characters hung from each boat. Cook fires glowed in metal pans on the tiny decks. When they passed close by, Alexander could smell the garlic and charcoal. He heard the sizzle of food on the grills and was obliged to swallow his hunger.

Most sampans carried a cave-like shelter of rattan that was stretched over an arched bamboo frame mounted on the stern. Alexander found himself looking into each one. He saw children playing, babies feeding at the breast, old men lying on mats smoking long flute-like pipes. On one he saw a pretty girl, perhaps his own age, wearing sandals and a tight silk dress slit at the side. An old woman was combing the girl's long black hair. Behind her in the cave he saw a pink lantern and pillows and cushions. Alexander felt himself stir. The girl raised her painted eyebrows and smiled. She touched her lower lip with two fingers and called to him, but he did not understand. His boatman cackled and wagged one finger when the girl sang a few words and called out again. Then they passed two houseboats moored end to end. Several Europeans in dinner clothes were sitting on one deck, playing cards and drinking. They ignored Alexander's sampan as it passed. The other houseboat bore a sign: TO LET.

The sampan passed the end of the magnificent illuminated street. It turned down a waterway that was narrower but nearly as busy as the river. As they drew close to the embankment, noise struck him like a falling wall: the cries of street vendors, warning shouts of carriers with long poles across their shoulders, horns and bells and music, a tumult of languages and voices, hammering and honking.

"Soochow Creek," said the boatman. He pulled in against a set of broad stone steps. When Alexander hesitated, the boatman handed him a small yellow apple and pointed impatiently towards the steps.

Leaning on his cane, Alexander stepped ashore and waved good-bye. He felt a bit unsteady now that he was back on land. He pressed down on the cane to keep his balance and stared up at the teeming embankment with the sense that he was diving into a high wave.

An old man in a blue cotton gown sat on the top step with a wooden birdcage on his lap. He was singing to the yellow bird, some sort of lark, Alexander guessed. It was like a dog walking his master, Alexander thought.

"Casino Belle Aurore?" he asked the old singer as he climbed the steps. "Casino Belle Aurore?" He received a thin toothless smile but no reply.

Alexander looked up and saw a sign: Szechuan Road. Many shops were fronted by tall signboards written in vertical black-and-gold characters he could not read. As he began to walk, he soon found that the sidewalks and the roadway were one. With every step, someone touched or jostled him. People rushed shoulder to shoulder in every direction. He stumbled against a basket stuffed with live ducks. Recovering himself, he saw four new wooden coffins stacked beside it. He could smell the freshly cut timber. Then he smelled something spicy cooking in deep fat and wished he had time to stop and eat, but he was in a hurry to find Pavel Krupotkin at his casino.

Taller than most of the crowd, Alexander held his walking stick up and a bit before him to open up a narrow path. It seemed to work. Still, every few paces he had to step aside for a charging rickshaw or an over-loaded single-wheeled barrow. The barrows carried baskets and crates or two people sitting on either side of the high wooden wheel. Some rickshaws appeared old and heavy, their seats filled with parcels and stacks of goods or large bundles. Between their traces the men pulling them were barefoot, older, with their heads down and shoulders pitched forward. Other rickshaws were clean and bright and painted yellow. Their canopies were up. Their rubber-rimmed wheels were taller and lighter. Running gently when they could, their youthful pullers wore what looked like cotton slippers. A Chinese man or woman rested inside, always looking straight ahead. Every rickshaw had several plates attached at the back indicating licenses in French, English and Chinese.

One rickshaw with a blue canopy approached slowly. A red lantern swung from the front of its awning. A slender woman sat inside. Her sleek black hair was lacquered like a panel of enamel. She caught Alexander's eye but did not turn her head. He had never seen such translucent skin, such shiny scarlet lips. Could she, too, be for sale? He felt excited at the thought, hot as a centaur. Until the revolution had come to the Academy, he had thought of little except girls and fencing.

As Alexander stared after her, the horn of a motorcar blasted just behind him. He heard the scrape of brakes and jumped back into the crowd. A two-door Studebaker pressed past him. "Idiot!" hollered an English voice. "In Shanghai we drive on the left!"

He came to a large cross street: Nanking Road. Needing to rest his leg, Alexander leaned against a wall. He stared at the richness of the shops while he ate his apple. Victrolas and phonograph records were displayed in the windows of S. Moutri Ltd., silver and glass at Tai Chong & Co., golf clubs at Hall & Holtz, pearls and diamonds at the Siberian Jewellery Store, and typewriters at the Office Appliance Company, with "Special Prices for Schools and Missions."

Two streetboys pressed leaflets into his hand. "Victoria Theatre. Pola Negri in *Mad Love*, " said one. "Lottery for the Benefit of the Russians. 40,000 Tickets. First Prize $20,000. International Committee for Assistance and Repatriation of Russian Refugees," said the other. Repatriation? wondered Alexander. He recalled all the disputes in Vladivostok and on board: whether to remain and fight to make things work in Russia, or leave and begin new lives. But reports of mass exterminations by the Reds had settled most debates. A new life was better than none.

An enormous dark man in pressed military khakis, shining boots and medals and a red turban and heavy black beard stood on a round platform in the middle of the street and directed traffic with a long baton and white-gloved hands. Some sort of British Indian, guessed Alexander, admiring his fierce authority.

Finished with his apple, he dropped the core. As he entered the Walk-Over Shoe Store for directions, he saw a barefoot boy pick the core from the street.

"*Pardon, monsieur,* " said Alexander to a European storekeeper in striped trousers and black waistcoat. "*Je cherche le Casino Belle Aurore, s'il vous plaît.* "

"If it's Frenchies you want, my lad, take a left and carry on." The man stubbed out his cigarette with a yellow thumb. "Hereabouts we're mostly English." Seeing the boy's confusion, the proprietor took Alexander by the elbow and led him to the doorway. He spoke more slowly. "Just take a left and let this mob carry you along. When you see Edward the Seventh, you're home."

"Edward seven, sir?"

"The road, boy, not the king."

In ten minutes, he was there: Avenue Edward VII, then the Rue du

Consulat. He passed along several narrower, more quiet residential streets lined with linden trees that stood before tall Parisian houses with mansard roofs. Two Europeans trotted past, posting briskly, dressed *à l'Anglaise* but mounted on short tough-looking horses with thick manes. Alexander admired their strong necks and powerful haunches. Hardy runners, he guessed.

He turned onto a broad busy boulevard, the Avenue Joffre. Here gendarmes in conical bamboo hats patrolled in pairs, their hands clasped behind their backs. Indo-Chinese, probably, like Captain Ricard's sergeant. Should he ask one of them? A Russian in China questioning an Annamese in French? He saw one coming his way. The policeman saluted when he approached.

"*Deuxième à gauche,*" the man advised. "*La Rue Lafayette.*"

It was a broad two-story villa, evidently converted to a higher use. CASINO BELLE AURORE said the sign in small bulbs over the door. Remembering his cadet training, Alexander paused for a brief reconnaissance under a tree across the street.

Two bearded Cossacks guarded the entrance. They wore rows of medals, tall cavalry boots with spurs and an exaggerated military costume. From time to time motorcars drew up, and occasionally a rickshaw. The guests were mostly European, women in wraps and long silk dresses, men in dinner jackets or dark suits. Many were driven by chauffeurs and attended by heavyset men in coarser clothes.

Finally Alexander was ready to go in. He wiped the toes of his boots against his scruffy grey trousers and tried to slick down his dark hair. He tucked in his shirt and brushed his jacket with both hands. He felt Viktor Polyak's broken pipe in one pocket and scowled. It gave him the courage he needed. He crossed the street and climbed the four steps to the doorway.

"Yes?" said one doorman, stepping in front of Alexander. The other Cossack looked at him as if he were the sort of beggar they had been hired to turn away.

"I am here to call on Prince Krupotkin." Alexander felt himself growing hot with a touch of his father's ready indignation.

"The prince is occupied," said the first.

"I am his cousin. I have a message from Count Karlov." Alexander stepped past the man into the brightness of the entrance hall.

A strong hand gripped his left arm. Nervous but furious, Alexander turned with both hands on his cane. "Touch me and Ivan Semyonov will rip off your beard," said Alexander.

"Semyonov?" Both men hesitated. "The hetman?" asked one, releasing him.

A woman in green silk passed by, a white fox over one shoulder and a black cigarette holder in her hand. She paused and looked at the two men and at Alexander. She was older, perhaps even forty, Alexander guessed, but her inviting roundish face had the pink and blond look of the country girls at home when they were still young enough to be fresh and pretty. And she had their body, too. The same high plump well-offered breasts that always caught his eye and that at night made him dream of rolling with one of them on the floor of the threshing barn with straw in her hair and her flushed pink nipples between his lips.

"Is anything the matter?" the lady said.

"This boy . . ." said one Cossack.

"I am a cousin of Prince Krupotkin, ma'am, and I have a letter for him from my father."

"I see." She smiled as she assessed him shamelessly from the head down. "Come with me. The prince is in one of the private rooms. Baccarat, I think."

Alexander followed her up the carpeted stair. He admired her high heels and the way her corsetted derriere drove from side to side like the smooth pumping pistons of a locomotive.

She stopped at a closed door and put one hand in the small of his back. "I'm Cornelia Litchfield. Be careful with those brutal Cossacks. Pavel uses them to collect his debts. No one ever wants to see them twice." She could see he was awash in her scent of perfume and brandy, and she smiled. "Perhaps I can show you something after you see the prince."

She opened the door and they entered a panelled sitting room warmed by a fireplace. Men looked up from two card tables. A female Chinese servant was replacing ashtrays. Alexander noticed a peculiar odor in the room, a smell that was not related to the smoke.

"Pavel, dear," said Cornelia to an exceptionally heavy, bald man in a dinner jacket, "this handsome boy says he's your cousin. Why can't you look like him?"

"Close the door, Corny. You never know who might come in." The man ignored the hand she put on his thick round shoulder. His neck and body were broad and soft, almost spongy, formless, giving the impression that if he removed his clothes his body would be released like fat pouring from a broken vat. But his face was hard, lit by small bright grey eyes and shiny with perspiration. The pores on his nose were like smallpox scars, large and pitted. A mottled burn scar marred his smooth head above one ear. He inclined his hairless head towards Alexander and said one word:

"Krupotkin."

"Alexander Karlov, sir. I have a letter for you from my father." Alexander reached into his jacket pocket. Horrified, he found it empty. He tried the other pocket, then both again. No letter, no money, he thought in panic. "I've been robbed." He looked up, red-faced, hoping to be believed.

"Pickpockets, no doubt." Krupotkin shrugged. He seemed indifferent to whether or not the boy was lying. "In Shanghai, everyone gets robbed. You just have to rob them first."

"My father and I arrived yesterday on the *Murmansk* from Vladivostok. He's still on board with three hundred men, Russians, our countrymen. He needs your help, sir, to make arrangements to come on shore. He sent me to bring you his letter."

"How do I know any of this? You could be anyone." Krupotkin wiped his lips with the back of his hand. "Every day unknown heroes and unheard-of relatives come to my door, begging for assistance. What do they think I am running here? Is this a casino or a church? Do I look like a priest?" His face shook and reddened. "Shanghai is crowded with rogues and imposters."

"How true." The lady winked.

"You and I met once before, sir, at Voskrenoye when I was young." Alexander held out his cane. "I can prove it to you, sir."

Krupotkin took the cane and, squinting closely, studied the bear heads on the the silver crest. He nodded and looked at Alexander with more care, but did not smile. Alexander could scarcely believe that this man was even a distant cousin of his mother.

"How old are you, boy?"

"Nearly eighteen, sir." Alexander now realized that the odor in the room rose from his host.

Krupotkin's hard eyes fixed on him. "How is your mother, my dear cousin? Alisa always was too good for your father."

"She was murdered on the Trans-Siberian," Alexander said quietly. "And the Reds kidnapped my sister."

"No." Krupotkin pressed his temples with one hand, for the first time showing what might be emotion. "Damn these devils! I am very sorry." He rubbed the scar above his ear. "We shall see if I can't find some position for your father here at the casino. But first he needs landing rights?"

Alexander stared at Krupotkin in surprise before replying. Who could imagine his father in such employment?

"Yes, sir, and for his men and friends," he said, not betraying his thoughts. "A French police officer, Captain Ricard, seems to be in charge. He says he knows you."

"Ricard. We know him well enough. He gambles here too often, never with success," said Krupotkin. "He pays by signing his worthless name. Perhaps we will let him clear a few chits. Your father and his friends could take on his debts. Write down the name of your vessel and we will see how this gendarme weighs his obligations. Duty or profit? A simple choice for a French policeman."

Krupotkin counted out some banknotes from his pocket. "Borrow this and find your way back on board." He pinched each bill between his fingers. "Try not to let anyone steal it. Here in Frenchtown, the Europeans own the buildings but the Chinese own the streets." He drew a black notebook from his pocket and wrote down the boy's name and a number. "And buy yourself some new clothes. If you are my cousin, you cannot go about like that."

As Krupotkin turned away, Alexander noticed a boil, hard and red as a radish, scraping against the edge of the prince's collar.

Cornelia came out into the hall with Alexander. "I hope I was useful," she said brightly, and took him by the hand. "Isn't he disgusting? He changes his shirt five times a day. You can see why I have to drink."

Before Alexander could respond, she led him down the corridor. "What a pretty stick you have." They entered a room with a billiard table and two shaded overhanging lamps.

"Are you a virgin?" she asked after closing the door.

Alexander hesitated.

"In Shanghai everyone pays extra for virgins," she added. "They're so rare."

"A, a virgin?" Alexander blushed as she slipped one hand under his jacket and ran her fingers across his ribs and stomach. He felt he was losing control over his body. He gasped for air as if running up a staircase.

"Are you a virgin?"

"I . . ." He remembered his father's irritating trick of avoiding a question with a question. "Are you?"

"Of course." Cornelia pressed him back against one end of the table. "Always." She lowered the single silk strap of her dress and narrowed her shoulders until the gown slipped down and her plump white breasts hung free like melons on a vine.

"Kiss me," Cornelia said urgently. She raised her left breast with both hands and guided her pink nipple to Alexander's lips. He noticed the blue veins beneath her pale skin. Then he closed his eyes and did as he was told. Squeezing her breast between both hands and sucking it into his mouth like a stick candy, he wondered if he was doing it right.

He lost her when she moved and he felt her fingers hurrying along the waistband of his trousers. A button tore loose. Her breasts pressed against his chest. He seemed to be drowning in a wave of brandy and perfume. She reached up and breathed on his neck before biting him fiercely below the ear.

Alexander jerked his head to the side. Leaning back to balance himself, he braced one hand behind him on the pool table. He was embarrassed by his own excitement.

Cornelia placed her right forearm between his legs. She straightened her own legs and lifted hard.

"Oh!" Alexander dropped his cane and fell on his back upon the table. He did not want to reveal the pain, but his knee felt as if it were bending in the wrong direction.

Cornelia lifted her skirt and climbed on after him. She straddled him with her knees. Her breasts rose and swung when she reached up and pulled the lamp cord. The room went black. Paralyzed with both alarm and ardor, afraid he was about to make a mess of things, Alexander clutched the leather side pockets of the table while she undid his shirt buttons and kissed his belly.

"How delicious," she said, pausing to work at his trouser buttons. "And what is this! My, my!"

Suddenly there were heavy steps in the hall. The door burst open. A dark figure filled the doorway.

"The prince needs you downstairs, Miss Litchfield," said one of the Cossacks, switching on the sconce lights.

"Tell him I'm coming," she said indifferently, her eyes still on Alexander.

* * *

On the way back to Soochow Creek, Alexander tried to reach the embankment by a shorter route, one less confusing, but instead he became lost. He soon found himself on a darker street called Blood Alley. It seemed to be a road of girls and sailors. Seamen sang and drank and vomited in the side streets. Women called to him from shadows and doorways in English, French and Russian. Twice Chinese girls slipped their arms through his and sought to lure him aside. They wore high-collared flowered silk dresses fitted tight to their slender bodies. Alexander kept one hand on the money inside his pocket. The girls left him when he showed no interest.

He had not gone far before he had to rest. His leg had been hurting since he had fallen backward on the billiard table. Although the evening air was cool, he sat down at a small outdoor café, Le Chien Rapide, with four round tables on the street.

"*Une bière, s'il vous plaît, et une omelette au jambon,*" he ordered. His mother would be pleased with his French. "*Baveuse.*"

A rickshaw pulled up outside a brick house across the street. Two red bulbs illuminated a small sign beside the door: LA SINGERIE.

An elderly Chinese woman in a high-collared dark fur coat gave a note to her puller and waited alone while the man knocked on the door to deliver the message. When the door of the Singerie opened, the rickshaw man bowed his head and went inside.

"Egg," said the waiter, setting down Alexander's soft ham omelette sprinkled with cilantro. His mouth watered when he smelled it. This would be the finest meal he'd had in months. As he ate, he recalled all his bad meals at school, on the train, in Vladivostok and on board. He mopped his plate with a piece of French bread.

"*Encore une omelette, s'il vous plaît.*"

He sipped his second beer while he waited. He felt like a man. At last he was doing something on his own. He tried to understand an

Italian naval officer who was negotiating with two girls at the next table.

"*Tout ensemble,*" the man repeated in a loud voice. He tangled three fingers. "*Terzétti?* All together, yes yes?"

The door opened at the Singerie. Three burly Chinese emerged. One walked to the lady's rickshaw and stepped between the traces. The small Chinese woman leaned forward and protested as the man lifted the poles. Her shouts held Alexander's attention as she cried out and tried to step down. The other two men rushed to the rickshaw. One of them pushed the woman back in her seat.

"*Au secours!*" she screamed as she attempted to climb down the other side. "Au secours! Help!" Again the woman was forced roughly back. "Help!" she yelled. Leaning forward quickly, she took her assailant's face between her hands as if caressing him. Then her fingers bent like claws.

"Ai! Ai!" She gave two fierce shrill cries and fell back into the far corner of the rickshaw. Bleeding red lines ran down both sides of the man's face.

Alexander stood and hurried across the street with his cane.

"What are you doing?" he said to the Chinese men as the woman screamed once more. "Leave her alone."

One of the men slammed his hand against Alexander's chest and pushed him into the middle of the street. Alexander stumbled but saved himself with his cane. A second man pursued him, swinging a long cosh attached to his wrist by a leather strap. Reacting quickly, Alexander avoided the blow.

"*Podlets!*" Enraged, Alexander took the cane in his left hand and drew the short sword. "Devil!"

In a vicious swipe, the blade flashed along the man's right arm and cut through his sleeve and strap. The Chinese screamed. The cosh fell to the street. Bleeding, the man cursed and rushed at him. One of his companions punched Alexander in the side of the head. Alexander staggered sideways into the street with the two men after him. But he had no time for dizziness.

He shook his head and stepped to his left so that he faced them with his sword arm. His heart was beating hard and he felt a slight shake or tingle in his joints. But he knew he was good with a sword. He remembered the speed drills and the bladework, trying to pierce a falling apple in the air with his epée. No one else in the class could do it.

He advanced his right leg forward as if in a duel, his left leg stiff as a bar behind him. Alexander knew he could not retreat, so he would have to press them. He flicked the short sword from side to side as if challenging two fencers.

One man feinted and rushed at him with a knife. Alexander raised his sword and braced against his left foot as the man came at him. The attacker plunged onto the blade and ran himself through the side. The man screamed and dropped his knife. Alexander freed the blade with a swift twist. Swinging instantly to his left, he clubbed the other assailant, nearly upon him, across the face with the empty cane. The Chinese yelled and staggered back, his nose flattened and bleeding. Alexander kept the tip of his sword raised between them. Again, the motions seemed easy and slow and familiar, like fencing of the early Italian school, with a sword in one hand, a dagger in the other. The third man fled.

The door to the Singerie opened and the lady's rickshaw puller appeared. Blood dripped from his forehead. His jacket was torn. He left the door open and ran to his mistress as the thug Alexander had stabbed was led away by his companion. The Chinese with the broken nose yelled something at Alexander.

Picking up the knife, the rickshaw man placed it in his cloth belt. He wiped his face on his sleeve and lifted the traces. Alexander saw that the puller had lost one straw sandal.

Alexander leaned on the side of the rickshaw and gasped for breath as he took the weight off his left leg. "Are you all right, *madame?*" he said to the lady. He noticed her rising wing-like eyebrows and saw her tiny slippered feet in the bottom of the rickshaw. They were sky blue and delicate as two robin's eggs.

"Thank you, sir," she said in perfect careful French. "Perhaps you saved my life. Those evil men are the enemies of my protector. They lured me here to exchange messages, then tried to capture me."

"It was nothing. I just . . ."

"No," the Chinese lady interrupted, shaking her head and glancing down the street. "You have a gallant instinct. That is rare."

"Thank you." Alexander blushed.

"Here is my card." Her voice softened, becoming almost intimate. "Please call on me."

The lady looked nervously down the road when a whistle blew twice in the distance. "Leave now." She touched his cheek with the blood-stained fingertips of one hand. "It is best not to talk to the police." Then her tone sharpened and she spoke rapidly to her puller in Shanghainese. With a lurch the rickshaw rolled away.

Alexander walked back to the café. He wiped his blade on his napkin and sheathed it. The waiter replaced the bloody napkin and affected to have noticed nothing.

"Bravo," said the nearby Italian quietly, raising his eyebrows, almost smiling, though he had done nothing to assist. Alexander was pleased with himself, exhilarated. He recalled shooting the Holland and using his penknife on the thief on the Trans-Siberian, and serving the machine gun. He wondered if he was developing a taste for this sort of thing.

He sat down to his beer. His leg was trembling. With a deep bow the waiter served his second omelette.

Not a bad day, thought Alexander, wiping two small smears of blood from his cheek. English courtesans on billiard tables, Chinese thugs in back alleys, not bad at all. And all his. "Becoming something of a swordsman, aren't we?" his father would probably say, if he knew.

As two Annamite gendarmes came running up Blood Alley, Alexander looked at the lady's card:

MADAME MEI-LAN WONG

CRAVATES SUR COMMANDE

69 RUE VOISIN

SHANGHAI

He recalled her touch, as delicate as the stroke of a sable paintbrush, but bloody. Neckties and scarves to order? He thought about where he was, the street girls and the Singerie and the woman's fear of the police. He wondered how Madame Mei-lan Wong was connected with that business. He must call on her as soon as possible.

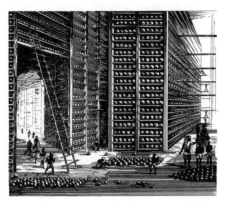

-9-

"Steady!" called Alexander. He squinted up at the sky and seized the swinging rope that hung from Rizhka's halter. Suspended by a canvas sling under her belly, his father's black mare flailed with her hooves as the ship's boom slowly lowered her to the sampan. Alexander guided the animal onto the narrow flat bottom of the skiff. He held the horse's head and stroked her nose before freeing the sling.

"Easy, Rizhka, you'll be ashore soon." The Cossack's horse was already secure in the other sampan, lashed to his for stability.

On the deck of the *Murmansk*, his father finished his good-byes, shaking hands with many of the men, Lancers and Dragoons and Hussars, kissing several old comrades on both cheeks, clasping others to him before he stepped to the rail. Gregori sat in the second sampan amidst their baggage. He held Osetra's head by the halter. Lieutenant Petrov waved down to Alexander. Vasily clapped and pointed ashore and called out something that his young friend could not hear. Alexander knew that Petrov and the others were depending on Major Karlov to arrange their landing rights.

"Soochow Creek," said Alexander to his father a few moments later. He felt like an old hand as they approached the waterfront. He recognized the smells of burning coal and garlic that seemed to shroud the port.

"I'm a bit old for this sort of work," said Major Karlov. "Starting a new life in a pirate town like this," he grumbled. "Whore of the East, they call it."

In fact, his father's eyes and voice were lively, as if he were a young officer on a fresh campaign. His tall black boots, wrinkled at the ankles, were polished as if he were visiting the Winter Palace. He wore a faded green tunic, well brushed but with no shoulder boards or decorations. A Russian officer always wore uniform, Alexander reminded himself, even when off duty.

Alexander himself could not wait to go ashore again. He wanted to attack, to learn every alley and corner of Shanghai. In one day he had learned more about women than he had in his lifetime in Russia. He thought of the silken girl on the sampan, the lacquered lady in the rickshaw, and Cornelia at the Belle Aurore. He had not told his father about the street fight with the Chinese, and the lady who had given him her card. His father once had told him that a man must keep certain adventures to himself. Alexander guessed that this was the sort of thing he had in mind.

"At least we shall go ashore like Russian officers," said the Count with determination.

Barefoot boys rushed to help when the sampan was tied up at a less busy spot alongside Soochow Creek. A crude narrow ramp of old boards nailed together was stretched from the embankment across the gap.

"I'll take the hetman's horse," said Alexander. With his father watching, he would have to lead the nervous powerful animal across to the other sampan and then up the steep ramp with his cane in one hand.

"No, Osetra's yours, Sasha. I won him for you, playing cards with

Semyonov," said his father casually. "We'll saddle them up while they're still in the boats."

Thrilled, Alexander saddled the horses while Gregori unloaded the sampans and directed the transfer of the baggage to two handcarts with large single wheels.

Another sampan tied up beside them. It was heaped with a struggling mass of trussed pigs. The smell reminded Alexander of the farms on the estate at home. The young swine squealed and resisted as they were lifted by their bonds and hurled up onto the stone embankment.

A factory siren suddenly blared and combined with the agitation and odor of the pigs to feed the horses' nervous excitement. Alexander could feel their flushed energy after the confinement of the ship. They were used to long canters and fast charges, not tight spaces and no exercise.

The Major paid the boatmen and climbed on Rizhka. The big mare was trembling, lifting one front hoof after the other. The sampans rocked as the horse pawed and fretted. Porters and coolies clad in baggy blue cotton paused and stared down from the embankment.

Karlov was not accustomed to taking nonsense from his horses. He leaned forward and gave Rizhka both spurs. The animal bolted up the ramp as if leading a charge. Sparks flew from her shoes when she scrambled onto the edge of the embankment. Fearful of the horse but seeming to enjoy the excitement, the crowd parted. The Major rode on without looking back.

Alexander knew he had to follow. Osetra, too, was trembling, and she strained against his hand. He gripped the agitated horse by the halter and stepped into the other boat. Stretching its neck, protesting, the big grey held back. Embarrassed as the crowd watched, Alexander slapped Osetra's side with his cane. Finally responding, the animal stumbled into his sampan, slamming against his shoulder and nearly knocking him into the water. He tightened the girth and lengthened the left stirrup while Osetra stamped from side to side. Veins stood out on the horse's neck. The boatman hollered down from the embankment, apparently concerned that the agitated animal would punch a hole in the bottom of his vessel. Alexander knew Osetra was not used to being mounted from the right, but with his left leg almost rigid, he had no choice.

Alexander took a handful of mane in his right hand and swung into the saddle for the first time since he had been injured. Immediately he used his heels. Goaded, Osetra sprang for the ramp. The horse stumbled once, its head plunging low, but then broke onto the embankment as if bursting from the start.

The Count had not waited, so Alexander followed him through the crowd at a trot. Gregori and the wheelbarrow coolies hurried on behind. They came to a bridge that led to the International Settlement and the French Concession. Squatting coolies whistled and solicited business with offers to help the rickshaws and carts up and down the steep bridge. Karlov engaged one of them to help push the barrows. The man's reluctance to leave their service made it clear the Count had overpaid. Alexander was relieved that he had caught up and had not become lost. The way his father rode, keeping up was part of the drill.

"Where are we going, Father?"

"We must make camp, Sasha, while we learn our way about the town." The Count stood in his stirrups and stretched. Back in the saddle, they were both once again at home. "After that, we'll let Shanghai know we are here." Alexander wondered what his father had in mind. From what he had seen so far, in Shanghai it was hard enough just to find one's way and stay alive.

They rode through the quieter streets of the Concession for two hours, searching for an affordable stable and accommodation. The few stables were crowded with racing ponies. The good hotels were too costly. Alexander grew more and more discouraged. His left leg was growing numb from the riding. Hungry, he smelled charcoal and roasting chestnuts.

"Time for a drink," said Karlov when they paused side by side at a street corner. "This damn town is impossible."

Alexander winced at the sight of the destitute Europeans in the crowd. Most wore fragments of Russian uniforms. They begged with the tentative awkward approach of the newly indigent. Lean and unshaven, some had rags bound around their feet. Several seemed drunk. A one-eyed man with a lieutenant's single stripe on his shoulder boards approached them and tried to sell his medals. Karlov handed the officer several coins but refused the medals.

"Should we go and ask Prince Krupotkin where to stay?" said Alexander, embarrassed for the old soldiers. He was growing more conscious of how much had been lost in Russia. "I know the way to the casino."

"Do you, indeed? The 'Prince'?" snorted Karlov. "Help from Krupotkin is too dear. Captain Ricard made me sign a pocketful of his gambling chits to buy our landing rights. We haven't set foot on the ground and already this cousin of yours has us in debt." Furious at the thought of his wife's grasping relative, the Count touched Rizhka with his heels. "Does Krupotkin still stink like a slaughterhouse?"

"Yes, sir."

"Then the sweaty swine hasn't changed. As one of Ricard's countrymen said, malice preserves one. *Mechanceté préserve.* Voltaire I think it was. Or Talleyrand? The French understand these things, Sasha."

"Yes, sir."

They rode along the edge of the Chinese city, the Boulevard des Deux Républiques and Chung Hwa Road. Finally, on a side street off the Rue Voisin, they found an inn with a red tile roof built around a cobblestone courtyard. Two grey ducks were painted on each stone gatepost.

"Time to unsaddle," said the Major. "Better here, boy, than be seen starting off in a second-rate European hotel." They rode in and dismounted near a palanquin that rested in a corner of the yard. His father went inside and made arrangements.

Once they were settled, Karlov and Alexander sat alone on the long narrow terrace that edged one side of the courtyard. The Count had sent

Gregori out for cigars and wine. Two bottles of Cos d'Estournel rested on the table between them. From time to time they nodded at a passing Chinese guest who bowed towards them. Alexander was excited, intrigued to be staying at a Chinese inn rather than a European hotel.

Karlov opened a bottle and poured both glasses. Then he said something that sobered Alexander.

"I do hope you understand, Sasha, that the only reason I speak rarely of your mother and sister is that it is too painful."

Alexander could feel his father growing maudlin as he drank.

"In her heart, your mother wanted to be a Decembrist, a gentle revolutionary. Did you know, Sasha, that the Decembrist wives were told that if they followed their husbands to Siberia they would have to leave their children behind? Any new child they had would become a serf, the property of the state." The Count filled both glasses. "And still they went to be with their husbands." Karlov squeezed his son's wrist.

"That is the sort of girl you need one day, Sasha, because you never know how life will change. Remember my words."

He released Alexander's arm and lifted his glass. "Your mother once told me that in exile in Siberia her grandmother's curls froze to her mattress, but she never complained about her new life. She was who she was, and her life was inside her."

Alexander could not reply.

"I know you miss Katia and your Maman, as I do, every day. Let us drink to them." Karlov touched his son's glass and drank. "We will search for Katerina when we can, Sasha, but you know there is no returning now to Russia."

Alexander's eyes filled with tears before he touched the wine. Where was Katia? He'd thought the matter over often on the boat. Might she still be in Siberia with a pack of Red Guards, treated like a woman of the camp, used by every Bolshevik for his pleasure? Or in a city with the Commissar? Or delivered by him to some prison for enemies of the new Russia, perhaps in Omsk, or even Moscow?

"Tonight, we drink and eat," said Karlov after a moment. "Tomorrow, we have three things to do."

"Three things?" asked Alexander, feeling like his father's friend, not his son. Here he was, drinking with him like a man.

"Find a way to live, help the others get off the boat, and put you in school." He raised three fingers one by one. "I'm too old to start slowly. And if we don't begin at once, soon we'll be two more Russian beggars dying in the street." Karlov paused and prepared a cigar before continuing.

"You think you know so much, Sasha." He filled the glasses. "So tell me. What do they need in Shanghai, and what do you think an old soldier like your father can do in a place like this?"

"Why, you could do anything, Papa. Anything. Pr . . . Krupotkin said he might find work for you at the Belle Aurore."

"What?" Karlov flushed and banged down the bottle. "You think I'd serve as a croupier to that toad of an *arriviste*? He was a cousin of your mother's cousin, and they all despised him."

Alexander had to agree. He remembered the stink. "I'm sure you're right, Father." He yawned. "Perhaps . . ."

"I know to do only two things, Alexander. I've done them both from Vilna to Vladivostok, and ended up with nothing. You know what they are?" He struck a match against the heel of his boot. "Riding and killing. These two, and telling other men what to do." Karlov looked up at Alexander with a gleam in his eye. "Perhaps we can find some way to put these fine talents to profit."

When Alexander awoke late in the morning, Gregori and his father were gone. Alexander had some tea, then busied himself as if he were in camp. He fed and watered Osetra, then cleaned their leather and weapons.

As he worked, he reflected on what his father had said last night about his mother's family in exile. Alexander knew that one hundred Decembrist officers, naive advocates of constitutional monarchy and improved conditions for serfs and workers, had been exiled by the emperor to labor camps in Siberia. Their wives, glittering ladies of St. Petersburg society, were declared widows by church and state. But Alexander's great-grandmother Katerina, like many Decembrist wives, had followed her husband by train and cart and foot to his camp in the wilderness. She had been permitted only four hours with him each week, and those in the presence of an officer of the state. In time, as the rules eased, the couple sent for their library and harpsichord and built a log house in Irkutsk near the shore of Lake Baikal. There both taught school. They instructed the local Buryats and three generations of less educated exiles in history and botany and music. In the evenings their small house was crowded and warm as Katerina, wearing her pearls, played Mozart with her students and her husband read aloud from Pushkin. Together they rehearsed amateur theatricals as if preparing for a house party at home. Alexander wondered if one day he would indeed find a woman like his great-grandmother.

At midday his father rode into the courtyard. A Chinese was sweeping the yard in even lines with a long straw broom. Startled, he looked up at the Russian horseman as if a unicorn or griffin had trotted up to him.

"Saddle up, boy," the Count said, his humor easier. "I've something to show you."

They rode to the edge of the French Concession, where they finally turned into the Chemin St. Bernard, a side street adjoining the old Chinese city. Gregori and two Chinese awaited them at the entrance to a large wooden building. They dismounted and the Major approached the two Chinese.

"It's big enough," said Karlov. "But is it cheap enough?"

Alexander looked about at the huge empty warehouse while the three men haggled. A long broken ladder lay on the floor beside him.

The two long walls, forty or fifty feet tall, were covered in wooden shelves from floor to ceiling. Flat wooden rungs were attached to one wall and led upward to a webwork of slender beams, woven like lattice, that crossed the great space and supported the roof.

Alexander stared up and wondered if his leg would be sturdy enough to let him climb to the top, and if his arms might be strong enough to let him cross the warehouse, swinging hand over hand. His stomach tightened when he thought of it.

A musty sweet odor hung in the air when one stood near the side walls. But at the end of the warehouse, where they were standing now, Alexander smelled something different. He reached down and collected some of the brown dust that covered the floor. He rubbed it between his palms and sniffed it. Tea.

"They're telling me this ancient wreck is cheap because of this stink," said the Count to Alexander. "They say in the old days thousands of balls of opium, the size of large melons, came here from Calcutta and Madras. They were unpacked and stored along these racks. Sometimes they repacked tea here as well."

The Count looked at Alexander, to make certain he was paying attention. "It was the British, of course, trading drugs to China and tea to India. If we had done that we'd still have an empire. Today nobody wants this place. The opium's not legal now, and it's too far from the docks for a warehouse."

Alexander watched his father sign a note and count out their precious francs and rubles. The Chinese took the money and the note, bowed and left.

"We have three months," said his father. "When you're not studying, Alexander, you'll be teaching here."

"What's it for, Father? I don't understand."

"A stable, a riding school, and a *Salle d'Armes*. We are going to teach these people how Russians ride and fight." He rested a hand on his son's shoulder. "And we are going to give the English the one thing they like best."

"A bar?"

"No, Sasha." The Count smiled. "A club. And you're going to learn how to start a business. The carpenters will be here soon."

"No good. No no no," said the master carpenter, interfering as Gregori prepared a fumigation fire on the hard dirt floor in the center of the warehouse.

The Chinese called over a carpenter who was drawing out the nails that held the shelves to the walls. The man dropped several nails into a bucket. Trying to help after his father had left him in charge, Alexander had been admonished to pull each nail out straight so it could be used again. The old shelves were being stacked for use as planks.

The carpenter took his instructions from his foreman and hurried out the door. Soon he was back with a wheelbarrow laden with branches and green feathery leaves and a smelly sack of butcher's scraps. He set a fire at either end of the warehouse. He dumped out the butcher's waste from the sack, but before feeding it onto the fires, the carpenter let the workmen pick out the edible bits from the slippery scraps of pork and pig intestines.

His eyes smarting, Alexander went outside to the open yard behind the warehouse. The workers sat nearby, chattering and eating noodles and bits of fish from small bowls with their fingers. Smoke soon billowed from both ends of the building. Alexander was confident that the greasy fragrant fires would do the job. The heavy gluey smoke should cling to the walls.

"What have you been up to, you young blockhead?" The Count dismounted and tossed Rizhka's reins to Gregori. "They can smell this in Hong Kong. It's worse than your cousin the prince. If you burn this place down, the moneylenders will skin us."

"You asked me to fumigate it, sir," said Alexander.

"What's in that stinking fire?"

"Bunches of wild garlic and green bamboo and pig guts."

That was too complicated for any but a Chinaman to think up, Karlov judged. "It had better work," he said, for once letting something go. "We open in one week. Tuesday. I've just posted an advertisement in the *North-China Daily News*. Soon you'll be teaching the *jeunesse d'orée* how to kill each other." He eyed the fires with an odd smile. "Should be a lesson they'll never forget."

"*À cheval, Alexandre!*" said the Count, as he did when he woke Alexander each morning by ripping the blanket off his son like a sergeant in the field. "Monday morning. Today we buy horses and weapons."

Accustomed to the slow pace of work on the estate at home and to the surly worn-out movements of the peasants, Alexander was astonished at how much had been accomplished. Somehow the energy of Shanghai's streets had been transferred to the Salle d'Armes. The framing and new layouts were done. Only the finishing work remained. Tomorrow morning the street hawkers would be selling the newspaper containing their advertisement, and the first clients should appear.

Alexander inspected the new stables. They had no roofs. "Mongol ponies live outdoors in the steppes through the winter," the Count had said. "Hardiness is their quality. Like soldiers, spoil them and what do you have? Old women."

Built from the discarded shelves, the stalls extended along the rear wall of the warehouse in the yard. Alexander noticed rat droppings in the corners. The creatures were already rearranging themselves within the building. He recalled seeing a street vendor with large traps hanging from his bamboo shoulder pole, and, for advertising, a dead rat suspended from the other end by its tail.

Windows and tall double doorways to accommodate a horse and rider had been framed at both ends of the long structure. The front end would be dedicated to fencing. Shelves had been pierced and rearranged to provide racks for foils, epées and sabres. Nails were driven into the wall as pegs for fencing masks and vests. Marks of charcoal indicated where the training mirrors would hang. The fencing floor was built from more shelf planks.

Eighteen feet above the oval riding ring, a narrow gallery ran along one wall. One end of the gallery led to two small bedrooms erected above the fencing space for the Count and Alexander. The green and crimson pennant of the Major's regiment was mounted on the wall above the main entrance to the Salle. Only at the very top of the warehouse did one level of the old shelves remain.

A village was growing in the rear yard behind the stables and the outdoor ring. On the third day a cook in baggy blue pantaloons had appeared with a sack of charcoal and two round tin pans. "Li," he announced, and that is what they called him.

In minutes Li had begun to prepare food for the laborers. By that evening Karlov and Alexander and Gregori were sitting on a stack of planks eating noodles and pork and prawns. Alexander helped himself again when the older men pushed their bowls aside.

"We'll have Ivan teach the fellow to make some proper food." The Major stood and lit a cigar.

The next day the cook's wife, Chung, arrived and swept the warehouse and picked up their dirty clothes. Her child played on the ground under the hanging laundry. In two days the family had created a shelter of bamboo. The walls of their hut were fashioned from intertwined strips of split bamboo secured to four bamboo corner poles set in the ground. The roof was made of bamboo and thatch.

An hour later, Alexander and his father tied up their horses outside a crowded stable. In a week's time Karlov had located and inspected all the equestrian establishments in the frantic congested city.

"Only one thing for sale here," said the short bow-legged Englishman who received them. Alexander guessed he was an old jockey, though the man's long face was creased like a sailor too long at sea. "China ponies. No proper hunters or racers, I'm afraid. Hop inside and have a look."

"You choose the horses," said Karlov to his son. "I'll do the bargaining."

Alexander thought it would work better the other way around. "Perhaps, Father ..." he began.

"Choose the horses, boy," said Karlov.

"Ponies for sale are down here." The jockey led Alexander inside past a line of stalls. "Mostly belong to chaps who're going home, or who can't pay their stable bills, damn their eyes."

"What's a China pony?" said Alexander.

The man shook his head at such bottomless ignorance. "You must be a griffin."

"What's a griffin?"

"New boys. Fresh out, first-timers in Shanghai. Mostly young lads here to pocket a fast fortune and catch a bit of naughty before they go home and die of boredom. We call young horses 'griffins' as well. Have races for them every year, the Griffin Plate. Where you from?"

"Voskrenoye, a village north of Moscow."

"What did your old gent do there?" the man asked in a hushed voice as he paused outside a stall and raised the latch. "He seems a proper stiff one."

"My father raised horses for the army, mostly blacks for the Guards. He was a major in the Hussars."

"Oh, I see." Changing his mind, the jockey closed the latch and moved to a different stall.

"What's a China pony?"

"First of all, one rule, laddie. Ponies are not small horses, they're a different animal altogether. Out here they're all Mongolians. A fresh lot come down from the steppes every spring. Buy them at auctions and use them in the races, in the Paper Hunt, in getting about, for everything, really. Short and tough. Plenty of run in them. Damned clever over open country and can carry lots of weight. Astonishing jumpers for such short legs." The man opened a stable door and stroked the muscular rump of a stocky dun. "When they get older, mind you, the Chinks and the Froggies chop them up and eat 'em. Prepare them differently, of course."

Alexander put one hand on the animal's withers, then moved it along her shaggy flank and down her buttock. He examined one gaskin, hock and cannon with careful tight fingers. She had better teeth than her English owner. Alexander checked each fetlock and raised her hooves one by one. The Englishman bridled her and brought out a light saddle. "Want to try her in the yard?"

"Mind if I don't use a saddle?" Alexander handed the man his cane. The jockey said nothing when the boy mounted from the right.

He took the dun for a short ride, circling and reversing in the ring, changing gait. He rode five more ponies while his father and the jockey smoked and watched. He checked the mouth of each animal and ran his hands down their legs.

"I'd say these three, Father," Alexander judged, and prayed he had it right. "The dun's the best of them. We can use the small fat one for children's lessons." His father made no sign of disagreement.

"One hundred sixty dollars for the lot," said the little man.

The Count counted out 120. "That will have to do," he said. "And forty more for two old bridles and saddles." He handed the man 160.

The man took the money gladly and shook hands with Major Karlov. "You ought to put that lad of yours in the races, but don't feed him so much. He's too bloody tall already."

Leading their new ponies, Karlov and Alexander mounted up and rode slowly home.

"I hope I picked the right ones, Papa," said Alexander, certain his father was comparing these ponies with the black stallions and mares in the paddocks at Voskrenoye.

"We'll see, Sasha." The Count smiled a bit. "But that little Englishman certainly thought you did."

-10-

For once Alexander was awake first. He lay on his back in the near darkness and listened to his father grinding his teeth as he slept next door. The sound reminded Alexander of a whetstone scraping old rust from a sabre. He was becoming used to the habits and sounds of life in the warehouse. But in quiet, private moments like this he missed his sister's laughter and his mother's music. He wondered if his father would ever play the violin again. Karlov had not opened the case since they had sailed from Russia. Alexander guessed that he found it too painful a reminder. Although she had often deplored the Count's lack of practice and finesse, Alexander's mother had loved it when her husband abandoned his evening game of whist and instead accompanied her while she played Fauré or Mozart on her Pleyel.

Alexander closed his eyes and dozed. He recalled lying late in bed on idle mornings, knowing his mother would be arranging the house for the day and planning meals with the cook, flower cuttings with the gardener and invitations for the weekends. Every morning she wrote letters. Every afternoon she played the piano, Mozart when she was at her happiest. Occasionally she would spoil Alexander herself, bringing him a breakfast tray of *chocolat chaud* and thin rolled blintzes with jellied fruit fillings and sour cream. He could smell the tray as soon as she opened the door.

Here Alexander's room had no ceiling. He stared up at the distant timbered roof of the warehouse and wondered again if he could make the climb. With his head near the wall he thought he could still smell the scent of the opium balls over the odor of the horses and the greasy clinging smoke of the fumigation fires. Today he would begin managing the fencing school. He reached under the sheet and ran both hands along his bare left leg. It felt cold. There was a ridged lump just below the knee and a thicker shorter bump above it. The calf and thigh seemed smaller than his right. His stomach tightened with a pang of worry. Who would want a crippled fencing master? What girl would like him like this?

As yet they had only foils and epées. His father's cavalry sabre, well-blooded, was too heavy for instruction and sport competition but would be useful in providing a sense of the weapon. After buying the three ponies, they had passed by Hall & Holtz, a shop that advertised cricket bats and jodhpurs in the *North-China Daily News*.

"For what, sir, do you require sabres in Shanghai?" said Mr. Hall, elegant in his English merchant way in tailored vest and trousers.

"For the Salle d'Armes," Karlov replied.

"The 'sale'? What?"

"To teach swordsmanship." The Count handed the Englishman his card. "Using only the foil, you teach ballet, not fighting."

Alexander was not certain he agreed, but it was impossible to argue weapons with his father. In Alexander's opinion the lighter fencing sabre, unlike the cavalry sword, required as much finesse and fingerwork as a foil.

"Sabre requires a strong right arm," added Karlov.

Mr. Hall read the *carte de visite*:

SALLE D'ARMES
4, CHEMIN ST. BERNARD
INSTRUCTION IN FENCING AND RIDING
BY
COUNT DIMITRI KARLOV
MAJOR, THE CZAR'S 5TH HUSSARS

"You are new to Shanghai, Count Karlov?" said Hall.

"Shanghai is where we live. Perhaps you will be kind enough to call on us for drinks."

Once outside, Karlov had explained his thoughts to Alexander.

"The English are good at three things: clubs, empire building and drinking, but they don't like to pay for any of them. They love to have others provide their food and drink. Splendid guests, witty and gracious, most of the time. Of course, they never speak a second language, let alone a third. Here at least you'll improve your English and learn some sort of Chinese."

"Do I still have to study French?" Alexander recalled biting his lips to stay awake in the high-ceilinged classroom in the old palace of the Knights of Malta, given to the Corps of Pages by Alexander I a century earlier. Instead of memorizing his French subjunctives, he would stare out the leaded window at the Maltese Cross atop the Catholic chapel in the garden and imagine the great sieges and battles the Hospitalers of St. John of Jerusalem had fought against the Saracens.

"Of course, Sasha," replied his father, "*pour te faire civiliser.* You must speak French well enough to be a gentleman, but of course never well enough to be mistaken for a Frenchman."

Karlov himself had always favored the Russian spirit of Moscow over the European style of St. Petersburg, where many of their friends conversed only in French. "But don't forget, boy, though you take your language from Paris, you must take your manners from London, at least most of them." Karlov recalled the English earl who had come to Voskrenoye for a shooting weekend and had stayed on for six weeks, borrowing his host's clothes and visiting the kitchen each morning to order his favored dishes.

Riding home, the Count had continued. "Mr. Hall cannot yet give us sabres, but he can give us clients. And we'll give the English a few new clubs to join."

The train of memories came to an end. Anxious about his first day, Alexander rose, made his bed and went downstairs. His leg seemed more stiff.

Chung had swept the ring and was on her knees polishing the fencing floor. Tea was on the boil. With reluctance Li had learned to serve the strong dark tea on which Karlov insisted. Alexander knew that the next step must be a samovar.

He led the horses from their stalls and secured them to the iron rings now set in the streetside wall of the warehouse. Now visitors and passersby would know immediately where they were.

"Polish your boots, boy," said his father sharply when he appeared downstairs. "An Englishman once wrote to his son that 'one can tell a gentleman by his linen and his leather.' Chesterton, I think it was, or Chesterfield. Those English names are all alike."

Karlov paced about, checking every preparation as if reviewing his regiment before battle. Chung took a pan of hot water from the edge of the cook fire and set it on the long rough table in the stable yard. An old belt was nailed to the wall nearby. The Count stropped his cut-throat razor with swift strokes and began to shave. Hurrying, he cut himself.

"Damn. I'm nervous as a virgin, Sasha. Come here and rip out these ugly stitches from the boat. They won't be good for business."

Nervous himself, Alexander held his father's chin with his left hand and sliced the tiny knots with the end of the straight razor. He carefully drew out the fine black threads. Dots of blood and a single cut recorded his work.

"I'm sorry, Father."

Karlov shrugged and rubbed his face with a splash of vodka. "Two plates of eggs, if you please," he called out to Li.

Alexander said nothing, but he was learning to prefer a Chinese breakfast of dumplings, soy bean cakes and congee, with a few red dates mixed into the rice porridge.

As they sat down to eat, Gregori returned from Bubbling Well Road with several copies of the *Daily News*. The two-column advertisement looked much like the Major's new calling card.

"Have some eggs, Gregori," said Karlov. "When you've finished, run down to the newspaper office and order five hundred copies of the advertisement. Have them send the bill."

"Five hundred?" said Alexander. "Isn't that more than we need, Papa?"

"Stop worrying about every bloody sou," said the Count. "We'll use them all. And remember, we don't have to pay now."

Alexander groaned inside. Soon it would be worse than the debts at home.

Then they waited for their first client. For four hours. No one came.

"Noon," said Karlov at last, buckling and unbuckling a bridle at the table in the yard. "Time for a drink." He poured Alexander a very small vodka so as not to drink alone.

Behind them, Semyonov was growling at Li by the kitchen fire. When one wanted low coals, the other required flames. The Chinese hunched his shoulders and muttered quietly while the hetman berated him.

Ivan set a large pan at the edge of the fire, stirring up grey ashes that settled into Li's wok of simmering oil. The hetman dropped a wedge of hard cooking fat into his pan and spoke to Li with loud careful clarity.

"*Khvorost*," he said. "Khvorost." Semyonov worked egg yolks, sugar, salt, vodka and vanilla into a bowl of flour. He rolled the pastries into thin sticks and dropped them into the hot melted fat. When the sticks grew brown and crisp, he removed them from the wok and sprinkled them with powdered sugar while Li stood moaning behind him.

At that moment a one-eyed man led three other men into the Salle. "Count Karlov?" he asked. Alexander recognized him as the beggar who had tried to sell them his medals on the street.

"Allow me to present my friends, all officers from the Fifth Reserve Grenadiers. I am Lieutenant Yeltsov, Andrei Yeltsov at your service, Major."

"Good day, gentlemen."

Alexander sensed obligation and wariness mixed in his father's voice. He tried not to notice the shadow of desperation in Yeltsov's tone or the lean frayed appearance of the men. They seemed torn between dignity and despair.

"My God," said Karlov quietly to his son. "There must be thousands like them."

"We are searching for employment, Major," Yeltsov said, "and wonder if we might assist you here. We can ride, fence, look after horses . . ."

"I regret there is nothing for you here, gentlemen."

"Perhaps clean the stable . . ."

"We have five horses and no clients."

Alexander knew his father was saving any positions for Petrov and the Cossack and for his own men still trapped on the *Murmansk*.

"But please step into the stable yard and we'll find you some breakfast." Karlov led the way.

The men ate eggs and pork with controlled hunger. Karlov busied himself with the horses, avoiding the entanglements of further conversation. But Alexander spoke with the Russians while they ate.

"How long have you been in Shanghai?" he said to Yeltsov.

"Almost two years. I was one of the first." Yeltsov wiped his plate with a crust of bread. "We have no passports and no consulate, so for the authorities we do not exist. We are at the mercy of the Chinese. All other Europeans, and even the Japanese, are protected by extraterritoriality, by the laws of their own countries. French courts try the Frenchmen . . ."

"Unless they've already bribed their way clear," added another officer. He tapped his empty plate with a fork while he spoke. "French courts exist to force you to bribe the French police." He glanced longingly at the cooking pan, but Li was already wiping it with a rag. "They say the *Préfet de Police* himself is a member of the Green Gang and protects the opium trade."

Semyonov stepped over, his shirt dusted with flour, and set down his platter of stick pastries between the men.

"Khvorost!" exclaimed an officer, smiling at the Cossack as they helped themselves. "*Spasibo.*"

"We Russians have no country," continued Yeltsov.

"That includes you, young fellow," said another officer to Alexander, not unkindly, as he rose to leave. "And now the Reds are sending out detachments to hunt us down wherever we go."

"May I suggest, Major," said Yeltsov as Count Karlov rejoined them, "that you permit me to add your name to the roster of officers in Shanghai that is kept by Colonel Trebinsky? It helps one's friends to find you when they arrive here."

"That way Katerina could find us if . . ." interrupted Alexander.

"If you please, Lieutenant." Karlov nodded and glanced at his son. "That would be most kind of you."

The men thanked their hosts and walked towards the entrance. Alexander saw his father slip Yeltsov some money.

"We have a dilemma here, Sasha." The Count shook his head and sat down on a barrel in the yard. He held a bottle by its cap and swung it back and forth with his fingertips, like a metronome.

"If we do not appear successful, we will not succeed. But to appear successful will be to incur costs that we cannot manage, such as these old soldiers."

"So what do we do, Father?"

"What we are doing, of course." He glanced towards the street again for possible customers. "What did I tell you to do when you can neither hold nor retreat?"

"Attack. Ura!"

In mid-afternoon, after a dozen more Russians had been turned away, the sound of a whining engine echoed through the warehouse.

"See who it is, Sasha. It's time you learned to say no. Don't think everyone has to like you."

Alexander left his father sitting in the yard with his drink and walked to the entrance.

"Pardon us," said a brisk English voice. The man raised a hand to his eyes against the sunlight and peered into the Salle. A young girl in a maroon school pinafore jumped down from the motorcar behind him. Alexander studied the handsome dark green Chandler with its tilt-up windscreen, whitewall tires and broad running board. The girl walked over to the smallest pony and stroked its nose. The man reached into the car and shook the shoulder of a sleeping boy before turning back to Alexander.

"Morty Hall tells me this might be the place to find some lessons for the children."

"Yes, sir, by all means," said Alexander with a smile. "We do riding and fencing and stabling."

"Matilda here is ten. She's due for the ponies. Harry's fourteen, needs something to keep him busy after school. Thought having a sword come at him might wake him up a bit."

A soft-looking youth with the paunch of an old man stepped from the car. He wore a maroon blazer with a school crest and mumbled lazily when introduced.

"Good afternoon." The Count appeared at the entrance and bowed. "Welcome to the Salle d'Armes." He smiled carefully at each child, as if their feelings mattered.

"Morris Templeton." The Englishman held out a card.

"Dimitri Karlov at your service." The Count clicked his heels in the cavalry way, like a gunshot.

Alexander remembered his father telling him that, once he was the count, he should never use his title himself.

Karlov took the calling card. "Where do your handsome children attend school, if I may ask, sir?"

"They're both at the Cathedral School," said Templeton. "Not learning overmuch, but it's sound on manners and strong enough on discipline."

"Just what my own boy needs." The Count nodded towards Alexander. "The men in our family never learn anything without discipline." Karlov thought of how he himself had lost his post as a Page of the Chamber after being caught gambling and drinking in the tower. It was on one such night that the emperor Paul, robed as Grand Master of the Knights of Malta, had stepped down from his life-size portrait and pursued Karlov and his comrades down the great hall of the Corps of Pages with hard echoing footsteps.

"If your boy can fence at all, Cathedral will be pleased to have him," added the Englishman. "The fencing captain's just sailed home to London with his family, and the team's a bit shy for the big match against the Lycée Français."

"He's handy enough with a foil," said Karlov. "Won the prize at school."

"I'll give you a note to the head." Templeton's face brightened. "It's that or the Lycée, and you know what the Frogs are like. Wouldn't want your boy turning out like that."

"I'd be obliged to you, sir," said Karlov. "Would you care to start your children's lessons now? The pony's already saddled. Your son could join the Fencing Club."

"The Club? Ah, there's an idea, but they don't have the kit with them. Perhaps tomorrow after school . . ."

"Your daughter could lead the pony around the ring. Get used to him. And we have a fencing jacket for the boy." Karlov smiled at the girl. "Would you like to be the first to join the Pony Club, Matilda?"

Never had the old soldier shown such interest in children, thought Alexander with annoyance. But he always seemed to smile into a woman's eyes, whether she were eighty or eight, for the instant appearing to see nothing in the world but her.

"Please, Daddy." Matilda looked up at him with big eyes. "Can't I?" She glanced back at the Count, then touched her father's hand. "Please?" Behind her, the Chinese driver wiped the Chandler with a chammy cloth.

Templeton paid for a set of ten lessons for each child. Holding a cup of tea, he leaned against a wall and watched.

In minutes, his jacket on a peg, Harry stood at one end of the fencing floor. Alexander rested his cane in a corner. He collected masks and a white jacket and two foils from the sword rack. He fitted out Harry and taught the boy the salute that precedes every bout. At first Alexander felt awkward. He had never taught anyone anything. His bad leg prevented him from stepping backward. But he supposed that if he could stab a ruffian in the street, he could teach a young boy how to begin.

He tried to remember his own first lesson with Achille Angelo at Kadnikov. The legend at the Academy was that Maestro Angelo had fled Rome after nearly killing a rival in one of Italy's last duels, which had been held in a paddock behind the city's race track. Apparently a crime in Rome was a credential in Russia.

Angelo, although a natural adherent of the Italian school rather than the Gallic, had tried to instill the best of each at Kadnikov: the finesse and precision of striking claimed by the French, and the energetic volcanic style of the Italian.

Years after leaving the Academy, Russian officers frequently returned to Kadnikov to refresh and advance their technique with the maestro. The master often said that fencing, the "mirror of the soul," contained all the lessons of life, that nothing else demanded such combinations of intelligence and athleticism, discipline and inspiration.

In the fencing hall, his teacher used to say, only the voice of the master should be heard. Alexander decided to begin his first lesson with the words that Achille Angelo often credited to an English lord.

"Let us have a conversation with the sword," said Alexander to Harry Templeton, putting one hand on the boy's shoulder.

"What, sir?" said Harry.

"Shake hands with your foil, Harry, like this, and put your two feet in the starting position, like mine." Alexander had the sense their two fathers were trying not to watch. Still, he felt at home when he put on his mask. He knew he himself would not be able to retreat. His left leg burned when he turned it sideways.

"*En garde*," said Alexander. He thought of all his training for warfare. Now, instead of turning his blade against the enemies of the czar, he was facing a fat English child.

Harry swung wildly, lunged at Alexander and lost his foil in the exchange.

Alexander picked up the blunt-edged sword and handed it to Harry. Unable to resist, recalling the scene, he stole a few words from his favorite writer.

"The foil is like a bird, Harry. Hold it too tightly, and you strangle it. Too lightly, and it flies away."

But his student did not heed Sabatini's lesson. The foil again flew from Harry's hand. Flushed and sweating, the English boy recovered his sword and began once more.

"Pity that fine lad of yours has a game leg," said Templeton in a quiet voice. "Is it something permanent?"

"Probably," said Karlov.

"How did it happen?"

"Accident on the Trans-Siberian."

"There are some fine doctors out here, especially one or two Huns," whispered Templeton. "Still, your boy's quick as a cat. Looks like that Douglas Fairbanks. I'd wager he can manage most anything."

Late in the afternoon Alexander and his father mounted up and crossed the Avenue Foch to leave the French Concession.

"The French know how to live," said Karlov, more cheerful with new money in his pocket, "but the English know how to dress." Alexander had heard this lesson before. "A man should learn to dress in London," his father added, "and a lady in Paris."

They rode slowly along the crowded streets of the International Settlement until they were stopped by an imposing bearded man in a red turban directing traffic.

"A Sikh," said Karlov with annoyance. "Hairy damned savages the British used when they stole Afghanistan from us."

In turn they visited a shirtmaker, a tailor and a bootmaker.

"You are recommended to us by Mr. Morris Templeton," said the Count, presenting his card to each Chinese fournisseur. "And perhaps you are acquainted with our cousin, Prince Krupotkin?"

"Of course, Count," said each man, bowing.

Karlov ran his long fingers over swatches and linings and lapel widths, leather samples and shirtings. It was the sort of care with which he used to check each hound before coursing after hares.

The Count ordered britches, two suits, a tweed jacket and evening clothes for Alexander, and more for himself. "No need for overcoats," said Karlov. "It's already December and mild enough. These people don't know what a real winter is."

Alexander's left leg, as he had feared, now measured a trifle shorter than the right. Fittings were scheduled. Before leaving the tailor, the Major dropped his last pair of faded Hussar trousers on the cutter's table. He turned one cuff inside out to reveal what was left of the correct color of the side stripes. "And one pair of these, if you please," he said.

At the shirtmaker, the Count ordered both English shirts and white blouses cut in the Russian style, with proper rounded collars, and wide sleeves and five off-center buttons.

"We must not forget who we are," he said to his son. "And when we give instruction, these Russian touches will be good for business, Sasha, provided they are never shabby."

Riding boots, shoes and jodhpurs were ordered for both, all save the ankle-high strapped boots in black as well as brown.

"Send the accounts 'round to the Salle," said Karlov as they left.

"Wasn't that awfully expensive, Father? How will we ever pay for it all?"

"That's why we did it all at once," the Count said lightly. "They'll never give us that much credit a second time."

Karlov tightened his girth and mounted Rizhka. "Now we need to prepare a party to give our little business a second opening. Instead of waiting for invitations ourselves, hoping these silly people like us, begging King Krupotkin for favors, we will invite them all first. The only problem will be hordes of our thirsty countrymen."

And paying for it, worried Alexander as they rode down Foochow Road to Caldbeck, Macgregor & Co., Ltd., "WINE AND SPIRIT MERCHANTS, ESTABLISHED 1864."

Alexander could almost hear his mother scolding while he watched his father select the spirits and the wine, cases of it. His mother had always been concerned by her husband's impulsive extravagance, his taste for the ruinous gesture. Instead, thought Alexander, she would have spent it all on her good works, trying to help the villagers.

The Count left Caldbeck, Macgregor carrying two bottles of Beychevelle for dinner. "To celebrate Shanghai," he said. At home he had always drunk it on his birthday. "I've always liked the label of the wine boat sailing on the Garonne, reminds me of Hannibal crossing the Rhône," he added. Alexander had heard this at least once before. When he was younger, on long winter evenings his father had told him tales of his namesake and of Hannibal until he had gone to sleep dreaming of slaughtered Persians and camp fires in the passes of the Pyrenees.

Karlov handed Gregori the parcel and turned back to Alexander.

"Tomorrow, Sasha, we shall have to stop by the Belle Aurore and ask that cousin of yours for help in getting the rest of our Hussars ashore. Better soak your handkerchief in cologne water."

-11-

"Welcome to the Belle Aurore, cousins." Krupotkin rose from a game of chemin-de-fer when Karlov and Alexander entered his *salon privé* in their new black evening clothes. Downstairs, a Cossack doorman had clicked his heels and held the door when they entered.

Mercifully Karlov had not seen the toad since the beginning of the German war, though he had heard rumors that Krupotkin had profited handsomely from government contracts for providing medical stores for the army, supplies said rarely to have reached the front. While his countrymen died for Russia, the only uniform Pavel Krupotkin had ever worn was the dark serge of commerce. The Count himself had not spoken to the man since Krupotkin had begged that Countess Karlov arrange for an invitation to the Winter Palace.

Karlov was aware that Krupotkin would carry a residue of resentment for the superiority that the Count had assumed towards him in the old days. Now he would extract a new deference from the Karlovs. The Count was prepared to yield something, even to sell a measure of apparent respect, but he suspected that Krupotkin's social insecurity ran even deeper than his resentment. So there might be some advantage in retaining a trace of social arrogance, in holding back a bit of recognition.

"Dimitri!" Krupotkin seized Karlov by both shoulders and twice leaned close as if to embrace him on each cheek. "Welcome, Dimitri!" The ripe stench reminded the major of the smell of the dead two days after battle. Twice Krupotkin's mammoth belly pressed against the Count.

"Thank you, Pavel, for your kindness to my son." A bit stiff, Karlov drew back and handed Krupotkin an envelope containing most of his last francs in reimbursement. At least he would begin with no indebtedness to this creature.

Krupotkin opened the envelope and glanced at the money, then shrugged. How like him to combine greed with feigned indifference, thought Karlov. The man's bald head had the tight, slightly moist look of a bladder under pressure. His soft mass seemed even larger than before. The open pores of his nose were draining oily perspiration. He was silent while he took out his notebook and crossed out the record of Alexander's obligation. Karlov noticed the taint of Krupotkin's fingers on the envelope.

"We trust you can join us at the reception to celebrate the opening of the Salle d'Armes?" said the Count. No doubt the man would be annoyed that the Karlovs were already established in Shanghai.

"*Naturellement.*" Krupotkin passed a hand over the red scar on his scalp. "*Avec le plus grand plaisir.* I understand you have been very busy, Dimitri."

"Well, well!" interrupted Cornelia Litchfield, entering the room and hurrying over to take Krupotkin's arm. "Who are your dashing friends? Oh, it's that handsome boy! And his brother?"

Alexander stared hungrily at her, still disturbed by the frustration of their first meeting.

"Dimitri Karlov, ma'am." The Count bowed, amused by his son's evident confusion. Perhaps they were entering a period when certain women might find both Karlovs to their taste. The Major returned his attention to Krupotkin.

"I would like to discuss, Pavel, how you and I can assist in liberating our countrymen from the *Murmansk*."

"Please have a drink." Krupotkin gestured at a sideboard. "Let us talk. We must speak first about your debts." He stepped to a backgammon table and sat down in the larger chair. The Count joined him without a glass.

Karlov recognized that Pavel Krupotkin was vulnerable. In the world of Shanghai, he would need Karlov's affirmation, or at least his acquiescence, that Krupotkin was indeed a prince. One sentence from his relations, even a word of humor, and his title would be replaced by ridicule. The pretension, however, carried some benefit for the prestige of the Salle d'Armes.

"A game?" Krupotkin lifted a leather dice cup.

"Paper rubles?" Karlov placed one die in his cup. He knew that the imperial paper currency, virtually worthless in Shanghai, could not be spurned by a Russian prince. "Two hundred a point?" He rolled a five for the start.

"As you wish." Krupotkin grunted and also rolled a five. He turned the ivory cube to double the wager. "So you have assumed Captain Ricard's gambling debts?"

"Some of them." Karlov rolled and played swiftly. "Only the chits I have signed, and they are more than enough."

"That is not what the French captain reports." Krupotkin rolled double fours and blocked two points. His cup was stained with the sweat of his grip. "And I understand you have been using my name, cousin, for credit at the shops."

"Wrong twice, Pavel." The Count looked Krupotkin in the eye. "I mentioned your name by way of introduction, never for credit." Now Karlov regretted even that. "But I need your help with this Ricard to get our other men ashore. We owe them that. They have been fighting for us all."

"Have they?" Krupotkin raised both eyebrows. "How many are there?"

"Over three hundred."

Krupotkin whistled and rolled. "That will be very expensive. Each man will be a living debt. Are you prepared to guarantee the cost?"

Karlov hesitated. "The men from my own regiment, yes, every sabre. About thirty. And two others I must care for. A Cossack, and one Vasily Petrov, a lieutenant in the Lancers who looked after my son. It will be their obligation, and my guarantee."

"Very well, Dimitri, on your word." Krupotkin leaned closer across the narrow table, his belly hanging on the backgammon board. His breath was like an open grave. "I will see what may be arranged. Of course, you will have to sign for them." He lifted the cube, encouraging the Count to double.

Karlov turned his dice cup upside down. He reached in a pocket while Krupotkin continued.

"But you must understand, my dear Karlov. This is not Petrograd, or even Monte. Here there is no nation, there is no blood. There is only money. In Shanghai a man must pay his debts. Every sou. Every *centime*. A man's credit is who he is." Krupotkin flattened the filthy worn banknotes and put them in his pocket. "And I, too, have obligations." He raised both hands and hesitated, as if expecting a gesture of recognition or respect. "How do you think I did all this in two years?"

"I do not know." The Count shrugged. "You can tell me if you wish, cousin."

"When it comes to money," said Krupotkin, "I have no relatives."

"As you say, Pavel." Dimitri Karlov had seen too much to be disturbed by such a man.

For a moment neither spoke. Karlov glanced at the bar where Alexander and Cornelia Litchfield were talking. They were standing close together, their posture partly concealed by a large globe set on a stand in a revolving frame.

"Your father is a most attractive man." Cornelia touched Alexander's hand as if by accident while she spoke. Standing near the drinks table, he looked awkwardly about the room while his father talked to Prince Krupotkin. She took out a gold compact and lipstick. After applying the waxy cosmetic, she stretched her mouth wide and pressed her scarlet lips together as if kissing herself. Alexander watched her lips part when she spoke again, separating bit by bit, as if reluctant to come unstuck.

"You both must miss your mother very much," she said.

Alexander nodded, not wishing to speak of his mother with this woman. He thought he could smell the perfume from Cornelia's breasts. He wanted to press his face between them. At the same time he wondered how his father was managing with Krupotkin. The prince would know more about money and business and cunning, but his father had the advantages of a man of action, of knowing when to take risk and how to get the hard things done.

Cornelia stepped between Alexander and the globe. She bent over the sphere and slowly turned it with one hand, as if searching for a lost continent. As she leaned forward, Cornelia's derriere pressed directly into Alexander's groin. He felt himself harden, filling the warm soft depression between her buttocks. She moved a bit left and right, accelerating Alexander's agitation. Another such movement, he thought, and he would embarrass himself. Then Cornelia turned to face him, scraping and pivoting her lower body against him while she straightened, the fingers of one hand still stroking the globe.

"I can never find Bangkok," she said with big open eyes as she separated from him.

"The prince tells me you already have a business in Shanghai, Count Karlov," said Cornelia when his father rose and joined them. "Some sort of school?"

"We are fortunate to be already active," said Karlov, recognizing the type. These roving adventuresses were one benefit of the British Empire. They had a gift for combining romance and realism. He had known one once in Paris. She had spoken of vast family holdings in the Rand and the Argentine even while having her bill at the Vendôme sent to his room with a rose.

"Perhaps you could teach me something," said Cornelia with wide eyes and an earnest set to her mouth.

"I would doubt it, ma'am." Karlov smiled and filled her glass before pouring himself a brandy. "But it might be my pleasure to try."

Alexander stepped back as the two talked and flirted. He felt uncomfortable, even a bit jealous. He had never seen his father courting a woman other than his mother, though Karlov always seemed to possess a magic way with them, from the most elegant beauties to the old babushkas in the villages on the estate. How did he do it? Generally hard and immovable as an anvil, with women he had the touch of a butterfly. "The Karlov touch," the Countess once had said in Alexander's hearing. She had sounded uncharacteristically ambivalent.

"I think I'll go for a walk, Father," Alexander said. He knew where he wanted to go: to see the rickshaw lady, to Madame Mei-lan Wong's. "Perhaps I'll go straight home afterwards, if you don't mind."

"Of course, Sasha." His father handed him a few dollars, different sorts of crumpled banknotes. "Don't forget tomorrow is your first day at school."

"Of course, Papa. Thank you." Alexander walked out into the hall as he flattened the old dollar bills in his hand, variously issued by the Yokohama Specie Bank, the Deutsch-Asiatische Bank and the Hong Kong & Shanghai Banking Corporation. He still did not understand how the Shanghai currencies all came to be based on the Mexican silver dollar.

Twenty minutes later Alexander found himself on the Bund. He paused to rest his leg and absorb the spectacle of the great riverfront avenue that he had first admired from the ship at dawn. His annoyance at losing Cornelia's attention lifted as he became absorbed in the nighttime atmosphere of the street. He set his back against a lamppost to avoid the pressing of the crowd. For an instant he found himself staring into the smiling eyes of a passing round-faced Chinese boy of four or five wearing a blue silk skull cap and mounted piggyback on the shoulders of an elderly servant. Wrinkling his tiny nose until it disappeared into his cheeks, the beaming child was a package of bonhomie. Alexander wondered when he had last seen a pure smile directed his way.

The great one-sided boulevard was even more grand than Alexander had imagined. To his right was a broad avenue, a sidewalk, a park and the Whangpu River, all of it a turmoil of noise and color and activity. The great buildings of the port street rose to his left like a fortress of commerce with ramparts of stone and glass and light: massive high-storied banks and domed trading houses, tall towered hotels and illuminated shops, consulates and government buildings.

He squared his shoulders, tapped his stick twice on the ground and set out, unhurried, intending to stroll as he had once imagined he would promenade in Paris. Would he ever know those boulevards that his family had loved for generations? Though Alexander felt on display himself, no one save the beggars seemed to notice that he was in evening clothes.

He found a slow pace did not serve him. It was like trying to bathe in a raging river. To avoid being ceaselessly jostled, he was obliged to hurry his steps to match the flow. Even then he was struck in the back and nearly knocked down by a bicycle laden with broad canvas parcels. Only the yellow-and-black tramcars moved slowly. Their bells rang steadily as they slid through the crowd that pressed against them as closely as water surrounds a fish. Things were calmer closer to the buildings, and he edged that way. There mendicants sat against the walls, porters rearranged their burdens and street cooks and vendors did their business.

The smell and sound of sizzling pork lard stopped Alexander near the French consulate. He paused on the corner and bought three spicy dumplings served on a scrap of newspaper, then three more. The ancient wrinkled street cook wore a conical straw hat tied beneath his chin. His old eyes were teary from the oily steam that rose from his simmering pan.

Hoping to buy a drink, Alexander entered a nearby building that he took to be a hotel. The uniformed doorkeeper was busy helping another man leave his hat and case.

As Alexander passed through a high-ceilinged lounge, he heard a din of male voices rumbling from an adjoining room. He followed two men through the crowded doorway and found himself standing near the longest bar that he had ever seen. He advanced to the black-and-white granite counter, only to be pressed against it by a group of Englishmen gathering behind him. A row of wooden ceiling fans stirred the smoke that clouded up from cigars and pipes and cigarettes.

"Double gin, whisky and soda, brandy and water!" They shouted faster than they could be served.

"A glass of red wine, if you please," said Alexander in slow English, waiting his turn.

"May I ask the account, sir?" said the Chinese barman.

"Account?" said Alexander, setting his money on the bar.

"Good God, boy, put that away!" said a heavy florid-faced man in a wing collar. "You're in a club, for heaven's sake." He pushed his empty glass forward, then turned to his companion. "Damned young griffins never know what they're about. Can't think why we let them in."

Embarrassed, Alexander picked up his money and, turning around in the crowd, almost knocked noses with a young man of his own height. With black brilliantined hair parted in the middle, the man had a long narrow face and an Adam's apple more prominent than his chin. English, thought Alexander.

"Not to worry." The fellow gripped Alexander's arm to steady himself. "Be my guest. Jo! Another claret for this boy and a glass of champers. Chop chop, Jo!"

"Yes, Mr. Hudson."

"Thank you," said Alexander. "I didn't know this was a club."

"It's The Club, my dear sir, the Shanghai Club. We've got the longest bar in the world, one hundred and ten foot, and the world's longest-talking bores." He gestured towards the far end. "The old taipans sit and grumble at the other end by the window. New boys like us, and the aging clerks like your chum there, grovel and fight for drinks down this end." He lowered his voice. Too late, Alexander thought.

"Haven't seen you about, have I?" Hudson reached a long arm past Alexander and seized his drink. "Cheers! What are you, fresh off the boat? Another Russki on the wing, perhaps?"

"Something like that." Alexander saluted with his glass, pleased to be wearing his new dinner jacket among this lot. "Alexander Karlov. My father and I sailed here from Vladivostok."

"Reckon you saw the Royal Navy thereabouts. We've been trying to give you chaps a hand against Lenin, from Archangel to the Crimea, but it doesn't seem to be working." He raised his hand for fresh drinks. "Hard enough to look after our own bloody empire without worrying about yours."

"Are you in the navy?" said Alexander.

"Lord, no. Discipline doesn't agree with me. I'd be getting the cat every morning. My family sent me out here three years ago to try and make a few guineas." He offered Alexander a cigarette from a silver case. "Told me someone in the family's got to do it every now and again. Ten years here, trading, light manufacturing, exports-imports, whatever, chap can go home and buy a proper country house. Only trouble is, one gets spoiled by the pheasants here, nothing like the same at home. Fellows go home rich and spend forty years dreaming about what they left behind."

"I thought there were plenty of pheasants in England?" Alexander coughed and put the Three Castle in an ashtray.

"Haw! Haw!" laughed Hudson. His Adam's apple bobbed up and down in his neck like a child's yo-yo. "That's a fine one. Out here, pheasants are what we call the jolly girls, the tarts."

"I see," said Alexander, attentively.

"These Chinese girls want to please you, not just excite you and have done with it. It's not their skill, though there's plenty of that. It's their attitude that's different." Hudson lifted a fresh glass from the bar and drank before continuing.

"Girls at home don't even know how to begin. Or how to finish, for that matter." He tapped a cigarette on his case. "The thought of returning to a lifetime of English sex is enough to make a chap dive into his gin."

The two drank and talked, exchanging cards.

"So you ride, eh, Karlov? We'll have to put you up for the Paper Hunt Club if you're any use in the saddle. Closest thing to war we've got out here these days. Nearly killed me last year. Best damn fun around this town, except for the sing-song girls," said Hudson. "Ah, here come my hopeless chums. Surprised they're still standing."

"Thank you," said Alexander. He found himself enjoying Hudson's quick changes of subject, but following him was a bit fatiguing. Ready to move on, Alexander set his empty glass on the bar. "I hope you'll join us for drinks Friday."

"You can count on that, all right, and I'll probably bring this thirsty lot along as well. They can smell free booze halfway to Nanking." Three young Englishmen joined Hudson and began clamoring for drinks. They were perfectly dressed but flushed and noisy as schoolboys.

"Until then," said Alexander, but Hudson was already too engaged to hear him.

Relieved to be outside and on his own, Alexander resumed his stroll. He walked past the Banque de l'Indochine, the German Club, Butterfield & Swire and the Russo-Asiatic Bank. He paused to read a brass plate mounted beside the front door of the Russian bank:

HEAD OFFICE
PARIS, 9 RUE BOUDREAU

LONDON OFFICE
64 OLD BROAD ST., E.C. 2

He wondered how long that would last with the Reds trying to take over every Russian business. Even the Russian consulate was closed.

When Alexander's leg began to trouble him, he climbed into a rickshaw.

"Chemin St. Bernard," he said several times. They came soon to the bright lights of Foochow Road, and abruptly he changed his mind. He had enjoyed Hudson's drinks, and now it seemed time for an adventure. He pulled a card from his pocket and, leaning forward, banged on the front edge of the rickshaw.

"Excuse me," said Alexander to the puller. "Sixty-nine Rue Voisin." He was not certain what he would find there, but he recalled the gentle touch of the older Chinese lady, and that her rickshaw had been parked on a wild street outside a house with two red lights. "Sixty-nine Rue Voisin."

He was not the first.

A carriage, several handsome automobiles and two rickshaws were drawn up nearby, none of them directly in front of the steps to number 69. The brick house seemed to be one of two built identically side by side, each a curious mixture of Chinese and what Alexander took to be Parisian. The doors and windows were framed in a tall substantial European way, but the russet tiled roofs turned up at the corners and pitched steeply to the center like a pagoda.

As Alexander climbed the steps, he heard a phonograph playing through an open window. Something light and modern. By the door he saw a brass sign plate: CRAVATES SUR COMMANDE.

The door opened. A burly retainer appeared in the soft pink light of the doorway. Alexander smelled perfume, or was it incense?

"Sir?" The man was neatly dressed in pressed blue cotton trousers and jacket, but his gaze was hard-eyed and his body solid and his face flatter and darker than most Chinese he had seen in Shanghai. Mongol, Alexander guessed. "Sir, I help you?"

Alexander heard laughter and two loud English voices coming from a room just off the entrance. He searched his pocket for the lady's calling card while the man blocked his way without aggression.

A voice directly behind him addressed the attendant in rapid Shanghainese. Alexander turned, and the second man bowed to him. Several stitches crossed the bridge of the man's nose. It was the rickshaw puller who had taken the lady away after the street fight. The doorman replied and stepped aside, now acknowledging Alexander with different, more respectful eyes.

An old bent woman in black silk welcomed Alexander in the hall. A tall comb was pinned in her white bun with the dignity of a tiara. She spoke some Chinese phrase of greeting and with graceful hands directed him into one of several sitting rooms. Alexander sat down in a carved rosewood chair. The room seemed a mixture of Chinese furniture and fittings set out in a comfortable European way. A servant brought him steaming aromatic tea and poured it into a blue-and-white porcelain cup, then walked out, leaving the door slightly ajar.

Through one wall he heard two Englishmen laugh and argue as they changed a phonograph record. "Something American," one said. "Irving Berlin." A needle scratched across a record before a new tune began. "Tea for Two." He could barely hear a girl's quiet sing-song laughter. His eye was caught by an unbound leather portfolio on the table before him. He opened it.

The first sheet of parchment bore an ink drawing of a young woman, Eurasian evidently. Large Western eyes framed in a delicate face, with fine long black hair hanging on bare shoulders, a suggestion of high unclothed breasts that cruelly ended at the bottom of the page. One word, Laria, was written in the lower right-hand corner, and below that the Chinese mark of the artist. Feeling his own excitement, Alexander realized that indeed he was finally visiting a brothel. He recalled an older boy at the academy, proudly recounting his adventures when an uncle had taken him to a house of shame in Paris.

Alexander turned eagerly to the next sheet. A very young girl, perhaps thirteen, possibly younger, slender and childlike save for very long pointed nipples. Neither Chinese nor European, he thought. Siamese, perhaps? Annamese? Chomna, she was called. Feeling guilty at the attraction, he turned to another page. Sisters, he guessed, Chinese, holding hands by the fingertips, one depicted in profile, the other from the front, both drawn from head to just below the waist. Buttercup and Daisy.

"I have been hoping you would call," said a quiet voice from the doorway. "I owe you so much, and I cannot close my eyes if I am in debt. Without your intervention, I would not have been seen again."

Alexander felt as though he'd been caught peeping. He quickly set down the portfolio. As he stood his knee knocked over his empty cup.

"It was nothing, Madame Wong, I . . ."

"You will please call me 'Mei-lan.'" The woman smiled, ignoring his confusion. Seeming with each step to balance herself on her tiny feet, she hobbled forward like a bird and sat on the edge of a chair. "But what is your name?"

"Alexander Karlov. My father and I have just arrived from Vladivostok. It was my first time ashore when I . . ."

"You are so elegant this evening," she said in a silky gentle tone, as if whispering something intimate. "Are you the Karlovs of the new stable, cousins to Prince Krupotkin?"

"Yes. How . . ." The advertisement had made no mention of Krupotkin.

Mei-lan's face was smooth, without expression, but Alexander thought he saw cunning in those bright eyes. "There are few secrets in Shanghai, though it is my trade to learn and to keep them. I know it is never easy to start a business. You must tell me how I may help you."

"Everything's all right," said Alexander, knowing better, thinking of the mounting obligations.

"If I cannot help you," she said softly, "then perhaps I can please you. But I do not know your taste." She gestured toward the portfolio with slender fingers. "And you are so young. Eighteen, nineteen?"

"Almost." He blushed. It was as he had guessed. She was the madam of this bordello. He saw now that Mei-lan was even older than he had thought, though what age he could not be certain. Her fine pale skin, though free of lines or even pores, seemed tightly drawn across her face.

"May I have you entertained?"

Near perishing at the very idea of being entertained, even more awkward than eager, Alexander stood and mumbled. "Perhaps another, I, tomorrow I have school."

"Very well." Mei-lan smiled and rose, ignoring a commotion when someone struck the wall in the next room. "But you must promise to come back for tea. Perhaps in the afternoon, after school? Please come to my own house next door."

Alexander nodded rapidly.

"Do you promise me, within the week?"

"I promise." He knew that he would think of nothing else. He bowed good-bye and walked to the door.

"Lin will take you home."

The night seemed cooler when Alexander stepped outside. He paused on the top step and Lin went for the rickshaw.

While he waited, a sedan chair came up the street. The two bearers were moving swiftly at a gentle trot. They set the chair down on its short legs at the bottom of the steps. The lead bearer held back a curtain. A young woman set one foot onto the pavement.

Alexander stopped breathing. He saw a perfect slender calf, then a green silk dress, slit up one side to the hip but sleek and tight as the scales of a fish. The Chinese girl straightened gracefully as she emerged, like a flower stalk recovering after a gust of wind. She had a tapered waist and the mere suggestion of a figure. A long slim neck rose from a mandarin collar to a fine oval face with black almond-shaped eyes and puffy bright red lips. Her smooth dark hair was sculpted to her head and gathered in a large glossy bun at the back. He stared at her. For an instant the entire world seemed to be still, without breath or movement.

He caught the girl's eye for a lingering second. Then she looked down and he stepped aside while she climbed the steps. Her fragrance embraced him as she passed.

Alexander hesitated and watched the door close behind her. He breathed quickly, overcome by her beauty. He recalled Hudson's words and swore to himself that he would see this girl again.

At that moment two black Chrysler automobiles approached the house.

"Hak Lee!" exclaimed one of the squatting carriers of the sedan chair. "Hak Lee!"

Both bearers jumped to their feet. They bowed once towards the automobiles before hurriedly carrying the chair across the street and setting it down once more. The two cars parked directly in front of number 69. Alexander saw Lin waiting down the street with the rickshaw, hesitating at the sight of the two motorcars.

All four doors of the lead car opened and four Chinese emerged. They wore baggy black cotton trousers, black Western jackets and dark American fedoras. The forward passenger seat of the second car opened. A thickset European with a hard lined red face got out and gave orders to the four men in clumsy Shanghainese. Alexander recognized the heavy Slavic accent. The man wore a grey chalk-striped suit over a white Russian blouse. There was a shiny dark red stain on his shirt. One of the Chinese climbed the steps to the house as Alexander stepped down, leaning on his cane. The other three spread out along the curb. One turned to watch Alexander as he began to walk away along the narrow sidewalk.

The Russian opened a rear door of the second Chrysler and a man descended. Standing upright, he faced Alexander on the sidewalk. Alexander had never seen anyone like him.

In his pointed European boots the Chinese stood as tall as Alexander.

He appeared almost shoulderless in his blue silk robe. Long thin arms swung loosely at his sides like ropes. One seemed to hang down farther than the other. His shaven head was long and egg-shaped, as if first swollen, then stretched. His face, a dull copper, was pitted by smallpox. His long uneven teeth were stained a yellow-brown. For a moment Alexander was held by his eyes. They were a filmy glazed black, almost without reflection. His right ear was enormous, at least twice the size of the left. Repulsed, Alexander broke the man's gaze and looked down. He stepped to the edge of the sidewalk to let him pass. The last thing Alexander noticed was the two-inch-long dark-stained nails that protruded from the bottom of each wide sleeve like the talons of a hawk.

Alexander felt the tall man's glazed black eyes on his back as he walked with his cane to the waiting rickshaw. As Alexander passed the second automobile, he noticed a figure sitting slumped in the backseat. It was a Chinese in a European suit. His arms were trussed with rope. Below one ear, the side of his face and neck were dark with blood. Two strips of tan material were tied around the man's head: a gag and a blindfold. Both were also stained.

"We go now, sir?" said the rickshaw puller.

-12-

"One more ride please, Mister Semov," said Matilda Templeton as the burly Cossack led her pony back to the entrance to the Salle d'Armes. Matilda ate a small marzipan tart as she rode.

"You will call me 'Semyonov,' young lady," said the hetman in his husky voice. He pinched the young girl's side until she giggled and smeared some of the Russian chocolate custard on her chin. "Sem-yo-nov, or I will cut off your pretty head." He tapped the hilt of his sword with his vodka glass. "Now it is almost time for the sabre rides."

The gallery and both ends of the warehouse were crowded with guests. The Templetons with four friends, Billie Hudson and a gang of smoothly boisterous companions, too many Russians known and unknown, and eighty or ninety others, Germans and Americans, Italians and Portuguese, many drawn by the advertising leaflets passed out on the avenues and at the clubs and restaurants by Hussars from the Count's regiment.

Captain Ricard stood with his pudgy wife and handsome blond son, a youth of about Alexander's age. The French boy was joined by a tall girl with very short, wavy blond hair. Alexander noticed that people seemed to avoid the police captain. Terse formal acknowledgments, rather than conversation, appeared to be the way to greet the Frenchman.

Young Ricard was not as tall as Alexander but more solid. He had broad shoulders and a strong neck. His blazer bore the crest of Shanghai's Lycée Français. The girl had a lively open face, sparkling eyes and a wide natural smile that Alexander appreciated from across the riding ring. He found himself staring at the girl, hoping to catch her eye. Instead, young Ricard glared back at him.

A bearded European had stationed himself outside the entrance. He was selling two-dollar lottery tickets for the benefit of Russian refugees. "Drawing at the French Mixed Court—Rue Stanislas Chevalier," proclaimed his flyer.

Cornelia Litchfield and Prince Krupotkin stood on one corner of the raised fencing floor, next to a basket of oversized green and yellow zucchinis. The two looked out over the other guests with different eyes: Cornelia with curiosity and invitation, Krupotkin with a keenness sharpened by flashes of recognition and resentment. "Here, Pavel, please." Cornelia handed Krupotkin a fresh white linen handkerchief from her crocodile pocketbook. The prince wiped his sweating face and dried his palms before dropping the linen in a trashbasket.

Alexander watched the pair intently. For a moment, on the billiard table at the Belle Aurore, Cornelia had loved him. She must have loved him. Now, horrified, jealous in his loins, he wondered how she could stand Krupotkin. "Women do what they must," his father once had told him. "And occasionally we do, too."

"Hullo there, young Karlov!" called out Billie Hudson. He approached with a cigarette in one hand and a tall drink in the other. "So this is where you Russkies teach your tricks with swords and horses." He grinned at Alexander. "Must be something to it. St. Clair tells me you're slaughtering all the lads on your fencing team at school. Seems once you slip on your mask you turn into Mr. Hyde. Says you start every drill like you're fighting for your life."

"Some of the boys are rather good," said Alexander. What had Angelo said at Kadnikov? "Once you pull the mask to your chin, you must look out through the steel mesh with the concentrated fury of a leopard in a cage."

"But those Lycée froggies will give you a sharp match. Meant to be bloody good at sabre." Hudson spilled a drop of his drink when he paused to wave at a friend. "Good thing you left the club early the other night," he drawled. "We ended up in too much mischief for a schoolboy like you." He leaned forward conspiratorially. "Started out smoothly enough at the Hotel Parisien for a bit of dinner dancing, then on to the Winter Garden and finally a jolly little crawl down Blood Alley. Ended up at that Yank sin house nobody ever admits they've been to. Girls all come from San Francisco, including that wild mama-san. Giving those cowgirls a crack at you is like being boarded by a gang of pirates with knives in their teeth. They have all the fun."

Before Alexander could reply, Hudson was off, saying something about ponies and refilling his drink. Alexander's mind was elsewhere.

He wondered what Hudson would think of his friendship with Madame Wong. Yesterday he had stopped by again for tea on his way home from school. Though he was still a virgin, Mei-lan had warned him against developing a taste for prostitutes. "It is a common inclination," she advised him, "of men who have something about which they feel insecure. Their pheasant becomes a reassuring refuge." He knew she was referring to Alexander's concern about his limp. He realized he was becoming dependent on her advice and friendship. He wondered if Mei-lan was always as nice as she was with him.

Alexander returned his attention to the party. His father expected him to be a most attentive host. Though usually more comfortable in uniform, Karlov himself was magnificent in new boots and herringbone tweeds, a braided leather crop in his left hand. He was touring the hall, kissing the hands of the married ladies.

Their Russian guests had already finished the *zakuski*, consuming the boneless anchovies, red salmon egg caviar, pickled mushrooms, liver paste and fillets of herring in wine before Alexander could get a bite. He had been looking forward to the familiar dishes of his youth.

Chinese waiters in Russian shirts buttoned up the side passed trays of canapés and drinks, vodkas and champagne, Pimms and Singapore slings. The dishes of Petrograd and Peking covered four tables in the stable yard. A pig was roasting on a spit over an open brick fireplace. Fat dripped and crackled on the coals. Li and a heavy Russian woman in a blue kerchief were still quarrelling over how the duck and cuts of pork should be prepared and served. Semyonov had warned the old baba that Li would not be easy. The bow-legged English jockey sucked his fingers and pinched scraps of crackling from the corner of the carving table. Two gypsy guitarists in soft leather boots and pantaloons, sashes and red bandanas strolled among the guests.

As the Count had feared, the Russians were devouring the food like locusts. They were thirstier than even the young Englishmen who drank as if just back from lifetimes in the desert. Only the English and their Celtic cousins were ever still drunk at breakfast.

"Send Gregori out for more wine and vodka," said Karlov to his son, worried about the embarrassment of running out.

"I doubt we can afford much more, Papa," said Alexander, though he himself had enjoyed more than a stolen glass or two. "They won't give us the credit."

"Don't be an old woman," snapped the Count. "You sound like your dear mother."

"Yes, sir," he said. Was his mother to be dismissed in such a way? He kicked at the sawdust scattered over the hard dirt floor of the riding ring. Old woman, was he? He'd see about that when he went back to Madame Wong's.

"I'm sorry, Sasha," added his father with rare remorse, squeezing his shoulder. "But you make only one first impression, and tonight is ours. Now we just need a bit of theatre so they won't forget us."

The Count turned and mounted the steps that led to the narrow gallery overhead. He made his way to the middle and gazed down over the center of the riding ring while he lit a long cigar. Far above his head the tattered flags and horizontally striped pennants of a dozen Russian regiments hung from cords stretched across the ring. Alexander had climbed the wall ladder and secured the ropes. In the center hung the white, red and blue banner of imperial Russia. Crossed swords and lances decorated the long wall beneath him. None had cost more than a few dollars, received with gratitude by the hungry owners. The flags of the United States and the great European powers were fastened to the opposite wall.

Karlov pulled a cord that rang the clapper of a large brass ship's bell secured to the wall. The din below subsided.

"*Soyez bienvenus!*" the Count called out in his clear commanding voice. Gregori and several other old Hussars began to guide the guests from the center of the ring. "Welcome to the Salle d'Armes, ladies and gentlemen. Now we will show you, if we may, how we ride and fence in imperial Russia."

A bugle blew from the entrance of the stable yard. Two Hussars tied large zucchinis to five ropes that hung from the latticed beams at the four corners and at the center of the ring. The big gourds swung slowly five feet above the floor, the height of a man's head.

Two cavalrymen, neatly turned out in full regimentals of boots and striped leggings and trim tunics, trotted swiftly around the ring. Both wore green plumed shakos. Alexander knew that several others had given up the best bits of their uniforms to outfit these two.

The riders paused at one end, drew their sabres and saluted the crowd. They spurred their horses with a yell: "Charge! Ura!"

Hollering as if in battle, each rider tore down one side of the ring and slashed with his sabre as he turned the sharp corner on his pony. Fragments of zucchini flew at the guests pressed along the edges of the ring. The horses wheeled, one faster than the other, and made for the opposing corners. Again the Hussars slashed at the swinging squashes. The crowd gasped and cried out as pieces of the gourds splashed onto them.

The faster rider pulled his excited resisting horse into a tight turn and made for the zucchini swinging at the center of the ring. But the other raced his pony against the rump of the leading horse. Harried, the first rider missed his cut. The second horseman slashed the squash in two. The crowd cheered and roared.

Karlov rang the bell.

"Would any of our guests care to try a ride?" called the Count as the zucchinis were replaced.

Three young Englishmen pushed Billie Hudson to the center of the ring. Alexander saw Hudson, flushed, stumble once.

"Hudson! Hudson!" cried the gang of friends. "Mount up, man! Ride like the devil!"

A Hussar dismounted and led his twitching horse over to the group. An Englishman held the prancing animal by its head. Another helped Hudson out of his jacket and waistcoat.

"Do we have another rider?" called Karlov. "Two bottles of champagne for the winner."

Captain Ricard's son stepped forward.

"No, François!" called out the boy's stout mother. But the tall blond girl seemed to be encouraging him.

Hudson and young Ricard mounted up. Friends adjusted their stirrups. The Hussars handed up two sabres.

François tested the heavy curved weapon in his hand, turning the blade left and right. Hudson paid little mind to his sabre but took the moment to steady his mount. He leaned low along the pony's neck, then stroked its shoulder as he made his seat well forward.

Alexander sensed that Hudson would be better in the saddle, but that young Ricard knew his weapon. Perhaps he was on the Lycée fencing team. "Come on, Englishman," thought Alexander. "Win this." Once mounted, Hudson seemed steadier.

Karlov rang the bell.

The two riders rode to one end of the warehouse. Alexander knew what it must be like for each horseman as he quickly tried to learn his horse, to maintain control of the animal with his legs and his left hand while preparing to use the sabre with his right. This was what he himself was born for. He wished he could have a try but his father had warned him that neither of them should ride or fence tonight. If they did too well, they would shame their guests. If they were bested, no one would want to take lessons from them.

The bell rang again. The two youths applied their heels. The ponies sprang forward.

Rushing the first corner turn, the French boy overshot. He jerked violently on his horse's mouth and leaned way out with his sabre, but was unable to reach the zucchini. The Englishman made the tight turn, close to the gourd, but failed with a clumsy cut. Hudson almost struck his pony's head as he completed the wild swing.

The crowd cheered and yelled, alarming the horses. Trying to settle their mounts, both riders turned and quickly trotted back to chop their first zucchini. Then they turned again and cantered along the two walls of the warehouse.

They cut down their second gourds at the same instant and made for the center.

Hudson arrived first at the last squash. He pulled in his pony and lifted his sabre, but wasted a moment when his horse reared against the bit.

Ricard was on him at once. The French boy raised his weapon. Ignoring the hanging gourd, he turned to the side with his shoulder behind the blow. His sabre parried Hudson's stroke. The clash of metal sounded across the ring like a gunshot. Shocked, Alexander understood that François had turned an equestrian event into a sword fight. Hudson's sabre fell to the floor with a heavy clatter. Ricard reversed his blade as he recovered. He sliced the fruit in two with a long backward cut.

"Bravo, François!" shouted several voices as the exultant young Frenchman rode once around the ring. "*Vive la France!*"

Flushed with triumph, the boy pulled roughly on the bit and tossed his reins to a Hussar as he jumped down.

Alexander doubted that today he himself would fare very well against such competition. But he vowed that when he faced it he would ride like Hudson and fight like young Ricard. If he were to play at sabre, however, he would need to strengthen his arm and shoulder. He could only hope his left leg would take the strain.

"Give him the champagne, Sasha," shouted the Count from the gallery. "The prize. Two bottles."

Smiling down at the rabble of strangers, Karlov thought of how the champagne had flowed at another party seventeen years earlier in St. Petersburg. Vol-au-vent à L'Impératrice had followed the zakouskis before toast followed toast at the banquet in the Marinsky Theatre celebrating the one hundredth anniversary of the Corps of Pages. Orthodox and Catholic, Muslim and Buddhist, officers and diplomats and government ministers, old Pages from every corner of the Russian Empire had returned for an evening of intense unique fraternity. The only thing shared outwardly by every man was the white enamel Maltese Cross on his left breast. The Count regretted that his son had not been able to complete his training as a Page.

Aware that the champagne was long finished, Alexander collected two bottles of Meursault from a barrel filled with ice and white wine. Leaning on his cane, he crossed the ring, careful not to slip on the sawdust. More than anything, he looked forward to meeting the tall blond girl.

"Congratulations," said Alexander with a smile. He held out the wine to François. "I apologize, but ..."

"What is this?" said Captain Ricard before his son could take the bottles.

"Is this what you Russians call champagne?" added the French boy. He ran one hand over his pale hair. His eyes still glistened with excitement.

"Perhaps this is how Russians pay their debts," said the police captain, contempt in his voice as he turned aside. "*Épouvantable!*"

Scarlet, momentarily speechless, Alexander set the two bottles down against the wall. He recalled how his father had taken on this Frenchman's casino debts in order to get his men ashore. Alexander would not permit himself to be humiliated by this policeman. He collected himself and directed his attention at the young woman.

"I am Alexander Karlov," he said in a clear voice and bowed his head. "Welcome to the Salle d'Armes."

"Thank you." She smiled, shaking his hand with firmness before he could kiss hers. "I'm Jessica James."

Ignoring the Frenchmen, Alexander returned her smile. For a moment, he held her eyes. He felt she was watching him as he turned and limped back across the ring. He guessed her accent was American.

"Congratulations, François," said Jessica after Alexander had left. She kissed the French boy on the cheek. "You were wonderful, fantastic with the sabre, but you could have taken the wine."

"It was an insult," snorted young Ricard. "You can't trust these filthy Russians. They promised us champagne."

Jessica looked at him before she spoke. "Isn't it a bit spoiled to be fussing about champagne when children are starving a few streets away?" she said slowly before changing the subject. "Perhaps you could take some riding lessons here, François."

"Riding lessons? Didn't you see me ride?" François stepped back and reddened and raised his voice. "These Russians are disgusting, that swaggering old count and his cripple son and all their beggar friends in rags of uniforms. Who do they think they are? The young one with the limp is staring at you right now."

Jessica looked around and quickly caught Alexander's eye.

When the evening finally ended, Alexander and his father sat with a few friends around the long table in the stable yard. Empty bottles stood near the lantern in the center of the table.

Alexander rested on a barrel. Leaning against Osetra's stall, he used chopsticks to eat rice and scraps from a bowl held close to his face like a coolie. He saw Chung rinsing glasses in a bucket. At the next table a man was sleeping, his face resting on the greasy surface. Other Russians sat quietly, two with their heads in their hands, moody in the shadows, as if one last drink had turned them from festive to melancholy. Alexander thought about François's girl. She was said to be a bit of a Bolshie, Hudson had told him, very independent, the only child of missionaries from the States.

"A handsome party, Dimitri," said Vasily Petrov.

"A little quiet." Semyonov covered the last crumbs of fruit cake with thick sour cream and lapped up the rich mixture. "Not enough women."

"Next time let my Lancers do the weapons drill," said Petrov. "Show these people how we stick pigs in the Crimea. We'll turn one loose in the ring and let the winner have the pork."

"It accomplished what was required," said Karlov. "We sold a few lessons, and these people are beginning to learn who we are."

Petrov drew a letter from his tunic. The blue envelope was already open. He cursed quietly while he leaned forward to read the letter by the light.

"Bad news from Paris," said Vasily after a moment, handing it to Karlov. To all of them news from Paris was almost like news from home. Only Paris and Constantinople held more Russian émigrés than Shanghai.

"Picked it up at the *Bureau de Poste* yesterday afternoon," said Petrov. They were all aware that the French postal service was the cheapest route for mail. To bind up the colonial empire, postage was the same rate as for letters sent within metropolitan France.

The men stared at Petrov as he continued. Alexander knew that none of these men expected to see their family, friends or property again. For many Russians, their boots were the most valuable thing they now possessed.

"Lenin's made that Polish devil Dzerzhinsky head of his new secret police, the Cheka. He already has agents killing Whites in Warsaw and Helsinki. They shot two officers in Paris who'd been recruiting men to fight with Denikin and Wrangel. Dumped them naked in the Seine near the public baths, *pour encourager les autres*."

"Have you heard what they're doing to our men if they capture someone from my regiment?" asked a lieutenant from the Guards.

Karlov shook his head.

"The Reds call us 'White Gloves' because of our uniforms. When they catch a guardsman, they cut a line through the soldier's skin all the way around his wrists, before forcing his hands into boiling water. Then they peel off his skin like two gloves, which later they use to strangle him, sometimes pulling on his skin over their own hands."

For a long moment no one spoke. Karlov filled their glasses.

"And now Dzerzhinsky is importing torturers from China," said Petrov. "He says no one knows the work like they do."

"Soon his men will be coming here to get us." Semyonov relit a thick black cigar.

"You're right." Karlov folded the letter. "But not by boat. They'll come by train. The Chinese Eastern Railway to Harbin, then through Nanking."

"Or the South Manchuria Railway," said Petrov. "We should have a couple of men watch the station." Li passed behind him carrying two wooden buckets of human waste and manure to leave by the entrance for the night soil cart that would shortly be on its rounds. In the morning Chung would be scouring the chamber pots with a bamboo whisk and soap and bunches of tiny sharp-edged clam shells.

"Sasha," said Karlov, his face grim and worn as he passed the letter back to Petrov, "time for you to strike camp. Off to bed with you now."

"Good night, boy," said Petrov when Alexander stood, too exhausted to complain.

The night sky was turning purple blue with false dawn, but Alexander knew it was not a matter of the hour. His father felt this conversation was not for him.

"The Red agents will be coming to Shanghai," he heard the Cossack say as he left. "It will be us or them. We will have to kill them first."

Alexander woke a bit later in the night, not feeling his best. Was that music, could the party still be continuing, or was he dreaming that he was home at the estate and his parents were playing in the music room? He sat up and reached for his bedside water flagon and drank from the bottle. It was music, one light but vigorous instrument. A violin. It was his father, playing at last.

Alexander climbed out of bed and left his room as the music stopped. He crept down the stairs. The riding hall was dark. A shadow in a chair leaned against the distant door frame in the dim patch of light coming from the stable yard. Alexander heard the sound of a glass knocking against a bottle. He crept forward and crouched near the wall.

Suddenly Mozart filled the Salle d'Armes. Not played with a perfect touch. Unevenly, lacking elegance, but with energy and feeling. It was his mother's favorite sonata for piano and violin.

Carefully, quietly, Alexander stretched out his leg as comfortably as he could. He leaned back against the wall and closed his eyes. He felt he was home again. He remembered the music room with its marquetry tables, Empire sofa and barrel chairs with peeling birch veneer. Soon his cheeks were wet. From time to time there was a slight pause or break. Perhaps his father was taking a drink or tightening the strings or struggling with the piece. At length he heard the third movement, and it was finished. Alexander sat still and opened his eyes.

Then he heard what was more painful and yet more beautiful to him than the music itself: the plunging sobs of his father echoed down the hall.

Alexander crept up the stairs and back to bed.

-13-

T he dense stink of the nearby tannery surrounded Jessica like a cloud as she waited for the small door to open. Excited to be on her own in the Chinese city yet anxious about police agents, she glanced down the narrow crowded lane but noticed only two barefoot children playing in the dust with the brown shell of a turtle.

The grille in the door slid to one side. A man peered at her. He turned and called over his shoulder. A second face appeared and nodded. The door opened and Jessica slipped inside. She heard the familiar *clack-clack* of the press as she entered.

Bundles of leaflets were stacked inside the door. She saw copies of the Chinese Marxist journals *Companions* and *The Communist* piled on a bench. Large identical posters covered the walls edge to edge like wallpaper. STRIKE! STRIKE! they demanded. A dozen workers from a tannery and the cotton mills crowded the small room. She was excited by the clatter and the oily inky smell of the printing press that came along the passage from the back room.

A Chinese blocked the hallway. He had no right arm. Jessica suppressed a shudder, though she knew him well enough.

"Welcome, comrade," he said to her.

"Good morning, Lin Teh," Jessica said. The union leader had been mutilated in a machine accident as a child of ten working at a mill in Chapei. She had heard that young Lin Teh had run alongside the loom conveyor, shrieking as he watched his severed arm being carried along to the next machine, until finally he collapsed by the spindler drive.

Jessica reached into a pocket of her blue cotton jacket and handed Lin Teh the twenty-five dollars that she had been filching day by day from the expense money at the mission office. He stepped aside and she entered the passage.

The old printer stood by his machine lubricating the cylinders and bearings with the long angled spout of an oilcan. Jessica relished the smooth powerful motions of the press that seemed to make her true interests come to life. She noticed the word "Birmingham" set in raised black letters along the base of the machine. No doubt the English workers who had built it had also been denied the fair reward for their labor. She nodded at the printer's wife, but the slight white-haired woman ignored her. With deft crooked fingers the woman continued to collect and stack the flyers in precisely even bundles. Jessica wondered for how long she had been imprisoned by this mindless work.

Three strike coordinators with red armbands stood with their backs to Jessica. They were taking instructions from a European in a heavy tweed cap seated at a small table in one corner of the room. Smoke clouded up from the table, and Jessica could just smell the man's heavy tobacco above the odor of the machinery. She liked its sweetness in the oily acrid air.

"Comrade," said Lin Teh nervously to the seated man, "this woman is a friend of our union, Miss James, from California in America."

The European looked up at Jessica with hard wary eyes. He did not stand. She felt herself take a half step backward. He was attractive, heavily built, solid as a fortress, with thick dark hair and a strong square tanned face.

"Why is this woman here?" said the man's deep voice in slow awkward Cantonese as he tapped out his pipe onto the table with hard knocks.

Jessica recognized the heavy Russian accent. She tried not to stare at him. A true comrade, a revolutionary from Moscow, perhaps a friend or acquaintance of Borodin or Trotsky or even Lenin himself. A man who must have come thousands of miles to help China. Like her parents, but without the moralizing vanity of missionaries, and with a practical program for improving lives and the future of a nation. A soldier of the people, probably a man who would offer his life for what he believed. And what risks he must have faced, here and at home. Jessica knew better than to ask names or put questions. With this sort of help, China might have a chance to make honest change, to build a real revolution. There must be some way she could assist him with his work.

"She helps us deliver our leaflets where otherwise we could not," said Lin Teh to the seated man as if apologizing for her presence. "The police will not stop her. And Miss James has been most generous."

"Useful," nodded the Russian. He swept his pipe ashes onto the floor with the edge of one hand. "Tell her to wait in the hall."

Embarrassed by the cracks in his boots and the patches in his tunic, Igor Trebinsky straightened his thin shoulders as he approached the food line at the Russian Relief Hall in the basement of the Orthodox Mission Church on the Rue Paul Henri. The faded yellow of his cuffs still reminded him, and a few others, of his regiment and of the 3rd Guards Infantry Division in which it had served.

At his age, and with his teeth and stomach, thick bread and thin borscht were all that Igor Trebinsky required. Every morning he left blood in his basin and blood in his stool. But the younger men were different. He understood why some took their own lives, and why others lay stupefied in the gutters. At least he had a full past, and a feast of memories on which to live. By the time Trebinsky had arrived at Shanghai Station, he did not have much of a future to lose.

"Won't you take your place here, Colonel?" said a far younger man, opening a space in line between himself and a friend. The speaker was dressed better than most. His wife was said to work as a dance hostess. "Please add my friend Nikolai Galitzkoff here to your roster of officers. He is from Tiflis. Lieutenant Galitzkoff commanded the Seventh Automobile Machine Gun Platoon. Fiat armored cars with twin turrets, you may recall, sir."

A bald young man in a flat almost-square cap and a leather jacket cut in the short Swedish military style clicked his heels and bobbed his head. His cheeks were hollow as two caves. "At your service, Colonel." The fold-down padded earflaps designed to reduce noise inside the armored vehicles had been cut away from his cap.

"Igor Trebinsky," said the colonel with his elderly gentleness. "Litovski Guards."

As one of the earliest White officers in Shanghai, Trebinsky had made a place for himself, and found a purpose, by maintaining a listing of officers as they arrived in the city, and by acting as a *poste restante* for mail that could not be delivered. The two small rooms he shared in a Chinese workers' neighborhood were filled with names and addresses from every part of Russia. Labelled baskets were nailed to each crumbling wall. "Artillery" said one, "Guards" said another. "Missing Wives and Children" said a third basket. All were nearly full with messages and letters. Sometimes he thought that the pain of Russia was his wallpaper.

While the line shuffled slowly forward, Trebinsky took his spectacles and a lined notebook from his pocket and prepared to make the latest entry. "Number 4" was written neatly on the cover. He asked the young officer for details of his family and service. The colonel was proud that though his eyes were poor, his hand was still steady.

After they were served the three went to a corner of the church hall.

There the colonel rested on the end of a bench. The two younger officers sat facing him on the floor with their backs to the wall. They waited to eat until the colonel's spoon touched his lips. The three men could hear the voices of the choir through the ceiling.

"I am looking for my wife and daughters, Colonel," said the young lieutenant between hurried bites and sips. "I believe they would have come by rail through Harbin."

"Many families are still trapped there," said Trebinsky. "But please come by tomorrow and search my records. Of course you will have checked already all the church notice boards and the newspapers."

"Yes, sir. I will see you tomorrow, then," said the armored-car officer. His bowl and bread were rapidly finished.

"Colonel Trebinsky," said a man with an eyepatch. "You might remember me. I am Andrei Yeltsov. I'm pulling a rickshaw sometimes now. I have fine new tires and a striped canopy." He tried to smile. "And I thought I might run you home, sir. No charge, of course, just for the practise of it. I'll do my best not to get you lost. I'm trying to learn the streets."

"That would be most kind and welcome," said the colonel, rising, his potato soup and one corner of his dark bread already eaten. He clicked his heels as he stood and faced his two earlier companions. "Good night, gentlemen. I am unable to eat all my bread. I hope you will help yourselves should you wish it."

A half hour later Lieutenant Yeltsov dropped the colonel at the entrance to the broken courtyard that contained his dwelling. There the old soldier gathered himself, his vision troubling him at night, and slowly made his way across the crowded space towards the doorway to his entry stairs. Laundry and dogs and children and clusters of Chinese families sleeping and cooking and quarelling made the short journey slow and lively.

Colonel Trebinsky climbed the stairs by placing one hand on the cracked sticky wall and both feet on each step. He could feel the grit and the breaks in the plaster through the hole in the sole of his right boot. He was relieved that his boarder, now a doorman in Frenchtown living well enough on tips and leftovers, would be at work for many hours more.

He pushed open the door, then closed it behind him, exhausted, his bowels painful. Comfortable in the darkness, he leaned his back against the door and tried to remember where he had left the candle. As he considered this, he smelled the thick tobacco in the air. Not his boarder's usual made-up cigarettes, but something better, stronger, sweeter. He looked down and saw a glowing pipe. A man was sitting on the floor in front of him. At last it is my turn, thought Trebinsky as the big shadow rose.

With astonishing agility the colonel turned to the near corner and lifted the old scabbard that leaned there. He was aware that some of his precious coal was burning in the grate nearby, a pot of water steaming above it. He gripped the handle of his sword and began to draw the blade. He heard the once familiar whistle of steel sliding swiftly from steel just as a powerful hand seized his neck and flung him violently to the floor.

Facedown, certain his hip was broken, Trebinsky cried out as a boot stamped on his right hand and his weapon was kicked away. Then he felt a heavy man sitting on his shoulders and pressing his face against the rough floor. The man raised Trebinsky's right hand and pinned the forearm between his knees.

"Welcome home, Colonel," said the rough, coarsely accented voice. "Your war will soon be over, White Glove." Trebinsky knew what this meant. He clamped his teeth together when he felt a knife cut the skin and tendons of his wrist and the speaker twisted the hand in one of his own.

"With all these names and addresses, you have already done much of my work for me," said his visitor, wrenching Trebinsky's hand towards the boiling water. "But there are things you will tell me now that are not in your baskets and in your notebooks."

* * *

"The colonel was naked," said Vasily Petrov, white-faced, as he sat down to join the others seated in the stable yard.

"His neck was broken. Looked as if he'd been burned a bit and tortured. His right hand was flayed, and the skin left in the empty mail basket of the Guards Infantry with the colonel's old gloves. Then someone dragged him out of his room and dumped him in one of the night soil carts by Soochow Creek. Right where they load it all onto the barges that go up-country to sell fertilizer to the farmers."

"Colonel Trebinsky was one of the first to make it here after the revolution." Count Karlov shook his head. "He kept the first roster of officers."

"That's missing, too," said Petrov quickly. "His notebooks and medals and all his correspondence from Paris and Constantinople. Nothing left but his sword and an old uniform of the Litovski Guards hanging from a nail on the back of his door."

"Poor devil was too cut up by his old wounds to defend himself," said Semyonov. "Wish they'd come for me instead."

"Patience, Ivan. They will." Vasily poured a glass of vodka and pushed the bottle towards the hetman. "Now they have all our names. They know our addresses. They even know what regiments we served with."

Semyonov filled his glass and drank the vodka. He was still angry after a meeting of the Cossack Relief Committe held at McTavish's Drug Store on the corner of North Soochow Road. Not permitted to come ashore, over a hundred refugee Cossacks had been living on the abandoned tramp steamer *Mongugai*. Sixteen had just been moved to hospital ashore. They were suffering from chicken blindness, the result of extended living in darkened holds. The others were so under-nourished that they were unable to eat the usual ten-cent meals provided by the refugee soup kitchens.

"Whoever it is that killed the colonel," said Karlov, "we must kill him first. It's just a different kind of battle."

Li handed Gregori a plate of speckled hard-boiled eggs and a dish of salt that the Count's old soldier servant set in the middle of the table.

"Did anyone at Trebinsky's place see anything?" asked Karlov.

"It's the sort of rooming house, sir, where everyone knows everything and no one sees anything," shrugged Petrov. "An old Chinese courtyard with a landlord wringing money out of rickshaw coolies who share the rooms in shifts and broken-down street girls who visit the hook lady for their last abortion. Can't imagine how the killer even found him."

"Let me go back and try. I gave the colonel his last ride home," said Andrei Yeltsov, who had begged from Karlov in the street several months before. Now the one-eyed lieutenant was the first of their circle to work as a puller. His face was older, drawn and hollow-cheeked, but he was lean and hard as a young coolie, and he was learning every street and alley. "I'll talk to the other rickshaw boys." Yeltsov took an egg from the plate and cracked the shell on the edge of the table. "The pullers know everything that happens in Shanghai."

"This should make it easier, Lieutenant." Karlov handed him a few dollars. "But if you hear anything, don't follow up on your own. Come back and tell us first. We don't want to find you naked with your neck snapped before you tell us what you've learned."

-14-

Whichever streets he took home from school, Alexander always tried to pass by the Rue Voisin on his way. If he did not, Madame Wong never seemed to mind. But if he did, she always received him with tea and something sweet, either tinned Scottish shortbread or madeleines or millefeuilles from her favorite patisserie, the Reine Claudette off the Rue Batard.

"I have learned that these Scots are a strange cold people," she lamented one afternoon over shortbread. "So difficult to arouse. Vigorous enough, in their way for a time, *mais pas de sensualité. Rien.* Yet who else can make a cake that is at once dry and crumbly, yet creamy rich?"

These visits were his secret pleasure. Not just for what Mei-lan gave him in clever counsel and womanly warmth, but always for the hope that he might meet the Chinese girl he had once seen stepping from the sedan chair.

Alexander was looking forward to a special afternoon. Mei-lan had asked him when would be his birthday. He had told her that his saint's day, his Russian name-day, was almost here.

"There is only one thing to give an innocent boy on his eighteenth birthday," Mei-lan had said in her soft voice last week. "It is time I introduced you to Sorcery Mountain."

Then she had sent a white-haired servant next door for the portfolio and an easel. "No doubt you will spend your saint's day with your father, but you will celebrate your birthday here as a young man should, perhaps a day or two before."

"*Mais oui*," he had said, "*certainement.*" But even the possibility of his first girl terrified him, though he thought and dreamed of little else each night.

"I am so pleased you speak French," Mei-lan had replied. "It is the proper voice of the flower world."

As if absent save for this task, the blue-gowned servant had stood beside the easel turning each page at Madame Wong's direction. The old man's eyes never flickered to regard the sheets that he was touching.

Mei-lan refilled Alexander's cup and pressed him with cookies. For some time she spoke absently of the qualities of each pheasant, occasionally with affection, commending the skin and suppleness of one, the explosive responsiveness of another. One girl, she said, pleased certain men by offering no movement or response whatever, by giving the client the sense that she was dead, or not even present. That, it seemed, induced such men to try harder themselves, and to be less inhibited. Most commonly, her European clients, especially the Americans, sought what Mei-lan called "*complaisance*," a sense of obligingness, an ease in giving pleasure to another.

As he listened, Alexander was reminded of a breeder selling dogs or horses, kind enough in word and manner, but ultimately a business owner used to instilling obedience and discipline, and with little tolerance for what could not be sold. He recalled the violent scene outside the

Singerie. Gentle and gracious as Mei-lan was with him, he felt certain that she knew when to use the switch or spur.

"Whomever you choose," she said, "will be yours five times. Less than that, you will learn nothing, and the girl will have no interest. More, you will become attached. The girl you select must teach you confidence rather than become your refuge."

Alexander tried to imagine what this would be like. He blushed when he felt himself grow ready. "Oh, thank you, five."

"The first time will be for your pleasure, to give you calm." Mei-lan paused. "The other four times to teach you how to give pleasure to a woman. That is a present no Englishman would understand, of course, but it is a gift that should serve you a lifetime, not a week." Mei-lan leaned forward and looked more closely into Alexander's eyes.

"Then you will make love with the art of a mandarin and the vigor of a Slav. The passion, of course, must come from you."

"I . . ." He felt hopeless, impossibly inadequate.

"Now you must choose," she had said, gesturing at the servant to turn the pages once again.

"They're all so beautiful," he managed, "but isn't there one more, another girl? I saw her once, when I first came here, stepping out of a sedan chair next door. There was a tall man, a Chinese gentleman, arriving at about the same time. With two cars and a Russian body-guard, I think."

A flicker of change, a touch of hardness, broke the serenity of Mei-lan's face.

"Mr. Hak Lee," she said slowly. "Always be careful of him. It was one of his old enemies who was trying to seize me when you and I first met. Mr. Hak Lee is the master of most of the old Chinese city, and of much that happens here. I am fortunate that we are old friends, for the flower world is not the garden it might seem to you. It is a pit of serpents. There are seven hundred houses of pleasure in the Settlement alone. Last week two had fires. Six pheasants died. Without his protection you would not find me here."

"But the girl?" interrupted Alexander.

"More debts are owed to Mr. Hak Lee than to any man in Shanghai. And here, uncollected debts are more powerful than the money itself." Mei-lan paused, waiting until her guest nodded his acknowledgment.

"This man is the leader of the Qing Bang, what you call the Green Gang," she continued. "Behind his back, Mr. Hak Lee is known as 'Big Ear,' the Master of the Mountain. You do not wish to owe him money, not one centime."

"But the girl was not with him?"

"No, Lily was alone." Mei-lan shook her head. Her gentleness returned. "She told me that she saw you. She found you most handsome."

Mei-lan wagged her forefinger. "But she is busy, shall we say, spoken for, with her own protector, a rich Scotsman, a grand taipan from Hong Kong. Now Lily takes English and French lessons every day and lives in an apartment at the Astor House Hotel. She can see the Bund from her window."

"Oh. She was wearing a green dress."

"But perhaps, if the old gentleman is away, with his family in Hong Kong, it may just be possible. We shall see." Mei-lan gestured towards the easel. "In the meantime, please select another pheasant for next week."

He had done so, and soon he would be back.

Alexander was beginning to enjoy his daily schedule: saddling up early and riding Osetra to school before the streets were busy, with his father, often red-eyed, trotting comfortably beside him. If they were early, they would stop for tea and dark bread at the Café König, where they would hand the reins and a few coins to a street boy while they sat and talked. In Russia he had never had such opportunities. There his father was either away with his regiment or busy about the estate. Here in Shanghai, when they were late leaving the Salle, usually because his father had just come home, they would canter until they came to Nanking Road, their horses fresh and eager in the crisp morning air. At such moments, Alexander felt that they could be anywhere, facing any challenge, that the two of them were a match for anyone.

Alexander was rarely certain what kept his father out all night, whether it was political meetings with his émigré friends or adventures with various distinguished ladies of the town. Count Karlov had become friendly with several of the elegant Chinese families of the city, ladies and gentlemen who dressed as readily for Paris or Peking, London or Nanking. At home they generally dressed for China, both the women and men in loose high-collared silk gowns, with the men adding vests in the cooler evenings. When out in the French Concession or the International Settlement, dining at the Ambassador on the Avenue Eduard VII or dancing at the Majestic Café on Bubbling Well Road, they conversed easily in several languages and dressed in dinner clothes.

Generally Count Karlov considered these Chinese to be more worldly and congenial than the smug European merchants with their bourgeois talk of trade and home. He found the women appreciative and quietly clever, the men intelligent and broadly interested.

One morning Karlov described the setting of his previous evening. His host, who dressed for the business day in a dark suit and watch chain, was an owner of coastal steamships and a collector of ancient antiquities. "At first I didn't recognize old Kung," said the Count. "Gerald was standing near the stone lions by the gatehouse of his walled compound, waiting to welcome me, with his hands tucked into the sleeves of a blue silk robe. Inside was a different world, something like a grand household at home, but with four generations living together, and all mixed in with a country village from a hundred years ago."

A servant had taken the Count's bridle in the entrance court. Then Kung had strolled with him along white pebble paths and under roofed promenades, over a garden bridge and past red pavilions and a small temple surrounded by shapely blue-grey rocks and small groves of shivering bamboo. Two rickshaws and a sedan chair rested under a bamboo shed. Nearby a barefoot servant was polishing a Paige Jewett touring car. A white-haired housemaid with bound feet and a broad sash bowed and stepped backward across the black tile floor when they entered the principal house, a long two-story structure with upturned roofs and red-lacquered doors and beams and ridgepoles. There the ladies of the household joined them, dressed that evening not for the Cercle Sportif or the Astor Ballroom, but in the pale powder and paint and jade pins of a different China.

"How was the food, Papa?" asked Alexander.

"I only remember the dessert. Spun sugar and whipped cream on top of powdered roast chestnuts and glazed berries. Peking Dust, I think they called it."

Alexander licked his lips.

"I have never had finer hospitality," added Karlov. "These people are successful and at ease in our world, Sasha, but they never forget their own, and we must do the same." The Count shook his head. "Of course, they have one thing you and I will never have: old ladies who keep the family memory. Widowed aunts and spinsters living in apartments on the courtyards, gossiping and teaching the children in the afternoons, and smoking opium and playing mah-jongg and cards all night."

Alexander and his father never spoke of Karlov's female companions, but increasingly the Count teased his son, though he never drew a response more than a blush.

"Don't think I haven't noticed you sniffing about Cornelia," his father said one morning over tea. "Not to mention your fluttering around that young American girl from the party. Remember to behave yourself, Sasha. Like a Karlov."

One morning Alexander woke early, his leg throbbing. He turned on his right side and picked up the two pieces of the Commissar's pipe from the bedside table. He thought of his mother and Katia and the Trans-Siberian. He recalled the instant when Viktor Polyak had broken his leg, the shocking pain, the sound of the bone cracking above his knee. He felt the enduring hopeless anger lodged like a stone in his belly. He sniffed the bowl of the pipe and smelled the dense odor of the sweet tobacco. He recalled the man's great strength when he had grappled with him in the train. He thought about the Commissar and fencing and François with the sabre and all that he must do. He knew he must prepare himself for many battles. He remembered Achille Angelo lecturing him at Kadnikov.

"In the end, the hand is the fencer," the slender Italian had said. "The legs provide mobility, but the hand controls the blade. Nothing your legs do can match the speed of the hand. But it must be strong enough so that you can afford to grip the weapon lightly, to guide the blade with just your wrist and fingers."

Alexander left his bed and put on his shirt and trousers. He limped barefoot along the gallery until he came to the fixed ladder that rose against the wall of the old warehouse. He must strengthen his hands and arms. He must know he could depend on them absolutely, if not on his legs.

He pulled himself up the ladder. At the top he reached up and gripped the first slender latticed beam that supported the roof. The beam was foul and sticky. Mice and birds or bats had visited before him. He wiped his hands one against the other and flexed his long fingers before he gripped the beam again. He released his feet from the ladder. He swung forward, so that he was hanging over the edge of the riding ring, perhaps fifty feet above the floor. To fall would break more than his leg.

Never looking down, he passed hand over hand, beam to beam. At first he felt free as he crossed the great space. His bad leg meant nothing. Then he felt a sharp pain as a large splinter lodged in the palm of his left hand. He tried to ignore it as he continued across. But each new swinging grip hammered the splinter deeper. It felt as if it was spearing through him from his palm to his armpit. Alexander concentrated and resisted the temptation to loosen his grip. He counted each swing out loud: one, two, three, four. He was almost there.

Then he realized he had forgotten that there was no ladder on the other side. Hanging suspended, he peered from side to side in the gloom. Exhausted, he swung a bit to his right and rested his good leg on the top of the highest shelf, the only one remaining. He let go of the beam completely and crouched down and sat on the shelf like a monkey on a branch while his trembling arms recovered. He gazed down into the gloom of the great hall below.

Here on his perch he could still smell the pungent odor of the opium balls that once had filled the warehouse. He spat into his aching bleeding palm and tried to wipe the black filth from his hand onto his sleeve. He squinted and used his teeth and fingernails to pick most of the splinter from his palm. He tried to dig for the smaller fragments but could not find them all. The effort made his palm worse, bloodier and more painful. He wiped the hand on his sleeve again, fearing lest his grip be slippery. After a few minutes he rose with his back against the wall and seized the first beam.

This time the passage seemed easier as he learned to use the rhythmic momentum of his swings to reach farther with each grip. He crossed the hall and slowly descended the ladder just before his father stirred.

From that day Alexander tried to rise earlier most mornings, so he could exercise his hands and arms and shoulders before the others woke. Sometimes he did it with his eyes closed as he swung all the way across the hall. Other mornings he would look down as he moved, until the height no longer troubled him. Mastering his fear, he became steadily stronger. Often he hung by one hand, confident in his new strength.

Once at school, he had a few hours of class and a wretched English schoolboy lunch, even worse than at the Academy at Kadnikov. Rather than borscht and dumplings, the diet was brown windsor and rice pudding. On special days, the treat was stuffed heart. The organ was filled with the diced remains of former meals, and bathed in a pasty white sauce that dripped thickly over the severed stump of the aorta. And yet, said Alexander to another hungry scholar, the English ridiculed the Chinese for eating monkeys and the blood of dogs.

School was in English, but at lunch or during breaks in the play yard there was a chaos of different languages. In two months he had found no real friends. Already in their final year, his classmates were set in their groups, banded together by sport or nation. They were like sailors in the same fleet but on different vessels. Only the Italians seemed to get on with everyone. Loud and scruffy, they boasted about girls, whispering about legs and breasts while the English boys talked cricket and planned their week around sneaky visits to the Chocolate Shop to feast on pork pies. He wondered what the boys would think if they knew where he took his teas.

Alexander received little attention, except on the fencing strip. He was too old and new to be befriended in mid-term, too big and worldly to haze. Even more than at home, team games were the glue of an English school, the test of who you were. Alexander was unable to join the sides and either take his beatings or lead his mates.

He did not play afternoon rugby or football or cricket with the other boys. Freed by his bad limb, Alexander would walk slowly home, Osetra having been led back by his father in the morning. Only on Fridays, when there was fencing, did Alexander stay late at school.

At first Vivien St. Clair could not conceal his disappointment when Alexander limped into the gymnasium with his cane. The fencing master, said to be half Maltese, was a wiry compact man with sleek flat white hair and a narrow dark face with peaked white eyebrows.

"Karlov, are you not?" St. Clair said. The master shifted his foil to his left hand and removed his glove to shake hands. The other boys stared at Alexander while they buttoned their white jackets. "I understand your father teaches fencing. Would you like to sit there and watch?"

"No, sir." Alexander was offended by St. Clair's assumption of his incapacity. "I was hoping to join the class."

"So you have fenced a bit yourself?"

"A little, sir, at the military academy at home, at Kadnikov." Not to mention, he thought indignantly, in the training hall of the Corps of

Pages, where the Knights of Malta used to test their steel without masks or button tips.

"Very well, Karlov, we'll set you up with Barini for today's drills. Your reach should help." St. Clair handed his own foil to Alexander, then a mask. "Barini, come forward, please. You two take the end of the line, next to the *piste*."

Once they started, ten boys facing each other in two rows of five, it was the universal language of the sword.

Barini was heavy for a young fencer, but not bad at sabre, slow but strong and determined. His face was red and sweating whenever he removed his mask. Alexander accepted the discipline of the moment: this was an exercise, not a competition. He concentrated on his form and timing. He did not try to dominate or show advantage, just to do it better, though of course he was not able to retreat. Even in practice, every stroke must matter.

"Beat, *coupé*, feint, lunge, *dessous, coulé*," called the master, "*doublé, fleche*, bind, tac and *pris de fer*."

Alexander was not impressed with the other fencers, except for one: Hideo Tanaka, a Japanese one year younger who brought concentration and the needed qualities of hand and eye and speed to the sport, and perhaps something else as well, a suggestion of a different and fierce culture of the sword, as if for him, too, it was more than just a game. Tanaka was the son of the Japanese minister to Shanghai. A black Daimler always awaited Hideo after school, the rising sun of Japan sometimes flapping on a small mast on the bonnet of the vehicle.

The following week, Alexander had shown St. Clair what he could do with an opponent. In foil drill, he had disarmed his adversary and defeated the school's former épée leader five-to-one. He realized that his dominance was not due to any new skills he had learned since Kadnikov. What had developed was his fighting spirit. His time with his father and the other soldiers, his taste of battle in Siberia, even the streets of Shanghai, had transformed schoolboy swordplay into a more mortal exercise.

He usually took different lanes or alleys walking home, hoping to strengthen his leg by the exercise. He was always excited by what he found. As if in a bazaar, shops were often clustered together by trade or profession. After the first two weeks Alexander could close his eyes and identify some of the narrow streets and winding congested alleys by their smells alone, by the aromas of the spice shops or restaurants or tobacconists, or by the stink of tanneries or the whiffs of coal or sawdust.

One afternoon he passed the open doorway of a tobacconist, Tabaqueria Filipina, 28 Nanking Road. Alexander inhaled the dense fragrance of unsmoked tobacco as he passed. He paused and looked at the window displays: pictures of John Smith and Sir Francis Drake decorated signs for Three Castles Virginia Cigarettes; Iphigenia Cigarettes, exclusively made in Cairo by Kyriazi Freres, Wallem & Company sole agents, said a poster; Balkan Sobranie—East is East and West is West, he read; and Old Dominion Cigarettes, Virginia, U.S.A., said another beside a picture of a grinning black field worker proclaiming, "I'se Here Boss!" What a strange country America must be, he thought.

Alexander walked on, but planned to return.

The following day he entered the store. He was received by a Hispanic gentleman wearing a red fez. "Can I help you, sir?" the man asked when it was Alexander's turn.

"Yes, please." Alexander drew the Commissar's broken pipe from his pocket. "Could you identify this tobacco for me?"

The man cupped the bowl in both hands and lowered his nostrils with the concentration of a sommelier challenged. He sniffed twice and turned to the shelves behind him.

"Aromatic," he mumbled, "very." The shopkeeper's fingers tarried over tins of cigarettes, racks of pipes and boxes of snuff. He took down a round quarter-pound tin and opened it and sniffed again. He nodded and beamed and passed the container to Alexander.

"One dollar, twenty cents," the man said.

It was the same sweet smell, but cleaner, not yet burned and bitter.

Alexander lifted the lid and saw a picture of an Ottoman soldier with a scimitar.

"Telkhis Smoking Mixture," he read, "The Ideal Blended Pipe Tobacco —Sweet and Cool—Tobacco de Lux."

"Do you sell much of this tobacco?" Alexander glanced at a rack of carved meerschaum pipes.

"Not recently." The man shook his head. "Mostly it is the taste of gentlemen from the Crimea."

Alexander chose a long-stemmed meerschaum carved with the face and headdress of a fierce Turk. He paid and walked home with the tin and the pipe in his pocket. He had thought about this for weeks. The tobacco would remind him of what he had to do, would keep him connected to the man he hated. Perhaps familiarity with the odor would one day help him to identify or pursue the Commissar.

His good leg was becoming stronger, and longer, but his left seemed always about the same, able to manage what was required but often tired and painful. He knew he was growing tall and wiry, like his father. One day he might have the same broad shoulders.

Today he could not concentrate in class. Tomorrow was his birthday, and he was expected at Madame Wong's for a special afternoon. At last he would be more than what Mei-lan called a "tea-guest," a prospective patron merely examining the offerings of the house. He wondered what girl she would provide. Could it be Lily?

Now he was on his way.

By the time he arrived at the Rue Voisin, walking more and more slowly, he was sweating like a miner.

He turned up the quiet street, not certain at which house he was expected. The closer he got, the more anxious he became, and the more he dreaded the need to undress and to perform. Fearful of what the girl might report to Mei-lan, he thought he would rather have another operation on his leg than carry on with the present obligation. At the same time, he felt lusty enough for an alley-full of sing-song girls. He just didn't want anyone to know if he embarrasssed himself.

The burly Chinese doorman was waiting on the top step of the establishment. He nodded and held the door when Alexander approached.

"*Bonjour, monsieur,*" said the bent old lady in black when Alexander entered. She handed him an envelope and a small ivory box. "*À la part de Madame Mei-lan,*" said the woman.

He opened the envelope and read the card: "To help bring your two worlds together."

He lifted the lid of the box and looked inside. A small bear carved from green jade rested on a red velvet cushion. Alexander opened his mouth and shook his head. He had never received a more thoughtful present. It was the sort of thing his mother might have given him.

Suddenly the shrill cry of a child in pain came through the wall and interrupted his thoughts. The scream was followed by a woman's voice, snapping cruelly in high angry Cantonese, rapid as a line of rifle fire, but suppressed, compacted as if not wanting to be heard. Madame Wong? Alexander was astonished by her change in tone. Then he heard two slaps, each one sharp and explosive like a breaking plate, followed by the crying of a young girl, a child, he guessed by her aching choky sobs.

While he speculated, the old lady in black interrupted Alexander's thoughts.

"*Mademoiselle vous attend dans sa chambre.*" She gestured towards the stairway behind her, then bowed with her hands clasped. "*Numero trois.*"

Almost frozen, Alexander put the present in his pocket and climbed the stair. A Chinese housemaid sat in a chair at one end of the hall. She was folding a stack of hand towels on the table beside her. She kept her eyes down and did not acknowledge Alexander. He hesitated and knocked at the door to number three. There was no reply. He knocked once more and waited. Nothing. He stood leaning on his cane and considered going back downstairs. This could be his chance to leave. He glanced at the maid. She nodded towards the door.

He turned the porcelain knob and entered a small bedroom with a large canopied bed and heaps of soft pillows and bolsters. The curtains were nearly closed. Four candles burned on a bureau. The scent of jasmine, and perhaps sandalwood, reached him through an open bathroom door. A lilting voice was singing softly, the words Chinese. He closed the hall door and wondered if he should bolt it. A green silk dress hung from a hook on the back of the door. Alexander caught his breath and slid home the bolt. The singing ceased.

"Please join me," said a girl's voice gently from the bathroom.

He leaned his cane in a corner and limped to the doorway. He felt he was going to die.

Bubbles flowed over the sides of an enormous porcelain tub that rested on brass lion's feet.

Lily's silky hair and black almond eyes and puffy red lips were floating on a cloud of scented bubbles in the candlelight.

Alexander had never seen or smelled such beauty.

"Please leave your things on the bed," she said, her voice demure.

He undressed and went back to the doorway. There he stood sideways, embarrassed, partly because of his thin left leg.

The girl looked at him with gentle appraising eyes.

"*Mon dieu*! Bravo! Please get in." Lily reached up one slender hand to touch him. "*Bon anniversaire, monsieur.*"

-15-

"Wake up, Sasha." Karlov kicked the foot of his son's bed. "You'll be late for the match. Peter's already saddled the horses. You can eat two hard-boiled eggs on the way."

"Sorry, Father." Alexander sat up blinking and swung his feet to the floor. It was Saturday, the day of the school's annual fencing match against the Lycée. He was filling in for the old captain of the Cathedral fencing team. "They're holding it at the Cercle Sportif."

"*L'exactitude est la politesse des rois*," said his father. "You've been late and tired all week. Perhaps I shouldn't have given you that name-day party," he grumbled just loud enough for his son to hear. "Too much of that *imeninnyi pirog*."

Alexander rose and washed his face with cold water from a basin. Too much of something, he thought, but not birthday pastry. If his father only knew. Although he was certain his father had enjoyed plenty of mischief when he himself was young, Alexander believed he would

deplore any inappropriate connection while they were trying to estab-
lish the Karlov name in Shanghai.

Alexander thought again of Lily and despaired that he would not see
her again. Madame Wong had emphasized that this liaison was at an
end. "Lily needs her taipan," said Mei-lan. "That is how she supports her
sick parents and her sisters. How could you help her do that?"

When he did not reply, Mei-lan continued. "Lily's time is not her own.
Each day she has her language classes. On the evenings when he does
not see her, the Scotsman requires her to take piano lessons until her
fingers ache. When he returns, he makes her play for him to show what
she has learned."

Alexander had nodded in bitter understanding. Like his father and
grandfather, he had always taken money for granted. Here in Shanghai
he was learning how much it mattered. All the same, money or not, he
had been hoping that their time together had meant almost as much to
Lily as it had to him. But Mei-lan had not been encouraging.

"Do not forget, *mon petit*, we women do not do this work for our
pleasure," she said, seeming almost to enjoy the point.

"But Lily liked you," Mei-lan had added, returning something. "She
said young men smell better."

"Young men?" Alexander asked. "Is that true?"

"I do not know," said Madame Wong with a slight shrug. "I was given
only older men."

He had been dreaming of Lily when his father woke him. Whenever
he touched her, Lily had the glossy smoothness, the perfect yielding
firmness of a shelled hardboiled egg. When they were lying idle, he
would close his eyes while Lily stroked him gently and entertained him
with tales told slowly in her lilting Soochow voice as they learned each
other's language, classic legends like "The Tiger of Chao-cheng" and
"The Fighting Quails." His favorite, "The Faithless Widow," she told him
each day. Always she avoided talking about herself and her obligations.

"Wake up, boy." Karlov handed his son a fresh white shirt. "You will be fencing for all of us," he said, with tension in his voice. They both knew all that was at stake. For them both this was more than just a schoolboy match, even more than a matter of the fencing reputation of the Salle d'Armes.

"I'm worried about the sabre," said Alexander.

"Sabre? Why would you do sabre?" The Count snorted. "It's difficult enough not being able to retreat in foil and épée. Sabre would push you back too hard on your left leg. Impossible. Let that heavy Italian boy do sabre, that Barini fellow. He's built for it, and it doesn't require the brains of foil and épée."

"I have to do it, Father. The two captains fight all three weapons."

"Madness." Karlov laughed harshly, but felt guilty for placing such a burden on his son. "You'll just have to kill him first with your foil." Then he shrugged, as if remembering a different, harder life. "On the other hand, why not? In battle, everyone fights wounded." He squeezed Alexander's neck with a strong hand. "It's all good training."

Forty minutes later they were there.

They rode through the wide gates of the French Club and left their horses at the stable. Karlov was carrying his son's foil and épée in his stained leather sword case. They walked past the indoor swimming pool and the columned clubhouse with its deep curving veranda and through the formal gardens. They heard the tap of metal balls. Four elderly gentlemen were playing at *boules*. A tray with white wine rested on a table to one side. One player was grumbling about the texture of the dirt playing surface as they passed.

"We could be in Bordeaux," said Karlov, amused. "Sit down here a minute, Sasha."

Alexander sat on an iron garden chair outside the tennis pavilion. Karlov knelt and pulled off his son's riding boots, for he knew how difficult that would be for him. He opened the canvas sword case and took out Alexander's fencing shoes. The traditional elk-soled shoes had no heels. Karlov slipped them on his son's feet and tied them with firm double knots. Then he lifted them one by one and dusted each sole with a bag of rosin. The shoes would provide perfect grip, but no insulation for his son's bad leg.

"Thank you, Papa," said Alexander, astonished. It was the sort of service that he would have expected to perform for his father.

They both stood. Karlov handed him the sword case and carried the boots himself as they entered the pavilion. Alexander sensed again the importance of the match.

A large crowd of parents and guests waited for them, seated in long rows of chairs on both sides of the black rubber strip, the narrow fencing carpet. The Lycée supporters sat on one side of the piste, the Cathedral on the other. Indochinese servants passed tea and coffee and petits fours.

As soon as Alexander saw the fencing strip, he began to withdraw within himself as the maestro had advised, to build a mental aggressiveness that he must conceal but hold always ready to be transformed into physical audacity behind the mask.

The junior school matches were nearly finished. Two twelve-year-olds in white jackets and trousers saluted with their foils. Then their weapons fell gently, silently to their sides. They could not be students of Achille Angelo, Alexander thought. "Let your enemy hear your steel," the old teacher used to say. "First show courtesy, then ferocity."

The two young swordsmen donned their masks and came to the en garde position. Alexander understood their nervousness. Even in informal swordplay, there was always the unstated element that the sport dealt in life and death. Remove the button from the sword tip, and it was a duel or war.

A juror stood at each end of the strip preparing to call the touches. The director and the jurors strode back and forth along the mat while the two contestants advanced and retreated. The young boys were evenly matched in skill, Alexander noted, if not in stamina. They flowed back and forth along the strip, lunging and retreating as if dancing together, connected by their clashing blades. The sound of the warring metal soothed Alexander, made him feel at home.

Finally one boy tired. His Lycée opponent pressed on and scored the fifth touch required to win the match. The loser removed his mask and tucked it under his sword arm. The boy's face was flushed and running wet. He gasped for air. After a moment of hesitation, he stepped forward and congratulated the winner with gritted teeth and shining eyes. The spectators stood and chattered and clustered around the fencers.

Alexander admired his father's demeanor as the Count strolled among the crowd. After three months in Shanghai, he had the presence of a seigneur at home, at ease in his own gardens. He seemed like a sleek high-stepping borzoi, lean and elegant but dangerous, stalking through a pack of lap dogs, though himself bred and ready to chase wolves. The long scar on his cheek did not diminish him. Men and women, especially women, came up to him, eager to be recognized. His father paused and bowed and kissed hands, remembered names and listened with ostensible appreciation. Occasionally he gave out a card.

Alexander, nervous, stood with Vivien St. Clair and the other six members of his senior team, whispering about their adversaries and helping each other button the left sides of their heavy canvas jackets. He glanced over at the French boys doing the same at the far end of the pavilion.

François Ricard stood with his back to Alexander. He seemed older, more fully developed than the others. He was loosening his muscles, bending side to side and rotating his broad shoulders. He spread his feet and repeatedly touched his heels with the knuckles of both hands clasped together. A tall fresh-faced girl with tawny blond hair approached him. Jessica James. Alexander was excited to see her. The match would give him a chance to show her who he was. The French boy paused and kissed her on both cheeks. They chatted for a moment before young Ricard resumed his exercises. Looking vexed, the girl turned away. Alexander thought she felt his gaze. She spotted him and waved one hand. They exchanged smiles. Then she found a cup of tea and took a seat beside Captain Ricard near the center of the front row of Lycée spectators.

The police captain nodded agreeably to Count Karlov, who sat opposite him across the strip. Seeing the girl made Alexander think of Lily, and of her intense delicate beauty compared to Jessica's vigorous outdoor look. He thought of Lily naked on her belly in the candlelight, her slender fingers gripping the rails of the bedstead, her sleek black hair spread like a fan on the white linen, her derriere raised in the air like a perfect pear waiting on a branch, smooth and dry only on the outside, chin-soaking succulent inside, its copper-toned skin caught in a ray of the sun.

The crowd grew still. The first senior match was under way, a foil bout with the winner the first to make five touches. Another such contest would follow, and then two matches each of épée and sabre. Alexander determined to study the French fencers to learn the techniques of their common training. He knew finesse and *élan* would be their code.

Alexander observed the Japanese minister watching his son in the second foil bout. The diplomat was dressed *tout à fait à l'Anglaise*, in striped trousers, a black jacket, wing collar and carnation. Young Hideo Tanaka was lean as an arrow, with none of the camaraderie or relaxed humor of his European or Chinese contemporaries. Tanaka's demeanor was as neutral as his father's, but Alexander knew he was focused as a microscope. His hand was fast, always in control. As a fencer he already possessed a sense of smooth violence. Tanaka had told Alexander about Bushido, the cult of the warrior, the samurai. When Hideo won his bout, five touches to one, neither the Japanese boy nor his father revealed the slightest satisfaction or emotion. Tanaka bowed once toward his opponent and once toward his father.

The Lycée split the foils but won both épées. They were leading three matches to one. Alexander had the sickening feeling that success in the contest would depend on him. He was already burdened by his father's words that morning, though doubtless they were intended as encouragement.

The schools split the sabres. Sweating like a fountain, Barini won his contest. "*Bravo! Bravo!*" hollered the Italians, traditional fencing rivals of the French, excited here as a row of magpies. The Lycée led four to two, with three points still at stake in the Captains' Match. Alexander would have to win all three: foil, épée and sabre. He guessed that François would find it embarrassing to be defeated by a cripple. For the French boy, it would be a *point d'honneur* not to lose.

Alexander stood and hobbled along the strip with his mask in his right hand. His left shoulder rocked up and down with each step. He thought he detected a murmur from the audience. Recalling Mei-lan's advice, and the advantage of being underestimated, for once he made no effort to diminish his limp. He handed the walking stick to his father and carefully drew Achille Angelo's old Pulotti from the sword case. He glanced at Jessica and saw her surprise. Like the rest of the crowd, she seemed startled to see a fencer who used a cane.

"Ah, one of those Italian grips, I see," said the Lycée's fencing master dismissively, observing Alexander's sword. He tapped the hand guard of the foil, then drew a handkerchief from his cuff and wiped his hands. "A short straight handle with a cross-bar behind the bell." He shook his head and tucked both thumbs in his waistcoat pockets. *"On est à Florence ici?"*

"That's the way I was taught, *Maître.*" Alexander tightened the martingale, the strap that bound the weapon to his hand. He wondered how many men this dandy had stabbed in trains and street fights. Maestro Angelo would carve him like a duck.

"Our handles are longer, you see, curved to fit the palm, with no cross-bar and no strap," said the French instructor as if lecturing an ingenue. "Gives one greater freedom of movement, of course."

"But less power and control," interrupted Karlov, hard annoyance in his voice. No one would lecture his family about weapons.

Alexander was aware of Captain Ricard and François's girl listening to the exchange. He feared his father's temper. And he knew that his leg would deprive him of the explosive aggressive style for which the Italian weapon was designed.

"As you wish." The Frenchman shrugged. "Of course," he added, raising his voice so that Captain Ricard could hear, "fencing did not come to your country until Peter the Great introduced it with the other civilized trappings he brought back from Europe. But no doubt the young Count Karlov knows how to use his blade."

"I am not 'Count' Karlov," said Alexander. He could see his father darken.

"But your father . . ." said the instructor.

"In our family, *signore*, the title does not pass until the father dies." Karlov absently touched the scar on his cheek. "And as yet, you see, I am still alive."

Alexander felt himself grow strangely cold. He could not imagine his father not being alive and with him. Life was lean enough without his mother and sister. He shook off the thought and tried to concentrate on what was being said.

"With us, the title passes only to the eldest son." Karlov nodded towards Alexander. "In your country, of course, every son of a count is a count, and on and on." He laughed lightly, almost taking the sharpness from his words. "So Paris swarms with counts, like rabbits."

"I believe that today in Moscow there are no titles whatever." Captain Ricard smiled and leaned forward. "May I introduce my son's friend, Jessica James, Count Karlov?"

"*Enchanté*," the Count said, ignoring Ricard's observation. He stared into the young lady's eyes as if briefly drowning in them, then smiled quickly and bowed his head when she stood.

"Good morning," said Jessica and Alexander to each other. Never had a girl gripped his hand so firmly. He wished he could hold hers gently.

"*Mademoiselle* James comes to us from California." Ricard sighed.

"Her parents are missionaries, dedicated to the elevation of the Chinese." He paused. "It is a substantial task, even for Americans."

Jessica frowned at the officer.

"Messieurs!" called the director.

Alexander limped onto the strip. At once he felt different: alert, at the center of what mattered. "Our art," his master had said, "was developed through the centuries in blood and death."

He nodded at his adversary as François strode onto the mat and ran his fingers through his blond hair. The director stepped between the two swordsmen and began a lengthy introduction. Could it be a coincidence, Alexander thought, that French was the universal language of both fencing and prostitution?

The director presented the opposing captains and explained the rules of the three-part match. The foil could score only by touching the torso with the sword tip. The tip of the épée could score on any part of the opponent's body from foot to head. The sabre scored anywhere from the waist up, with either the cutting edge or the tip of the blade.

Alexander knew foil was his own best weapon. At both Kadnikov and the Corps of Pages, foil was considered the highest form of the art and science of swordsmanship. Weighing under one pound, thirty-five inches of fine steel from bell guard to button tip, the foil combined strength and reach, balance and an infinite capacity for speed and lightness of touch.

But Alexander knew he could no longer do much that he once had done. Now his right hand must replace the speed and strength that his almost rigid left leg could not provide. His back leg could no longer furnish the cobra-like coiled spring to give distance and force to his lunge when he attacked. He could not retreat when pressed, or continue his own attack with a swift reprise, for now he could only drag himself slowly forward, never backward. Nor could he retain his balance if he brought his feet together in the *rassemblement*. His favorite simple attack, the *balestra*, a forward jump followed by a full lunge, he would never do again. Now his defense must be perfect, his thin blade as solid before him as a wall of steel. His own attack must be steady and continuous, always forcing his enemy to attack under the worst conditions. He himself must rely on point control and the precision of his hand. As the taller fencer, he would have the advantage at a distance, but in close work the shorter arm would have the edge.

Fortunately, Alexander had begun to adapt his game during the lessons he had been giving at the Salle, and his morning exercises in the rafters had greatly strengthened his hand and arm, though during the past week he had abandoned those disciplines for others, with Lily. In his early mornings at the warehouse, he had occasionally closed his eyes and rested suspended from the ceiling by one arm or the other to force himself to depend on that single strength. Had he now been weakened by the softer rigors of the boudoir? Sometimes he wondered if it was madness for a cripple to undertake the fastest of all sports. At least in the saddle he felt the equal of any man.

"Messieurs!" called the director. The guests took their seats. Alexander pulled on his leather glove and flexed his long fingers. He took deep measured breaths, preparing for the only activity that required him to make lightening conception and execution simultaneous.

The two boys faced each other four yards apart at the center of the strip. Alexander knew that the five yards behind him would never be used. He must either hold his place or advance.

The two stood with their left arms hanging at their sides, holding the masks by their padded tongues. Their right feet and shoulders pointed forward, their bodies in narrow profile to each other, presenting smaller targets. Their left feet pointed left, at right angles to the right. This position, once comfortable and instinctive, was now painful for Alexander. Each boy held his sword pointed towards the ground just to the left of his right foot as he prepared for the salute.

Alexander stared François directly in the eye. He bent his right elbow until the tip of his foil pointed at the ceiling with the blade before his right eye. The French youth did the same. Alexander heard his own blade whistle as he swiftly lowered it, what his instructor called "the opening note in the symphony of fencing."

The two fencers saluted the judges and the audience. Glancing at his father, Alexander saw the tension in his face. Tight furrows had replaced his nonchalance. Alexander resolved not to look at him again.

Alexander drew on his mask with his left hand and pulled the tongue down firmly behind his head. He was surprised to see François assist this motion with his armed right hand, an indelicacy against which Angelo had warned. "You must respect the sword." Could it be that the French boy was trying to avoid messing his hair? Vanity could be a distraction, but also a source of resolve.

Alexander's mask transformed his world: now he was isolated, totally alone, focused like a racehorse at the starting line.

"En garde!" called the director.

Both fencers assumed the beginning en garde position with their foils and bodies in line and their sword tips at eye level. Alexander was careful to remember a detail about which he had occasionally been slack. He arched his left arm behind his head with both elbow and wrist bent. "Like a scorpion's tail," he had been instructed.

He felt his body quiver with tension and concentration, the fuel of nervous energy that was required to alternate with periods of deliberate relaxation of the muscles during every match.

"*Prêts?*" called the director. "*Allez!* Fence!"

François touched blades, lunged and attacked.

Alexander parried hard, spanking his enemy's blade down and holding it briefly with the strong middle of his sword, the forte, against the weaker end of his opponent's weapon, the foible. Then he disengaged, stood still and watched his adversary recover.

Already, all the complicated lessons of his youth, the training in false attacks and stop thrusts, the *riposte, remise, redoublement*, the *inquartata* and the *passata sotto* of the Italian school and all the rest of it were absorbed in the hot instincts of desperate combat. If his legs were slow, his hand and blade must be fast.

Alexander advanced with a short step of his right foot, then immediately restored his balance by drawing his stiff left leg forward behind him. He kept his feet close, in balance, so as not to widen his guard. Once again the two touched swords, beating and circling their blades. Alexander felt a trembling in the other's foil. He sensed François was about to lunge. Anticipating and interrupting his opponent, he advanced once more with two quick short steps, then counterattacked just as the French boy straightened his sword arm and threw his front leg forward to attack. Alexander parried lightly and touched François's right shoulder in that instant of vulnerability that follows every failed lunge. Then he immediately relaxed his arm and grip.

"*Touché!*" said the nearest juror.

They resumed the en garde position and began again.

Instantly Alexander replaced relaxation with speed and ferocity. Conscious only of the combat, he saw nothing but his enemy's foil and the target of his torso. He repeated the pattern of swift short advances, then pressured his adversary with double advances. He knew François had the strength and fighting spirit of a fencer, but did he have the point control and concentration? Did he have the sense of distance to be certain that an enemy's lunge could not quite reach him and thus let him stand steady to counterattack when his adversary was extended? Alexander knew that soon the two would have no secrets from each other.

Alexander's pairs of forward steps followed like the inevitable rapid even ticks of a metronome. He kept François's foil engaged, beating it to the sides and down, enveloping it, binding it with clockwise and counterclockwise circles with his sword. He could sense everything through the touching blades: not just pressure and evasion and strength and speed of stroke, but even irritation and frustration, uncertainty and anger, and perhaps a little fear. Five minutes on the strip, said the maestro, will teach you all there is to know about a man.

With each exchange, the two fencers moved farther down the piste into François's five yards of mat.

With a flash of recognition, Alexander understood for the first time that his own handicap was not his alone: it was shared by them both. For just as Alexander could never retreat, so it was impossible for François to advance. The French boy, too, had lost half of the fencing strip before he started. To advance he would have to knock Alexander down. As long as Alexander's hand was swift enough to keep his own sword tip between them, François could not move inside his guard to press him closely with the strength of his body.

Alexander suddenly realized that to win he must continually transfer his disability to François Ricard. He must make his will prevail. He must fence with "second intention," planning his moves ahead like a chess player.

In one close exchange, with both fencers touching, François won a French juror's call to get a touch and make the score four to one. Alexander recalled the instruction: never let a doubtful call distract you. He stepped forward quickly when they resumed: double advance after double advance. With such small steps and little backward pressure, his leg did not much trouble him. He pressed François farther and farther down the strip. It became Alexander's ambition to force his opponent so far down the piste, to the very end, that neither one would be able to retreat. He was used to that condition, but François would not be able to accept it. With the movement of their legs largely taken from the match, it would be purely a matter of the swifter steel. But it did not come to that.

"Touché!" exclaimed a juror as Alexander's blade bent against its target. "Foils bout *pour Monsieur Karlov et la Cathédrale.*"

The school match now stood at four to three for the Lycée. Two events remained.

As Alexander removed his mask and limped over to his father, he noticed that Jessica James was watching him intently.

Karlov took his handkerchief from his breast pocket and handed it to his son. Alexander wiped his face and returned his Pulotti to the sword case. He drew the épée and flexed the more rigid blade in both hands. Half again as heavy as the foil, this was less his weapon. But he felt he had gained an advantage of confidence over young Ricard, even though, with the different rules of épée, François could now score on any part of Alexander's less nimble body.

When Alexander took his place for the salute, he saw Billie Hudson slouch into the pavilion and stand behind the third row of seats on the Cathedral side. Dressed in a checked hacking jacket and a dripping foulard, the Englishman lifted a silver flask to his lips. He toasted towards Alexander before he drank. Alexander knew what Hudson thought of his own former adversary, the young French swordsman.

Again there was a close touch by both. Again Alexander lost the call. St. Clair rose briefly from his seat in protest. Alexander returned to his rhythm of steady small advances, binding the opposing weapon with whistling circular and diagonal semicircular parries and aggressive movements with his swift sword tip. But with the épée it was harder work, and harder on his leg. One to one, then, with a cunning feint-*coupé* attack, two to one for Alexander.

He felt the smothering fog of sweat and hot breath inside the cage of his mask.

Three to one for Alexander, then three to two with François growing steadier, more aggressive when they met with the strong inside parts of their épées. His legs and arms now vulnerable, Alexander was obliged occasionally to twist his body and lean back. His leg began to ache and pulse with pain. His left knee felt as if it were coming apart. Between knee and hip the bone seemed thin and hot, like an electrical wire overcharged and glowing, ready to burn through.

Four to three for Alexander as the crowd applauded a lightning parry, double attack and touch. But this time François held his sword in line when Alexander advanced and just beat him to the touch. Four four.

It was time to change, to hazard, to fight *con passione*. Ura!

Alexander extended both arms. Immediately he stamped his right foot farther forward, an *appel*, risking instability. Dragging his left leg, he lunged as best he could, desperately attempting to attack in a single increasingly fast forward movement with his arm rigidly extended and his wrist unbroken. It was shameful: the slowest, most painful lunge that he had ever made. But it still gained some speed and reach. Surprised, François was late with his parry and suffered a touch to his forearm. He removed his mask and stepped back as the Cathedral supporters applauded. His face was flushed and dripping like a diver emerging from the sea.

"Touché! *Les épées pour Monsieur Karlov.*" He had won both foil and épée.

But Alexander knew he could not lunge like that again. Had he failed, he would have been vulnerable to both touch and injury. To recover from the lunge Alexander would have been obliged to thrust his shoulders backward while pushing back with his advanced right leg so as to get the necessary momentum to regain the en garde position, altogether an exercise of hopeless exposure.

The school match was now tied at four to four, with only the captains' sabre bout remaining. The crowd sat forward expectantly. He saw his father square his shoulders and briefly close his eyes.

Alexander dried his face and borrowed a weapon from a schoolmate. He concentrated and collected himself. This Shanghai school meant nothing to him. He was fighting for Russia and his family, and especially for his father.

The sabre seemed unduly heavy in his hand. Four yards distant, he saw the gleaming blue reflection on his enemy's broad blade. This time the cutting edge, too, was now capable of making the scoring touch. He recalled how fiercely Ricard had used this weapon on horseback, and braced himself. Whatever his body felt, he must vitalize his blade. Every resource he possessed must be alive in his sword.

After they saluted, François immediately set on him like a Cossack, with heavy sweeping strokes, bearing hard down and across with every blow. Alexander felt a cruel strain on his left knee.

One point for François, then one more. Cheers filled the pavilion.

Alexander's left leg trembled. Let him come to me, he thought. Use your arm strength, not your legs. François bore forward again with slashing strokes. Alexander shortened his arm as François came in. When the French boy started a stroke, his blade too wide for half a second, Alexander turned his hand and caught him with his tip. Two-one.

When they began again, François pressed him, their sabres meeting halfway up the blade. He kept the contact and leaned against Alexander, infighting, with only their bent arms and blades between them. Alexander resisted the weight and superior strength of his opponent's body, though his leg felt as if it were being hammered down by a maul. Ricard's blade nicked his shoulder.

Three to one for the Lycée.

"Bravo!" cried several Frenchmen. "Bravo, Ricard!"

Alexander glanced at the crowd. For the first time in his life he saw what might be fear in his father's face. Somehow, he decided, he must use his hand speed before François could exploit his strength.

This time Alexander advanced with tight steps and short blocking strokes of his sabre. The pavilion rang with each blow. François tried to retreat and then extend his arm, but Alexander caught him halfway back with a finely timed and well-placed whip to his opponent's forearm.

Three to two, then four to two for the Lycée. One more touch and the match was lost.

By now Alexander could no longer feel his leg. He tried to keep his weight forward as the combat resumed, rapidly changing the angle and height of his blade, short stroke to short stroke, edge to edge, using speed, preventing François from utilizing his advantage. Delivering the blows with the strength only of his right arm and shoulder, at first he kept François at a distance, as if with foils.

But François came on with his own small steps, hacking short chopping blows with his curved cutting edge. Finally he pressed the flat side of his blade against Alexander's and forced it so close that, nearly mask to mask, *corps-à-corps*, Alexander heard the other's heavy panting breaths as if they were his own. François pressed both blades up, then extended his arm and punched them forward with all his weight. His blade axed down onto Alexander's right shoulder.

Something snapped in Alexander's leg. He collapsed to the side and tried not to scream as he lost his sword and fell onto the edge of the piste. The side of his mask hit the floor. He looked up through the steel mesh and saw his father rushing towards him. Jessica rose from her chair, both hands to her mouth. Alexander groaned and gasped and bit his lower lip. He felt a different kind of pain, as if a molten rod had pierced the tendon behind his ankle and stabbed upward to his calf.

After a moment he sat up on the strip. He kept his mask on to conceal his tears and the weakness in his face. He hoped they all thought that he had merely slipped.

"Are you all right?" said Jessica. She bent over him while his school-mates gathered around.

"I'm fine," he said forcefully, but he knew better. "Thank you." He wiped his face with his sleeve as he removed his mask.

François gripped Jessica's shoulder. He drew her back before he reached down to shake his adversary's hand, a bit too hard, Alexander thought.

"Congratulations." Alexander smiled up at him.

"Five matches to four. *Le Lycée a gagné!*" called the director as spectators stood and cheered. "*Merci, messieurs, mesdames. À l'année prochaine!*"

Karlov placed his hands under Alexander's arms and lifted him with care. His son put his left arm across the Count's shoulder. Hudson took Alexander's other arm, and the three walked slowly from the pavilion.

"I am so sorry, Father," Alexander said quietly, leaning on him.

"Not at all, Sasha." The Count shook his head. "You honored all of us."

-16-

"There will be no more of that damn monkey climbing in the roof till your leg mends," said Karlov, sitting on a new bench near the entrance to the Salle d'Armes. "And the doctor says we must have a surgeon get in there and fix you up properly."

"It's better already, Father," said Alexander, surprised that his father knew about, and had permitted, his exploits in the rafters. His leg was as bad as ever, or worse, but at least the cast was off his ankle. After months of tightening and atrophying, his Achilles tendon had ruptured under the strain of the match and separated the muscles in the calf of his leg from the bone of his heel. Pulled back down and stitched back together, after four weeks the cord of tissue was still sore and tight. He recalled a detail of his father's youth.

"Didn't you play games blindfolded on the stable roof when you were a boy, Papa?"

When I was a boy, thought the Count, I did some things too foolish for a circus performer, and others too unbecoming for a satyr. He carried on as though Alexander had not spoken.

"In the meantime, Sasha, you're taking a quiet train ride up to Mongolia to buy us a few Shanghai ponies. Right up on the steppe, on the edge of the Gobi Desert, where Genghis Khan bred his herds and the Manchus had their imperial pastures. Keep you out of mischief and give you a chance to rest your leg."

"Yes, Father." Alexander was thrilled at the adventure and surprised that he was being allowed to do it on his own. But then he recalled the tales of his father in Poland buying stallions when he was young, and stories of his grandfather on his grand tour when he was eighteen. Wandering in Italy for nine months, instead of letters he had sent home cases of sculpture and crates of paintings, trophies that included the chubby pale nudes that adorned the smoking room at Voskrenoye, and one or two others too outrageous to hang in a domestic household, though they had found their place in a dark corner of the wine cellar.

Slightly self-conscious, Alexander took out his tin of Telkhis Mixture and began to fill his meerschaum. The sweet odor joined the smells of horses and other tobaccos that always filled the stable. But he was confident he could distinguish it amidst a thousand smells.

"Don't get too excited," the Count said dryly. "You won't be the first Russian on the steppes. The czar sent men to Mongolia three hundred years ago."

"Cossacks, of course," interrupted Semyonov, setting down a plate of mushroom piroshki. "During the Napoleonic wars we used Mongol ponies in our breeding stables on the Don, and after that, a few English thoroughbreds to give them size."

"Then it was our tea trade, many long years before the British ever drank it, of course," resumed Karlov, ignoring the hetman as the Cossack left to begin a sabre lesson with a pupil. "Hundreds of thousands of chests a year, packed with bricks of pressed tea leaves, first by sea from

Foochow, then by riverboat and muleback, finally across the Gobi by camel and oxcart and on to Russia."

Alexander reached out and took one of the small flaky puff pastry pies, nodding while his father spoke.

The Count accepted the folded newspaper that Vasily Petrov handed him. The Russian paper *Shanghai Zaria* was mostly a listing of new arrivals, a record of brutal tales told by the latest refugees and a schedule of services at Shanghai's five Orthodox churches. Small notices published the names of those searching for surviving friends and relations.

"Bolshevik butchers." Vasily tapped a story. "The Cheka has ordered peasants to be shot in any district where they aren't keeping the snow off the railroad tracks. Their agents have murdered more Whites in Paris and Constantinople."

"No need to worry," said Karlov, knowing better. "There are too many of us in Shanghai. The *duroki* wouldn't know where to start."

"The Cheka has a newspaper called *Red Terror*. Here's something reprinted from their first edition." Karlov and Alexander remained silent while Vasily Petrov continued.

"'Comrades! One need only go into the kitchen of the accused and look into his soup pot,'" he read. "'If there is meat in it, then he is an enemy of the people. Stand him up against a wall!'"

For a moment no one spoke. Alexander remembered his grandmother saying that the peasants never ate meat, except at Christmastime and Easter. What they had, they cooked with linseed oil. Cabbage and buckwheat *kasha* and black bread were what they ate. At Eastertime, Katia and their mother painted eggs to give to the village children. The Karlov household itself, of course, after seven weeks of modest Easter fasting, would celebrate midnight mass in the family chapel, then feast on goose and suckling pig.

"The Red agents are getting closer." Vasily handed the paper to Karlov. "Someone shot Prince Ledyev in Harbin. Their assassins will be here next."

"They already are." Karlov tossed the paper aside and rolled a cigar between his fingers. "Poor Trebinsky. 'White Gloves' indeed," he muttered before turning to his son.

"If you leave early, Sasha, you'll have the pick of the ponies in Mongolia. A lot cheaper than buying here from those thieves at the horse auctions, bidding against the taipans at the Shanghai Horse Bazaar." Alexander knew business was growing quickly. But he guessed their debts were growing faster.

"I could leave soon, sir. The school holidays are almost here," said Alexander, puffing on his pipe. His father had not commented on his new habit. The white meerschaum was already turning a pale yellow-brown. "How many ponies do we want?"

"Six or eight for us, and perhaps one or two more to sell. They won't let you buy any stallions, of course, only mares and geldings." The Count began to clean a bridle with an oily rag. Although Karlov had done such work often since the Salle had opened, Alexander was surprised each time. In Russia he had never seen his father handle tack. "You'll want full pockets, Sasha. We'll have to borrow a bit more against the Salle. You'll need silver. Mexican dollars are best."

There was a crash behind them. A sword struck the wall and dropped to the floor. An Englishman cursed and pulled off his mask, his face red as a pepper.

Alexander turned to see Ivan Semyonov, sabre in hand, glaring at a student on the strip. Breathing hard, the young client recovered his weapon and faced the Cossack again with the eyes of a man trapped in a tiger's cage.

"Steady, Ivan," called the Count in Russian. "It's a lesson, not a duel. Dead students don't pay." Karlov lit the cigar and returned his attention to his son. "If you do your job up there, we'll have something to bet on in the races."

And to ride in the Paper Hunt, thought Alexander. He had not told his father the details of yesterday's ride with Billie Hudson. It had been his first time back in the saddle, and he had made Osetra lather like a washboard.

"In England, we chase red foxes. In East Africa they gallop after jackals. Here in China we have scraps of paper," Hudson had explained yesterday morning over scrambled ducks' eggs and Black Velvets in the stable yard. "Paper hunting began out here sixty years ago. Got the idea from lads who'd been in the Crimea fighting you Russkies. Now the paper hunt boys lay a long trail across the countryside, sort of rough route a fox would take, and then go after it like blazes, riding hell to hounds. Just like we're back in Lincolnshire. Stirrup cups, angry farmers and all."

Billie poured more champagne on top of the dark stout in his glass. Black Velvet. Alexander was disgusted by the morning-after English drink, but he liked Hudson no matter what he drank, or how much.

Hudson had put up both Karlovs for the Shanghai Paper Hunt Club, but they had not yet ridden. They were still waiting for their black hunting kit to come from the tailor. Only the old winners such as himself, Billie had informed him, were allowed to wear red, which Hudson persisted in calling "pink." That afternoon Billie showed Alexander where the hunt had run the previous day.

The two had trotted out of Shanghai into the countryside north of the city. Scraps of blue and yellow paper still marked the route laid down for the weekend's chase. Green paper marked the bridges. Purple marked the wades. Hudson whipped his pony and raced ahead. "Let me show you how we did it," he called over his shoulder to Alexander.

Cantering hard, they splashed through rice paddies and across the sharply curving railroad track of the Nanking Railway. Clumps of dirt flew up from their horses' hooves. They passed yellow temples set in bamboo copses and farm hamlets encircled by moats. They turned a tight corner around a small red Buddhist shrine with a steep tiled roof. A short wrinkled village crone stared at the riders when they slowed for the turn. The woman's left eye was clear and white as an egg. Her right stared at them as if they were devils from another world.

He had trouble keeping up with Billie. Hudson's pony had the short legs, long body and thick hocks that Alexander now recognized as typical of the Mongol breed. Osetra was fast enough, but seemed big for this type of riding, heavy, too much of a war horse. Alexander finally pulled even as they approached a steep humped-back stone bridge.

"Tally ho!" yelled Hudson, challenging Alexander over his shoulder as he whipped the China pony. Only one rider could pass at a time between the narrow stone walls of the bridge. Alexander imagined what this would be like with forty half-drunk riders using their spurs and whips. The answer lay directly in front of him. Hudson was charging for the bridge like a man riding for his life.

But Alexander thought his grey gelding could probably make it first, shouldering Hudson's pony aside at the last moment if need be. They galloped closer, Osetra one stride ahead. This victory was too easy, Alexander thought.

Unexpectedly, he found large uneven stepping stones set into the ground just before the bridge. Osetra's left forefoot struck a slippery stone and, driven by his powerful hind legs, slid forward. The horse plunged down to the left just as they came to the final stone step that led onto the bridge. Alexander's right stirrup sparked when it grazed the edge of the bridge. They stumbled down the soft steep bank of the stream and splashed into water up to Osetra's belly. The gelding struggled on, almost swimming. Alexander heard Hudson hallooing as his pony clattered across overhead and scrambled down the far side of the bridge. Osetra clambered up the opposite bank, puffing, dripping water.

"Got your boots wet, did you?" called Hudson as they trotted on. "Rubicon Creek, we call that one. No going back." The thick russet coat of his pony foamed with lather.

"All good training," said Alexander, out of breath, thrilled to be back in the saddle and no longer preoccupied by his leg.

They followed the trail through family graveyards planted with cypress and junipers. They rode through old plantings of beans alternating with stalks of cotton, their green and brown striping the landscape. They continued through orchards of pear trees and aisles of broken wheat cut through the grain fields by the hunt. They galloped past villages of angry Chinese, reminding Alexander of the surly peasants at home. Hudson paused near a round stone well. Four Chinese farmers were waiting in faded blue trousers and jackets. One of them led a black pig on a cord.

"We always promise to come back and look after things when the hunt is over," Hudson explained to Alexander, handing the bowing men a handful of coins. "Otherwise, they mess up the trail by digging pit traps and moving the paper about before we start. Then someone breaks his back or a pony snaps a leg. Can get a touch rough."

Karlov interrupted his son's reminiscence of yesterday's ride.

"Here's someone to see you, Sasha, unless I'm mistaken."

A bicycle pulled up at the entrance to the stable. A young woman in fitted tan trousers dismounted and carefully rested her machine against the wall. A long parcel was tied to the back of the bicycle.

"Good morning, Count Karlov," said Jessica James. She did not look at Alexander.

"Good morning to you, young lady." The Count stood. "You may remember my son, Alexander. This old Lancer is Vasily Petrov, and that is Ivan Semyonov on the piste."

Alexander stood and smiled, his cane in one hand. He remembered Jessica's concern when he had fallen at the fencing match.

"Will you teach me?" She looked at him with bright forthright eyes. For the first time he noticed that she was wearing a bit of makeup. "I'd like some private lessons."

"I'm afraid I can't," he said. "I'm not giving fencing lessons just now."

"I will teach you what you like, miss," growled Semyonov, sword in hand, grinning like a pirate.

"No, thank you." Jessica smiled at the Cossack while she opened her package and took out a pair of short riding boots with overly pointed toes. "It's riding lessons I'm after. Are cowboy boots all right?"

"By all means," said Alexander, perhaps a trifle too eagerly, hoping she had chosen this stable because of him. He knew his father would disapprove of the boots. "We can start in the ring. Dressage or cross country?"

"Cross country, please, and I'd like to saddle my own horse, if you don't mind. I did a bit of riding at home when I was little."

He led her across the ring to the stable yard. He did not mind her seeing him using his cane, perhaps because she had already observed how he could fence.

"Everyone says you're brilliant with a sword," she said, as if sharing the thought. "I hope you are all right."

"I'm fine, thank you," he said, quickening his steps.

"I love the smell," Jessica said when they arrived at the stable yard. She closed her eyes and inhaled. "It reminds me of when I was young in California. I always loved horses, but my family moved around so much I could never have one of my own."

They chose a horse and a saddle. She brushed the animal's back before she saddled it. Alexander only had to help her with the bit. Then he sat on a stool in the center of the ring and watched her ride around him.

"You have a lovely seat," he said, catching his breath as she posted in her tight trousers and cotton shirt, her breasts adjusting to the motion. "But keep your heels down." Despite her inappropriate American boots, she looked even more attractive than he remembered. For the first time he could appreciate her figure. Unlike many women, Jessica did not dress to emphasize her curves. Perhaps during these lessons she would take his mind off Lily.

As he watched and instructed, Alexander was aware of a rickshaw pulling up outside.

A Chinese in blue cotton trousers and the black jacket of a European bank clerk stepped inside and approached Dimitri Karlov. The man bowed and handed the Count an envelope. Then he looked around the Salle with care, counting the horses and the swords and furnishings and writing notes on both sides of a card.

Alexander could not tell what was being said or read, but he could feel his father's anger as the man continued his inspection. Karlov stalked through the warehouse and sat in the stable yard with a vodka while he reread the enclosures. Then he came back to the riding hall. The visitor was still at work.

When the Chinese touched the hilt of the Count's own sabre and began to draw the blade from the rack, Dimitri Karlov spoke to him.

"If you draw that sword, you will have to use it."

Startled, the man dropped the weapon back into its slot. "I am doing only what my master requires," he said, both fear and firmness in his voice. "If you wish to speak to Mr. Hak Lee, he is outside." The visitor turned and hurried to his rickshaw.

Count Karlov strode to the door of the Salle and squinted into the bright daylight.

A gleaming black motorcar was parked near the entrance. A burly Russian stood smoking nearby. Watching the Count approach his master's Chrysler, he hesitated before dropping his cigarette and grinding it out with one heel. Karlov ignored the man as the bodyguard followed him at a distance towards the car.

A rear window slowly lowered. The rickshaw rolled away.

"Good morning, Count Karlov," said a quiet voice through the open window.

"And good day to you," said Karlov without lowering his head. He was unable to see more than a suggestion of a long and pitted copper-colored face. "If you are Mr. Lee, your man has been disturbing my business."

For a moment there was no reply.

"There is my business here as well, Count Karlov," said the voice at last.

"Your business is my business. Nung was only attending to mattters that concern us both. I must know the security that supports your debts. Understand that I wish you only good fortune. Then we will both have the money that should be ours." The speaker paused. "But mine, I will have."

"Good-bye to you, sir," said Karlov as the window rose. He controlled his temper and strode away, unseeing in his anger, until he reached the entrance. There he stopped, slowly focusing on watching his son teach the young lady to ride around the ring. The boy seemed to be enjoying himself.

Reluctant to have the lesson finish, Alexander had let the time run on.

"Thank you, Alex," Jessica said at last, stroking her horse's shoulder. "I really want to get better. Perhaps one day I can teach you something." She dismounted and paid the Count for five lessons.

"What's the matter, Father?" said Alexander while Jessica led her horse back to its stall. His father did not seem himself.

"Your damned cousin Krupotkin has sold our debts to the Chinese moneylenders. That way he gets his money quickly without being seen to squeeze his own relations. The svinya has sold our notes to some Chinaman called Hak Lee. And these Chinese usurers are even more ruthless at collecting."

Alexander's heart stopped when he heard the name: the tall man with the swollen ear about whom Madame Wong had warned him.

Karlov drained his glass. "They've already raised the interest on all our overdue notes. The man who was just here said they'll be stopping by every two weeks. I dare say they won't all be as civil as that chap you saw." He folded the envelope and stopped speaking when Jessica approached. He did not wish to upset his son by reporting the conversation with the Chinese at the car.

Alexander recalled Mei-lan's tale about how the young Hak Lee had once worked in the same house of pleasure as herself, but as a plaything for the former imperial eunuchs. That experience had led him to pledge that no man would ever touch him again, even with a handshake. The neutered courtiers would arrive by sedan chair, cunning and hugely fat and soft as pillows, carrying their dried testicles in small porcelain boxes that hung by silk cords from their waists, treasures waiting to rejoin them in their next life. After enduring unspeakable abuse, of which his unhealing infected ear was one reminder, Hak Lee was said to have murdered the worst of them, and to have left the shrivelled glands inserted in place of the man's eyes, to discourage anyone from helping to pursue him. The missing eyes were found in the porcelain box left between the eunuch's soft thighs. No one cared to chase the killer. Only the legend had followed Big Ear.

Years later, Mei-lan had recounted, after the street hijacking of an opium delivery, an enraged dealer had chased Hak Lee down a narrow alley. Unarmed, the young Big Ear had abruptly stopped and seized a razor from the hand of a street barber. As his pursuer stumbled onto him, with one scything motion Hak Lee had cut the man open from navel to throat like a perch. Then he had wiped the blade on the dying man's sleeve and returned it to the trembling barber with apologies. When he walked down the lane another day, men bowed when he passed. Soon he began to lend money, choosing his first borrowers from this alley where they knew him best.

"Can I ride you home, Jessica?" said Alexander after a moment. "Osetra could use a little exercise. I'll lead your pony back."

"That would be lovely. I'll pick up my bicycle tomorrow," she said, careful not to sound too eager. "We live just off the Rue Batard."

They mounted up and Alexander led the way. He was proud to have her riding with him.

"I'm amazed how well you know the streets," she said when he took a shortcut. He was hoping to find a way to spend more time with Jessica. On the way they stopped at Le Chien Rapide for tea. Alexander had not been back since he had met Madame Wong.

"I've never been here," she said, noticing Alexander's strong hands and long fingers resting on the table. "My parents tell me to stay away from Blood Alley and parts of Foochow Road." She frowned as if resenting their instruction. "But I want to explore all these sort of places, find out everything about Shanghai. Especially the Chinese city. None of my friends wants to do it with me. They just don't care about how the real Chinese live and eat and do things. All they know are servants and compradores."

"Shall we do it together?" asked Alexander, pleased by his boldness, excited that she shared his sense of adventure. Always attack, he thought, ura!

Jessica looked at him before she replied. "Let's start Friday," she said, smiling, "after my next riding lesson. I can't wait." She lifted a tea cake from the plate. "May I ask what happened to your mother, Alex?" she inquired carefully, trying not to put too much curiousity in her voice.

When he hesitated, she added, "It's just that you and your father seem to manage so well together, as if you've always been on your own."

"Well, I've been away at school, and my father's been away in the army, but my mother died last year, on our journey to Vladivostok." He could not say more.

"I'm so sorry," she said, reaching for his hand, understanding that his self-reliance was less solid than it seemed.

Alexander's attention was distracted by a burly Chinese who stared at him from the doorstep of the Singerie across the street. He returned the stare and paused before speaking.

"Do you ever get home?"

"To California? Not in three years." Jessica took another cake, oblivious to her messy fingers. "My parents are so busy, visiting the missions, working with the converts. Now my mother's getting into the fight against child prostitution."

Alexander groaned inside. He thought of the drawings he had considered at Madame Wong's, and what might be going on in the building just across the road. The man standing there folded his arms and kept his eyes fixed on Alexander. Finally he turned and went inside.

"Some of the girls are twelve or thirteen, even less," Jessica continued. "It's horrible. Their parents sell them, and the gangs and warlords are all mixed up in it." She paused and looked at Alexander, as if judging him, disappointed that he had not responded with concern. He was so attractive, but she hoped his privileged childhood and recent hardships had not inured him to the suffering of others. "It's so awful what they do to women here. One doesn't know where to begin. Foot binding, child prostitution, drowning baby girls, concubines ..."

"Baby ..." he interrupted.

"Yes. The Chinese've been doing it forever. An Italian missionary, Father Ripa, said in Peking they used to throw the female babies outside the city walls. Once he saw a hog eating one of the little girls."

"When was that?" Alexander said, the horror honest in his voice, her concern reminding him for an instant of his mother.

"The early eighteenth century. But they're still doing it today." Jessica paused and sighed, her face red. "I've learned all sorts of disgusting things. The Mandarins used to bend the spines of their sons to make them appear more scholarly."

"Have you ever been to Inner Mongolia?" he said, wanting to change the subject. At least they both loved horses and were excited about Shanghai. Unconsciously, he straightened his own back. "I'm going next week to buy some ponies."

"No, but I'd love to. It's meant to be very wild, and the Mongols never believed in foot binding." she said, standing. "I'd better get home, Alexander. Thank you."

"My pleasure, Jessica." He wished he could take her with him.

She sucked the sugar from her fingertips, watching him all the while. "Call me Jesse."

-17-

They were the only Europeans, and Jessica was the only woman. The Chinese at nearby tables acknowledged them with their eyes, not with word or gesture. To the surprise of the waiter, it was Jessica who discussed the menu in comprehensible Shanghainese, though Alexander had chosen this unusual Cantonese restaurant and was now able to converse a bit. Two motionless green turtles, the tasty symbols of longevity, waited their turn in a shallow stone pool in the center of the wooden dining room.

"Let's eat something different," Jessica suggested with a mischievous smile, hungry after her second riding lesson.

Alexander nodded while she ordered. Jessica was pleased that he let her do it. She glanced at him, trying to determine what made him so attractive. They did not share that much, she felt, other than a passion for the life around them. She was glad Alex had his father's craggy face and long wiry body, but without that deeper hardness that seemed just beneath the old Count's courtly charm. She had never seen eyes as hard as Count Karlov's after he returned from speaking to the man in the car outside his stable. It was as if he were containing some savage outburst. Somehow these Russians, both White and Red, seemed to have a wild side that reminded her of the fresh energy of some Americans at home. The two nations had something in common, she thought, that the Asians and Europeans of her acquaintance did not share. But with the Russians it was not pioneering vigor, she recognized, but something more troubled, almost angry. Perhaps Alexander would help her understand what it was.

"Chrysanthemum tea?" she asked.

Alexander nodded again and wiped his hands on a steaming hot towel. He thought she had declined owl and chameleon, and some third dish beyond his Shanghainese, possibly pangolin. He was pleased that Jessica was not squeamish about the unusual suggestions. He liked her bold spirit, if not all the feverish opinions that came with it. But he was habituated to arguing with his sister, and there was something of Katia in Jessica's edgy independence. Katerina used to enjoy baiting him with her opinions, like a fencer lowering a trembling foil, teasing with the button tip, looking for a weakness, trying to get under his easy dismissal of her views. Anyway, thought Alexander, it was nice to be alone with a girl, a comfort just to be talking with a woman.

Their chopsticks soon danced over the food, seizing morsels of eel and blowfish, sliced duck gizzards and baby pig's feet in plum sauce. They drank and smiled, warming to each other as they spoke of horses and schools, parents and friends, Kadnikov and San Francisco. They laughed, and after a time their laughter became conversation.

As she spoke and touched his arm, Alexander felt himself growing warm. What would it be like, he wondered, to assay with her some of the refinements to which Lily had introduced him after school? He could not believe what he had learned and done with her. But it was fading away, like distant music that still moved him but was becoming just a dream.

He guessed Jesse was a virgin. Would a girl like her ever do such things? He knew Jesse liked to think she was a modern emancipated woman. Might she extend this liberal philosophy to Bohemian sexual adventure? What would this American girl say if he suggested that they try the Devil's Knot?

"My parents have gone up to Nanking. They're always travelling," Jessica said, interrupting his thoughts. She sensed how much he missed the women in his family. "My father's worried about the safety of the missions and our clinics, with all these warlords fighting in the countryside, and now the Kuomintang regiments trying to control everything around Shanghai."

"If you think the politics are troubling here," said Alexander, "you should see what's happening at home. The Soviets are making lists and killing everyone who disagrees with them, even each other. Every day we hear more stories from refugees and in letters from Paris."

She listened as he continued, his love for Russia animating his words. For these Whites, restoration was a bitter and hopeless mission, a crusade, and it was the opposite of hers. She hoped that Alex did not share too much of it.

"The Reds started with the aristocrats and the officers," he said. "Then they moved on to the priests and what they call the 'bourgeoisie,' then the Anarchists and the Socialists. Now it's the *muzhiki*, the richer peasants and other Bolsheviks." He paused, then summed up angrily, "The Communists are savages."

"But what about the serfs?" she responded aggressively. Jessica restrained herself from asking if the Whites, after centuries of class domination, were not responsible for any evils that followed them. "Weren't your peasants just like slaves?" she added. "You know they're better off now."

Alexander's stomach tightened. He didn't want to argue with her, but he couldn't stand this sort of talk. The Reds had destroyed his family and his country. But what would this girl say if she smelled the dark inside of a peasant's hovel at Voskrenoye, and saw also the perfect kennels and the blacksmith shop, the chapel and the gatehouse and the garden pavilion, the entire self-contained world of their estate? Would she see the hardship and the luxury only as an ugly contrast? Or might she be willing to understand the relationships and the harmony of a different world?

"We ended serfdom years before you Americans ended slavery," he said hotly. "The Bolsheviks, on the other hand, are filling new slave camps in Siberia while you and I are sitting here at dinner." He had not told her about the Commissar who had killed his mother, but the raw memory made his voice harsh and bitter.

"Well," said Jessica, backing off a bit but not letting go, "I don't know about all that, but in China the Communists are not so bad." She herself had grown concerned at some reports from Russia and hoped that the worst of them could not be true. "All the Reds are trying to do here is end the tyranny of the landlords and the moneylenders and the warlords. Somebody has to do it."

"Sun Yat-sen's already said all that, and the Kuomintang are trying..."

"Chiang and the Kuomintang are just more of the same, Alex," she said dismissively, waving one hand. "Don't you see? They're working with the warlords and their bandit gangs, and some of those bandits still practice cannibalism. Do you know they hang the hearts and livers of their enemies in the cookshops in the villages? Sometimes the bodies are cut and salted and hung in the sun before broiling. It just happened in Sau Yau. Our French missionary friends know all about it."

"Jesse." Alexander stopped when she touched his wrist. He was about to ask her why the Reds were bringing Chinese torturers to Moscow. How much cruelty did they need? He breathed slowly and tried to contain himself while she continued.

"It's only the university students and the unions and that Mao Tse-tung who are ever going to make a difference. Only the Communists will do it." She gulped some of the sugared tea, her cheeks bright and her voice rising. She was aware of his annoyance, but she was determined to express herself. "Next time we'll go to one of their meetings. You'll see."

He was about to retort, but he saw Jessica's breasts pressing against her dress in her excitement. He forgot about his food and the argument. She had a generous but fit figure, not like Lily's slender stalk-like body. He was astonished by this American's crazy political beliefs, but he remembered his father's advice: don't win the argument and lose the girl.

"Are the chicken feet next?" he said after a moment. "Or the deep-fried pigeon eggs?"

"You'd better eat everything," she said, relaxing, as if stepping back from the barricades. She smiled, wishing to enjoy him again. "Tomorrow you're going to Mongolia."

At the table behind Jessica, four men ate eagerly and noisily as they crunched fried cicadas and drank rice wine from small silver cups while they ate tiny rice birds wrapped in leaves. The waiter worked around the table, ladling soup into blue-and-white bowls. Alexander saw a small paw being served to one diner. He could just discern its shiny curved nails in the broth. He glanced quickly at Jesse and was relieved that she could not see it. Then the waiter took away a large platter from the center of the other diners' table, revealing a hole beneath where the dish had been. The man spread small plates of seasonings between the diners, probably cilantro, ginger and what looked like sour chili.

"You have such amazing eyes," said Jessica. "They're so different. The left one is so green."

"They're just like my sister's," said Alexander, flattered that Jesse had noticed. "My twin, Katerina," he added, and suddenly felt a sharp pang. At unexpected moments like this he was reminded of how much he missed her.

The waiter stepped back from the nearby table and blocked Alexander's view. He noticed a second waiter entering from the kitchen with hurried steps. The man was carrying an awkward object swaddled in a towel. Something was hanging out the bottom. It looked like the tail of a cat. Alexander was watching the second waiter bend under the table when Jessica asked:

"Where is your sister?"

"We don't know. Somewhere in Russia." He was certain that Katia was still alive. "The Bolsheviks kidnapped her."

"I'm so sorry." Jessica reached out and touched his hand.

"Katia's a bit like you," he said after a moment. "Always worrying about anyone who's disadvantaged. I think she got it from my mother." Unfortunately, he thought, the Bolsheviks had now turned such innocent social concerns into a brutal philosophy, and Jessica seemed to be infected.

Just then the four diners at the adjoining table gave small clucks and cries of delight when both waiters stepped back.

Alexander saw a small long-tailed monkey secured in a wooden frame beneath the table. Its thin hairy limbs were trussed behind its back. Its elegant grey tail flicked against the cage. The pale shaved crown of its skull poked through the hole in the table like a boiled egg in a cup. A moist red line circled the skull like a fine necklace.

Holding a broad-bladed knife, one of the waiters leaned over the table. Alexander was disgusted to see him skim off the loose cap of the creature's skull and set it upside down onto a plate. One of the diners poked the cap with his chopsticks before sucking the tips of the sticks. Then the four reached out with slim long-handled porcelain spoons. With exclamations of delight the gentlemen helped themselves to raw brains from the living skull.

Shrill moans rose from beneath the table.

Alexander was appalled. He had thought the monkeys were meant to be drunk and gagged before they were served.

Jessica turned to see what was drawing his eye. At that moment a spoonful of white brains and pulsing blood vessels touched one of the diner's lips.

The little monkey sighed and moaned as another diner served himself.

"No! You can't!" Jessica cried, rising abruptly from the table, one hand to her mouth. "Kill it! Kill it!" She gagged and choked as she ran for the door.

Alexander stood and followed her.

He found Jesse leaning over a railing and vomiting into the night. Embarrassed for her, feeling guilty, Alexander hesitated, then went back inside. Standing, he quickly finished his tea, apologized and paid the bill.

"How could you? You did that on purpose, didn't you?" she said when he came back outside. "You just wanted to see if I'd be shocked." Her cheeks were hollow and her eyes narrow with anger.

"Not exactly, Jesse," he said. "I didn't know they were serving monkey tonight. But I did think they'd be serving dishes that might disgust you, and I thought that in a way that was what you wanted."

"That's why the Communists are right," she said, her face contorted, almost ugly as her voice rose. "All these old barbaric ways have to stop. Everything. Selling children. Eating live animals. Beheadings. Cannibalism. The Reds will change it all."

Alexander's bitterness returned with a rush. "I was on a train in Siberia when your beloved Reds took a wounded White officer and threw him into the furnace of our locomotive."

Jessica stared at him and was about to speak.

"Why do you think the Bolsheviks are bringing Chinese torturers all the way to Moscow?" he added.

She pressed her lips together and shook her head violently.

"Too much." She trembled. "It's too much. I'm going home."

Jessica turned and held up a hand. A rickshaw drew forward. She climbed in without speaking another word.

* * *

Shanghai Station was a swirling bedlam of jostling travellers, porters, soldiers, vendors, thieves and beggars. Each person pursued his activity with an intensity that Alexander had seen only in Shanghai. At home the workers and farm laborers had seemed to trudge, hoping only to delay their toil, weariness and resignation heavy in their demeanor.

He watched a thin old man hurry past him on straw sandals. His torso bent parallel to the ground, the man was laden like a mule under a canvas pack. He gripped a leather strap in his teeth and hands, binding his burden to his back.

Vasily Petrov carried Alexander's bag as they walked to a first-class coach of the Nanking Railway. Alexander was looking forward to being on his own. He would watch China pass by his train window like a motion picture film, then take the ferry across the flooded Yangtse-kiang, and finally bargain like a gypsy with the Mongolian horse breeders.

He remembered another world, when horse breeders and cavalry agents visited in the spring to buy black horses from his family. His mother would receive each of them with the hospitality for which the estate was celebrated. Cold lunches and wine from the vineyards of friends in the Crimea were served on elegant tables set between the paddocks. Pressed linen tablecloths, French china and spring flowers welcomed the diners on the grass. He could see his mother in a long high-collared summer frock, her green eyes smiling as she directed her guests to their places. Later there were strolls in the informal English park and tea and poetry in the gazebo. At night the guests, sometimes scores of them, slept wherever there was space, several of the young men on the low wide wall-to-wall ottomans in the divan room, built by his grandfather in the Turkish style after Russia's conquest of the Caucasus. Others stayed up till dawn, drinking and chatting over backgammon in the smoking room beneath wall racks of long-stemmed Turkish pipes. Upstairs, personal servants slept on pallets in the halls outside their masters' bedrooms.

Alexander took a seat in an empty compartment, sighed and lowered the window by its thick leather strap. It reminded him of the shattered window of the train in Siberia and of watching Katerina being carried off on horseback. Alexander shook his head, determined to put the last train ride from his mind. It was an image he had recalled too often.

Vasily stood on the platform below, smoking, wearing a pair of worn breeches with the faded pale blue stripe of the 2nd Lancers down the outside of each leg. He seemed older and quieter, less confident than when Alexander first met him in Siberia. Alexander checked that his money belt was tight. Reassured by the hard weight of the silver dollars, he stood and leaned out, resting his arms on the windowsill.

A tall girl came pushing through the crowd with a wicker basket in one hand. She saw Petrov and advanced quickly to Alexander's window, breathless. Seeing her, Vasily waved and walked away.

"I'm sorry about last night." Jessica gazed up at Alexander with big eyes. "I just couldn't stand it."

"I don't think I'd like you much if you could." He was glad she had come. He loved the way she looked, flushed and excited.

"It's just China," she said, "and you and I look at it so differently." She reached up and placed one hand on his arm. "It really wasn't your fault."

He nodded at the basket. "Are you coming with me, Jesse?"

"No, but I thought you might be hungry." She smiled and handed up the picnic basket. "We didn't have much dinner."

"I hate to think what you've put in here," he said lightly as he set the basket on the seat behind him.

"Sweet and sour borzoi," Jesse said, trying not to laugh. "How long will you be?"

"About two weeks." He noticed another passenger entering the compartment. "Mongolia will be empty without you."

"Mongolia is always empty," she said, pleased by his gallantry, wanting to say she would miss him. "Please get me a pony. I'll pay you back."

The whistle blew twice. Doors slammed until the train trembled and nudged forward.

"Good-bye, Alexander Karlov."

He recalled some advice Mei-lan had given him during one of their afternoon teas. Always leave a woman with an unfinished promising memory. He bent down and took Jessica's face between his fingers. He looked into her eyes. For the first time Alexander kissed her on the lips. When he released her, she smiled at him with a dreamy sense of attachment and admiration.

"Good-bye to you, Jesse James."

She merely stared after him, not waving, until Alexander could no longer see her.

The short train slipped slowly from the station. They passed other trains on either side. Along the curve of the track he watched his train approach the complex of sidings and turntables on the edge of the city.

He looked out the window to his right, at an empty cattle car, its wooden slats broken and decrepit. Then another cattle car, and another. But this one was filled. With young girls, perhaps eleven or twelve years old, all scrawny, half-naked in the wind and shivering in rags.

"My God," muttered Alexander, recalling what Jesse had said. For an instant he thought of Katia, horrified at what might have befallen his sister.

The car passed slowly, so close to his window that the starving girls appeared like framed pictures hanging on a wall. They stretched their thin arms through the slats, appealing for food. Alexander reached out and passed one of them a coin. The nails of another girl scratched his arm as the car pulled away. "Me, too!" she called out in Chinese.

"Country girls," said the Englishman who shared his compartment. "Farmers up north are all starving after the floods, you know. Starving. Families sell the girls for ten dollars to work in the sweatshops or brothels in the city. Always happens in the bad years." He stood and closed the window. "Of course, Chinamen love virgins, and with a little chicken blood, they'll all be virgins again and again." He pulled out a silver flask wrapped in leather and sat down. He glanced at Alexander's picnic basket and held out the flask. "Care for a starter?"

"Thank you, sir." Alexander took a longer drink than he should have and returned the flask. After the disturbing sight of the girls, and the sharp reminder of his abducted sister, he did not feel much like a chat. He rested a hand on the basket. Turning his thoughts to Jessica, he resolved to pursue her when he returned.

-18-

"Might as well finish all this up, if you don't mind. Stuff'll only spoil." Alexander's travelling companion reached back into the hamper for the last duck breast. "I'll be leaving you soon at Soochow. Venice of the East, they call it. Venice of the East. Others say it used to be the Athens of China."

The Englishman picked a scrap of crisp shiny skin from his waistcoat and popped it in his mouth. "Course, for me it'll be the silk factories, then a houseboat party on the lake, unless I can sneak off for a bit of sing-song playtime. Prettiest little things in China. Soochow's famous for them. Famous. But I suppose you're a bit young for that sort of mischief?"

When Alexander did not reply, he continued. "The emperors used to come to Soochow to find their courtesans."

"Aren't those cormorants?" Alexander stared out the window as the train slowed.

"I said courtesans, not cormorants," the traveller said impatiently. "Actually, they were concubines."

"Aren't those birds cormorants?" said Alexander, pleased that he was reacting only to what he wished to hear.

Wide sampans floated low in the water of an oval green lake close to the tracks. Rows of dark long-necked birds gripped the gunnels of each vessel with webbed feet. On the far side of the lake he saw pink and brown pigs foraging in a field of mustard grass and purple clover.

"Ah, yes. Cormorants, all right, young man. Fishers. Keen and well-trained as falcons. That ring around the throat stops 'em from swallowing the fish after they catch them. So they just peck out the eyes and gobble them down like oysters. Gives the birds just enough to keep them at it."

A fisherman with a basket between his feet jabbed one bird in the breast with a bamboo pole. The cormorant rose in the air, then tucked in its wings and dove into the water. Nearby a bird soared from the lake, flapping furiously as water streamed from its body and sparkled in the sunlight. When the creature settled onto the edge of another boat, the boatman squeezed the brightly-colored swollen pouch beneath the bird's mouth. The cormorant opened its curved bill and disgorged the living fish into a basket.

"No one trains animals and women better than the Chinks. No one." The silk dealer shook his head. "Who else would have such patience?" He rummaged in the picnic basket. "Ah, mind if I have one of these?" He lifted a round chocolate pastry from the basket. "Looks like you have two."

"Please help yourself," said Alexander, still hungry.

"You should see the women at those big wooden hand looms. Set in their filthy dark huts right on the dirt floor. But they always keep a basin of water handy to dip their fingers and keep the silk clean." The Englishman sucked at his fingers. "Thud-thud of the shuttle like a drum all day long. Thud-thud. Civilized person couldn't stand it. But a good weaver turns out five feet of brocade daily. Five feet, perfect yard wide. Nobody else can touch them. Nobody. Most of the women can't straighten their backs when the day's done. But they're at it again the next morning soon as there's a ray of daylight."

The train pulled into a station at the northern edge of the walled city. Small carts and donkeys with bells under their chins and teams of coolies with straps hanging from their shoulders waited at the edge of the crowded platform.

"If you'd like to go on outside, I'll pass down your bags." Alexander lowered the window while the silk dealer took two suitcases from the overhead luggage rack.

"Much obliged." The man put on his hat and brushed off his waist-coat. "Much obliged. They use those donkeys here because the old city lanes are too narrow for carriages and rickshaws."

Relieved to be alone in the cabin, Alexander handed down the bags to his informative companion. They exchanged good-byes twice. Men-dicants and missionaries passed along the side of the train, pressing begging bowls and religious tracts on the first-class passengers. Alexander accepted a pamphlet from a Chinese student assisting one of the missionaries.

"Soochow University," declared the front page. "An Institution of the Southern Methodist Churches of the United States." He thought of Jesse and wondered if her parents could be involved. Or had she said they were Pres-byterians? He wished she were with him. He ate the remaining chocolate pastry and finished the butt of the French bread and a bit of cheese while he waited for the train to leave for the next towns and Nanking.

Finally the whistle blew. Doors slammed. The train jerked forward. Alexander stood up and leaned out the window looking at an immense pagoda that towered over the ancient walls and at the steep stone bridges that arched over the waterways surrounding the city. Nearby he saw a man with a wooden yoke around his neck from which twenty or thirty live chickens were suspended by their feet.

Glancing ahead, he saw another train moving towards them, sliding slowly from Soochow south towards Shanghai. It advanced unevenly, almost stopping and starting as the two trains approached on close parallel tracks. The word "Harbin" was painted on the front cars, on others "Nanking." Most appeared to be third-class, cattle cars or box cars, rough and unfinished. All were crowded, packed with lean Chinese with hard hungry faces. The last two cars were first-class, with only a passenger or two in each compartment, mostly Europeans and one party of Japanese.

The oncoming locomotive slowed as theirs gained speed. Alexander looked at the quickening faces of the other train's passengers as they passed four feet from his.

A man smoking a pipe faced him for an instant. A big-framed man with a rugged square face and thick wild brown hair, the passenger was alone in his compartment.

Alexander stopped breathing. He stared as the figure slipped past and out of view. The trains moved faster.

Was he mad? He felt a chill come over his entire body.

No. It was him: the Commissar, Viktor Polyak.

Alexander turned and jerked open the cabin door and rushed down the narrow hallway. It was no use. By the time he reached the door at the end of the corridor, his train was moving far too fast for him to jump. Polyak's train was already out of sight.

Alexander leaned his head against the window of the door and closed his eyes. He felt the thumping of his heart. This was the moment he had been dreaming about as he lay half awake so many nights. A second chance at the Commissar, for his mother, for Katerina and for himself. He trembled while he tried to consider what his father would want him to do. "Patience, Sasha," his father once had said when Alexander grew too urgent during a hunt in the forest. "Patience is the hunter's greatest weapon."

He walked slowly back to the cabin as the train started to follow the line of the Grand Canal that led north to Wusih, Chinkiang, the Yangtse-kiang and Nanking.

"Would you mind putting your things in the luggage rack?" said a woman with what Alexander now knew to be an American accent. Two young red-haired children, a girl and a boy, sat quietly facing each other beside the window. The woman put a book mark in her Bible and nodded at Alexander while he closed Jesse's hamper and lifted it to the rack. The woman's Bible was protected by a white cloth cover bearing a large cross and the words, "China Inland Mission Hospital."

Alexander sat down opposite the missionary and tried to concentrate on what he should do about the Commissar. He knew he must send a wire to his father and shorten his trip as much as possible. Then, beginning to doubt himself, he considered the moment again. Was it really Polyak he had glimpsed, or was he just too obsessed with what had happened on the other train?

"It's time for prayers, children," said the woman, standing.

"Excuse me, please," said Alexander. "I think I'll go and take some lunch."

As he closed the cabin door behind him, he saw the two children kneel on the floor and clasp their hands and place their elbows on their seats. He smiled, remembering his impatience when his mother made Katia and him say their lengthy prayers at home. Perhaps he should be grateful that Jesse was interested in politics rather than religion, in Marx instead of God.

"Please you take seat?" said a dignified Chinese maître d'hôtel, leading Alexander to a table for two on the left side of the smoky restaurant car.

A heavyset man with a lined red face sat in the opposing seat. He glanced at Alexander's cane. "I hope you do not mind facing backward when you eat?" the man said with a German accent, reaching across the table to fold up a set of engineering drawings he had spread across Alexander's place.

"Not at all." Alexander took a menu and smiled at the waiter.

"And I hope you do not mind French wine." The German filled Alexander's glass from a bottle of white burgundy. "They got here first, so there is nothing from the Rhine."

"It's lovely," said Alexander, pleased to be served a drink.

"The French bring wine to China for the Europeans," smiled the German. "But we bring machines for the Chinese."

"Machines?" said Alexander, eyeing the menu.

"For everything. Grinders for the cotton seed mills and the bean oil plants, generators for the steam filatures and rollers for the cigarette factories. The only thing we can't replace are the cocoons of the silkworms." He paused and refilled the two glasses. "How far are you going?"

"Nanking," Alexander said. "Then a few more trains on to Taiyuan."

"Taiyuan? *Mein Gott!* You'll be damn near in Inner Mongolia."

"Will I find telegraph stations on the way?" asked Alexander.

"Plenty of stations," snorted his dinner companion, "but not many working. Like Italy. Truth is, communications out here worked better in the days of the Great Khan. Fourteenth century or thereabouts."

"You don't say," said Alexander, not meaning to provoke amplification. His English companion had already taught him all he could stand for one day. These itinerant lecturers were worse than his father.

"Well, yes," nodded the German. "The Khan's postal runners ran station to station, day and night across the steppes. They wore bells tied to their belts to warn the next runner as they approached each station. Next man had to snatch the mail pouch and run on without missing a step. If the bells stopped ringing the Khan would have his head."

"Thank you," said Alexander as the man emptied the bottle into their glasses.

"First you will have fun crossing the Yellow River. The old Hwang-ho has burst its banks again and flooded half Shansi province. They say it's the ninth time the river has changed its course and found a new mouth to the sea. Millions of the little yellow devils are starving or drowned, washing up hundreds of miles downriver."

The German waved at a waiter. "Red!" He tapped the empty bottle with his spoon and turned back to Alexander. "You'd better eat up while you can. I recommend the brown windsor soup and the mixed grill. When it comes, I'll exchange you my liver for your sausage."

"Mixed grill, if you please," said Alexander to the bowing waiter. Thinking of the soup served every Monday at school, he added, "Nothing first."

Later Alexander recalled the German's words. He was sitting in the bow of a crowded sampan, rucksack on his lap, while the craft crossed miles of flooded rice fields northeast of the great river. The slowly moving water was yellow-brown and thick with loamy soil.

The sampan passed farm implements and coolie hats bobbing on the surface. Here and there he saw small hills rising above the water, islands usually crowded with clusters of peasant families in faded blue cotton trousers and jackets. The men wore conical straw hats, the women strips of white cotton bound around their heads. Many waved their arms like scarecrows in the wind, appealing for food and help as the sampan floated past. Behind them on some hilltops, frail bamboo shelters and small houses of grey brick and ochre tile looked down on the rising water.

Alexander was amazed that even in normal times the bed of the river must be higher than the surrounding fields and villages, that the Yellow River's earthen embankments ran through the land like two tall winding walls, waiting for the accident of rainfall to either starve, feed or flood the province. He ground his teeth when he saw the swollen naked body of a child floating facedown some distance from the boat. Several rats with long whiskers swam urgently towards the body, as if racing for their share.

After an hour the sampan came to a raised village on a hill surrounded by high walls of thick dried mud. As the vessel glided forward, Alexander glanced down and saw orange centipedes and black scorpions slithering up the bank and climbing onto broad green ferns that spread like a skirt over the edge of the lapping water. A long green snake swam with its head above the surface. A fat black beetle was struggling in its mouth.

The sampan bumped to a stop. Alexander climbed out onto the soft bank, awkward on his cane. He climbed carefully between tight rows of small pumpkins and water spinach. He avoided an old woman who was bent over the plants, harvesting each one just before the water reached it and collecting them in a sling that hung from her shoulders. She turned her head to one side without raising it and looked at the stranger as if not seeing him.

Alexander walked around the island village. He was the only Westerner. Barefoot children followed him, not begging but thin as little wooden stick dolls. He came to a market square set between mud walls in the center of the village.

On one side half a dozen mongrels with mangy coats and prominent ribs lay whimpering on their sides, their legs trussed together with knots of straw. The white-and-pink carcasses of skinned cats hung by their colored furry tails from a rack above the dogs. A grey heap of long-tailed rats twitched in a basket to one side. Occasionally the basket rocked with angry agitation.

Alexander thought he had already seen enough in his life to leave his boyhood squeamishness behind, but now he felt even more sick than hungry. He walked quickly across the marketplace. Just before he entered a narrow lane, seeking his way back to the sampan, he passed a butcher's stall where long cuts of meat were displayed on a counter made of split bamboo. The cuts could not be pork or mutton, and he knew these Chinese would not be eating beef. My God, he thought, can it be? He glanced down as he passed. In a basket behind the counter he saw what could only be the long bones of two thighs.

Somehow not sickened as he thought he should have been, Alexander considered all the horror he had experienced since leaving the Academy. Only one thing truly stirred him now. He concentrated again on the haunting fleeting face in the train window. He felt certain it was him: the Commissar.

-19-

Taiyuan was the beginning of a different world. Mongol camel drivers with long sticks squatted by their beasts, awaiting goods and baggage for the long return journey to Inner Mongolia and the Little Gobi. Others unloaded heavy baskets of lime and coal from the backs of their kneeling beasts. The thick coats of the animals were patchy where they had started losing hair with the coming of spring. Studying the condition of the camels as he would a horse, Alexander noticed that the humps of the younger healthier beasts were upright, fat and firm. One camel, crippled, was being sold for meat.

Wandering about the open market, he found that millet was used as commonly as bamboo in the south. Women, cooking over fires made from the roots, were selling it in seed cakes and puddings to hungry clients who ate it with their fingers where they stood. Mules and ponies were eating the cereal as feed. Stalks of millet fencing, eight or ten feet tall, enclosed small herds of sheep. Children squatted on the ground, binding the shorter stalks to be sold as brooms. Alexander smiled, wondering if Jesse would object to their labor.

He watched the dark-skinned Mongols carry their pelts, skins and wool from stall to stall as they bartered with Chinese traders for boots and saddlery, bolts of thick felt, glass snuff bottles and brass Buddhas. Others traded stiff sheepskins for ladles and copper kettles, for sacks of salt and flour. Itinerant Chinese tanners loaded the hides onto two-wheeled carts.

Squealing animals and the odors of fresh blood and offal drew Alexander's eye to a team of Mongol butchers who were slaughtering sheep and dissecting carcasses of mutton with the swift strokes of men locked in desperate battle.

Nearby a row of cages hung from long bamboo poles. Oblivious to the adjacent slaughter, Mongol larks sang from them as if in competition. White-haired men studied the birds with their ears close to the cages, listening to the songs and making encouraging sounds with their lips. Alexander considered buying a songbird for his father on the way home. Or would that make the old soldier feel old?

He was surprised to find a Chinese vendor, perhaps the representative of one of the old Russian Asiatic trading houses, selling Russian loaf sugar and boots and Japanese fans and matches. Silver coins from different countries seemed to be the only currency the traders accepted.

While he observed the busy life around him, Alexander became aware of a group of lamas watching him. The four men had the dark lined squinting faces of Mongols, but they wore the long pleated robes of Tibetan monks and tall narrow hats with raised ear flaps. The lamas fumbled with their beads and looked down and aside when he returned their stares. They walked slowly with self-created dignity. Perhaps it was true, he thought, that it was the influence of Buddhism that had tamed the Mongol warriors of the Khans and made them too soft for war against their more numerous neighbors.

Alexander walked on to a group of battered open lorries that were surrounded by scores of short-tailed sheep. The dented metal panels of the doors and sides of the trucks were alternately burnished and rusted as if they had been scrubbed with wire brushes. The dense curly coats of the animals were brown with dust and grit. Wary buyers clenched the fat of the creatures' necks in one hand while they poked the ribs of the bleating animals with the other.

He stood and watched Chinese in long cotton robes haggle with the Mongol drivers over the price of each animal. Worthy adversaries, he had been told. The Mongols were said to be tenacious bargainers, but the Chinese enslaved them with perpetual interest on petty debts. Were he and his father Mr. Hak Lee's Mongols? Alexander was reminded of Krupotkin when he saw an elderly merchant enter a note in a small book as he accepted some payment from a Mongol. The old Chinese still wore the pigtail required by the Manchus but prohibited by the Revolution of 1911.

Alexander went from truck to truck, wondering at the mechanical condition of each and examining the height of the sides of its bed.

"Mongolia? Ku-yang?" he said to a driver who stood in the long bed of a Chevrolet, scraping out a carpet of hard black sheep droppings with the side of one pointed boot. "Ku-yang, to buy horses. Return Taiyuanfu?"

In two hours, the sheep had been sold and Alexander sat in the bed of the Chevrolet with his back against the cab. The driver and two other Mongols sat in the front. They had secured a bit of canvas to the forward end of the wooden frame that rose from the truck bed. Alexander rested on the filthy folded tarpaulin, but was certain he would soon be using it for protection against the wind and cold.

For ten hours they motored on over hard dirt tracks, into the blow of a strong dusty wind. Whenever the vehicle slowed, Alexander raised his eyes and squinted ahead, hoping to spot a telegraph station where he could send his father a cable about the Commissar.

In the evening the driver made a fire by the side of the track. He grilled a rack of fatty sheep ribs over a smoking bed of wild garlic and passed around a bowl of thick sour milk. Alexander had never eaten better or drunk worse, he thought as he licked the thick grease from his lips. He shared one of his father's cigars with the men. Then all four lay down under the canvas in the bed of the truck. The smells of the sheep overwhelmed the thick odors of his companions. He fell asleep while the others talked and laughed.

Alexander was woken during the night by the crackle of sandy grit striking the sides of the truck like hail. The canvas rippled and cracked overhead like a sail in a gale. He rose and climbed down from the lorry to relieve himself, surprising a furry marmot that stood sentry at the end of a burrow beside its gravelly casting.

The night was cold and star-filled. A cutting wind had risen, blowing hard and harder from the northwest. This was not the balmy weather of Shanghai. The sand howled horizontally across what he guessed was the beginning of the Mongolian plateau. Now he understood what had stripped the paint from the sides of the Chevrolet, and why the oily coats of the sheep were layered in brown sand, and perhaps why the Mongols had sunken eyes protected by high cheekbones.

He climbed back in the truck and lay down beside his snoring companions. He stared up at the sand-obscured stars through a tear in the buffeting canvas. Tomorrow they should be driving through a gate in the Great Wall and entering Inner Mongolia, the Land Beyond the Passes, the home of warrior horsemen. *Mong*, he knew, meant bravery. He could not wait to ride their ponies.

Hunched in the bed of the lorry, cold, Alexander lay awake and wondered if his father could have imagined what this mission would be like. Perhaps that was what he had in mind, Alexander concluded, still concerned that the telegraph office in Nanking had been closed and he had not yet sent a message to Shanghai. But he had been assured that the telegraph extended into Mongolia and that he would find an office from which to send his wire.

* * *

Pressing the jointed bit against the pony's clenched teeth, Alexander forced the thumb of his other hand between the hard gums at the back of the young mare's jaw. His cane rested against a post of the makeshift corral beside a twelve-foot pole with a large leather loop at the end that the men had used to catch two stallions. Round felt tents were clustered behind the fencing. Three young boys, no more than seven or eight years old, riding bareback with ropes for reins and bridles, were galloping back and forth, racing each other on the far side of the corral.

The shaggy Mongolian dun twitched her head violently from side to side in her stubborn fight to avoid the bit. Her long black mane and tail flared sideways in the slicing wind that swept the steppe. After a winter on the plain she had a coarse bear-like coat over a smoother wooly undercoat.

Alexander ignored the critical mutterings of the dark-faced Shara tribesmen watching him. He ground the knuckle of his thumb into the animal's toothless gap and the jaw snapped open. The boy slapped in the snaffle and buckled the jaw strap. He lifted an almost hairless sheepskin pelt from the rail of the corral and set it well forward on the creature's bony back. A stripe of dark hair ran along its spine.

Then he settled a steep U-shaped wooden saddle onto the sheepskin while the pony danced with short hard stamps of its hind feet. The edges of the Mongolian saddle were trimmed in beaten silver metal. Tooled leather thigh wings painted in crimson and yellow hung down over the stirrup leathers. Long thongs swung from the silver medallions that decorated the base of the saddle. Condensation steamed from the pony's nostrils as Alexander looped the thin rawhide reins over the high front of the saddle.

One of the Mongol horse dealers stepped forward to hold the animal's bridle. A long whip swung from his wrist. It was the same man who had explained that the thinness of the horses was only the temporary result of the long hard winter on the steppe. Alexander shook his head and the man stepped back without expression. It was not so much that Alexander wished to show them that he could manage on his own, but rather that he wanted to see how he and this pony would work together.

Sand swirled up from the hard dry plain and slashed across the open corral. In the far distance, dark snow clouds swept lower and lower across the sky like sails collapsing from a mast. Finally the clouds shrouded the white mountains that guarded the horizon. As far as he could see, there were no trees or other vegetation save for tufts of some short hardy grass sprinkled with the blue and yellow wildflowers of early June. The white bones of sheep and horses were scattered on the steppe, the wild pastures of the Mongol emperors. He knew that horsemanship had begun somewhere on these treeless plains that stretched several thousand miles to north of the Caucasus.

Here there were no lamas, and Alexander sensed that Genghis Khan could still recruit his horse warriors. Their curled bows and long quivers would be light on their shoulders as they leaned into the wind, each rider leading three or four shaggy spare ponies for the long ride to the Danube. Under their saddles might be a slab of raw horse flesh, slowly being salted by the sweating animal and pounded by the rider, eventually to be eaten raw in the Tartar style.

Nearly as tall as Alexander, the owner of the mare raised the worn felt and fur collar of his long quilted coat. His winter skullcap, spiked at the top, was made of crimson silk and frayed gold braid. A silk sash belted his waist, securing a pair of leather gloves at his side. The pointed toes of his embroidered felt boots, practical only in the saddle, curled sharply upward. The other men, their deep-set eyes squinting, the leather of their faces cracked and burned brown, seemed to notice only the Russian boy as he prepared to try the horse. The long skirts of their padded coats flapped in the wind. A large black dog, shaggy as an old bear, limped amongst them, its bulbous nose to the ground.

Nearby, four mares and three geldings were already tied to the wooden rail of the truck bed. The lorry would not hold more than eight. He thought he knew which one would serve for Jesse. It was a young gelding that would require constant little disciplines by the rider. Without being dangerous or too difficult, this one would make Jessica a better horsewoman.

Short-legged, between twelve and fourteen hands, the ponies had coarse muzzles and heavy heads and shoulders, but their barrels were long and deep and they had promising hocks and quarters. The two sturdy stallions secured to corral posts were not for sale. To sell a stallion was to sell the business, to sell Mongolia itself. Alexander wondered if it were true that for generations the Manchus had taken the bigger ponies to China, thereby causing the Mongolian breed to lose a bit of height.

He prayed his father would be pleased with his choices, and with the price, but he thought this mare he was saddling must be the best. A handsome grey-brown, she was perhaps a hand taller than most of the others, yet carried their strong proportions. A few scraps of scarlet silk were braided here and there in her heavy mane. A coil of red cord bound the base of the dun's thick low-set tail. Hoping the mare's owner would not discern his interest, Alexander had saved her for last.

He clucked gently while he reached under the mare's belly to grab the girth. The leather band was smooth and dark, stained by the sweat of many horses. Alexander tightened the girth and pulled down the stirrups. Not wishing to fuss with the length, noting the height of the pony's owner, he lifted the reins and checked the saddle. With a nod at the owner, he set his right boot into a stirrup and mounted up, wincing as he swung his left leg high to clear the tall arched back of the saddle. The men stepped away in anticipation.

As his weight touched the mare's back, the animal lowered her head, hesitating for an instant as she shifted from one front hoof to the other. Then, stretching her short neck forward as if reaching for air, the pony tore from the corral while Alexander's left foot was still searching for the stirrup.

The hard dry grassland of the steppe stretched before them into the mountains, opening to them like an ocean parting as they plunged into it. The bitter sharp air, laced more and more with sand and snowflakes, struck him like a freezing wave. Exhilarated, feeling born to it, knowing that he could not hold the horse, Alexander gave the mare her head. For now, he would ride the pony, not fight it. He kept just enough rein, neither slack nor tight, for the animal to know that he was mounted and in touch. His rigid left leg was too long for the stirrup. Instead of struggling or riding unbalanced, Alexander freed his right foot and rode as if bareback, gripping with his thighs, his legs hanging long.

They galloped, and there was no corral, no Mongolia, no long return to Shanghai, no childhood lost in Russia, no Polyak, no other soul or animal, only the wind and his oneness with the horse.

The pony continued longer than Alexander thought possible. The first excited pitch of her gallop gave way to a long settled run towards the mountains while the snow thickened. After a time he could not feel his face or his hands. He leaned forward just enough to ease his balance and lower himself in the wind, not enough to encourage a still faster pace. As they ran up a slight slope in the steppe, white now with a skim of late snow, he set his stiff right hand on the pony's shoulder. Though frost tinged her thick coat, he could feel the warmth beneath, as if an engine in perfect balance was devouring just the energy it needed to continue.

A river, half frozen, wound below them. Across it, a wide brush of whitened poplars and alders extended to the foothills. It reminded him of winter at Voskrenoye. Alexander squinted into the thickening snow and thought of the long train ride across Russia, of the dense endless wild forest that had surrounded them, the taiga of Siberia. With the snow in his face and the pony beneath him, he almost felt he could gallop home.

His attention briefly lost, Alexander felt his mount slide as one foot slipped on the frozen ground that bore downhill towards the river. Chilled and distracted, he was too slow in pulling up her head. The pony plunged forward on one shoulder, falling and rolling as Alexander was flung from the saddle.

Stunned, he slowly gathered himself until he was sitting upright on the hard ground. Snow covered his boots to his ankles. For a moment there was no feeling in his leg. He wiped his face with stiff hands and looked about for his mount.

The pony was standing near the river. Her white body steamed from nose to tail. Her chest pumped in and out. The reins hung down at the edge of the stream as the horse leaned out and brushed her lips along the thin edge of the ice crust until they reached the flowing water. Slender shoots of some plant rose around her feet, perhaps wild rhubarb, pink and white in the snowfall.

Alexander rose slowly, feeling his stiffness and anxious not to disturb the pony. He did not wish to chase her. It would be a long walk back across the steppe without a cane. As if hunting, he limped towards the river in front of the horse, rather than directly at her. Though seeming to ignore him, she stepped back a few paces as he approached the stream. The boy swept snow from a rock and sat down with his feet near the river, not looking at the pony, his left leg stretched straight forward. He raised the collar of his jacket as the blizzard gusted around him and the animal relaxed. Alexander's hands and face grew numb.

For all its strength and will, Alexander knew, a good horse was a social animal. A good horse liked people and other horses, and already he was certain that this was a fine one. They were far out on the steppe, alone in the swirling sand and snow, and she would come to him if he let her.

He recalled how he had always loved the first winter storm at home, how he would help the grooms drag the troika from its shed and listen to the polished harness bells as the big sleigh glided across the fresh snow to the shooting lodge. Bundled in wolf rugs, he and Katerina had once arrived there for lunch to find his father and a forester bending over the carcass of a large black bear, working with their skinning knives. Each man pulled back the heavy winter pelt with his left hand while his right worked the knife along the open edge between the underside of the skin and the white membrane that covered the flesh and muscles. Only a small circle of blood surrounded them, a scarlet halo in the snow. On their way home, two snow-covered woodcutters bowed as the great sleigh slid past. Icicles hung from their shaggy white beards.

Alexander sat erect and squared his shoulders. This was a day for Russians.

Hungry, cold to the bone, he rummaged in his pockets and found two wrinkled yellow apples he had bought in the market at Tsining. Through the wind he heard a snort behind him. He turned and saw the mare not five yards away. He took a bite from one apple to release its smell. Then he stepped slowly towards the pony with the apple in the flat of his hand.

"Taiga," he said gently, thinking of his old horse at home. "Taiga."

The mare raised her upper lip, snorted steam and took the apple.

Alexander lifted the reins from the ground and tightened her girth with stiff fingers.

In a few minutes he was in the saddle, cantering towards the corral with the wind and the snow at his back. Passing a thicket of dwarf willows, he disturbed a party of small antelope, white as ghosts. Alexander wished he had a rifle, perhaps the light Mannlicher .256 left to him by his mother's father. Snow streamed from their coats when the animals bolted.

The Mongols seemed surprised to see him. He knew they were used to races across the steppe of ten to thirty miles. He bargained for Taiga and the saddle and the bridle. The tall man accepted the heavy silver coins but was too proud to count them. His own stallion was saddled nearby.

Then Alexander helped the men move the ponies into the truck.

Before he left, they shared with him a bowl of koumiss and chunks of cold horsemeat. The fermented mare's milk burned his throat and warmed his belly.

The weather softened as the truck drove back by a different route,

Alexander and the driver alone in the cab. They passed the skeleton of a camel.

"Telegraph," Alexander demanded repeatedly, and after a time they came to a mud-walled telegraph station. First he had felt guilty that he had done nothing when he saw the Commissar, and now he had been unable to warn his father as he should have.

Three round huts made of wooden posts and thick pale grey felt stood outside the walls. Large rocks were scattered on their roofs to secure the felt and hide coverings against the wind. Small plots of onions and cabbages grew between the huts. A travelling cart with tall wheels and a felt roof stood nearby. A wooden placard leaned against an unused signpost.

"Imperial Chinese Telegraph Administration," Alexander read in faded English. Recalling his father's words, he was pleased that Russians had been here first.

The telegraph agent met Alexander at the entrance to the compound. Several camels and a yak loitered inside the walls. Walnut shells were scattered about the courtyard. A dark-faced girl sat in the dust milking the yak into an earthenware bowl, her hands lost in the animal's shaggy belly.

"Telegraph to Shanghai, please?" said Alexander, his mind again on Polyak.

A heavy man in a long double-breasted quilted red robe, the agent smiled and shook his head. He led Alexander into the small building, of which the mud walls of the compound formed two sides. He proudly showed Alexander his machine, but explained that the line was not working because wandering gangs had been cutting down the telegraph poles for firewood. Soon new poles would rise and the machine would work again, for pole theft was now a hanging offense, as Alexander might observe as he drove on, the man advised.

"Tea," said the agent forcefully, taking Alexander by the arm. The truck driver followed them as they entered the largest of the three yurts.

A fire of camel dung heated and illuminated the center of the dwelling. Scraps of felt, hemmed and stitched together, carpeted the floor. The agent directed his guests to sit on two square wool rugs. A copper prayer cylinder rested on a low table between them. Several saddles and small chests were set against the circular walls.

The agent took a three-legged metal basket and set it over the center of the fire. He placed a kettle of water in this fire cage and threw in a handful of tea leaves and a chunk of white mutton fat. Seated cross-legged on a red-and-yellow cushion, he served the dark tea in brass bowls and sprinkled in salt with gestures of dramatic generosity. Then he passed around a dish of yogurt covered with sweet clotted cream. The agent and driver ate noisily while they debated the condition of the grass on the steppe. When they were finished, the telegraph agent offered his guests snuff from a bottle and would accept no compensation other than Alexander's last cigar.

That afternoon the Chevrolet passed a column of oxcarts. The spring-less vehicles reminded Alexander of the tarantasses at home, the four-wheeled farm carts mounted on poles that were used by the peasants at harvest time. Each cart they passed carried one long telegraph pole set diagonally across the wagon, sometimes with stacks of hides piled beneath the pole. Soon the lorry passed rolls of telegraph wire waiting alongside the road. But they would be too late for Alexander.

He was glad he had come to Mongolia. Not just for the test of an adventure on his own, but because the steppes and the horses and the uncrowded wildness had reminded him of home. Yet somehow he was looking forward keenly to Shanghai, as if that also would be like coming home.

-20-

"Who is it?" the man growled through the heavy door on the second floor. The air in the stairway was thick with fiber dust from the first-floor shop that stitched jute sacks for bagging rice and spices.

"Comrade," called the girl. She raised her voice above the hammering of iron on hot metal that came from the monger's workshop in the alley. Squatting men were mending woks and pails over small charcoal fires. "Comrade! It's Jessica James, the American woman. I have two letters for you that were delivered to the printing shop."

Viktor Polyak opened the door to the narrow room and stood back against the wall as Jessica entered. She almost touched him when she passed. The Commissar was wearing coarse gray trousers held high at the waist with a wide belt, and no shirt. He had a hard rounded belly, powerful arms and heavy shoulders and a broad chest covered in black curls. Jessica smelled the old sweat of his body over the tobacco smoke as she passed him. His fierce presence filled the room.

"Sit down." Polyak pointed at the single wooden stool. It was set beside a small open window near the head of a bare mattress on the floor. He must have been watching the street while he smoked. A long narrow shelf ran along the wall above the mattress. A revolver, a bottle of clear liquor, a bowl of rice, several pipes and a few books rested on the shelf. Two long strips of some salted fish hung from the far end like produce in a Chinese market.

A torn photograph of a bearded man with full white curly hair was pinned to the wall above the shelf. A monocle hung from a cord around his neck. Beside the photograph was a smaller picture of a narrow-faced man with thin receding hair, a short pointed beard and a small mouth with narrow lips. The intense heavy-lidded eyes of a fierce believer stared through round spectacles.

Jessica felt awkward and prissy in her long ironed skirt and low-heeled shoes recently polished by her amah. She noticed a copy of *Aurora*, the theoretical journal of Peking's Communists, lying on the floor.

"Karl Marx?" she asked, pointing to the larger picture as she perched herself uncomfortably on the stool.

"Of course." Polyak poured some vodka into a tall Chinese tea cup with no handle.

"And the other man?"

"He is the cardinal of Marxism, the man who is keeping our revolution pure at home. I am one of his priests." Polyak spoke without looking at the photographs, Instead, he kept his eyes fixed on Jessica.

"He is Feliks Dzerzhinsky, founder of the Cheka, the father of the Red Terror. Lenin said we needed to find a Jacobin, and he did. Dzerzhinsky is our Robespierre. Our Savanorola. Some would say our Torquemada." The Commissar drank before continuing. He spoke like a missionary, dispensing fervor. "As one of his departed enemies said, he keeps alive the dry flame of fanaticism. When I grow tired, I think of him, like other men think of Christ."

"Where does he find such strength?" asked Jessica.

"When the Revolution came in 'seventeen, his hard labor in the czar's prisons had just been extended another six years. Before that, Dzerzhinsky was a Polish aristocrat." Polyak's voice quickened. She could feel the power of his admiration. "He passed his youth in the dungeons of the Citadel in Warsaw and in the Butyrki prison in Moscow. Now he lives like a monk in the Lubyanka prison while he does his work. Sleeps on the floor in his office beside the telegraph machine and refuses to eat anything but dark bread and potatoes, like the poorest laborer. In the mornings he coughs up blood."

"Have you ever met him?" She glanced at the picture and felt that Dzerzhinsky was in the room with them.

"I saw him once. At the end of an interrogation. He was more exhausted than the prisoner, who could not stand. I only heard him say one thing: 'We don't want justice. We want to settle accounts.' That is the religion Dzerzhinsky taught us." Polyak paused as if concerned he had exposed too much of himself.

"Now tell me who you are while I eat. My name is Radinsky, Viktor Radinsky." He handed her the cup, then took a knife from his belt and sliced off slivers of dried fish that he dropped into the rice bowl on the shelf.

"I'm about to start here at the university." She sipped the harsh drink and tried not to reveal any reaction when it burned her throat. "My parents are missionaries, Presbyterians." She saw the Russian slip his knife into its sheath without cleaning the blade. "They're always travelling, so I never have to tell anyone what I'm doing." She watched him eat, the bowl raised too close to his mouth, rice falling from the chopsticks as he used them like a scoop. His uneven teeth were stained yellow by tobacco. "I try to do errands and deliver things to help the union and the strikers."

"A pigeon."

"What? Oh, you mean like a carrier pigeon, delivering messages."

Polyak nodded, wiping his mouth with the back of one hand.

"A little rice and fish?" He offered her the bowl and reversed the chopsticks in his other hand. "Have you eaten?"

"No, thank you." Jessica took another sip and set the cup on the floor. "Well, no, I haven't eaten, really." She noticed the broad muscles of his forearm as he continued to hold the bowl out to her.

Jessica took the bowl, trying not to hesitate as she accepted it. His thick fingers touched hers. His nails were dirty and broken. He drained the cup and refilled it while she picked at the cold salty dish with his chopsticks.

"Have you read Marx?" Polyak asked, his voice softer. He handed her the cup and took a pipe from the shelf.

"Only *Das Kapital*," said Jessica between sips, feeling more comfortable with the acrid taste. "I just finished it. I bought the *Manifesto* yesterday. Do you think he was right? Will capitalism destroy itself?"

"It doesn't matter." Viktor sat down on the mattress near her. "One more revolution will make Marx right. It will save us fifty years. That is our job in China."

He filled the pipe from a round tin and tamped down the dark tobacco with his thumb. She noticed Moorish figures on the container.

Jessica felt the vodka burn through her, and with it the excitement of her proximity to revolution. For the first time she felt that she was not wasting her life. Not wasting herself in school, at prayers or in teaching bandage rolling and domestic sanitation at a mission, or in trying to persuade old men not to wash their armpits with urine. Hundreds of millions of Chinese needed to be freed from the Three Exploitations: abuse by the landlords, abuse by the moneylenders, abuse by the capitalists. Only revolution could do that. She set down the chopsticks across the rice bowl and accepted the cup from his hand. A thick cloud of smoke rose from his pipe when he spoke. It reminded her of a picture she had seen of Lenin.

"When I was a boy, it all seemed hopeless, as if nothing could ever make a difference. Russia was so vast, the oppression so complete." Polyak leaned back against the wall and drew deeply on the pipe while he scratched his belly. "Now a few thousand of us are changing the world."

"I hope I can help."

"In Russia today, some are young women, not older than you. A few come from grand families, and sometimes those can be the most useful."

Jessica wondered if he were thinking of a particular young woman, but he said no more.

"Where are you from?" she dared to ask in the silence.

He leaned forward and filled the cup before replying.

"My father was a naval stevedore in Petrograd, when there was work. He waited every day like a workhorse in a stall, not knowing when he would be needed, until the military told him what they wanted him to do. In our Russia, everyone will have work."

Viktor shrugged. "I never knew my mother. She left us after I was born. Perhaps my father was too rough. He told me that every time he touched her she called it rape. What did she expect him to do?" Polyak paused and looked at Jessica as if he wanted her to respond. He drank from the bottle before continuing.

"My father was exhausted and angry when there was work at the docks, hungry and furious when there was not. In the summer, when food was cheap, he bought sacks of beets and potatoes and onions. By the time we got to the bottom in the winter they were always rotten. We ate them anyway. Often he was too drunk to boil the water to cook them in."

Powerful and building like a drum beat, Viktor's deep voice mesmerized her.

"Finally his legs were crushed when a cargo net broke at the docks and crates of ammunition fell on him. After that there was no money, not for food or doctors or even for vodka or proper crutches." Polyak drank and filled the cup. "I made him crutches from the scraps of old packing cases we used for firewood. When he was very drunk I took away the crutches so he could not get to me and beat me."

Jessica was dizzy from the smoke and the drink, but exhilarated. With this man she felt that she had reached the core of what she wanted from life: to be at the center of what mattered. With her help, change would radiate from his efforts, from the power of his inspiration.

"Are you truly prepared to help us?" He tapped his cold pipe upside down against the wall and looked at her with his dark absorbing eyes as the burned tobacco fell to the floor. "To be something more than just a pigeon?"

"Yes," she nodded eagerly. Mindful of keeping her balance on the stool, she was careful to drink modestly before setting down the cup.

"I must travel a great deal. Harbin, Nanking, Peking, and I need someone dependable here, to carry messages, to arrange meetings, to translate," he said. "How is your Shanghainese?"

"Nearly perfect, and I speak a little Mandarin."

"Very well. I will tell you this once." The Russian looked her in the eye. "This work is dangerous. The more you learn, the more you do for us, the more dangerous it will become."

"Religion is the opium of the masses," Marx had written many years ago, and so in truth it was, thought Viktor Polyak several mornings after the American girl came to his room. The Russian sheltered beneath a plane tree and listened to the voices of the choir rising from the church of St. Nicholas. Their song was a reminder of the most seducing bond during his country's age of slavery. He stared up at the tiled onion dome before spitting out the yellow residue from his pipe. To Polyak, the hymn was not an uplifting joy, but an anthem of tyranny and hunger. The Orthodox church considered the czar to be God's chosen ruler for his country. The synod and the patriarchs were nothing but heaven's whores on earth.

Polyak recalled another Sunday long ago. Trembling with the cold in his bones, standing across the street in the crusty frozen snow of St. Petersburg, as a young boy he had watched the priests waiting at the top of the steps to welcome the rich to Easter service. Hoping for a coin, several boys Viktor knew ran to assist them. The great ladies were helped from their sleighs. They moved with caution and self-concern, as if even that simple descent were a hardship. Then the ladies paused to observe the other arrivals, chattering together in their furs and muffs. Their soft fat escorts paraded after them in long black wool coats with wide curly astrakhan collars. Ignored by priests and parishioners, old women with rounded backs and thick kerchiefs used stiff straw brooms to sweep away the snow before the feet of the churchgoers. For Viktor, the interminable music and liturgy that followed meant only an extension of his hunger. When the service was finally over, he and a swarm of other boys ran around the church to the doorway of the basement soup kitchen. There they fought for places in line like a pack of wolves tearing at the carcass of a lamb, knowing there would never be enough for all. There, as a boy of fourteen, Viktor Polyak had nearly accomplished his first strangling, his friend spared only by the intervention of two older youths who had pried his fingers from the other boy's throat.

Polyak raised his collar against Shanghai's warm rain and lowered the broad brim of the grey hat over his eyes. Once again, he was waiting at the back of a church, though this time not for thin potato soup, but to continue his life's work. Feliks Dzerzhinsky demanded terror, and terror he would have. These nests of revanchist enemies were gathering in cities across the world, each one becoming a resource for the enemies of the revolution, a cesspit where men and money and propaganda festered and still threatened everything the Bolsheviks had achieved. Wherever there was opposition, said Lenin, mass terror must be introduced at once. Though he was fighting alone and far away, Viktor Polyak would do his part.

To bring the red terror into every émigré parlor and bedroom, each killing must advance a purpose of its own, thought Polyak. Each violent act should be as efficient in its way as if it were part of the coming socialist reorganization of the means of production, like the collectivization of the farms and the seizure of the factories. The spirit of the refugees must be crushed in every town where they were gathered, from the Seine to the Whangpu. Fear and horror must pursue them, said Dzerzhinsky, like bats hunting mosquitoes in the night, and exterminate their dreams of counterrevolution. Instead of developing small new fortress colonies of their own, each supported by church and officers and aristocrats like the tyranny of the czar itself, the émigré families must suffer enough to be driven into their holes like rats.

Here in Shanghai there was so much to be done, and no one but him to do it. With no Soviet consul and over twenty thousand Whites already arrived, the revanchists were building their own Little Russia here on the China coast, centered on the Avenue Joffre: five Orthodox churches, two newspapers, their own schools and restaurants, and now even a White Russian regiment in the Shanghai Volunteer Corps. Most of his countrymen were as idle and useless here as they had been at home, but the women all worked like coolies, no matter what their former class. The attractive young ones did what they had to, and the old dry ones did what they could, opening bakeries and cosmetic shops and language schools.

Women, he knew, must be fuel for the engine of the revolution, both here and at home. The worse they had been treated, if proletarian, or the more they had been isolated and pampered, if aristocratic, the more fertile the opportunity, said Borodin, and so it seemed.

Polyak pulled his pipe from a pocket and recalled the young Karlov girl he had captured in Siberia. She was ripe as a plum warm in the sun, both ideologically and physically. That first night in the forest camp, when she was crouched shivering with the other prisoners, he had brought her bread and a mug of soup, the same ration as his own men received. As soon as she had finished, he had seized her by the wrist and led her deeper into the woods. There he made her sit beside him on his overcoat and help him drink his last bottle of vodka. She was silent until he began to touch her and rip her clothes. Then the girl had screamed and fought him with ferocity, compelling him to be violent before he was able to take her. During the night she sobbed and trembled. But by the fourth evening, not needing another beating, she seemed used to it. She was sullen and stiff as stale bread, but unresisting.

For two months it had been the same. At mealtimes the Karlov girl gathered firewood and worked with the cooks. Every evening, before the meal, she attended political talks around the camp fire. She herself was made to address the others about the suffering of the peasants on her family's estate. She confessed that in the winter her personal maid rose before dark, abandoned her own children and trudged through the snow to rebuild the fire in Katerina's room. By the time they were approaching Moscow, the girl was joining eagerly in the discussions, intensely critical of the abuses committed by her class, and seemingly sincere. At night she was silent as a plank, but her hands were no longer clenched when he seized her.

Thinking of how it had been with her, Polyak rubbed the pale meerschaum against the sides of his nose. The oil was good for the wood.

In Moscow he had placed Katerina Karlov in a party reeducation school for special cases, under a new name, of course, to make it impossible for anyone to find her. The school itself was not the usual institution for young Communists, the Komsomolski. It was even more than that, the first academy for a new generation of Soviet agents, young women and men trained to dedicate their lives to changing the world. A few came from counterrevolutionary families. The Karlov girl had not resisted when he himself had tied the red scarf around her neck before they took her photograph. Perhaps the shock of her physical union with him had helped to break her connections to her past. One day, he believed, Katerina Krassilnikov would be in the women's vanguard, her mannered education replaced by revolutionary zeal. When he left for China, she had been neither cold nor affectionate, but as indifferent to his departure as a glass of lukewarm tea left behind on a table, and he had wondered if she might be pregnant. He considered what it would be like to be a father.

The rain thickened and slanted in the wind. Polyak put his pipe in a pocket and walked closer to the back of the church. He approached the two open-sided bicycle sheds that served the building. One appeared to be reserved for the children of the Sunday school. He stepped into that shelter and stood against a post that supported the single long beam of the roof.

While he waited, Polyak thought of the men who had demonstrated the courage, and the stomach, to do what had to be done last year at Ekaterinburg in Siberia. With White officers and the Czechs nearing the city to rescue the royal family, the Reds had butchered in the cellar not just the czar himself and his wife, but also the emperor's four beautiful daughters and his sick young son. That was the magic of it. It was the murder of the children that meant there could be no turning back for either side. You could smell their blood, one hero later said, thick as liver on the floor and walls. Relentless thoroughness was essential to the mission. Thankfully the following night the job was completed when the czarina's sister and five more Romanov princelings were slaughtered nearby at Alapaevsk. The Whites must have "no live banner" around which to rally, Lenin himself had insisted.

The same was true wherever the Russian bourgeoisie and aristocracy gathered to survive and intrigue. Here in the frenzy of Shanghai, it was less easy to identify their leaders, but the roster maintained by Colonel Trebinsky had already helped. Polyak touched the bulging pocket containing the notebooks of the White Glove. It had taken some days, but he had found the example he wanted: the grandchild of General Rikovsky, one of the last enemy commanders to fight on in the Crimea.

At that moment two young girls came skipping around the corner of the church, holding hands, squinting and laughing in the rain. Both wore headscarves. As they neared the shed, Polyak was not certain if one of them was the child he required.

"Angelika?" he said in his most gentle voice as the two entered the shelter and shook the rain from their cloaks. "Angelika Rikovsky?"

"Yes, sir," said one of the girls, perhaps twelve, looking up at him with an open face, her bright eyes ready to smile. "I am Angelika."

Polyak backhanded the other child with a blow of his right arm that knocked the girl from her feet. She crashed down in a jumble of bicycles and lay still. One of her shoes remained where the girl had been standing.

"What are you doing?" screamed Angelika. Polyak seized her by the throat and her scarf fell to the muddy ground. He grabbed a jumping rope from the basket of a bicycle and wrapped the doubled cord around the child's neck. Silent, resisting only with her little hands, the red-faced girl was helpless as he bound the rope about her slender neck. One long pigtail was caught inside the cord. He tightened it until the soft skin of her neck was pinched together in tight lines like the twisted knotted rubber at the bottom of a balloon.

He flung the red wooden handles of the jump rope over the beam above his head. Hauling on the handles, he lifted the child from the ground and tied a strong knot. Angelika's feet swung and kicked in the air as she raised both hands to her neck. Her face swelled. Then her eyes bulged and stared and her arms fell at her sides.

Polyak glanced at the other still unconscious girl. He must finish the job. It would only take a moment. He bent over the second child and dragged her towards him by her bare foot through the mess of tangled bicycles. As he reached down for her throat he heard the cries and laughter of other children. He could not kill them all. Cursing, Polyak stood and hurried to the second shelter. He climbed on a bicycle and turned onto the slick shiny cobbles of the Rue Corneille as the merry children emerged around the corner of the church.

* * *

Jessica dropped the leaflets she was carrying and pressed herself against the wall. She had heard shots fired somewhere in the distance.

Like a tide reversing, a rabble of union demonstrators came running back past her down the street. She saw men tear off their red armbands and fling them away. Others threw down signs and rolls of posters. Straw sandals were littered here and there. A man bleeding from one shoulder paused and leaned against a shop wall opposite her, his eyes closed. He sat down slowly, smearing blood on the wall as he sank to the ground. Jessica wanted to run to him but dared not cross the street. The shop owners had already bolted their doors and boarded up their windows. There was no place to hide. Feeling exposed, she felt her own outrage change to fear.

Brandishing truncheons and pistols, a line of Annamese policemen commanded by a French officer appeared around the corner, neat and quick-footed as a band of dancers. The crowd fled before them. The officer blew his whistle and raised his pistol. Men fired their weapons. Two workers fell. Others ran on wounded. The officer whistled twice. The police paused in a line across the street well before they came to Jessica. Three mounted Europeans in uniform and several trucks loaded with men in military outfits appeared behind the policemen. The horses pranced nervously while the trucks pulled up. Jessica was horrified to recognize the English regiment of the Shanghai Volunteers. Small Union Jacks were fixed to the vehicles.

Jessica guessed that one of the mounted officers must be Alexander's friend Billie Hudson. Didn't these otherwise decent young men realize what their soldier games were doing to the innocent Chinese, to thousands of mill workers and their starving families? They all seemed to think the regiment was some sort of sporting fun, like weekend cricket or the Paper Hunt. Now they were being used as the Cossacks of Shanghai, to protect the ruling class from the wretched coolies who made them rich. Jessica resolved to do everything she could to fight this barbarity.

As the last of the fleeing demonstrators ran past, jostling each other and stumbling and falling, a gang of Chinese rushed forward from an alley across the way. Just like at the factory speech, she thought, probably a team of strike breakers from the Green Gang or one of the other Triads that was working with the Kuomintang and the warlords. They were armed with long staffs and curved broad-bladed swords. A man in a black American gangster hat stood at the corner of the alley holding a big revolver. He fired his pistol and the gang charged into the mass of fleeing strikers.

Paralyzed, Jessica watched men being beaten and shot down. One tall coolie paused in his flight to aid a fallen comrade. As he bent down two strikebreakers clubbed him across the neck and back. The man fell amidst a swirl of swinging weapons.

The running crowd thinned. The swordsmen stepped among the fallen strikers and worked two-handed like farmers harvesting grain. One raised his sword to the side, whipping the weapon in an arc as he hit a striker who had stumbled and fallen at his feet. The man's head fell onto the street. The stump of his neck gushed darkly as the body collapsed and the head rolled and came to rest on one cheek. Jessica closed her eyes. She slumped down against the wall and lost herself.

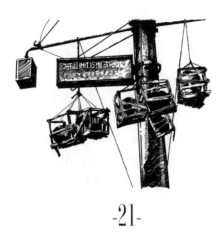

-21-

"You! You and you!" said Alexander, pointing with his cane, picking his men from the crowd of porters that teemed at the gate when the Nanking Express pulled into Shanghai Station. "And you!"

He led the four men back along the train to the first baggage car. He tipped the freight master and pulled back the bar that secured the center door. He opened the door slowly and stepped from the platform into the near darkness and the hot horse smell of the freight car. It reminded him of winter at the stables at home, when the snow was too deep and the cold too bitter to exercise the horses. The stable smell would grow stronger as the snow deepened. He would sit in the stall with Taiga and feed his horse cellar apples while he spoke to him about the dark white winter outside.

Alexander had no doubt that he smelled just like the railroad wagon itself. Last night he had slept in the car with the ponies at Nanking Station, both because he was wary of thieves and because he was keen to have the horses become accustomed to him. He had spent much of the night awake, thinking of all that awaited him in Shanghai, especially the hunt for the Commissar, and how he must warn his father at once.

Then he had thought of Jesse, of her lively face and exciting figure and her dreadful politics, which he hoped would not divide them. He admired her spirit and he was curious about her determination to be a modern woman, to participate in the world, but she worshiped the very people he loathed and her orientation reminded him of the Left Bank student politics that he was told infected Paris. Yet he recognized, too, that there was in Jessica's attitude something of his own mother and her grandmother, of their concern for the suffering of others, perhaps even a touch of the pluck and independence that had distinguished the Decembrist women.

Finally, asleep and half asleep, Alexander's mind had turned to Lily, and he was tormented again by the sexual fulfillment followed by denial. Was it always that way on Sorcery Mountain, or was it usually the other way around? Or both? Either way, he did not want to believe that by the end she did not care for him. Lying near the horses, he had dreamed of Lily and their fifth and final meeting. She had not removed her tight green dress. "This afternoon you must love me as you first saw me," she said in her soft voice, "in my green silk cheongsam."

First Lily had undressed him and teased him with her tongue and aroused him with the puffy red pillows of her slick lips. She had pulled up her dress the little bit required before sitting on him, her back towards his face, before settling down ever so slowly and absorbing him with her moist tightness, teasing and pinching him as she moved fractionally down and up. Then she turned around, without losing him, and leaned forward over him. She smelled of jasmine. Her thick black hair shrouded his face like a dark silk tent. Her lips touched his ear. "Good-bye, Alex-san," she whispered. As she spoke Lily tightened and his entire body rose violently from the bed as if exploding, ripping the green dress up the side seam in one long tear.

A week later he had asked Mrs. Wong if he might purchase one more interview with Lily, whenever her Scottish taipan was absent in Hong Kong. Mei-lan shook her head. "Do not confuse education with romance," she said with gentle firmness. "You are too young and strong to develop a taste for sing-song girls. That is a weakness common to gentlemen who have something about which they feel insecure." They both knew to what Mei-lan referred.

Alexander recalled the hardening conversation that had followed. Embarassed at the memory, wanting to believe that Lily had found him special, he had pressed Madame Wong again.

"What do you think?" she had reminded him with a touch of impatient sharpness that he had not heard before. "That she sees you for her pleasure? Men are work, and a rice bowl for her family." Mei-lan tapped her tiny silk shoes with irritation. "Why must men always want something more? Something for their vanity and comfort? If you go to a restaurant, must the fish on your rice love you when you eat it?"

"I understand," said Alexander, not wishing to. "I didn't mean anything like that. I just ..."

"Do you think it was up to me when I was a girl, sold by my mother and starting my training at ten with less choice than a child in class learning her sums and alphabet?"

Alexander could feel Mei-lan restraining herself as she continued.

"On my eleventh birthday, my own body not yet ready, but already taught massage and other skills, they took me to a dark room. An old Mandarin lay on his back as if dead in the lantern light, his body in tight swollen folds like a jade buddha. He hardly moved as I rubbed his soft skin with warm oils and worked to make the blood stir in his veins. Whenever he liked my touch he slowly lifted his long opium pipe to his lips without opening his eyes."

Alexander had not replied when Mei-lan paused. Her calmer demeanor gradually returning, she continued more gently.

"How can these girls do what they do and care for you as well? Men come here to have women without complications. Then they demand the complications. They're like children, expecting us to make their lives complete. But my girls are like surgeons. If they were sensitive to each person they could not do this work."

Alexander shook his head at the memory as he rose. He recalled that only once had Lily talked to him about herself. "Do you think I could be a film star?" she had asked him as she turned sideways before the mirror and cupped her small breasts upward with both hands. "How would I look in moving pictures?" Too well, he thought.

Now the eight ponies stamped nervously in the wagon, backing and shouldering against the walls, straining and pulling on the lead ropes that secured their halters. Straw and manure and spilled wooden water buckets littered the floor. He took a bale of straw from the end of the car and spread it on the station platform just outside the doorway. Then he passed slowly among the ponies one by one, clucking and whispering, stroking their shoulders, cupping his hand over their soft whiskered mouths.

Alexander paused by the wooden birdcage that he had suspended from the ceiling of the car. The lark was silent, motionless, sitting on the floor of its cage, apparently disturbed by the stench and the extended darkness. Worried, he whistled, but the small brown bird did not respond. He took the cage outside and handed it to the most elderly porter. The man smiled and cooed and clucked as he stroked the thin bars like the strings of a violin. Alexander returned to the car and approached his mare.

"Taiga," he said gently, pressing his face into the pony's neck. He undid the rope that was tied to a nail in the wall. "Taiga." He held the bridle close to the young mare's head and led her out into the shadowed light of the railway platform. He handed the bridle to the sturdiest of the station coolies. "Hold her while I get the others."

One by one Alexander led the ponies onto the platform until each nervous porter held two by the head. Then he brought out the steep

Mongol saddle and its smooth sheepskin and set them on Taiga's back. He lengthened the left stirrup.

"Stay close behind me," Alexander instructed the porters, using gestures to assist his awkward Shanghainese. He took Taiga himself, his cane in his free hand. "One by one in line." He gave his rucksack to the man with the lark. He felt proud and confident as a Cossack as he led his column through the crowd and onto the streets of the Chinese city, Chapei, making for Soochow Creek.

In the chaos in front of the station all China seemed to be doing its business. Stacks of baskets stuffed with flapping fowl were being loaded onto handcarts next to mounds of goods wrapped in burlap sacking. Pole porters were balancing bulky loads before lifting them to their callused shoulders. Men dickered beside pyramids of melons and crates of common porcelain. Straw sandals were being sold from wicker baskets, pickles from unglazed brown pottery jars.

Alexander walked at the front of his line of ponies and led the nervous animals along the edge of the hard-packed dirt street. They passed tradesmen, mendicants and busy practitioners of medicine, gambling and barbering, all laboring in makeshift stalls made from bamboo frames and thatch. He breathed in the odors of charcoal and garlic and cooking oil. After the emptiness of Mongolia he was happy to be back amidst the clamor of Shanghai. He was home.

Trying to be a good officer, he paused repeatedly and checked the men and horses following behind him. Only one man seemed in danger of losing control of his pair of ponies, provoking curses from a streetside dentist engaged in pulling teeth with an ancient set of angled pliers. The porter with the lark followed at the end of the column. The long hind claws of the bird gripped the swinging perch as it switched its head from side to side, inspecting Shanghai.

Alexander exchanged one of the prancing animals for another man's, then mounted Taiga. He was determined to arrive at the Salle d'Armes on horseback. After his wintry ride back to the corral in Mongolia, he trusted that Taiga would not run away with him again. But he could feel the straining power of the horse, anxious to fill her lungs and stretch her muscles. He imagined the nightmare of Taiga galloping out of control through Shanghai's noisy crowded streets, with the other horses breaking free and following her in a stampede.

He sawed gently on Taiga's mouth, pulling back with one hand, then the other, to prevent the pony from setting the bit in her teeth and sensing the freedom to run straight forward. Once or twice, startled by a horn or a screaming Chinese, Taiga capered sideways against the bit, pulling her chin in tight and switching her head from side to side, preparing to bolt. Alexander kept the mare in check as they approached the more orderly built-up section of Chapei near Soochow Creek and the International Settlement.

He was startled to see something hanging from the lampposts just ahead. The objects looked like birdcages. But as he rode closer, his eyes almost on the same level, he saw that in these cages there were no birds. There were human heads. Gory, blood-stained heads with their eyes open. A red rag was often stuffed into the cage, sometimes in their mouths. He wondered if Mr. Hak Lee was involved.

The human remains of violent politics reminded Alexander of the first thing he must do when he got home. He was excited as he turned the corner onto the Chemin St. Bernard and saw the entrance to the Salle d'Armes.

"Welcome home, Sasha!" cried Count Karlov, hurrying out and holding Taiga's head as Alexander dismounted. Karlov gave his son a strong embrace and a prickly kiss on either cheek. Alexander smelled the vodka on his breath. Somehow his father seemed older, but Alexander knew that was not possible after only three weeks away.

"This gray looks like a proper runner. Duns are often the hardiest." The Count ran his hand down one foreleg and admired the four black stockings. "Good withers. Shoulders like a bull. What's she called?"

"Taiga, Papa," said Alexander, thrilled to be home and with his father. "She runs like the wind on the steppe."

"Taiga, eh?" Karlov smiled at his son. "We'll put her in the Derby," he added as he paid off the coolies. "Let's get the rest into the yard and have a better look at them. But what's this?" He pointed at the birdcage when the creature began to sing.

"A present for you, Papa, a Mongol lark."

"So I've become a lonely old Chinaman, have I, in need of a companion?" said the Count, a bit of tartness in his voice. "Li will love it."

Alexander started to smile, then stopped as they led the horses through the Salle.

"Father, there's one thing I must tell you," he said. "I tried several times to send you a telegram, but there was always something wrong with the lines."

Hearing the change in his son's voice, Karlov handed the leads to Gregori. He looked his son closely in the eye.

"What is it, boy?"

"I've seen him, Father." Alexander felt his stomach harden. "The Commissar, Viktor Polyak, the man who killed Mother and kidnapped Katia." He spoke rapidly, eager to pass the burden to his father.

"I saw him in the window of a train in Nanking, bound towards Shanghai. He was smoking a pipe. He must be somewhere in the city." Alexander paused, then continued, keen to free himself from the guilt of his own inaction. "Our two trains were passing so quickly. It was too late for me to get off and follow him."

"That's all right, Sasha," said Karlov in a low hard voice. "This is not for you. Settling accounts is business for your father." His face was white, a red patch on each hollow cheek. "And we've had nasty trouble here while you've been away. I wonder if it was him."

"What happened, Papa?"

"Another killing, young Angelika Rikovsky, the general's granddaughter."

Shocked, sensing it was Polyak, sick that he had not helped, Alexander took a moment to speak.

"Do you think it could be him," he said finally, "the Commissar?"
The Count shrugged. "Angelika, too, was strangled."

"You must stop worrying about your leg," said Mei-lan. "When you think of it, you make everyone else more aware of it. Otherwise, they would be concerned with their own problems, not yours." She leaned forward and poured the tea. A smile creased her smooth glazed features. "Do I offend?"

"No." Alexander blushed, feeling offended. "Of course not. But how can I not think of it?"

"Let your leg give you an advantage, both with men and with women. Men will underestimate you, and no woman who likes you will ever find it troubling. We are not as superficial in our admiration as are you men." Madame Wong paused. "Our concern must be for security, which means money, usually someone else's."

Alexander nodded, not certain that he wished to hear much more. Since their last conversation, he had not thought of Mei-lan as quite the same gentle and affectionate lady.

"You must make the way you live with this leg one of the things that makes you more attractive, not less," she continued. "Deal with it as if you are indifferent to this problem, not as if you are struggling to overcome it."

Mei-lan lifted a small porcelain bell from the tea table and rang it twice. "Don't you understand? Do not be so self-conscious. No one else cares if you have a problem. Why should they?" There was a rare shadow of crossness in her silky voice. "Think of me for a moment. Do you believe that I am as nimble as I might wish?"

A maid appeared.

"Remove my slipper and unwrap my foot," directed Madame Wong.

In a moment the maid returned with a low padded stool, and Mei-lan placed her tiny right foot on it. The servant removed the red brocade slipper and unwound a ten-foot wrapping of fine white silk. Alexander tried not to watch.

"Please do not be embarrassed for me, young Karlov." Mei-lan spoke with a suggestion of sternness. She nodded and the servant left them.

"This was done when I was a very young girl, in the eighteen fifties." She smiled. "The period when our emperor gave the Europeans the mudflats that are now your Shanghai, when the foreign pirates built their Treaty Ports. In those days, our bound feet had nine gradations of beauty." Mei-lan gazed down at her foot and turned her ankle with a touch of vanity, first one way, then the other. "Everyone did it. They say the poor imitated the rich, and the rich imitated the courtesans."

She leaned forward and extended one hand towards Alexander.

"Do me one kindness. Please." Her voice was even again, with measured softness. "Do not be distant. You must understand. Touch my foot, please, my golden lotus. It is so sensitive. Through it, I can feel everything."

Alexander hesitated.

"Mine are perfect, perfect. Not like the Duck Feet of some women. When I was young, I used to attach small silver bells to my heels, to draw attention," she said demurely. "And, on the tops of my shoes, silk butterflies with pearl eyes and moving wings that fluttered when I tottered with my little steps." Mei-lan sighed like a lovesick schoolgirl. "Men perished with lust when they saw my tiny feet. When I went out, before I had a chair, I was carried on my servant's back." She looked at Alexander as if at an admirer, as if she were making love.

"Take my foot in your hand. Please. That is meant to be a pleasure for us both. You must understand that I am making you a gift, *mon cher*." She raised the fine angled black lines of her eyebrows. "It is the ultimate intimacy."

Reluctantly Alexander knelt. He took Mei-lan's foot in both his hands with all the gentleness that he possessed. It seemed barely warm, without life. Once, he remembered, he'd picked up a baby thrush, the size of his thumb, downy soft, that lay abandoned on the floor of the forest after its nest had fallen in a windstorm.

Mei-lan closed her eyes and raised her chin.

He had never seen or touched such skin. It seemed too fine and smooth to be alive. It was thin as a film of gelatin, translucent like the glass of a lightbulb. Her foot was four inches long at most.

Alexander could feel the thin bones of her arch and upper foot bowed upward like the bars of a miniature birdcage. He thought he felt little ridges in the bones where they might once have been broken or compressed. Her four smaller toes were a cluster of tiny bumps under the edge of her foot, like small snails without their shells. Only the big toe, permanently bent up at the first knuckle, had a nail.

He tried to ignore the smell, pungent yet strangely inoffensive. Never before had the body odor of a Chinese caught his attention. Even to Westerners, the Chinese always smelled less than did similarly exercised or unclean Europeans.

"Thank you," she said, and Alexander set her foot back on the stool. "Though this was done to please men, no European man has ever wished to touch or smell them. But to men of old China, before our ways changed when the dynasty fell ten years ago, such feet were a garden of eroticism." Mei-lan smiled as if she were young again, and desirable.

"The smell of unwashed bound feet, rich as a French cheese in the sun, aroused them," she said without embarrassment. "Our crippled toes were pink and crowded together like the petals of a lotus bud, a symbol of sensuality. The lotus grows in mud but flowers as perfect beauty."

Alexander rose and took his seat. Mei-lan rang the bell. The maid returned and replaced the bandage and the slipper.

"What you must do, Alexander Karlov, is to stop fighting against your leg and trying to fence, which can only make it worse. Instead, put your energy into what you can do well, so that this problem makes you excel, not struggle. Then you will turn both handicap and concentration to your advantage."

"I . . ." Alexander began, shaking his head.

"Please listen." She paused and looked at him, smiling once more. "But I am so foolish. Why would a handsome young Russian boy, even you, listen to an old Chinese woman, even me?"

"I am listening."

She shook her head gently. She had so much to teach him. "You Europeans waste people whom you think have problems. You try to cure their abnormalities instead of using them as advantages. You hide such people away at cost to you and misery to them in hospitals and special homes. In China we use such people. We find a purpose for everything. In the drawers in a medicine shop are two thousand different herbs and substances. Sea horses and fossils, bark and insects. To us everything is useful, everything is food." She filled both cups before continuing.

"You put a blind man in a home. We train him to be a masseur, to use his two advantages. Since he cannot see the bodies of his clients he is necessarily discreet. He leaves them their privacy, even as he touches them, and his hands are more sensitive than any other man's. Who else would concentrate so hard and do this job so well? Every blind person is a master of touch. He sees with his fingers, finding the deepest secret knot buried in your muscle. What other masseur can rival that?" Mei-lan paused. "And what is a bad leg compared to blindness?"

"Of course," said Alexander, embarrassed now by his attitude, not his leg. "I . . ."

"I think you will understand better if you do something that will show you what I cannot express. At the full moon, my driver will take you to Turtle Beach, north of Shanghai."

"What happens there?"

"The turtles. After seven years wandering at sea, the females return there to the exact beach where they were hatched in the warm sand, where they first scrambled to the surface after they broke their eggs and rushed down into the sea before the gulls and sand lizards could eat them. It is said that to return to the beach, they follow the moon across the oceans for years like lost lovers. Perhaps these reptiles will teach you what an old woman cannot." She paused. "But at the beach you must not interfere with what you see."

"May I ask you something else, Mama-san?" said Alexander.

"Please. You have never asked me enough to repay you. I look forward to the day when you will."

"I would like to engage your artist, the man who does the portraits of the sing-song girls, to sketch a picture for me, the face of a man I need to find."

"Too easy," said Mei-lan, without asking for explanation. "He is next door now, drawing one of the new pheasants, a quiet well-formed child from Soochow. If you can wait, he will be at your service."

"Here they are, Father," said Alexander four days later. He dropped two thick bundles of printed sketches on the table in the courtyard.

Karlov picked up one sheet and studied the face.

"So this is our Commissar," he said, handing copies to Semyonov and Petrov and Andrei Yeltsov. "So this is Viktor Polyak." The Count looked up at his son and spoke more slowly.

"But is it truly him, Sasha? How close a likeness is this?"

"Very," said Alexander. "We did it three times, and this is exactly as I remember him, Father. Even the eyes are his."

"At last, gentlemen," said Karlov. "Time for the *règlement des comptes*. Now we must find Polyak before he kills more of us. Be careful. Remember Colonel Trebinsky. We don't want any more broken necks or flayed hands." He handed a sheet to Vasily Petrov. "Here, Lieutenant, take this to the young Bukovsky girl and see if she recognizes him from the bicycle shed."

"Yes, Major."

Dimitri Karlov handed a large bundle to Yeltsov.

"Distribute these to the rickshaw boys, if you please, Andrei, and tell them the man who helps us find him will receive twenty dollars provided he mentions it to no one." His hunter's instinct told Karlov that the scoundrel was not far.

-22-

He lay on his belly in the sand grass and stared out from the low dune at the East China Sea. Jessica lay close beside him, her face a silvery blue in the light of the moon. He felt they were alone in the world. The water was calm, rippling with gentle swells at that moment when the tides were in balance. At the far edge of the ocean, the moon was reflected in a perfect circle, clear and round as a white dinner plate. From the moon itself a column of light, golden at the core, silver-blue at the edges, cut directly across the water towards his eye, broadening like an avenue as it came to them from its narrow source on the horizon.

Alexander could feel Jesse breathing under his arm, which lay across her back. After a time she began to shiver with the cool of the night. He lifted his arm and took off his jacket, then spread it across her shoulders while she murmured a protest. Jessica turned on her side and placed one hand on his cheek and the other behind his head.

"When can I ride my new China pony?" she asked.

"Whenever you please your riding master."

"Oh, Alexander." She pulled him to her. "Alexander."

He saw her eyes bright and huge as their faces came together. Then they kissed and shared the warmth of their bodies. His hand felt the slope of her waist and the smooth dip of her spine. He felt within himself the tension of measured intimacy, the restraint that came from liking her too much while not wishing to provoke resistance by pressing her too fast. But her breath was hot on his neck, and she pulled his shirt from his trousers and ran a cool hand up his back. He felt himself stiffen against her, and she did not shrink from him.

Then she was on top of him, the movement hers, her head dark against the bright night sky. Her eyes caught the reflected sparkle of the moon as she looked down at him with hungry eyes. He was surprised by her, astonished by her boldness.

"Keep still, Alexander," Jessica said in her clear daytime voice, "and let me kiss you my way." She hesitated. "Are you a virgin, too?"

"Always."

Her lips parted, slightly smiling, she put one hand on his cheek and lowered her head. Her other hand began to search the front of his trousers.

"Good Lord," she exclaimed, stopping, staring out to sea. "Good Lord." She slipped off him. Alexander rolled onto his belly and gazed across the water with bitter disappointment. He could not believe that he was being cheated of this moment. After all this time, they were finally about to enjoy each other, and he knew she had been sharing his excitement, putting all her usual other nonsense to one side. When would they have the chance again?

A long dark shadow cut the smooth rippling surface of the moon-bright sea.

Armored like an immense beetle or an Indian rhinoceros, its dark scalloped carapace reflecting light like the black shield of the devil, the creature grew larger as it glided forward to the beach. Whirlpools disturbed the water where its feet paddled powerful strokes at its sides. A second monster broke the surface behind it, then to the sides another and another as the prehistoric invasion made for land.

The first giant turtle paused at the water's edge and paddled a final almost useless stroke as her heavy bulk settled into the soft wet sand. She rose on her feet and forced her weight forward uphill toward the dry sand beyond the tide line. Perhaps six feet long, the massive beast paused after each painful advance as she slowly dragged herself up the beach towards the dune. Alexander had never seen a creature so cruelly awkward outside its element. Was this him without a cane?

Jessica glanced at Alexander and took his hand, which rested between their faces on the sand. He felt content again, close to her and excited by what they were sharing.

They stared down in silence between the waving blades of dune grass. The turtle climbed slowly towards them. Behind her the animal left a broad flattened path perhaps three feet wide, with a deep track on either side where her webbed feet had struggled to propel her forward. After a time they could hear the scrape of her claws against the sand and the hollow rattling gasps of her exhaustion. Finally, turning sideways, she arrived at a small basin in front of the dune, a protected place where the tide would never reach and where the sun would bake the sand each day.

There the turtle stopped and rested. After a time she began scraping away the sand behind her with her hind feet, slowly digging a hole at the base of her shell between her rear legs. Then she extended her head on its thick neck. Stretching, she pointed towards the sky as if crying to the heavens. The beak of the turtle's mouth opened like a hungry bird's in a nest. A stream of jelly, a mixture of eggs and some porridge-like material in which they settled, poured from her rear into the hole. A final clutch of eggs fell into the depression. More jelly dripped down. Jessica squeezed Alexander's hand.

The huge turtle extended her hind legs to the sides and swept the piled sand back over the hole, then packed it down artfully with her powerful webbed feet. Again she paused, worn out by the labor. She drew in her neck until only her broad scaly face was visible. She began dragging herself awkwardly down towards the rising tide, stretching all four legs ahead, then rising and pulling her body forward as if rejoining them. The turtle paused between each ungainly effort, rallying her strength. Alexander could feel the animal's exhaustion. Along the beach to either side seven or eight other beasts were at various stages of emergence, ascent and egg laying.

The first turtle finally reached the damp sand. She tucked in her legs and waited.

Water lapped against the front of her shell. Her head reappeared, swinging from side to side as if welcoming the touch of the sea. The first wave splashed across her length. Then another and another, until only the top of her shell showed clearly. At last the sea covered her. The turtle extended her legs and took one powerful stroke. She shot forward like an eel, again strong and graceful in her element, returning to the ocean.

Jessica released Alexander's hand. He turned and looked at her. Her eyes were filled with tears. She sobbed once, then cried openly as he hugged her.

They stood to go, Alexander unsteady on his cane in the sand. Jessica stretched and gazed out over the ocean.

"No!" she screamed suddenly. "No! They can't!" Without warning, she began running down the beach.

Alexander turned and looked after her. He saw three men, their baggy trousers rolled up to their knees, struggling with a turtle as it sought to return to the sea. Two carried long poles. The third held an axe.

Limping heavily from side to side, feeling useless, Alexander made his way to the harder damp sand and awkwardly hurried down the beach. He saw two more groups of Chinese going after other turtles. A handcart waited at the edge of the dunes.

Two of the first set of men jammed their bamboo poles under the turtle as Jessica ran screaming towards them. They levered the giant reptile up onto the edge of its carapace and tried to topple the animal over onto its back. The third man punched the hard underbelly with the flat of the axe head. The blow echoed down the beach. The female fell onto her back as Jessica came to them. "Stop that!" she shouted with fury.

The axeman raised his weapon to strike at the head where it shrank inside the shell. Jessica pushed him violently. He cursed and stumbled and fell over the beast. One of the others struck Jessica across the shoulders with his pole.

She screamed and turned to face her assailant with her fists just as Alexander came up behind the man.

"Damn you!" Alexander raised his heavy cane and struck the man across the side of the head. The man fell and lay still. The third Chinese rammed Alexander in the stomach with his bamboo pole. Alexander staggered backward, gasping, as the man with the axe cursed and got to his feet.

As the Chinese raised the axe, Alexander drew his sword and lunged. The man cried out as the blade passed through his right arm. Alexander freed his weapon as the axe fell beside the turtle.

At the same time Jessica had lifted the fallen pole and slipped it under the overturned beast. Threatening the unwounded Chinese, Alexander demanded that he assist Jessica to right the animal. "Help her!" he yelled. With two poles levering, the turtle was flipped back onto her belly.

Alexander looked along the beach. The other two crews were watching the scene. The wounded axeman screamed at them, and they all began to advance towards the turtle that had been overturned.

Jessica collected the second pole. Alexander lifted the axe and put his sword arm around Jessica's trembling shoulder as the men came towards them, muttering threats as they advanced.

Just then a gunshot rang out from the top of the nearest dune. It was Madame Wong's driver, standing and shouting in his American hat with a pistol in one hand. The turtle hunters gathered in a knot and made quickly for their cart. Seeing them flee, Alexander hurled the axe into the ocean.

"You were wonderful, Jesse." He took her trembling hand as they climbed the dune.

"So were you, Alex. I'm glad you can fence."

"You can thank my grandfather," he said. "The sword cane was his idea. He used it one night in Padua."

She squeezed his hand, then sighed. "But you can't blame those men, you know. We were breaking their rice bowl."

At the top of the dune they paused and looked back. The rising tide had engulfed the giant female where they had been fighting. They could just make out her dark shadow in the water as she took her first stroke and slid swiftly back beneath the sea.

Andrei Yeltsov was relieved his work was almost over. He leaned between the traces of his rickshaw, arching his back and lifting and resting one foot after the other. He remembered that he still had a few flyers of the portrait stuffed under the cushion of the passenger seat behind him. He removed two and folded one into each of his shoes. The balls of his feet felt as if he were running on nails. The base of his spine was a red coal buried in his back.

He had learned this was a young man's game, like war. As they grew older, the Chinese pullers turned to rice wine and opium to ease their pains. Growing weaker as their debts increased, they could stop neither work nor habit. Unable to compete with the younger pullers, they worked longer hours as they grew weaker and required still more opium to ease their toil. Shanghai's prostitutes, Yeltsov knew, whether Chinese or Russian, suffered a similar decline, going from a few rich clients to many poor ones as they aged and the cost of their work began to show.

He would make one final stop tonight, his usual last try for business, at the Vienna Garden Ballroom on the corner of Bubbling Well Road.

Drunken gentlemen always tipped the best, especially when they were leaving with one of the young hostess dance partners. It always saddened him if the girl was Russian.

Tired and slow, he was a few minutes late as he turned at the corner onto Majestic Road. The Latvian doorman whom he usually bribed had left. Yeltsov was relieved to see one client still standing before the darkened doorway. The man appeared to be a bearded priest in a white cassock, but nothing was surprising in Shanghai at night. Andrei cursed when a second rickshaw suddenly emerged from the shadow of the street trees and hurried towards the waiting figure. But the priest waved off the other rickshaw and pointed at Yeltsov's, perhaps noting that the puller was a European. Not Orthodox, evidently Catholic, the big man quickly stepped into Andrei's vehicle when it came to rest.

"Monsieur?" asked Yeltsov. "Where to, Father?"

"Number four, Chemin Saint Bernard," said the priest to Andrei's astonishment.

The rickshaw rattled on in the silence of Shanghai's nearly empty streets. Andrei tried to ignore the pain bruising the balls of his feet. Once he thought he heard the rustle of papers behind him in the hands of the priest.

Finally they turned the last corner. The rickshaw drew up near the entrance of the Salle d'Armes.

"One half dollar, please, Father," said Yeltsov, beginning to turn his head as his passenger leaned forward and seized his throat.

Mei-lan was correct, Alexander reckoned, his thoughts full of Jessica and the turtles as he walked slowly home from her house after their long evening on the beach. The moon was sinking fast. The first blue light was brightening the early morning sky. The night soil carts were finishing their work, leaving empty wooden buckets beside the doors of the dwellings they served. Alexander paused to light his pipe in the doorway of an herb shop and smoked thoughtfully while he continued his walk. For once the smell of the tobacco did not lead his thoughts to Viktor Polyak.

Life would indeed come more easily when he was in his element, doing what he was good at, he reflected. His father had found a way to keep doing that, and it seemed to be working, though debts still threatened to overwhelm them. For himself, Mei-lan was right. On horseback he was like the turtles in the water, but fencing magnified his weakness, like the turtle struggling to climb the beach.

He was surprised to see a rickshaw pressed against the outside wall near the entrance to the Salle d'Armes. Lieutenant Yeltsov's by the look of its striped canopy. Was that him asleep in the seat?

"Andrei!" Alexander called out. There was no reply. He stuffed his cold pipe in a pocket and walked to the rickshaw.

It was Yeltsov, dead, his neck at a peculiar angle, his Russian blouse torn, a horse's bridle strapped over his head, his teeth broken where the bit had been jammed into his mouth. His one eye stared. A handful of torn leaflet portraits was scattered on the floor of the rickshaw.

Worried for his father's life, Alexander rushed into the Salle. He drew his sword and started up the steps. From the roofless room he heard the familiar nighttime grinding of teeth, as if his father's jaw were cracking stones.

He knocked loudly on the door. "Papa!" he called before entering, waking him for once. His father rose as swiftly as a leopard on a branch. As if woken by an alarm in camp, he stood facing the door with his revolver when Alexander entered the room to tell him about Andrei Yeltsov.

"Let's see, Sasha," he replied in a steady voice. He followed his son downstairs in his nightshirt.

Karlov removed the bridle from the head of his friend. Then he handed Alexander his pistol and lifted the slender body in his arms. "Soon it will be our turn to go after them," he said.

Alexander wondered if it would ever end.

-23-

"I must come, too, Father," said Alexander as the Count and Semyonov cleaned their pistols at the table in the stable yard. "Please." The seven-shot cylinders of their revolvers rested on an oily rag between an open box of 7.62mm bullets and a plate of *pelmeni* sprinkled with dill.

Alexander knew that this evening his father would be leading the hunt for Viktor Polyak. Having distributed hundreds of portrait flyers to Shanghai's rickshaw boys, and offered a $20 reward to any puller who helped with the chase, they already had reports of several sightings. And yesterday the Bukovsky girl, hysterical, had confirmed to Vasily that the man in the portrait was the killer of her friend, Angelika.

"No, Sasha. *C'est à moi.*" Karlov squinted up at the sky through the long barrel of his Nagant. "This is my work, for your mother. She would not forgive me if I let you soil your life with vengeance."

Alexander grumbled to himself as his father continued.

"Tonight we are going to check every place where someone has reported seeing the Commissar. The night-shift factories in Chapei, the labor market, the wharves, even the Casino."

"There is more going on in Shanghai tonight than just our little wolf hunt, Major," said Vasily Petrov, cleaning the bloodstained bridle they had found on Lieutenant Yeltsov's head. "The police have cancelled leaves and all the Shanghai Volunteers have been called up for duty in the morning. The Light Horse, the American Troop, the Jewish Company, even the Japanese."

"How did you learn that?" said Karlov.

"An old Hussar in the Russian Regiment told me. They're the only Volunteer troop that gets paid, so when the Municipal Council calls them up, you know it's serious. They're expecting trouble in the Chinese city. The Kuomintang has sent in two troop trains from Nanking, and the Triads have been organizing all week. Something to do with the Communists and all that talk about a general strike."

"What do the secret societies or gangs care about strikes?" said Alexander, thinking of Jessica's passion for the workers. He picked up another of the shell-shaped morsels of noodle dough and chopped beef and dipped it in the small bowl of sour cream before nodding his approval at Semyonov.

"Until the Reds came along, the Triads used to control the cotton workers' union and many other trades," said Petrov. "Now they're losing money and power to the Communists." He shrugged. "So whose side do you expect them to take?"

"Just the time to kill our Commissar." Karlov nodded. "With all that going on, no one will miss one more Red, if we get lucky and catch the devil."

Alexander was aware that his father knew far more than he was letting on. It was no secret that the White Russians were natural allies of the Kuomintang and the taipans in fighting the Communists. The more dangerous the Reds became in Shanghai, the more closely their enemies would work together.

"If we catch Polyak, boy, we'll bring a piece home for you." Semyonov grinned at Alexander. "I'm tired of these long services for our friends. First the colonel, then Yeltsov and the Rikovsky girl. Too many old bearded priests in tall black hats. Too much incense and praying. It's bad for the soul."

The Cossack slapped the chamber back into his Mauser and wiped his oily fingers on the top of his boots. "It's time we buried a few Reds instead. At least those bastards don't want anyone to pray over them. Shallow graves will do."

"I've had enough of this screaming, Ivan," said Count Karlov several hours later. A dark cigar between his teeth and the heel of one boot raised against the wall behind him, he leaned against the back of the bicycle repair shop. Bent handlebars, broken wheels, fragments of chains and the bones of some animal, perhaps a pig, were scattered at his feet.

Smothered screams and the sounds of a man sobbing could be heard through the wall. Karlov guessed they were using bicycle spokes on the wretched man, said to be a runner for the Chinese Reds. He had been caught with two bundles of *The Labourers*, a journal of the city's Communists, tied to his wheelbarrow beneath a stack of bamboo fish traps.

Have I really come to this? thought Karlov, tasting the stale dryness of vodka in his mouth. Encouraging thugs to torture coolies in a Chinese slum so I can hunt the killer of my wife? Must I dishonor myself so in order to do the honorable thing? Sometimes the contrasts of his life seemed impossible. At other moments they made him laugh. Privilege and violence had been his life. With more curiosity than concern, the Count wondered with which it would end.

He recalled attending a dance reception at the Winter Palace when he was Alexander's age, a recent graduate of the Corps of Pages: the acres of marble floor bright as a young girl's eyes, the two sets of violinists alternately playing Liszt from opposite ends of the ballroom, the sudden silence when the czarina entered and passed between lines of bowing officers and curtseying ladies, hundreds of them, all dressed like figures in an opera. He remembered the lights of the chandeliers reflected on the toes of his boots. And he remembered the soft stillness of the great courtyard hours later when he emerged into a cloud of snow settling over St. Petersburg. The waiting carriage horses, nostrils steaming, were white statues in the night. By heaven, he thought sadly, how little there is left, and what a life I am giving to my son.

On the other hand, he himself had learned to find pleasure and satisfaction in both extremes of his life, in the hardships and brutal realities of the campaigns and in the traditions and luxuries of his days at court and at Voskrenoye. Perhaps Alexander, too, would learn to relish his different worlds.

"Go inside, Ivan, and make certain they learn what we need to know. Otherwise these damn Chinese gangsters will dissect the man alive just to pass the evening." Karlov stamped out the cigar. "In Sichuan last year, they slit open the shoulders of captured enemy soldiers and pressed candles into the wounds. The men were forced to kneel at an altar while the candles were lit. When the flames reached their skin, they were hacked to death."

"Makes an old soldier feel at home." Semyonov shrugged. In five minutes the Cossack rejoined Karlov. There were no more cries from the shop.

"He said the Russian Reds have been sleeping in an old opium den behind a cigarette factory at the other end of Chapei. They've been holding meetings in an empty godown next door." The hetman kicked a broken bicycle seat that knocked against the wall. "They're organizing the strikers into shock brigades to take the streets, just as they did at home."

Karlov and Semyonov strode to the other side of the building where the old Morris taxi waited, the Russian driver asleep in the backseat.

"Wake up, Vlad!" The Major banged his fist on the hood of the automobile.

The dark streets and alleys were nearly deserted as they drove by the light of the single working headlamp. Occasionally a figure dashed across the road before them. They heard the crack of gunfire from the direction of Shanghai Station to the north.

"That'll do it, Vlad," said Karlov finally. "Back into that alleyway next to the factory and turn off your lamp. But stay in the saddle. Leave the engine running and one back door open." A glow of light reached the street from the second floor of the cigarette factory.

"We're too late, Major," said Semyonov when they came to the narrow doorway. "The Triad chop-men must have got here first." The heavy wooden door of the den hung open, the long top hinge torn from the frame. A smear of paint stained the door. They could smell the dense odor before they entered.

Holding his revolver in his right hand, Karlov touched the paint with his left. He squinted in the dim light. Green paint stuck to his fingers. "The Green Gang's left its mark." He stepped inside. "And not long ago." That Chinese monster, Hak Lee, the Count thought at once, reminded of his debts.

The two men paused while their eyes adjusted to the darkness. Deep shadows outlined the double-decker bunks of the opium beds that stretched across the long narrow chamber from end to end.

"*Pyos!*" Semyonov cursed as he stumbled over something on the floor. "Dog!"

"Drag him outside," said Karlov, in case it might be Polyak, "and we'll try to see who it is." He wanted to take the Commissar alive, so as to learn what had happened to Katerina. But dead would be better than not finding him at all.

Semyonov hauled the body out by one ankle and they examined it in the low light that came from the factory. It was a young Chinese, barefoot, in the worn blue cotton of a day coolie. A red band was knotted around his thin left arm. His right arm was severed at the elbow, the forearm and hand missing.

"One clean cut. Looks like they still use those old broadswords." Semyonov bent on one knee in the dust and sniffed and squinted at the wound with the appreciation of a connoisseur. "Probably about one hour ago. You can still smell the fresh blood."

The Cossack rose and the two men went back inside. The Count lit a long cigar match and they looked about the opium room. Four more bodies were draped across several of the bunks, evidently flung down there by their attackers. Bloodstained leaflets and a red banner were strewn about the space.

The Count found a small notebook on one bunk. He slipped it in a pocket and held a match to the face of each dead man. Only one was Caucasian. "Check this one," said Karlov. Semyonov pulled a sketch of Polyak from a pocket of his tunic. He lifted the man's head by his hair and turned the face towards the flickering light with the flyer held close beside it.

"It's not the Commissar," said Karlov. "But he's Russian, by the shirt and the face. One less comrade."

They motored home across Shanghai, the Count disapppointed with the hunt. They tried to avoid a block of low workers' dwellings that were blazing in the night, but the adjacent streets were blockaded by piles of packing cases and overturned buses and tramcars. Shanghai's police and volunteer firefighters were absent. Shadows darted through the smoke like dark ghosts. Several bodies lay beside the barricades.

A man leaped from an alley and swung at the car with a long bamboo pole. Semyonov fired at him out the window of the Morris just as the windscreen shattered. Karlov closed his eyes too late as fragments of flying glass struck his face. The assailant fell as the car turned sharply and escaped down a narrow passage between two godowns.

"Take us to Dr. Yukhnin, Andrei," said the Count. "Avenue Foch. I have glass in my eye." He covered his left eye with one hand to prevent it from blinking. Thin lines of blood leaked between his fingers.

* * *

Two hours later they found Alexander waiting at the entrance to the Salle, a pistol in one hand.

"Any luck, Papa?" he asked in a tight eager voice as his father stepped from the Morris. Then he saw the black patch that covered his father's left eye. He knew better than to inquire about this latest wound.

"Not tonight, Sasha." Karlov shook his head and removed a gray notebook from his pocket. "But I think the Commissar lost a few comrades, and we found a *carnet* that may help us catch a few more."

"Vodka!" called Semyonov, leading the way into the stable yard. Gregori was asleep with his head on the table. The sky was brightening above them.

"Good morning, master." Li bowed in the shadow of his dwelling. "*Chai*? Tea?" He removed the cloth that covered the lark's cage and hung it from the bamboo frame that held his pots. He replaced the water in the creature's porcelain bowl. The bird hopped about on its bar and turned its head from side to side, blinking and looking about before it began to sing.

"Vodka, tomato omelettes, tea," said Karlov, fatigued, setting his revolver on the table. "If you please, Li."

The men sat down and pulled off their boots as new voices approached through the hall. Gregori stirred, then rose and returned with a tray carrying vodka and small slender glasses.

Vasily Petrov and two others joined them.

"Good hunting, Vasily?" The Count accepted a *papirosy* when Petrov held out a packet of the Russian cigarettes with hollow tubes at one end. "Did you play hunter to the Green Gang's hounds?"

Petrov took a moment to reply, as if disinterested, yet resigned to what had to be done. "Killed a few Reds, but they were all Chinese. Mostly union organizers, and one student leader," he said. "We found this nonsense inside his shirt, another magazine of Shanghai's Bolsheviks.

We must find that damn press." Vasily dropped a copy of *New Youth* on the table before filling his glass.

"The gangsters didn't really need our help, though we had to do our share, show a taste for it so they would invite us along next time. They knew who they were after. The lucky ones were only beaten," he said with faint disgust. "Stripped from the waist down and clubbed with bamboo rods until their swollen thighs looked like bloody chopped meat."

"That's their old-fashioned way," said Karlov mildly. "The Chinese love tradition."

He watched Chung serve omelettes and boiled potatoes to his friends, and congee and dim sum to his son. Alexander went at the rice gruel like a starving coolie. The Count reminded himself to make certain his boy did not go too far native. Then Karlov drained his glass and opened the notebook before eating himself. He turned several pages and stared hard with his good eye as the light improved.

"It's all in code. Only numbers, no letters. But it looks simple enough," the Count said at last. "We'll give this to the mathematics professor at Saint Boris Academy." Karlov handed the notebook to his son. "He broke German codes for the army."

Alexander flipped open the notebook from the back. A small photograph was pinned facedown to the final page. He drew out the pin and turned over the picture. His hands trembled.

A young woman with long dark hair stared back at Alexander. Her face was thin and she wore a drab ill-fitting workman's shirt. The dark kerchief of a young Red cadet was knotted around her throat. He could not tell from the black-and-white photograph, but he knew that the girl had one green eye, one blue.

"What is it, Sasha?" His father adjusted his patch and reached for the picture. "Have you seen a ghost?"

"Yes, Father." Alexander nodded and handed him the photograph as he spoke.

"Katia."

* * *

Viktor Polyak shook his head and cursed as he read the first letter the American girl had brought him. More accustomed to him now, Jessica finished her second vodka as she stood by the window watching him. He dropped the letter and pulled some notes and a block of paper from the shelf above his head.

"Are you ready to work?" he asked in his thick rough voice.

"Of course," she said. "Anything. What can I do?"

"Once you start this," he said slowly, the note pages in his hand, "it becomes more dangerous for both of us."

"You can trust me, Viktor," she said with fervor, setting her empty cup on the windowsill.

"Very well. Sometimes you remind me of another young comrade new to the cause." He paused and looked at her more carefully.

"Here," he said, slapping the soiled mattress beside him, "sit here and see if you can make this out. Yesterday the revanchists stole my code book. We will have to make another."

Jessica took the pages and the pad and sat where he had indicated. She decided not to ask Viktor of whom he had been speaking. She wondered if it was a woman. Instead of inquiring, she set down the cup and read the notes, surprised to find that they were in fair English. She was thrilled by their content and its message. Polyak sat beside her while she studied them. He read the second letter as if she were not present.

His left arm brushed Jessica's breasts as he reached across to lift the bottle from the floor. She was startled by the touch, but he only poured more vodka into the cup, drank and passed the drink to her. Then he struck a match and held out both letters until the flames caught them. Black ashes settled to the floor between his feet.

For two hours they worked side by side, drinking and creating a new code book from his notes.

"Now you know more than you should." He took back the pages and examined each one before setting it on the shelf. "More than you can ever tell. You have put yourself in danger."

Dizzy, smelling him, she turned her head to look at Viktor Polyak before replying. She felt thrilled and validated by the intimacy of the danger they now shared.

"Already they are hunting for me," he said. "Yesterday they came close. But they will learn who is the hunter, who has brought our Red terror to Shanghai."

"You can trust me," she said again.

He seized her short hair in one hand, turned her face to meet his and kissed her hard on the mouth.

At first Jessica tightened her lips against his kiss, then she felt her mouth open and she received his thick tongue between her teeth.

Vodka, fish and tobacco joined as the embrace continued. Polyak ignored her attempts to push him from her. She felt his hard hand scrabbling hungrily under her skirt and she struggled to avoid him. Soon wet, she felt the rough rub of his fingers as he found his way through her underclothes. With one swift motion he pulled them down to her ankles and pushed her back upon the mattress. He bent over her and buried his head between her legs.

"No!" Screaming in protest, Jessica seized his thick hair in both hands and tried to pull away his head. But again he ignored her resistance. She felt his beard scratch her thighs when his tongue discovered her. She kicked violently and screamed again.

Polyak drew back. He stood up and opened his belt. He fell on her. Jessica cried out, resisting and pummeling him. Overwhelmed, she pressed her fists against her eyes, then finally gave up. Her virginity pierced as if it were nothing, she felt that she was being taken by some animal. Polyak grunted and rolled with her onto the wooden floor.

At the end, he rose, pulled up his trousers and sat half-naked on the stool with the empty bottle swinging between his fingertips.

"Welcome to the Revolution, comrade." He watched Jessica with cold eyes. "Now you are one of us, in mind and body."

Trembling, she sat up on the edge of the mattress. Fear and humiliation and anger boiled together inside her. She stared at him, shocked to realize that he was undisturbed, that Viktor saw no shame in what he had done to her.

Then Polyak stood, stepped to the mattress and threw himself on her a second time.

"No!" she cried in a hard voice. Disgusted, infuriated by the insult and betrayal, Jessica fought him with her fists and nails. Rolling away from him, she drew the knife from his belt. She held the point against his belly when he tried to pull her to him. He released her and stood back.

"Suka! Stupid bitch!" He lifted the stool in one hand. "Give me that knife!"

Jessica stood and quickly adjusted her underclothes and skirt. Breathing fast, she stepped to the door before turning back to face him. Her lips were tight with anger. She opened the door and flung the knife into a corner of the room. Polyak set down the stool and spat as she left the door open behind her.

-24-

"She's still a little wild, Papa."

"Who do you mean, Sasha?" Half-hidden in smoke, there was no smile on Karlov's lean scarred face, but Alexander knew when there was humor, even affection, behind the astringent tone. The black patch was gone, but Karlov blinked frequently and his left eyeball was still marred by two blood blisters from the broken glass of the windscreen.

"I was speaking about my horse, Father, not a girl," said Alexander, almost achieving the Count's absence of expression.

"It's all the same, boy." Karlov rose and stepped to the samovar for more tea and hot water. Crowned by a brown English teapot, the tall metal urn rested on a table near the cook fire. Many of the old soldiers had banded together and presented the well-used samovar to the Count on his name-day to thank him for his hospitality at the Salle. Now even Li and Chung were using it.

His father sat down again and unfolded the *North-China Daily News,*

July 20, 1919. Alexander noticed one of the headlines: "Anarchists and Bolsheviks Fighting in Moscow."

Baby Lu was playing near the Count's chair, drawing in the dust with the point of one of the Major's old spurs. The clear round face of Li's daughter was bright with delight, her narrow eyes almost closed by the fullness of her smile. Perhaps the girl reminded his father of Katia. Alexander had seen no children as engaging as the Chinese. It made him wonder all the more how they could kill and sell such girls. He remembered Jessica's indignation when she showed him photographs of young girls for sale in a Chinese newspaper. Although he teased her for it, he was beginning to admire Jesse's American optimism, her sense that things could always be improved.

"Taiga is running even better," Alexander said. "But it's still hard to make her run my race instead of hers. She's always flat out from the start."

"Sounds like a Hungarian," said Karlov. "Magyar girls always boil quickly, before the turnip is cooked." He reached down with two fingers and idly pinched the child's ear until she squealed.

"But she will be ready, Papa. I just wouldn't wager too much on us in this first race." He was still concerned about making it harder for Taiga by not balancing his weight evenly in the saddle. Other jockeys raced with short high stirrups and both legs bent double. But Alexander's stiff leg made him ride too tall and erect in his stirrups. The longer left stirrup tended to shift his weight from the center.

"*Trop tard*, Sasha. I have bet already. Mostly winnings from the French dog races at the Canidrome. There were fifty thousand people there on Saturday." The Count shrugged. Every day was a gamble. "We are in China, Sasha, the paradise of punters. The Chinese wager on everything, from the chili crop to cricket fights."

"Well, please tell the others not to bet too much." Alexander thought of the old Russian soldiers who were shining shoes and pulling rickshaws. Every day one or two came by to borrow a few dollars from his father. Many nights several slept on the floor of the riding hall, always with the understanding that they would be gone by sunrise and that no man could ever spend more than two nights. With a groan Alexander realized they would all be betting every penny on him. "Perhaps they should bet to show, Papa, not to win."

Alexander rose and walked to the larder at the back of the yard near Li's dwelling. He picked out two carrots and went to Taiga's stall with a bridle. While the mare chewed he lifted her hooves and cleaned them with a pick. Then he curried her and slowly ran both hands down each of her legs, following every bone and tendon. She was in fine form, muscled and shiny, with just a touch of extra weight. She was slightly restless in her stall, full of energy from white clover and alfalfa. Now that he knew Taiga better, he was more conscious of the smallness of her eyes, especially of the little sockets, which seemed to be a feature of these Mongol ponies that in Shanghai everyone called "Chinese." Perhaps, like the well-sheltered eyes of the Mongols themselves, they were a protection against the wind and flying sand and snow of the steppes.

"I'm going to give her a short ride," he said as he led Taiga past his father.

"Only two days till the Griffin Handicap," said the Count, though he knew there was no need to make his point. "Leave a bit of edge on her."

Alexander mounted and trotted down the Chemin St. Bernard to the corner. Then he rode through the busier streets until he came to the Confiserie Charlotte. He waited his turn behind a nest of precocious French schoolgirls. Already coquette, they whispered when they saw him. Embarrassed but tempted, he decided to leave things with a "Bonjour, mesdemoiselles." He recognized one flirt as the sixteen-year-old sister of the fencing victor, François Ricard. That reminded him. He had not been able to see Jesse since the night of the turtles. She'd even missed her last riding lesson. He wondered if he had done something wrong.

He bought a box of bittersweet chocolates and rode on to the Rue

Voisin. He handed the reins and a coin to a boy at the door. Two American automobiles were parked at the corner. A burly Chinese was wiping them with a chamois cloth.

Madame Wong received Alexander after a moment.

"*Quelle gentillesse!*" she exclaimed, untying the ribbon. "*Des bonbons superbes.*"

"*De rien.*" He selected a chocolate heart when she held out the present. "What an amazing dragon," he added, admiring her green silk dress.

"I wear these embroidered dragons to please the foreigners. They expect it of us." Mei-lan shrugged. "I hear you are riding on Saturday, the big race."

"I didn't know you followed the races."

"An old friend told me. He'll be down in a moment."

Alexander wondered what might be happening upstairs. He ached when he thought of Lily and her puffy red lips. His hostess, revealing a rare sense of mood, seemed a trifle on edge today. Before he could reply there was a shuffle at the door.

A tall thin Chinese entered the room. He stood taller than any Alexander had ever met. He recognized the low shoulder and the hugely swollen right ear and remembered when he had seen the man before. Alexander recalled the bloodstained figure trussed and blindfolded in the back of the big Chrysler. A second man, thickset, dressed in a European suit and holding a hat in both hands, waited outside in the hallway.

"Allow me to present my young Russian friend," said Mei-lan. "Alexander Karlov." She spread out both hands and dipped her head. "Mister Hak Lee."

"Good afternoon, Mister Karlov." The Chinese nodded sharply but did not extend a hand. He seemed to sigh when he spoke, as if he were always short of breath. Alexander thought of tuberculosis, the "White Scourge" of China. "I am acquainted with your father, the Count Karlov."

"Good afternoon, sir." Alexander bowed, remembering that this man was rumored to be at the top of the pyramid of lenders who now held his father's debts. Mr. Hak Lee was even more striking than Alexander had recalled. Gleaming black boots, slightly pointed and with riding heels, emerged from the bottom of his blue silk gown. His face, the deep color of dull copper, was long and pitted. The irises of his dark eyes were amber and widely veined. He wore a blue silk skullcap over his high forehead.

The three sat, and a servant poured tea. For a moment no one spoke. Alexander was conscious of the silence, aware that the black eyes had settled on him like a cloak. When the man lifted his cup, Alexander did the same and tried not to look at the very long yellowed nails of the older man.

"Do you find Shanghai agreeable?" Hak Lee breathed deeply as he spoke in slow pidgin English. He nodded without turning his eyes from Alexander. The man in the hall quietly closed the door.

"Shanghai is our home," said Alexander.

"Madame says that you are at your best with swords and horses."

"That is our living here, and what we did in Russia."

"Mei-lan has told me that you saved her life."

"Well, I . . ." Alexander hesitated, though he was comfortable that they now seemed to be conversing in a mixture of pidgin, Shanghainese and French.

"She once saved mine," said Hak Lee with less wind in his voice. "So you have paid a debt to her that I have not been able to." He regarded Mei-lan with a look that on a different face might have seemed benign, even affectionate. As Hak Lee spoke to him again, Alexander wondered if once they had been lovers.

"In China we do not forget our obligations."

"In Russia, too," said Alexander, hoping this Chinese, the Master of the Mountain, was not referring to his father's debts.

"There are many ways to discharge an obligation," said the tall man, apparently comfortable with the silence that followed his words. Finally he spoke again.

"I understand that you are racing on Saturday, in the Griffin

Handicap. I am told that you are well mounted, that you chose this pony yourself, in Mongolia, from many others."

"It's her first race," said Alexander quickly, "and mine as well."

"I have a weakness for the races. If I were not rich, they would make me poor."

Alexander was not certain if this was humor. He dreaded the idea of this man betting and losing on him, and then perhaps pursuing his father's obligations until they were truly ruined. Equally, if he discouraged a bet that might have become profitable, Mr. Hak Lee was not a man to cherish missed opportunities. He knew rickshaw boys had had their knees smashed when they tried to rent their conveyances from a different purveyor.

"How will this Taiga run?"

"She'll run well, sir, especially off the mark, but she doesn't know how to race, and neither do I." He was concerned that Hak Lee already knew the name of his horse. He must have had someone at the timed trials on the cinder track, or perhaps watching the early morning gallops.

"But if she can run, young man, and if you can ride the way they tell me, then for three-quarters of a mile fortune may favor you." Hak Lee looked at Mei-lan, who nodded. Alexander was certain that with him she always did.

"If I were your brother," sighed Hak Lee, "how would you advise me to wager?"

"If you were my brother, sir, I believe you'd mount another horse and race against me." Alexander started to smile, then caught himself.

"If I were your brother," said Hak Lee with no change in his voice, "how would you advise me to wager?"

"Sir, I . . ." Alexander knew that only the truth would do, and that even that might not suffice. "I would bet on Taiga to show, but not to win."

Alexander waited, but received no reaction from Hak Lee. "Of course it will depend a bit on the condition of the track," he added, "and the rest of the field."

* * *

Never had Alexander seen such a tight integration of Europeans and Chinese. Nothing bound Shanghai like greed and gambling, closer links than common humanity itself. Chinese and Europeans could walk the same streets, breathe the same air, eat the same food, sometimes sleep with the same partners, but until they placed their bets they were in different worlds.

Thousands were gathering in the stands and on the center lawn, generally the site of cricket games and polo matches. Englishmen with shooting sticks studied form sheets over drinks in the Members' Enclosure. On the lawn, poodles and terriers and shepherds and pekinese were walked by owners who shared their nationalities. Nannies wheeled dark blue perambulators. Amahs held their straining charges by the hand. Chinese merchants were dressed for London or Peking, and often for somewhere in between. An owner of cotton filature factories where ten-year-olds labored with bleeding hands strolled amidst the crowd wearing pinstriped trousers and a blue cotton jacket. He bent, smiling, and handed sweets to a pair of young French twins. It was the season's first meeting of the Shanghai Race Club. Hurdle Races, Steeplechases and Handicaps were on the card.

As Alexander stood beside his father on the terrace of the Members' Enclosure, he regretted that his race would be last and that he would not be able to relax. He had left a note for Jessica, hoping she would come to the track, but he had received no response. Recently she had seemed to be avoiding him, and the last time he saw her she had been strangely distant, almost angry or withdrawn. She had not even kissed him on the cheek. He feared he had been too forward on the beach, though she had seemed to be at least as keen as he. Was she embarrassed? He wondered if something could have happened to her, or to her family.

Count Karlov was at his borzoi best, carrying himself with a lean silken hardness, distinguished but accessible, to a point. He wore twills and a bold tweed jacket over a high-collared Russian blouse, the buttons off center to the left, a paisley scarf knotted easily at his throat, a small yellow rose in his buttonhole. The ladies who came up to Dimitri Karlov, and many did, carried opera glasses, their escorts bearing trim black binoculars. The Count, however, had hanging from his neck a pair of heavy gray Leitz field glasses. Captured from a German officer near Osterode, the large lenses were designed to study distant formations and to identify targets for bombardment.

Tired of complaints about the face-losing reputation of the Russian tarts and idlers who shamed the other Europeans of Shanghai, Alexander appreciated the antidote provided by the easy distinction of his father's demeanor. It also rendered ridiculous the Russian pretenders who decorated themselves with fraudulent titles and medals. On Easter Day, during the endless service at St. Boris Cathedral, when the choir, the most celebrated singers in Shanghai, had shook the stones with "Christ is Risen from the Dead, Trampling down Death by Death," he had heard old Countess Pilski chattering like a hen to her companion. "Look at that devil Karlov, will you," sniffed the countess, now a piano teacher. "He had the most dreadful reputation in St. Petersburg when he was young." Always mourning someone, Countess Pilski was dressed in her habitual black and lace. "But I must say, now he shows them all what it was to be a Russian."

"Say, there, Karlov," said an Englishman in the Enclosure. "We could use you on the Interport polo team. We're off Tuesday on the old *Empress of Russia* to take a crack at Hong Kong in the Keswick Challenge Cup. We need a handy Number One, or Two."

"Thank you, but I'm afraid I'll be on duty here at the Salle," said Karlov. Alexander looked away, knowing the truth. His father would be concerned he'd have trouble getting back into Shanghai without a passport.

"Damned shame the stewards just banned half-breed ponies," said Morris Templeton, gin in hand. "Whole point of racing is to improve the breed. Why not give our ponies a bit more height and speed, eh? No one agrees on what's a China pony, anyway."

"Rubbish," answered another Englishman loudly, his face flushed and shiny under his Curzon topee. "Stewards know what's what. They verify the China ponies every day, for the races and the Paper Hunts. 'Bout thirteen hands and hairy with a bad head and piggy eyes. That's it. From Mongolia, of course. Anything else running here would be the death of amateur racing. Spoil the whole show," he concluded. "Boy! Two double gins with a splash of that Montserrat Lime Juice."

"Nervous?" said Karlov after the men had moved off.

"Yes, sir," said Alexander, wishing he could ride with his father's confidence and grace. "I'm worried about everyone losing money on me."

"Of course," said the Count, never one to coddle. "You should be worried." He took a few crumpled dollars from a pocket. "Why don't you go to the Pari-Mutuel, Sasha, and see if you can lose a little yourself."

Alexander knew some of the riders and horses. Planning to spread his bets over them, he went and joined the line during the tiffin hour. Directly before him in the queue, two Chinese, perhaps assistant compradores at some British trading house, shuffled forward in their three-piece suits, studying racing forms and time sheets and calculating odds on an abacus.

Impressed by their deliberations, Alexander changed his mind and decided to wager only on the one race in which he knew the runners best: the Paper Hunters' Cup, open to all China ponies that had done two Paper Hunts during the last season but had never won more than one official race.

Taiga had been in only one Paper Hunt so far. She had not taken to it well, galloping from the start, balking at the wades and generally getting in the way of several senior riders, one of them an important client of the Salle d'Armes. "Steady, young Karlov!" the Englishman had hollered like a sergeant-major. "Steady on!"

Both Alexander and his mount had been confused by the large field of ninety excited ponies scattered over a ten-mile course and by the cheering laughing crowds standing on Chinese grave mounds near the most dangerous jumps, waiting for misfortunes. Both Taiga and he were distracted by the refusing steeds, by the limping riderless ponies, by the false trails laid by angry villagers, and by the blinding clouds of dust. A Norwegian shipowner had broken his back in a nasty crash with the Japanese minister at the edge of an otter pond near Artery Creek. One pony had to be put down by the Master with a pistol. At Iron Spine Bridge, dangerous enough with missing stones, irate leek farmers had menaced the riders with hoes and long wooden ladles filled from buckets of night soil.

For his father, of course, the Paper Hunt was all too relaxed. Wearing the pink coat of his earlier victory, Count Karlov rode with ease along the frantic course, scattering the hostile Chinese like Turkish camp followers, occasionally pausing to collect an abandoned animal, or dismounting to assist a fallen rider and steady her pony while she remounted. To the other riders, it was a harrowing breakneck adventure to be reviewed over a month of cocktails; to Dimitri Karlov, a carefree outing after many lost battles.

The Meet was so English, Alexander had thought as he rode slowly home with Taiga steaming and puffing under him. Meant to be just a game, but somehow more than that. As his father remarked later, the British made a sport of war, and the opposite as well. "All we have in common with these English is a love of drink and horses," he had heard his father say more than once. "The English need drink to permit themselves to get excited, then later to dull themselves to sleep. How can such people understand us, our Russian madness?" Alexander nodded dutifully, thinking of his mother's warning, that melancholy and passion ran in their veins like blood.

One pony, Wild Night, had impressed Alexander in the Paper Hunt, though the gelding had thrown his rider at the Suez jump and hadn't finished, leaving Captain Sassoon on Desert Gold to reach the finish flags first.

Alexander came to the betting window and placed all his money on Wild Night to win, then went for his weighing in. At 167 pounds, he was ten over the eleven-stone-three-pound racing weight. When he left the weighing room in his green silks he heard cheering and discovered that Wild Night had won the Paper Hunters' Cup. At three to one, he was well pleased. The Count was waiting for him at the racing stall, where he was checking Taiga's girth and bridle. He left the uneven stirrups as they were.

As Alexander handed his father the winning ticket, Pavel Krupotkin and Cornelia strolled past the stalls.

"Gambling again, cousins?" said Krupotkin. Alexander noticed a cluster of small boils just above the prince's collar, fresh and red as a patch of wild strawberries.

"Good afternoon," said the Count. Annoyed by the reference to his debts, he continued to attend to Taiga.

"Cousins, indeed! That bucket of night soil must be very generous to her," Karlov said after they had passed. "You'll learn as you get older, Sasha. The trouble with going out is that you see more people you don't wish to see than people you do want to see."

Alexander nodded absently, more worried about the race than about Krupotkin. Nervous, he led Taiga from the stall.

"Good luck, my boy." Dimitri Karlov took his son's cane and gave him a boot up. "Remember, you ride for all of us."

That was more than Alexander wanted to hear. As he rode slowly to the starting line, calming Taiga with hushes, one hand stroking her shoulder, he saw Billie Hudson, thrown in the day's first steeplechase, now leaning on a cane himself and chatting with Jessica James. Hudson was pink-faced and animated. Alexander felt a rush of jealousy. Hudson raised his stick and yelled something Alexander could not hear. Jessica waved and blew a kiss. "Sorry I didn't answer your note," she hollered. Perhaps nothing was wrong, after all, he thought hopefully.

The field of thirteen gathered at the start behind the flag. Alexander had already checked the grass course, still slightly damp from yesterday's rain. It would be a bit slow and heavy, probably helpful to a powerful pony like Taiga. He knew only two other riders: his Japanese schoolmate, Hideo Tanaka, and François Ricard, nicely mounted today on Esprit, a handsome roan. The young Frenchman, too, had to be well over the weight. Alexander recalled François's hard ride against Hudson in the sabre race at the Salle. The French boy had been bold, but not much of a horseman. Tanaka, intense as ever, glanced over and answered Alexander's smile with a stiff salute, but between François and Alexander there was nothing.

Taiga capered sideways as Alexander held her in just before the starter dropped the flag. Alexander knew he must ration her speed, for the last quarter mile would be the race.

They were away. After a few strides Taiga was already in her gallop, sharing the early lead with a cream ridden by a British officer from the naval station. The other eleven were bunched in two packs as if in races of their own. François Ricard was caught in the first pack, several lengths behind, where he sought to carve his way forward with whip and spur.

With half a mile to go, Alexander tried to steady Taiga without fighting her, not wanting to waste the mare's energy in a struggle against him. He leaned back, and for once she seemed to accept the restraint. The cream pulled away and he could hear the lead pack gaining on him as he stayed on the inside rail. The cheering of the crowd in the center lawn filled his ears. The first three horses in the pack were closing and coming even.

Alexander saw François coming tight alongside, slashing with his whip, pressing to the center as they made the turn together. The cream was still showing them his hooves. Soft clods of dirt and grass flew up into Alexander's face.

Annoyed by the ponies gaining on her, Taiga began to stretch.

Alexander felt the trembling of her bridle reaching him through the reins, then the relentless breakaway pull he remembered from the steppes. He released her, trying simply to help Taiga, to keep still and stay out of her way. He held the whip through both hands and used it to touch her right shoulder lightly, just enough to keep her balanced, running straight, instead of either veering away from the other ponies or crowding in to head them off.

Alexander was surprised to see another pony, a chestnut with a short and slender rider, a proper jockey, coming up outside François, shoulder to shoulder with them both for the next furlong. Then the chestnut began to pull away and started to close with the cream, which had lost a bit of the spread. Almost stirrup to stirrup, Alexander could see François goading with his spur. Blood slicked the flank of his roan. Desperate not to come in fourth, Alexander leaned forward as they passed the cream and began the final straight.

"Run, Taiga!" he cried, wishing he were fit to ride with shorter stirrups, but riding with his hands forward above her neck, his face in her thick flying mane, his muscles joined with hers, their hearts pounding together. Now half a stride ahead of François, surging, straining with speed, Taiga was shoulder to shoulder with the chestnut as they crossed the finish first.

Suddenly there was a commotion at the rail just before him.

A small dog dashed onto the track, its long leash streaming behind it. Alexander pulled on the right rein. A blond boy bent under the rail to pursue the dog, then stopped, staring up from his crouch at the thundering ponies. The tan spaniel flattened itself on the track, its nose in the air. Taiga stumbled, planting her right foreleg, then rolled forward on one shoulder and threw Alexander on his back into the path of the following ponies.

For a moment he could not see. He lost sight and wind. He felt one blow on his shoulder, then another to a leg as something struck him like an axe and the rear of the field passed over him. A moment later

Alexander tried to sit up, catching his breath, his mind almost clear. He blinked and looked down the track and saw another pony crash into Taiga and go down. He felt a dull pain in his right ankle. He saw his father and Jessica running towards him before he lost consciousness again.

-25-

"One more day, Papa," said Alexander as his father pushed his high-backed wicker wheelchair into the stable yard, "and I'll be out of this thing." He felt lucky that all he'd suffered a few days earlier was a badly sprained ankle and a bruised shoulder. "At least Taiga wasn't hurt."

"Too bad she didn't roll over that little brown bitch," grumbled the Count. "I thought you won, but those drunken English stewards called it even."

"She's ready to run again," Alexander said, "and I promise you we'll win the Shanghai Derby, Father." He wore a Chinese slipper on one foot, a polished brown jodhpur on the other. He could smell the hetman's golubsty browning in their bacon fat.

"Soon it'll be time to get on with what Doctor Danziger said, Sasha, opening up that left knee of yours and seeing what they can do." Baby Lu was sitting at the Count's feet, drawing in the dust on the toes of his boots. "It's time you gave that leg a proper chance."

"I'm not sure there's much point, Father." Alexander hated the idea. He was certain his knee would never bend and work again. The leg was shorter, and always stiff, but he had learned to get around, and he'd tried to listen to Mei-lan and accept it as it was. "Danziger said he didn't know if they could really make a difference."

"Who taught you to be so stubborn?" snapped Karlov, dreading the idea of surgery even more than did his son. "You'll have an operation if I have to do it myself." Muttering, he set the wheelchair at his own place at the head of the table. At the ironing shelf behind him, Chung spread her lips and sprayed the Count's best shirt with water spat between her teeth.

"The doctors can't make it any worse, Sasha, and even a little movement in your knee will make everything easier. Surgeons can do a lot today, especially these Germans. They've had so much practice."

"Papa," said Alexander, eager to talk about something else. He knew one subject that would hold his father's attention. "What are we going to do about finding Polyak? He won't stay in Shanghai forever, and if we don't catch him we'll never find Katia."

"We'll find him soon, boy." The Count waved one hand at Gregori. "We know the Shanghai Communists are planning meetings with the Soviet agents, and that should be the time to catch him. Then it will be a pleasure to wring the story out of him. I'm sure Semyonov will want to help. Everyone answers Ivan's questions."

"Major?" said Gregori, looking weary from his evening job in a Russian restaurant.

"Two glasses and a cold bottle of the Montrachet, if you please, Gregori."

"Rice is ready," announced Li, meaning as usual that the meal was prepared. Alexander wondered how much squeeze the cook was collecting each day from the household's suppliers.

"Lunchee, master?" Li bowed at the Count's elbow. He put down plates of sweet pickles and baby cabbage rolls to go with the drinks, then began to set two places.

"After this, Li, you can start us off with your Chinese blintzes."

"Pancakes, Father . . ." Alexander stopped as someone walked towards them through the riding hall. He did not like people seeing him in the wheelchair. It was not the ankle that mattered, but the sense of confirmation that, further disabled, he was physically even more incomplete. If he didn't already have one bad leg, he would have been on crutches instead of in this chair.

"Good afternoon, gentlemen," said Jessica James, presenting a bunch of yellow roses. She dreaded what the Karlovs would think if they knew about her working with a Russian Communist. When she looked at Alexander, at the eager affection of his greeting, she felt confused again, no longer quite so intent on preventing any man from touching her. She thought of all she had been reading about the emancipated Bohemian ladies of Paris, and wondered what it would be like to have a real lover who cared for her.

Repelled by Viktor, but still excited by the ideal of revolution, Jessica had decided that the cause was more important than her own brutal experience, than her personal hatred for the man who could help change China. Yet she felt that she would never be the same, that she had lost not only her innocence, but something of her core of dignity and self-possession. Despite the pain and horror, she had determined to put the rape behind her and to continue their work together.

"Welcome, Miss James." Dimitri Karlov rose. "You will make our lunch a party. Another glass, and one more place, Chung, if you please, and a vase."

"Who should I give these to?" Jessica held out the flowers between the two men.

"I think my father wants them, Jesse," said Alexander, thrilled that she had come, and reminded of his father's firmly captivating manner with even the most difficult women and horses. Alexander had been upset by her recent coolness.

"Of course." Jessica handed one rose to Alexander without touching him, then gave the bunch to Count Karlov. "I've brought my parents' car. I thought I'd take our jockey for a drive." Seated between the two men, she compared their long Karlov noses.

"How are your parents?" The Count smelled the roses and passed them to Chung.

"Yesterday I got a wire from Tientsin. They sound fine. My father's been asked to serve on the Board of Revisers of the Old Testament Scriptures in Mandarin."

"In Peking?" asked Alexander, hoping this dreadful toil would keep her parents away for some time. He was happy that Jessica seemed to be more herself again, though she was still avoiding the slightest kiss or touch. But perhaps if they were on their own, he would get a chance to finish what they had started on the beach.

"I don't know, Alex," said Jessica a bit testily. Her face tightened. "But I keep hearing terrible stories about what's been happening to missionaries in some of the wilder provinces when the warlords and their gangs take over the villages. Somewhere up in Jilin they caught a lady from the China Inland Mission and cut open her stomach and did horrible things until she died."

Alexander had heard the tale. The rebels had wrapped the missionary's intestines around a weaver's spool and slowly wound her guts onto it while she and the villagers watched.

"In China you never quite know what's true," he said, hoping to head off a row, "or how long ago these things happened." Alexander feared his father would lose his good humor and not tolerate Jessica's habit of using every horror as an excuse to advocate world revolution. Or would he remember his own injunction to Alexander: never argue with a woman?

"You two probably don't agree with me," said Jessica, glancing at the Count, "but that's why everything has to change in China. We're never going to get rid of these brutal old ways without a complete change, a revolution, really."

"You can bring the pork after the blintzes, Li," said Karlov sharply, turning to face the kitchen. "And I think we have some open red."

For a moment there was silence at the table as all three understood that it was time to change the conversation.

"There's something I want to show you, Alex," Jesse said later, after she had helped him into the green Humber and packed in his crutches. "It's a sport that doesn't depend on fighting or abusing horses. A real game."

"Cock fighting?"

"Don't be funny." She pressed the ignition button until it screamed. "You understand very well."

"Does that mean you don't like what my father and I do?" he asked, already annoyed. Abuse horses? When he'd got in the car, he had been thinking only of kissing her. Now Jesse was back on the barricades and rolling out the tumbrils. Meanwhile she was driving like a bank robber in an American film, using the horn as if it were music, nipping in and out between handcarts and pole porters and rickshaws.

"I admire you both, because you're so good at what you do," she said. "But sometimes when I watch you and your father with your swords and horses, especially him, and some of the other old Russians, too, it's as if what they're doing now isn't important to them, because nobody's getting killed, and so it doesn't count." She ignored a coolie with pots hanging from a shoulder pole who shook a fist and spat as they hurtled past. Alexander started to reply, but Jessica continued.

"I think it's the boots. Why must these Russians wear boots all the time? It's as if they're always ready to leave that instant for some battle or campaign."

"My father is a soldier," said Alexander hotly, "who no longer has a country to fight for." He was determined not to apologize for their life, nor for what they'd lost. "I wish I could be more like him."

Jessica turned her head and glanced at him before she spoke.

"You're too much like him already."

"Please stop the car," he said, determined to get out. "Please stop the car."

"What?"

Before he could reply, Jessica turned off onto the edge of an open field just past the municipal electric plant. European men were gathered in two clusters near a wire frame at one end of the large open space. Dirt paths that had been worn into the surface of the field connected four small squares of canvas pegged into the ground. Men with leather gloves were tossing white balls back and forth while others swung long wooden sticks.

"Baseball," said Jessica with a smile, her mood changing.

Still angry, Alexander did not speak as she helped him to get out.

"Here, Alex, put your arm across my shoulder." She handed him one crutch. "At home everyone plays baseball. It's the only team game that isn't violent."

He looked more carefully at the men standing about idly with big gloves on their left hands. "I think I'd prefer to go badger digging. Billie and his mates were off before dawn today with dogs and shovels." And a bottle or two, he thought, and probably after being up all night. Over Jessica's shoulder he saw one team of men scatter across the field as a player began to throw balls from a high dirt mound.

"Badger hunting is disgusting. The poor badgers don't have a chance."

"They don't? Tell that to the dogs with their throats torn open." He watched a man swing a stick and hit a ball farther than he could have imagined. One player ran to retrieve the ball. He hurled it to a teammate as the batter ran and a line of spectators cheered and yelled insults and advice.

"The boars, the big males, have hides like rhinoceros and teeth like tigers. Their jaws clamp down like the winter in Siberia. They burrow faster than six men with picks and shovels can dig them out."

"You're just trying to upset me again. How could you like all that? It's horrible."

Relaxing, feeling almost even, Alexander gave it up.

"Who plays this game out here?" He was happy to be resting for a moment with one arm across her shoulder, the other over his crutch. It was the first time she had let him touch her since that night at the turtle beach. "Where do all these men come from?"

"The ones in the field are a mixed team of sailors from the *Carolina* and Marines from our Yangtze gunboats. The men in gray, batting, are the Shanghai Amateur Baseball Club, the Yanks, everyone calls them. They have over five hundred members, mostly American cotton traders, silk buyers and missionaries. There are Chinese teams, as well."

"Really."

"Next week we're playing one of the Japanese teams, from the South Manchurian Railway. They just beat Formosa. The man batting now is called Kingman. He's ruining some games by refusing to play on the Sabbath, but they say he's the greatest ball player in Asia."

"Is he really?"

Jessica glanced at Alexander, uncertain if he was being sarcastic. It was that same unhelpful even tone he must have learned from his father.

The sound of a bat and ball cracked again. Men cheered and hooted. The baseball flew.

"From the Halls of Montezuma to the shores of Tripoli," sang a group of Americans in blue uniform. Several of them were eyeing Jessica with broad smiles. He was pleased that she looked away.

Proud to be with her, beginning to enjoy the game, Alexander glanced at Jessica and thought he saw a tear in her eye.

"Does watching this make you homesick?" he asked her.

"I never thought about it like that, but, yes, I think it might," she said, a bit defensively, knowing it was both that and her recent abhorrence for unwanted male attention. "And sometimes I wonder why we're all here anyway. How can we ever really make a difference in a place like this?

And our Shanghai isn't even China. Here things are easy, compared to the interior." Jessica turned her head to look at him directly. "Why do you ask, Alex? Don't you ever get homesick?"

"Every day," he said, looking down.

"How about a seat on our bench, you two?" said an American sailor, stepping over and smiling at Jessica.

Alexander wondered if it was the crutch or the girl that drew the invitation.

"Thank you," Jessica said, and they both sat down. "Is there any way I could buy a pair of baseball gloves and a hardball? I want to teach my boy-, my friend here, how to play."

"He looks like he's been playing already," the sailor said cheerfully, nodding at the crutch. Alexander was late in smiling.

"Oh, I'm sorry. Here, you can have this ball," the young American added, handing one to Alexander.

"What do you think?" Jessica smiled at him. "Two old mitts?"

Alexander knew Jesse would get what she wanted, not in the coquettish flirty French way, but with her open direct manner. All the same, of course, it would be hopeless if she weren't so attractive.

"Well, no, miss, it's all U.S. Navy issue." The sailor winked at her. "But we're sailing for Manila Bay tomorrow, and they've got enough balls and bats down there to outfit the National League. Our Filipino stewards swipe the stuff all the time anyway. So perhaps I can slip you a couple of old gloves from the spare bag."

"You'll have to let us pay for them," said Jessica.

"Now that I can't do, miss. I can lose some of this stuff, but selling it would mean the brig."

"Thank you very much." Alexander held out a hand. "My name's Alexander Karlov. This is Jesse James."

"The robber from Minnesota?" The sailor grinned and shook hands.

"The Robin Hood from Missouri," said Jessica.

"Do you have time to let us buy you a drink after the game?" said Alexander, wondering about whom they were talking.

"Well, yes, but I don't think your lady friend will like the sort of place the fellas have in mind. Blood Alley and all that."

"She'll love it," said Alexander before Jessica could speak, teasing her, but proud of her spirit of adventure. He took a pipe from his pocket and began to pack it from his leather pouch.

"I thought you didn't like soldiers," said Alexander after the sailor grabbed a glove and ran onto the field.

"He's not a soldier. He's a sailor."

"I wonder why intelligent women are so literal," said Alexander as if truly curious. When she did not answer, he lit his pipe before speaking again.

"Do you play this game, Jesse?"

"Sort of," she said, embarrassed by her reply. "In America the girls play softball. This is hardball."

Alexander turned the baseball in his long fingers while he smoked.

"You could be a pitcher," she said. "You have such lovely strong hands."

Each knew the other was thinking about his leg. He considered telling her about the operation he might have, but said nothing.

"I like the smell of your tobacco," she said without thinking. "It's so sweet."

Then she blushed and said no more, as she realized where she had smelled it before, and who had been smoking it. Perhaps it was a favorite among the Russians. She had bought a tin of Telkhis for Viktor.

-26-

"It's tonight, Major." Vasily Petrov sat down wearily and reached for the vodka. "The *sobaki* are meeting on that pleasure boat on South Lake. Apparently they were afraid of a raid by the gendarmes if they met again in the Concession."

"Who will be there, Vasily?" The Count was relieved that Sasha was absent, certain his son would want to join them if he were at the stable. He was probably taking the American girl to dinner, perhaps even to the weekly *diner dansant* at the Parisien, not too pricey at three dollars a cover. Although the James girl had no background, and too much tedious pedestrian intelligence, at least she wasn't Chinese. Her naive social sympathies reminded him of the women of his wife's family, but she seemed to have what was needed to build a new life in a place like this: spirit.

"How many men?" added Karlov before Petrov replied.

"Six of the bastards, sir. Chinese organizers of the Socialist Youth League and two travelling butchers from the Far East Secretariat of the

Comintern, that baby-face Nikolsky and our friend Polyak." Petrov seemed excited, more himself, thought the Count, once again the determined officer who had made a life of soldiering, only to become a useless refugee in China. Although it was rarely mentioned, Karlov was still grateful to Vasily for looking after Alexander on the Trans-Siberian.

"The Green Gang's going to give us a little help," Petrov continued, "fishing sampans and a diversion, but this time they want us to do the sharp part."

"It will be a pleasure," said Semyonov.

"We'd better leave now," said Vasily, "and we'll need to dress for the party."

"Li!" called Karlov. "Lend us three coolie hats, if you please, and some old cotton jackets and trousers." He wished there were time to collect two or three more men. He was determined to capture the Commissar and question him about Katerina.

While the Russians cleaned their weapons, Li set out the clothes. Only Petrov, thinner and more homesick every day, was slim enough to fit properly into both trousers and jacket. Karlov wore a pair of Li's patched pants. They rose high above his ankles and were roped around the waist. Not inappropriate for a fisherman, he reckoned. Semyonov set a bamboo coolie hat on his bumpy shaved head and grinned as he held up the blue garments. "For children," he grumbled as he pulled off his old boots, unthinkable for a Cossack.

In an hour, they parked near a market in Jiaxing as dusk grayed the old fishing town south of Shanghai. The others waited outside while Dimitri Karlov entered the Golden Rabbit Teahouse. He felt awkward in his hat, but if a foolish appearance would bring him vengeance, he would play the clown.

Men sat around tables on black wooden benches playing cards and smoking from long bamboo pipes with metal bowls and mouthpieces. The Count glanced around through the thick tobacco smoke and took in the chatter of the card players and the clatter of mah-jongg tiles. This was not the Bund. Bustling waiters served white cups of cheap brick tea made from leaf scraps and tea dust.

One corner of the room was sectored off by a railing. Inside it men stood holding small perforated wooden boxes and betting eagerly on a cricket fight taking place on the round table in their midst. Some clucked with their tongues and tapped rhythmically on their boxes to stimulate the tiny waiting warriors.

Their gambling spirit was what Karlov liked best about the Chinese, but this once he put aside the temptation to pause and place a wager.

A thin Chinese seated in the opposite corner with two other men raised a hand and nodded at Karlov. The Russian joined the three at their table.

"My honored uncle has sent me to assist you." The man, slender as a crane, rose and bowed. He withdrew his fingers from his sleeves and shook hands in the Western manner. His hollow cheeks were pitted. His wispy mustache and fingers were stained yellow.

"Your uncle?" said Karlov.

"My uncle is Mister Hak Lee. You are fortunate that your enemies are his enemies," said the Chinese in pidgin as his companions nodded. But less fortunate, thought the Count, to be a debtor of that yellow devil. Yesterday he had learned that Hak Lee was known for sending coffins to the dwellings of his principal enemies and delinquent debtors. "Yang here will provide you with a fishing boat. Chin will watch your automobile. There are five men on the boat, not six. Two are from your country."

"How will we know their boat?" asked Karlov.

"It is long and painted red. The front roof of the cabin is high and curved and covered in bamboo held down by painted boards. There are eight square windows along each side." He clasped his hands and spoke more firmly. "I am asked to say one more thing."

The Count raised his eyebrows.

"My uncle does not like leftovers. So remember to leave blood for the drums."

Karlov nodded, familiar with the expression for the Chinese tradition of massacring all prisoners and survivors. And today in Russia, with military chivalry as dead as Ivan the Terrible, things were little better. His own hands, too, would never again be clean, he thought as he recalled tortures sanctioned and so many prisoners never seen again. Even the campaigns in Central Asia and the brutal wars against the Turks had not been as merciless as these last two years of civil war.

"When your work is completed," said Hak Lee's nephew, "it would be best to extinguish all the lights on the pleasure boat and to smash a hole in the bottom and close the doors so the vessel sinks quietly in the night with all its guests inside."

"We will need Yang to help us approach them," said Karlov, nodding, almost boyish with eagerness. Yang looked displeased.

"As you wish." The thin man glanced sternly at Yang. "You should leave now. And my uncle recommends that you be careful."

Hak Lee would not wish to lose a debtor, thought Karlov before he and Yang and Chin walked to the car. Yang directed Semyonov to drive to the north end of the lake. There fishing boats were tying up, unloading their catches and spreading long nets to dry on poles. Others were preparing for night fishing. Men were lighting paper oil lamps and pushing off in their sampans.

Wearing coolie hats and too-small straw sandals, their weapons tucked in belts beneath their shirts, the three Russians followed Yang to a boat where two barefoot fishermen squatted on the stern of a sampan somewhat larger than the others. Their blue trousers were rolled up over their knees. One of the fishermen, acting as captain, welcomed them with a few words. A large net was folded in a pile across the bow. Yang and the Russians rolled up their trousers and walked across a boarding plank onto the boat. Karlov sensed that here all his experience would count for little, that today his only advantage would be surprise.

One fisherman untied the sampan. The captain used a long boat hook to push off from the stone embankment.

With the hardy weariness of an old campaigner, Dimitri Karlov felt revived by the tense exhilaration that preceded every battle. But this time he felt he was engaged in piracy and murder, not soldiering. On the other hand, he had something to kill for. This time he was fighting for his family, not the Romanovs.

He recalled his first battle, in southern Romania in '77. A keen cadet of seventeen, even more terrified of doing the wrong thing than he was of the enemy, he was wearing the new boots that his father had bought for him in Paris. Before bright clusters of colored tents and pennants, the Turks were waiting for them with their backs to the Danube and Bulgaria. The Alexandriyski Hussars had advanced as if on parade, a screen of lancers in the front, another regiment on either flank, Cossacks and Dragoons, a wave of Russian black and green and white. The easy creaking of leather, the jangling of spurs and weapons, and the snorting and slow hoofbeats of the horses were like the first gently tumbling stones of what would become an avalanche. Soon, responding to the trumpets, the horsemen trotted and then cantered before galloping and finally breaking line with that mad fighting lust for which the czar's cavalry was feared. That dawn every man and horse had started fresh and unwounded, the cold steel still bright and each bit of leather gleaming from bridle to boot. After the charge, the surviving animals and men looked as if they had been scrambled in a pit of mud and blood. In all the world, and he had seen it, there was nothing to excite a man, to suck the stomach from him, like the pounding stirrup-to-stirrup din of a charge of cavalry. His own father, wounded in '56 before the Redan at Sevastopol, had once told him that the only horsemen who could face a good Russian regiment were the British heavy cavalry he had seen leading an enemy advance in the Crimea.

Count Karlov glanced down at his straw sandals and white ankles and considered the point to which he had come. He patted the bone handle of his pistol.

The lake was brightened by lights from the shore and from the score of floating vessels. The surface of the water was calm, but a modest current ran from north to south where a stream emerged and fed a large canal. A long houseboat or pleasure craft was anchored towards the southern end. Interior lights illuminated its square windows through thin hanging coverings. The Count strained to discern a shadowed profile through a curtain.

He sat in the stern of the sampan. Petrov and Semyonov were in the middle of the vessel under a bamboo canopy. Semyonov carried his *kinjal* stuck into his rope belt like a fish-cleaning knife. But the long straight blade of the Caucasian Cossack was designed for different work.

Rows of perch and bass hung from cords edging the canopy along both sides of the boat. The Major leaned forward and spoke quietly to his old companions. "Remember not to kill Polyak," he said, knowing Semyonov's ferocity once engaged.

Yang stood near Karlov and took the long stern scull under one arm. The captain and the other fisherman crawled onto the bow and began to play out the long net from the starboard side. The current grew slightly stronger as they approached the center of the lake. The captain swung a gently glowing fishing lantern on a pole off to port. Insects crackled in the lamp.

Not directly, but as if crossing the lake from side to side, they approached the anchored stern of the red pleasure boat.

Karlov reached under his shirt and gripped his revolver. He could see a man standing on the deck of the red boat with a pistol in his waistband. The sentry leaned against the wall of the long cabin and lit a cigarette as he looked around the lake.

"Monkey!" cried the captain of the sampan in loud Chinese that carried across the water. He lay on the bow and stretched out an arm as he screamed at his crewman. "Idiot monkey!"

The long fishing net had come loose and was being carried south by the current. Small sections of bamboo buoyed its edges on the surface.

The captain reached out with the boat hook but was unable to secure the drifting net as it approached the anchor mooring of the pleasure craft. He jumped up and scrambled aft with the hook. The front end of the floating net caught in the anchor rope of the red boat. The net began to swirl and tangle along its port side. Following the net, Yang guided the sampan closer. The sentry on the boat drew his pistol and screamed at the sampan's captain, gesturing for him to pull away.

The captain scuttled to the stern, hollering and pointing at the net. Arriving next to Karlov, he handed him the boat hook as the two vessels almost touched. The stern of the sampan bumped against the red boat as the fisherman still in the bow began pulling on the net, drawing the two boats closer and closer together. The sentry crouched on the gunwale yelling orders down at the captain.

Karlov reached up with the hook and caught the sentry behind one knee. He pulled him into the water between the boats at the same moment that the man's pistol fired and struck the sampan's captain in the belly. Entangled in the net, the sentry's head broke water. Grunting, Semyonov leaned over the edge and plunged his kinjal into the base of the man's neck. The sentry thrashed about in the bloody water as Semyonov held his head down and twisted the long blade before pulling it free.

Two more armed Chinese appeared on the rear deck of the big boat just as Karlov and Petrov were climbing on board. The Count lost his small sandals as they clambered up. Before Semyonov could join them, the sampan fell away downstream.

The Cossack stood up in the small boat. "Chyort!" he cursed as he hurled his dripping knife at one of the armed men. The double-edged blade lodged in the thigh of the gunman in the same instant that Karlov hit the man with a bullet from his Nagant. Semyonov drew his pistol but was unable to fire lest he hit one of his companions as the distance grew between the boats.

The other gunman exchanged shots with Petrov near the forward entrance to the cabin. At that moment a European with a short double-barrelled shotgun stepped from the stern door of the cabin and raised his weapon at Karlov. He was a slight dark-haired man with the soft open face of a disinterested schoolboy.

"Major!" warned Vasily as he dropped his pistol and fell wounded to his knees. Karlov turned and saw a Chinese step to Petrov. The man put a revolver to Vasily's head and pulled the trigger.

At the instant the shotgun fired, Karlov shot his pistol at the European as he himself was blown from his feet, struck in the legs and stomach by the gun blast. He fell against the gunnel with his bleeding legs stretched before him. Vasily Petrov floated dead in the water. Struck in the chest, the European with the shotgun collapsed backward into the doorway.

The Count glanced down at the red porridge that was his lower abdomen. He had seen enough killing wounds to recognize this one. He felt like an old wolf caught at last in the steel teeth of a rusty trap. He sighed once, as if fatigued. He regretted his bare feet. It would not be a soldier's death.

A big European in a Russian blouse stepped over his fallen comrade and grabbed the shotgun from the man's hands. Standing in the cabin doorway, he examined the scene.

Karlov tried to collect himself. Slowly he raised his revolver from the deck. It seemed impossibly heavy. If only he could add one more bullet to the thousands he had fired in his lifetime. He blinked and thought he heard a cavalry trumpet in the distance.

"Polyak," Karlov said quietly as the big man stepped towards him and fired before he himself could shoot. There was an overwhelming flash and shock like a cannon shell exploding at his feet.

Karlov's right arm was nearly severed at the shoulder by the shotgun blast. He wheezed and began to gargle with the blood that was settling in his lungs. For an instant he thought of Alexander. Thank God the boy had not come.

The Commissar walked over to the Count and looked down at him. He leaned the empty shotgun against the gunnel.

"At last you have found me, Major Karlov," said Viktor Polyak. "But with those legs, I don't think you will ride again." He bent down and lifted the Nagant from what was left of Karlov's right hand. He examined the blood-slick pistol and checked the chambers.

"I have enjoyed your daughter, Katia," Polyak said, putting the gun in his heavy belt. Karlov's blood smeared the front of the Red's trousers. "She gave me such pleasure on the way to Moscow whenever I had time for her."

Red bubbles frothed on the Count's lips when he moved his mouth. Only his eyes and brain were still themselves.

Polyak knelt beside Karlov and took the Count's head between his hands. His palms cupped Karlov's cheekbones. His strong fingers squeezed the Count's temples.

Dimitri Karlov stared up at the Commissar with blood dripping from his lips. He tried to raise his left arm.

"Soon I will kill your son," said Polyak, moving his enemy's head a bit, as if cocking it. "That will be the end of the Karlovs."

Polyak turned Karlov's head to the left, then violently twisted it back to the right. The Count's neck cracked like a gunshot.

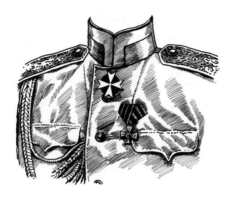

-27-

The double-eagle flag of the Romanovs and the green and crimson pennant of the Hussars shrouded the bottom half of the coffin. The top section was open. The Count's eyes were closed. A touch of his favorite cologne covered any odor of his remains. Many of the mourners, some friends, some not, leaned over in the Russian manner and kissed Dimitri Karlov on his forehead near the prayer band that crossed it.

Alexander had rejected the cosmetic attentions of Messrs. Lafont et Humaine. The celebrated embalmers of the French Concession, often accepting jewelry in lieu of currency, were said to have filled more than one safe with enough earrings and snuff boxes, enamel decorations and brooches to garnish a ball at Czarskoe Selo. For such trifles Monsieur Humaine would transform a crone into a fresh young princess, an exhausted old man into Valentino. Instead, a Russian military surgeon had cleaned and stitched Dimitri Karlov's body after cutting away his destroyed limbs.

Rather than rosy glazed perfection, the Count's damaged face revealed who he was, and what his life had been. His cheeks seemed more hollow in death. But his strong features, the creased brow and long nose and knobby cheekbones all remained. The prominent recent scars of the civil war were clear marks below both eyes. But more defined now in death than in life, with obscuring color replaced by revealing pallor, were the less evident traces of distant campaigns and older battles: shrapnel from Poland, a bullet crease from the Ukraine, a bayonet scratch from Tannenberg.

The green tunic was patched and faded, but clean and well-pressed. Only the Cross of St. Vladimir and the Order of St. George and the small white Maltese Cross of the Corps of Pages were attached to the breast of the jacket. The major's right sleeve was pinned up at the shoulder. His cavalry boots, handsomely polished and boned by Alexander, rested in the darkness of the lower half of the coffin. The Count's long trousers were empty. His dress sword was attached to the brass rings on his high belt. Alexander had thought that his father's sabre might still find a purpose. As for the wounds, Alexander felt they were his own. He was lonely in his soul.

He had been alone at the Salle d'Armes with baby Lu when Ivan Semyonov had returned late in the morning with his father's body. Chung had already gone marketing and Li had left for the snake shop to buy a powder for the wind in his bones, as he called his rheumatism. Alexander was sitting in the yard writing a note to Jessica, whom he had not seen in a week. Playing at his feet, humming to herself, Lu had begun to whine as heavy steps approached through the Salle. Suddenly she started to cry.

Alexander had risen and turned around as Semyonov and two others emerged into the daylight carrying a bloody blanket, with two bare feet hanging out one end. They lay the remains on the table as Alexander cried, "Papa!" He threw back the sodden blanket and pressed his face against his father's, his arms about the damaged body as sobs tore him and he felt the slick drying blood between their cheeks.

Finally, Ivan had pulled him back and the others had wrapped the body and taken it away with the Count's best uniform. Alexander collapsed on a bench beside the stained table. His face and hands and shirt were dark with his father's blood. He stared at the Cossack with questions in his eyes.

"It was him, Polyak," Semyonov had said grimly, his own eyes red. "We nearly got him, but the bastard killed your father first, shot him and then broke his neck." He hesitated. "It's my fault. I was useless, drifting away on the other boat. By the time I returned with a few of our friends, the Reds had abandoned the boat. We never found Vasily's body."

Alexander had not spoken. His mind had passed to Voskrenoye, and their last picnic in the English garden. Linen and blankets and silver, wine and lemonade and heavy hampers were waiting when they entered the glade beside the stream, but no servants, as his mother preferred. Katia was off, collecting wildflowers. Alexander had gone deeper into the woods on his own, to look for game tracks and gather mushrooms in a napkin. He had not been allowed to bring his new .410. When he returned along the stream, about to throw sticks at the geese, he looked at the glade and saw his mother and father as he had never seen them, embracing on a blanket like young lovers.

Now smoky clouds of sweet incense hung in the crowded candlelit gloom of the nave of the Cathedral of St. Boris. Bearded Orthodox deacons in black gowns and squared-off hats guarded the poor boxes and swung incense salvers from long silver chains. Mourners from a dozen countries shared gossip as they stood amidst the rituals of a vanished empire. Blue Chinese robes and high-collared white Japanese naval uniforms set off the fashions of the Faubourg St. Honoré and the fitted suits of St. James's.

Jessica stood by herself to one side in a black dress and scarf of her mother's. Overwhelmed by the haunting power of Shanghai's most celebrated choir, she watched Alex pass among the standing mourners. She felt guilty for some of what she had said and felt about his father.

Though his eyes were tired and his face drawn, his cheekbones more prominent, she had the sense that Alexander was growing even as she now observed him, kissing hands, forcing a smile, doing his duty. Three days before, she had rushed to the stable as soon as she received the news. She knew that Alex had no one else. She found him in his father's room, sitting on the floor, working on the old Count's boots. He looked up at her, speechless, far away, his sunken eyes filling when he saw her. She felt him realize that he needed her. She sat down behind him and wrapped her arms around him, until his crying became hers. She had forgotten her new aversion to being touched.

The church filled. Russian men, several hundred in uniform, or fragments of uniform, spoke in low tones about the old days and another world. In the dim uneven light one might imagine that their uniforms were not tattered and frayed, that their medals and decorations were complete and appropriate, that the Czar of All the Russians still reigned.

Their ladies, some old and dignified, with backs straight as guardsmen, only a few still able to present themselves in pearls and lace, extended lightly perfumed hands to be kissed. Others, younger, the celebrated Russian beauties of Shanghai, the next generation of survivors, compared gowns and whispered against their rivals.

Ivan Semyonov and two other bearded Cossacks stood in a dark corner, growling of revenge. They wore their boots and spurs as if their stamping steeds were waiting outside for the ride that would bring them satisfaction.

"Damn shame they don't have pews in these Slav god-boxes," said Billie Hudson to a racing friend, neither of them altogether sober. "And just take a look at these bearded chaps in black, will you. Look like Druid priests. All this mystical mumbo-jumbo is worse than the Holy Romans."

"Nothing like this left at home in Mother Russia," said Hudson's companion. He yawned and leaned against a stone column as wax dripped on his shoulder from a sconce.

The white-bearded archbishop, scarlet vestments hanging from his bowed shoulders, stood at the head of the nave and raised his silver-topped staff. Faster than an auctioneer, the deacon recited the rich liturgy of lengthy prayers and readings in Church Slavonic. "Give rest with the saints, O Lord, to thy servant who is fallen asleep." From time to time the choir reinforced him, their tenors rising to crescendo behind the carved stone screen of the transept. Chanting followed, and more prayers and lessons.

"Dear lord almighty," whispered Hudson loudly, "one could bury an army in less time. How's a fellow to sleep standing up?" He paused and glanced around, lowering his voice. "But just look at these Russkie Jezebels! Crikey! Wish I could afford two or three."

His friend stared at a red-haired mourner and rolled his eyes as if he were being strangled. "Each of 'em could break your heart while she sucked the gold from your teeth. That beauty there is ten cents a dance at Delmonte's Cabaret. They're open all night. Don't know how she does it."

When the service was finished, Alexander stood at the head of the cathedral steps by the door, the archbishop beside him. Even as he received the mourners, he could not believe that his father was truly dead, that now he was alone. He could not bear to think of Katerina. He felt hollow and cold, but fortified by the clarity of what he had to do. He remembered the way his father had hugged him when he had turned and seen him in the barracks at Vladivostok, and of how they had struggled in this city to start again together.

"Thank you, Colonel. Thank you, ma'am," he said, bowing repeatedly, wishing that Katia were at his side. "Father would be honored that you came."

"You have the sympathies of Japan," said the minister of that country. Dressed in a morning suit, the lean diplomat held a black silk hat and white gloves in his left hand.

"I am so very sorry, Alexander," said Hideo Tanaka with formality, dipping his head, as he followed his father in line. "You have our regrets and you have our respect."

"Call on me, Count Karlov, if there is anything that I can do. Anything," said one old friend wearing a Maltese Cross, an officer and Page to whom Dimitri Karlov had lent more than he should have, and then more again. "Your father was the last of us."

"Join us at the Salle d'Armes afterwards, if you please, Major," replied Alexander to each kind word. He hoped his father would have been pleased by the reception he had prepared to follow the service. Caviar and champagne on credit were just what the old cavalier would have demanded. Conscious of a rank odor at his side, Alexander turned to acknowledge the next commiserant.

"Young Karlov," said Pavel Krupotkin grandly. "You must call on me at the Casino, cousin, just as soon as your mourning is somewhat behind you." He paused for a long silent belch, as if emptying himself, then wiped his mouth. "Perhaps tomorrow afternoon." Alexander was reminded of a torn sack of rotting onions once left in a corner of the root cellar at home. Even the lean winter rats had left the bag alone.

"I am aware of the heavy debts your father left you on that stable. Impossible for you, really. Even the tack and ponies cannot be yours for long." The man spoke to him as if he were a child. Alexander thought this might be to his advantage.

Dressed in black, but still provocative, Cornelia Litchfield stood in line behind Krupotkin. She shifted her dark shawl across her breasts and distanced herself from the prince just a bit. She seemed to wink at Alexander when she dabbed her eyes while Krupotkin continued.

"I wish to help you, boy, so that our family will not be embarrassed. We cannot have your father shamed. You must permit me to make you an offer to relieve you of your debts by selling the Salle d'Armes." He moved his head closer. "You really have no choice."

"Thank you for your prayers," said Alexander, drawing back. His face and tone expressed nothing. He clicked his heels lightly but did not extend his hand.

"Let me know what I can do for you," whispered Cornelia, her lips moist and sticky against Alexander's ear when she kissed him. He looked past her and was pleased to see Jessica last in line, waiting, he hoped, to go back with him to the stable. As she approached, he turned and looked at his father for the last time.

"*Ty vsegda exdish verkhom s mnoi*," he said quietly. You will be riding with me every day.

A cordon of Hussars was scattered along the sidewalk and wall outside the cathedral, mostly men that Karlov had liberated from the icebreaker the year before, now scruffy survivors of the long battle of Shanghai. Alexander was familiar with the tradition: at home they would have been in full dress uniform, three paces apart in line, with their backs to the church, their white gloves clasped behind them. Here, these unshaven thin men wore only scraps of uniform, perhaps a regimental cap and a pair of tall worn boots, or an army belt or leather harness. But most of the buttons and the leather shone. Many of the Hussars would be hungry. All were thirsty. Soon they would banquet at the Salle d'Armes. Two Annamite gendarmes kept their distance at the corner.

Parked across the Rue Corneille were two black Chryslers and a curtained sedan chair. A burly Chinese in a pinstriped black suit and a Chicago hat leaned against the second car. He lit a cigarette as he counted the mourners filing from the cathedral.

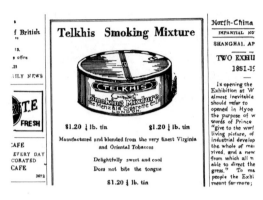

-28-

"No, Viktor." Jessica glared down at him and pulled away her arm with difficulty. She had been free of him for a week while he was absent in Nanking, recruiting cadres for the fight against the Kuomintang. "I told you last time. That's not going to happen again. I was drunk and you forced me."

"Forced you?" Polyak grunted and looked up at her from his stool by the window. He lifted his drink with his left hand and plunged two fingers of his right inside the belt of her cycling trousers.

"Forced you?" he repeated with contempt. "You sound like my mother. Women always say that." He pulled Jessica towards him with two rough movements until her waist was near his face. "You seemed to be enjoying it."

"Stop it, Viktor!" Jessica demanded, her anger hardening, her glass untouched. "You are lying." She resisted forcefully, gripping the edge of the raised window, determined not to let him take her again. "You know I never wanted to. You raped me."

Polyak turned his head sideways. Pressing his face into her crotch, his mouth and teeth jammed against her, he kissed her wetly with hard moving lips.

Unable to step backward, Jessica swung her right hand and smashed her glass against the side of his head.

"Suka!" he screamed, releasing her and rising as he banged his drink down on the windowsill and put one hand to his left ear. "American bitch!"

Scarlet red and breathing hard, Jessica stepped back against the wall. Snatching up his vodka bottle in one hand, she prepared to slam him in the head and scream out the window.

Polyak moved towards her. His jaw muscles twitched and his fingers curled as he raised one hand to her neck.

For a moment she thought Viktor was going to grab her by the throat and strangle her. She saw his powerful fingers spread and stiffen. Then he stopped and clenched both fists. He stared at her with new assessing eyes. He tore the bottle from her hand and, cursing, returned to the stool. He filled the glass, drank it, and filled it again, finally setting it down without offering any to her.

Jessica folded her arms across her chest as she regained control of her breathing. "You repulse me, Viktor, but I came back because I still believe in our work." She spoke slowly, as evenly as she could, checking her anger. "And because I know that you believe in it as well."

Polyak shrugged and scratched himself. "You are just too bourgeois. Like those idiots, your parents."

"If I were like my parents, I wouldn't be here. I'll help you with your work, Viktor. That's what matters. You don't care about me, anyway." She now knew that was true, but she would not have minded hearing the contrary. There were things about his life that she could not help but continue to admire. He avoided her eyes when she stared at him, waiting for his response. His newly trimmed, pointed beard reminded her of the man who had freed his country after arriving at the Finland Station in

St. Petersburg, alone save for his courage and beliefs, after a lifetime of flight and exile. She still saw more than a bit of Vladimir Lenin in the character of Viktor. Lenin was said to be a hard man, too.

"Leave downstairs by the back way," said Polyak finally, handing her three envelopes. "And bring back the message from Ng Hanjun."

Odious as Viktor was, Jessica's immersion in his cause prevented her from resenting him completely. It was not easy to organize a movement of workers and intellectuals while being hunted by the *Sûreté* and the warlord gangs. Every few days he was obliged to move and change his appearance, and she knew he could not sleep with the chatter and the whirring wheels of the pottery workshop downstairs. Each night there were meetings with different cadres and with leaders of Shanghai's Marxists and those from other cities, determined intense men like Liu Renjing and Zhang Guotao and Bao Huiseng, men who were risking everything to build a new world.

She still felt fortunate for what she had, this connection to a great important work. And she knew it was only the value of her contribution to the revolution that might make endurable what she had suffered from this man's abuse.

As her parents had urged her to see human suffering embodied in the life of Jesus, so Jessica now sought to see her rape as a link to the degradation of the Chinese, especially the women. Like many revolutionaries, including Viktor, she must find strength in her personal injury and anger.

At the same time, disgusted and outraged as she was, rough and demoralizing as the experience had been, Jessica was not entirely displeased to have lost her innocence. Hideous as it had been, part of her did not want to think of this man as having truly raped her, though of course he had. At least what he had done to her had removed the issue of losing her virginity, that old-fashioned preoccupation of so many of her friends. Perhaps now she could enjoy physical experiences the way women were meant to today, without repression or abuse. Perhaps this was all part of her initiation as a revolutionary. She sensed the difference in her understanding. Now she just wanted a fresh start, to feel clean and in charge of herself once more.

Jessica thought of the moment she and Alexander had embraced briefly at the cathedral, and how she had felt when she saw him sitting so alone on the floor, cleaning his father's boots. For the first time, she began to feel what it might be like to give all that one could to one person, rather than to disperse oneself across broad charities. But she knew she was not ready for that change. The difficulty was not in choosing between Alexander and Viktor, it was in working out what she wanted most, both now and tomorrow. For the moment, she still wanted both men in her life, or at least what they represented.

What Jessica regretted was that she had not shared her loss of innocence with Alexander, their loss of innocence, as she thought it might have been. Nor could she ever tell him what had happened and with whom, for that would betray Viktor's safety and would offend Alexander's sense of his Russian duty.

Fortunately, Viktor had already taught her not to wallow in good-byes. Jessica did as he said, without hesitation or looking back. As she left, she noticed a priest's white cassock hanging from a nail on the back of the door. In the narrow passage downstairs she lifted her new bicycle over the brown shards of broken pots and bowls. She placed her schoolbooks, bound in a leather strap, into the wicker basket, one message in each book. She was excited, a little frightened, but she felt born to it. Sometimes she was not certain which of her two lives she preferred, but she felt proud and fortunate to have them both.

Jessica put on her blue beret and pedalled down the crowded lane under over-hanging laundry strung between the two-story brick tenements. She noticed with dismay the long narrow cloths of foot bindings hung out to dry, a canopy of suffering. She stopped at two stalls for baked rice cakes and some bright green vegetable sauteed in a pan that flashed with flaming oil when the street cook flipped it in the air.

As Jessica made her way to the first address, a fruit merchant off Fong Pang Road, she thought of Alexander. She was pleased she had been seeing more of him again. He needed her now, and she admired his courage. With both parents dead, Alex was truly alone. He had more responsibility than any boy of eighteen should carry. She had heard rumors that his father's death had been an ugly brutal one, but Alexander had not told her how it had happened. Like all these Shanghai Russians, Alex seemed to carry a sense of unfinished business, as if there were something desperate that each of them still had to do. She knew he had left school to run the stable, and his father's debts were common knowledge, partly due to the profligate largesse said to be one badge of these fatalistic émigrés.

Alexander seemed more like the old Count every day, taking chances, looking back, even a bit extravagant, more certain now of who he was. She hoped he could acquire his father's ability to survive and carry on, without quite that inner hardness that had seemed to come with it. Alexander already looked sturdier, still more handsome, his clothes smarter, more starched and neat. He seemed excited by the struggle of his life. That, she also understood with admiration. She wondered if she could find a way to reconcile her affection for him with her personal sense of what she had to do.

She would meet Alex after delivering her messages. Perhaps she should seduce him at last, even use him to replace her pain with pleasure, to begin a fuller kind of life. She knew he would be a shy and awkward lover, inexperienced, of course, but at least he would respect her.

"What floor?" she had asked when they agreed to meet at the Great World Amusement Palace on the Avenue Edouard VII. Jessica was still amazed by the colonial peculiarity of this street, that the south side of the grand avenue was French, in name and administration, while the north side was English, and spelled "Edward." The French police directed the westward traffic, and the International Settlement police controlled the eastbound traffic.

If Shanghai was famously frantic, the Great World was its molten core, a teeming mixture of Dante and Breughel. The World had six seething floors, each a crowded madhouse of different entertainments and activities. The higher up, the more frenzied and outré. Alexander and Jessica had already met there once, on the first floor, amidst swarms of magicians, birdcages, acrobats and slot machines. Exhausted, they had agreed to explore the upper floors on later visits, one by one.

"Second floor?" she had suggested, thinking they might meet in one of the noisy restaurants on the level otherwise crowded with midwives, barbers, cricket vendors and pimps. The midwives were said also to serve as abortionists.

"Four," Alexander had replied. Now she made her way up the broad staircase, itself an avenue of display and bargaining, laughter and haggling. She paused on Three and stood against a wall near the head of the stair. Jessica took out her new compact and redid her lips. Nearby stood a row of exposed modern flush toilets. Bold young Chinese were delighting in testing this new amenity in public as they lowered their trousers and practiced the different posture it required. She turned and began to climb again.

Hot from the struggle of ascending the crowded staircase, Jessica arrived on Four amidst the dense smoke of incense and tobacco. She looked about but did not see him. Keeping one hand on her money pocket, she strolled slowly between the revolving wheels and the shooting galleries, the acupuncture cabinets and fan-tan tables and massage benches. The scarlet-lipped sing-song girls wore shiny tight high-collared cheongsams slit to the waist. Some wore their hair in soft permanent waves copied from the film magazines. Others had short black lacquered hair sculpted tight to their heads. They did not seem pleased to see her. The girls ignored their own countrymen and instead hunted the occasional parties of laughing red-faced Europeans wandering about with their ties loosened and jackets slung over their shoulders.

Then she saw Alexander. He looked strong and elegant. Tall and lean as his father, he was swinging his dark stick and wearing cream linen trousers with a Russian white shirt. His boots shone. She liked his high bridged nose.

Alexander was standing at the edge of one of the small square dance platforms, watching Billie Hudson dancing to a three-piece jazz band. Hudson's taxi-dance girl was something in addition to Chinese, the way Billie liked them, perhaps a bit of Thai or Cambodian in her mix. The two seemed to be enjoying each other, Jessica thought with a touch of envy that surprised her. Hudson held a strip of dance tickets in his bad English teeth.

Jessica stepped up behind Alexander and slipped her hands along the sides of his hard waist.

"Buy me winee?" she whispered against his ear in pidgin. "Small glass for velee friendly girlee?"

"No-ee." He shook his head without turning around. "Me nicee boy. No drink with bad girlee."

"That's not what I hear, Karlov," she said after he turned and kissed her. "A friend of mine thought she saw you going into a house on the Rue Voisin where nice boys never go." She wagged a finger, though she was curious about the truth. "Shame on you."

"A young man in my position has many obligations," said Alexander without hesitation, a touch of drink in his voice. "I'm shocked to hear you know about such places."

He took Jessica by the hand and led her between two tatooists and a lottery vendor to the next restaurant, done up like a prison cell with a three-prisoner cangue hanging from one wall. Old wooden manacles hung beside the Chinese stock. A fortune-teller was reading an English sailor's palm at the corner table. A girl Jessica guessed was Russian stood behind him stroking his neck with both hands. Jessica wondered if Alex would enjoy the same attention.

"What shall we eat, Jesse?" Alexander said after ordering vodka slings. "One of their specialties? Still living new-born mice?"

"Don't be disgusting."

"But they are so real, Jesse, so Chinese. People claim the lively little ones are so tasty because they're still hairless, like Prince Krupotkin."

She laughed despite herself and noticed again the varied colors of his eyes.

They finished their drinks and ordered another. Alexander had the sense that his life was accelerating, like everything at the Great World, and that he should make the most of it. He felt emboldened, as if by a sense of fatalism, as if the charge his father sometimes spoke of had begun, with the trumpets blaring and the mounts, spur to spur, moving together into a trot, and the unstoppable do-or-die madness only a short canter and gallop ahead.

"Are your parents still away?" he said. "Saving China?"

"They're always away," she said. "Are you saving the Salle d'Armes?"

"I hope so." He thought of the message he was sending to Mr. Hak Lee tomorrow and frowned. "I'm doing my best." He prayed the second race would go the way he judged. The steeplechases seemed easier to predict. Fewer horses running, and very few of them good jumpers. "But you've just given me a new idea."

"I have? Will you give me a prize if you use it?"

"Do I charge you, Jesse, for your bad ideas?" He smiled, but she didn't smile back.

"Perhaps if I want to save it, I should make the Salle d'Armes a bit like this madness, the Amusement Palace. With something always going on. Just look at this place. Instead of closing each afternoon when the ponies are back in their stalls and the swords in their racks, why not extend every day with different events and competitions? Especially anything people can gamble on."

"Good idea," she said. Her face changed as she considered it. "But is the gambling really necessary? It destroys so many of these Chinese families."

Whom should he please? wondered Alexander to himself, almost amused. Jessica, or Mr. Hak Lee?

"Two more slings, if you please," he said to the waiter, although Jessica had not finished hers. "And some paddy crabs and rice and cabbage, any way you serve them." He grinned at Jesse. "Cabbage makes Russians feel at home," he said, a saying that had annoyed him whenever his father repeated it.

"Will you always be like this, Alex?"

"How do you want me to be?"

"Just like this," she said after a moment. "More or less." She lifted her chopsticks and touched the side of his face with them. "Don't change too much."

"Don't worry." He smiled as he rested his hand on hers, then took a sip before he looked her in the eye and spoke again.

"I'd like to invite you to the Twin Ducks this evening."

"Who are they?" she said, feeling a bit light-headed. Fortunately, Viktor had taught her how to drink.

"It's an old Chinese inn, not far from the Rue Voisin. It's where my father and I stayed on our first night in Shanghai."

Jessica hesitated, taken by his new boldness. After all, she had come here thinking of seducing him. She felt ready for an adventure, something she would want to remember, something that would put that first horrible experience behind her.

"Have you been back?" she asked.

"No, I've been saving it for something special." He tapped her hand. "For the American bandit, Jesse James."

"Do I get my crabs and cabbage first?" she said.

"Waiter!" he called, almost spilling his drink. "Waiter! What's happened to our dinner? And I'd like to buy a bottle of vodka, if you please."

"Did you know that mandarin ducks are the symbol of inseparable lovers?" She took his hand in both of hers. Alexander shook his head.

In twenty minutes, they were in a rickshaw. As he took Jessica's face between his fingers he saw the yellow moon, nearly full, waiting for them at the end of the next street like a guiding lantern. He kissed her, for an instant thinking of their unfinished evening on the turtle beach. He trusted tonight would be different.

"I thought you were a virgin," he said during the night, as he watched the moonlight stripe her body through the window slats. For the moment Jesse had left her politics on the floor with her clothes. In bed, she had been eager if not resourceful, responsive more than provocative. It would improve when they were more comfortable, he thought. He was keen to find that mixture of affection and excitement, passion and relaxation, that Mei-lan had said must be the goal.

"I was a virgin," she confirmed, her ankles still resting on his shoulders. She considered how different he was, how unlike Viktor. Not more innocent, as she had anticipated. More sophisticated, more generous, more ready to take pleasure in her pleasure, the last thing she had expected in a younger lover. As if following her mind, he moistened one finger between her lips, then touched her gently and slowly circled her live center, first with the finger, then with his tongue.

"It's like a little volcano," he said as she trembled. "You have three volcanoes," he added after a moment. Shifting his attention, he touched the center of one nipple, then the other with his tongue.

"You surprise me, Alex," murmured Jessica, closing her eyes again as he gave her first volcano more attention. "When did you learn all this? I thought you were a nice schoolboy. Oh, yes. Right there. Oh."

He raised his head. "I went to school at Kadnikov. I was a cadet."

"I think your classroom must be somewhere in Shanghai," she said with langour. "I love your touch."

Jessica felt as if she were being unwound. Suddenly her body trembled outward from its core. She gasped and almost kicked him away. But he pursued Jessica with his touch and tongue, not letting her escape the waves rolling through her body.

"Oh, Alex. No," Jessica said finally, gripping and pulling his hair with both hands above his ears, lifting his head and pressing his cheek hard against hers, unable to accept any more. She could smell herself on his mouth and face. "No. Please. I can't stand it." She gasped, her eyes closed as she opened her mouth wide for air. "Please, stop." Then Jessica cast back her head. She opened both eyes, staring at him before she whispered.

"You have a tongue like a pangolin."

Alexander sat back, grateful for his training.

Jessica lowered her feet and sat up against the wall with her legs crossed while her breathing slowed. She felt eager to talk. Afraid of the completion of intimacy, she wanted to retain something for herself. She had to think. What sort of woman was she becoming? She held up one of her feet and wiggled her toes.

"Don't you think it's horrible what they used to do to the little girls, and still are doing in some places, binding their feet, scrunching their toes sideways under the soles and bending their heel bones down under their ankles until they look like the hooves of a deer or a pig?"

"I wouldn't know," he said, careful not to disagree, but thinking of Mei-lan and her pride in her perfect tiny lotus feet.

"They're the only girls in the world who can't run and play, the only women in the world who cannot walk. They say the pain goes on until they die. Often the feet never heal. The skin is always rotting. Infections come and go forever. Sometimes one foot rots off."

Not meaning to, instinctively she shrank away from Alexander on the bed. Confused about her feelings and behavior, feeling she was losing something of her own control, she was aware that her words were breaking the pattern of their intimacy. Perhaps that was what she needed now. With Viktor, her loss of control had come from his violence. With Alex, it came from something he had found within her. But with both men, she felt a loss of power.

"And the foot binding's all done to please the men, of course," she added, "and to keep the women trapped at home."

Alexander could feel Jessica retreating into her talk. Annoyed, he thought of Lily afterwards, his head in her lap, her hair silky on his shoulder, his eyes closed while she waited for him to rally and she traced his lips with cool gentle fingers and told him again "The Tale of the Faithless Widow," a story of a son's reunion with his vanished father, a pawnbroker in Nanking. Instead of retreating, Lily gently extended the sense of intimacy as far as he felt like going, adjusting to his mood and pace, always available, never pressing. This must be what Mei-lan had meant by "complaisant."

"The men think the crippled feet are sexy," persisted Jessica. "They believe the way it forces the women to walk makes their thighs bigger and softer, and their vaginas tighter, like virgins." Jessica noticed the urgent indignation swelling in her own voice. She was aware she was using this candid language as a challenge, to assert herself.

"Do you think it's true?" he said with little interest.

Jessica looked at him. Irritated, her temper hardening, she was determined to say all of what she wanted to express.

"The men put the tiny feet in their mouths, filling their cheeks with them. Then they bite them and chew them and suck them, caring nothing for the woman's pain. Some men even make the women grease their feet and force them up their behinds. Can you imagine? And they make little cups to put into the four-inch shoes so they can drink from them. Sometimes they drink the water used to wash the feet."

"How can you love China so, Jesse, if you hate everything about it?" said Alexander. Exasperated, he felt used by this excuse for her withdrawal, the way he'd heard women often felt when men turned away too quickly after making love. Only with Jessica James it was political speeches instead of cigarettes.

"What do you mean? I don't hate China."

"You do. The food, the politics," he said, standing and looking for his trousers, "the customs, the corruption, the courtesans, the old religions, the slums, the child labor, the rickshaws." He pulled on his shirt and boots.

"You hate it all, Jessica. What is all that but China?" He stood by the door, tapping his stick on the floor and watching her dress. "For you it's just a place to try and make other people be like you, to work at making things the way you want them to be, like a hospital or a crusade, or some place for you to enjoy somebody else's damned revolution."

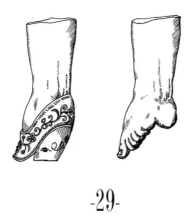

-29-

"You're the last person alive who saw him, Ivan." Alexander handed the old flyer to Semyonov. "Does he still look like our sketch?"

The Cossack drank and lifted the picture in both hands.

"It's him. The face, damn near, but more hair and a thick neck. Except now he has a beard. Not a real one, a small pointed one, like the devil himself, Lenin." Semyonov stroked his thick tobacco-stained mustache. "Polyak's a powerful big bastard, like me." He set down the flyer and emptied his glass. "Maybe bigger." He looked at his friend's son with weary red eyes.

"It was my fault." Semyonov shook his head. "I should have made it on board with your father and Vasily. The boats pulled away so fast." The hetman filled his glass before speaking again.

"Promise me, boy, that you won't try to finish this without me."

Alexander paused. It was the second time that Ivan had blamed himself and made the same request. He was aware that Semyonov felt an obligation to look after him. But he himself had two duties: catching the Commissar, and saving the Salle d'Armes. He knew only one man who could help with both.

"I'll do my best, Ivan."

In half an hour, Alexander was at the Tabaqueria Filipina on Nanking Road, where he hoped he could make a connection to Viktor Polyak. He loved the embracing smell of the unburned tobacco that perfumed the shop. Newly arrived Jean Valjean Coronas were featured in the window.

"Good morning, *señor*," he said to the proprietor. "A tin of pipe tobacco, if you please, your Telkhis Mixture. Four ounces."

"*Con mucho gusto.*" The man adjusted his fez. "One dollar, twenty cents, please."

"May I ask if you've had much call for this? Has anyone been buying it recently?"

"Not this week, sir. If you don't mind my saying so, it's a bit pricey for most of the refugees," he said, glancing at Alexander's starched Russian blouse. "But a young lady bought some a few days ago. I believe she was American."

"Thank you." Alexander wondered if it could possibly have been Jessica, buying him a present? He was very pleased with the notion, but how would she know the brand? Perhaps his father had told her, although that seemed unlikely.

He left the shop and remounted Osetra. Calmer than Taiga, not disturbed by traffic after the din of gunfire and artillery, Osetra was a sound street horse. Carrying his cane like a crop, Alexander rode slowly to the Rue Voisin, along his way enjoying the shade of the London plane trees that lined so many streets in Frenchtown. He was disappointed that his trip to the Tabaqueria had not brought him any closer to Polyak.

He thought of his last conversation with Madame Wong. Finally he had asked her for the return favor she had always offered.

"I need your help," he had said, "to find the Russian who killed my father and mother and seized my sister."

"I cannot help you myself," Mei-lan had replied. "But I will do what you are doing, free a friend from obligation by calling on the favor I am owed."

As he approached on Osetra and saw the waiting Chryslers, he knew that Mr. Hak Lee was already at her house. If anyone could find Viktor Polyak, it was the Master of the Mountain. The Green Gang had four thousand members who did what they were told.

The Russian bodyguard was waiting on the top step. Alexander had seen him at the service. For the first time the two acknowledged each other with a nod. Joss sticks were burning in the hall. Hak Lee was waiting for him alone, while taking tea in one of Mei-lan's sitting rooms.

"Good morning, Count Karlov. I was sorry to learn about your distinguished father," sighed the Chinese, bowing slightly in his seat. The pupils of his eyes were larger and darker than ever. "I am told that I might have the honor of providing you a service."

"Yes, sir, if you would." Alexander passed the flyer of Viktor Polyak into Hak Lee's long yellowed fingers. "I need to find this man. He killed both my parents and he has kidnapped my sister."

Hak Lee pulled back his head and squinted from a distance. "A strong face. Do you require him alive or dead?"

"Alive, so he can tell me how to find my sister, Katerina."

"This I will do," said Hak Lee as if it were an easy matter. "I will find this man. With no obligation passing between us."

"Thank you. For this I would do anything."

A spark of interest brightened Hak Lee's eyes. "Would you?" He leaned slightly forward. "Anything?"

"Yes, sir," Alexander said at once. "Anything."

"For this service I will ask you nothing. But you must understand I do this not for you, but for Madame Wong and for my obligation." Hak Lee's robe shook like a curtain while he settled his narrow sloping shoulders, as if trying to equalize their height. "And the task is congenial enough. These Communists are my enemies as well. I am assisting the commander from Whampoa, General Chiang Kai-shek, in this duty. As the general says: China's other enemies are a disease of the skin, the Communists are a disease of the heart. Better to kill a few Russians now than many Chinese later. Kill the teacher, and what can the students learn?"

"Yes, sir." Alexander nodded with relief, as if all China were now on his side.

"First you must provide me with more copies of this picture."

"How many?"

"Two hundred."

"Of course," agreed Alexander. "You will have them today."

Hak Lee folded the flyer and slipped it into a pocket of his robe. "But you and I now have other business of our own."

Alexander dreaded what this must be. He could envision a mountain of chits signed by his father: a lifetime of obligation.

"I hear that you have given up your school."

"Well, yes."

"Have no regret. There are many schools," Hak Lee said dismissively. "I myself cannot read or write. I never attended what you call school, yet the French consul general has just appointed me to their *Conseil Municipal*, though I speak few words of French."

And I hear you've returned the honor, thought Alexander, by giving the French chief of detectives an appointment with your gang as the protector of the opium trade. "There is so much to do," he said. "I have to manage our stable, and . . ."

"Your stable, your famous hall of arms, is not truly yours, though they say it has become the center of Russian life in Shanghai, the heart of Little Russia. Every day the creditors come to me, to what some round eyes would call my compradors, trying to sell me discounted obligations of your father's. Debts are worth more to the man who has the will to collect them, and they insist my agents will do better at collecting what is possible. Already I hold more debts than your stable is worth."

Big Ear almost whistled when he sucked in air before he continued, as if preparing himself to speak at length. Mei-lan had warned Alexander that, if he favored you, Mr. Hak Lee liked to teach. If he did not favor you, you would receive a different sort of lesson. "Listen to him with respect," she had said. "Let him speak. It will be less costly."

"Debts for oats and straw. Debts for wines and vodka, saddles and horseshoes, bootmakers and tailors, for lamp oil and luxuries, and for the great cost of buying the warehouse itself." He rolled the fingers of both hands in the air, as if these burdens had no end. "That debt Prince Krupotkin sold me first. Some are notes signed by your father's hand. Others are just mounting petty obligations, recorded only by the suppliers. Even the night soil carriers have received no tip in three months." His tone hardened, as if this was work he knew too well. Agitated, he pulled at his swollen ear, aggravating an inflamed abscess.

"Do Russians believe we should collect their waste each night for nothing? Shanghai is known for the quality of its night soil, as rich as the city, they say, but can the Russian be so special?" He paused and breathed again. Alexander was alarmed at the touch of bitterness, even of contempt in Hak Lee's voice.

"All over Shanghai your proud countrymen are ignoring their obligations while their beautiful sisters sell themselves in houses far worse than the one next door." He paused and wheezed. "If you yourself sold everything, the hall itself and every sword and horse, you would have nothing left. Yet you and your father have been living like grand gentlemen, as if you had suffered no revolution."

Offended by the tone this gangster used toward his father, but aware that he was being tested, Alexander sat straighter but did not reply. He knew the man was right. He thought of his own school bills, which could not amount to a pittance of all that his father owed. He expected Mr. Hak Lee to continue, and he did.

"I mean no disrespect, but we must understand each other. All Chinese admire the loyalty of a son. And there is one thing I learned about your father that makes me think his son and I can do business: they say he always kept his word." Hak Lee squeezed and scraped his ear with pointed yellow nails. Alexander tried not to notice.

"So what are we to do, young Count?" He turned one hand and looked under a nail.

"I will work to pay off every debt, sir," said Alexander. "The Salle d'Armes is doing rather well, especially our clubs, and will be doing even better. I have some ideas. Next week we are holding our first boxing match, with champions from each navy. Even the Japanese, competing in the flyweight."

"That will mean much new wagering." Hak Lee nodded, a little fresh brightness in his eyes.

"I just need time."

"Time?" There was something like humor in his voice, or at least an appreciation for the droll. "Time is costly. It is the most precious thing we have. The more time, the more you owe. Perhaps you will manage to pay your new bills, day to day, but I cannot have much hope that you will be able to pay the old ones that I hold, and the interest." Hak Lee shook his long thin head from side to side without taking his eyes from Alexander.

"Debt is something I know as you know horses, as a farmer knows his field, as some men think they know women. Debt is in my bones. Of course lending is easy. Collection is the art. I can look at a man, ignoring his protests, ignoring his promises, and know what he will pay and when."

Alexander believed him. "I . . ."

"For you, hard work will not be sufficient. It rarely is. All over Shanghai men are running day and night in the traces of my rickshaws, thinking to work off their debt, running to exhaustion with the dream of buying their own vehicle. But they grow old and weak just paying the interest each day. Some run to pay the interest on the interest. I look at their feet and the bend of their backs and I know how many more miles each can run." Hak Lee gave a wheezing chuckle. "No, we must find another way to clear your abacus." Big Ear stopped abruptly, forcing Alexander to face the silence.

"I don't ..."

"Horses," Hak Lee said in a louder voice, finding fresh vigor as he knifed to the bone of business. "Horses. You know the races are my weakness, and I am tired of the embarrassment of losing when I bet. Today there are so many ways to gamble in Shanghai, from pelota and boxing and baseball to the new Stock Exchange. When I was a boy, younger than you, earning a few coppers in ways Mei-lan would not wish me to recount, I was always hungry, living on stolen melons and rotten rice so I could wager every coin I touched."

Alexander did not speak when Big Ear paused and wheezed.

"But I never understood these animals of yours, or what made some horses win. It was not size, or strength, or even always speed. What was it?" continued Hak Lee. "Instead, I just learned how to gamble, and then to lend, and finally to collect. But you, they say, you know horses better than any young man in Shanghai."

Alexander realized that he was with a man who had a more complicated code and history than even the worldly old Russians with whom he was familiar.

"So perhaps you will advise me when you have ideas about the races. That is your world. It might be only a few words about a horse or a rider or a stable. Or better still, just your sense of luck or instinct. Soon we will talk about the Shanghai Derby," continued Hak Lee after taking breath. "For this, I can carry your debts. Then, to clear them, from time to time I will call on you for something greater, but never for something that you cannot do."

Alexander hated to think where this might lead. What would his father say? Proud but practical, elegant but hardy as an old bear, somehow he had always managed despite his habits of presumption and improvidence.

"I need some time to consider this," said Alexander.

"Who can afford time? Do you not wish my assistance promptly in this other matter, now, before this Russian you are hunting leaves Shanghai? Who will find him for you then?"

"Well, yes, but I thought the two matters were separate, sir."

"They are, and they are not. Nothing is unrelated in this world. If we understand each other about these debts and your assistance when requested, then you can keep your father's stable, and it will be my pleasure to help you earn peace for your ancestors."

Peace, indeed, thought Alexander. He dreaded what a reckoning with this brutal Chinese might cost one day.

-30-

"I don't have very long, Viktor," said Jessica, trimming his hair with the barber scissors she had brought from home. She was impressed with the way he had already applied the bleach.

Now Jessica felt uncomfortable with even this sort of intimacy, but she still wanted to assist his mission while avoiding every other complication.

Things must be getting more dangerous for Viktor, she suspected, judging by the condition of his new quarters and the abruptness of this latest move. The small space smelled of garlic and old cooking oil. There was no window, just a narrow room above a rag shop in a brick tenement on the Chinese bank of Soochow Creek. No longer were there dried fish hanging from Viktor's bookshelf. No pictures of Dzerzhinsky and Marx decorated the walls. Only his pipe and revolver were still visibly at hand. A tin of Telkhis and an oily rag and a small box of cartridges rested beside them on the table.

"Just one message for you to take," Polyak said.

"Of course, Viktor. My bike's downstairs."

"But be sure and deliver the letter before you go to that foolish meeting."

"I wish you could come, too," she said, knowing he never would. "The Unbound Foot Association has been fighting for change in China for twenty-five years. It could support all your other work." Annoyed, she put down the scissors. Not wishing to touch him, she flicked the bunches of hair from his bare shoulders with a dirty towel. "I thought the Communists were opposed to foot binding, and to all the other abuses that require a revolution in this culture."

"Of course we're against foot binding, and all the rest of it," he said impatiently, as if speaking to a child. "You know that. But building our cadres and changing power must come first. We must win the bigger battles, comrade, before we make more enemies by fighting the small ones."

Jessica understood, and admired his resolve, but she could not abandon her daily causes.

"Are things all right, Viktor?" she said after a moment. "The *Daily News* says the police have been jailing some of the union leaders, and I hear the Green Gang is working with the Sûreté and Chiang Kai-shek."

"What do you expect?" He stood and pulled on a starched English shirt with the brass collar buttons already attached front and back. A dark suit hung from a nail on the wall. The cassock hung beneath it. "Sometimes jail is part of the work. It could happen to you."

"Me?" She was shocked at the idea. "What have I done?"

He shrugged. "Whatever they think I have done, you have been doing, too."

Perhaps he was counting on this new hold over her to replace the sexual control that had not worked, she thought as he continued. One of the exciting things about Viktor was this hardness, his unblinkng deliberation. He needed her, but without concessions. It reminded her of what a boy Alexander sometimes still seemed to be.

"Leon Trotsky was in prison nearly twenty times," Polyak continued. "Today, instead of starving among lice and rats in an unheated cell in Odessa, he is commanding the Red Army from an armored train with a printing press, a telegraph station, a library and a bathtub."

Apparently that was Victor's notion of a grand hotel, she thought, no longer quite so taken with his perspectives. Sometimes she now saw life through Alexander's eyes.

"There are worse things than prison." Polyak shrugged and handed her a starched white collar. "Help me with this."

Jessica attached the collar at the back, feeling like something between a valet and the dresser of an actor. He needed a bath.

"Would you like me to start your pipe before I go?" She twisted the lid off the tobacco tin, hoping that the offer might diminish his resentment of the new distance between them. She had come to enjoy the little ritual of the pipe. It was the only personal detail that she still welcomed. Somehow it had become part of her role. Josef Stalin and all the other Soviet leaders seemed to smoke a pipe.

"Do it right," he said, his chin high as he finished threading a striped tie through the collar and buttoning the front. "Don't pack it down so tight."

Jessica ignored his difficulty in knotting the necktie. She struck a wooden match against the brick wall and sucked a long blue flame into the pipe, enjoying the sweet smoke that filled her mouth and clung to her. She took a few puffs until the bowl was hot. Passing the pipe to him always made her feel like an Indian chief sharing a uniting gesture.

Polyak accepted the pipe and looked at her through the smoke. After a moment he set it down and began to clean his pistol with the rag.

Jessica felt a chill, as if she herself were now in danger. She put the scissors in her pocket. Then she stood and nodded at Viktor and left with the letter. Determined not to be late for her job at the Mission, and hoping to see Alex, she hurriedly walked her bicycle through a cluster of women selecting rags with which to make their mops and shoes. As she rode, Jessica considered her two Russians, and what the Reds and these White aristocrats had in common. Only two things besides vodka, she realized with satisfaction: passion and a contempt for the middle-class values of the bourgeoisie.

The twin Chryslers were parked on the Rue Lafayette outside the Green Dragon Teahouse next to a street-side money changer's table that was protected by a wire screen. The two drivers were fussing with the coachwork like stablehands grooming a royal team. Alexander knew it was Mr. Hak Lee's custom to hold court each week at various centers of his power. Coffins were stacked like mah-jongg tiles in front of the coffin-maker's shop next door. The smell of the fresh-cut wood reminded Alexander of the first day he had come ashore in Shanghai ten months before.

He found the teahouse crowded. Tiles drummed on the black tables. Men were chattering over tea and cards. Known as a hangout of the Green Gang, the Dragon was quieter, more subdued than most tea-houses that Alexander knew.

An ear cleaner squinted through round spectacles as he attended to a customer in one corner. His tiny tools were laid out on a cloth on the client's tea table. In one hand he held a duck-down duster. With the other he worked a slim metal pick into his customer's left ear. The client's head was inclined on his right shoulder. His eyes were closed as if he were enjoying a secret dream. Columns of smoke rose from his nostrils.

Alexander saw the bodyguard standing at the back by the door to a private room. The Russian's heavy lumpy face resembled that of a stone buddha staring through the smoke. A line of men waited silently against the wall nearby. None of them seemed to pay attention when a mama-san slowly paraded six young girls between the busy tables. She left only one behind her in the teahouse. Perhaps twelve, pretty and powdered and brightly painted, the slim satin-clad girl stood behind her heavy-bellied client, waiting to attend him while he finished his hand of cards. Calm and without expression, there was nothing of the playful child in her demeanor.

Alexander thought of Mei-lan's account of how her Western clients sought what Chinese men had always required in their women, a spirit of complaisance, a pleasing, flattering acceptance of their roles. By itself, submission elevated the other party. "It is that, and our smooth skin, that European men enjoy," she had explained. Alexander wondered what it was that certain rich Chinese sought, the clients who patronized the two bordellos staffed with girls from America. The contrary, perhaps? Girls who were older, more spirited, and with a different look and touch and smell?

"*Dobroye utro*, Count Karlov," nodded the bodyguard, ignoring the line of Chinese supplicants and informers. "Mr. Hak Lee is in there working with his debt collectors." He indicated the door behind him with one thumb. "You are next, sir."

A burly Chinese stepped from the room, leading a smaller man by one elbow. The waiting men looked elsewhere as the two passed. The smaller man was trembling. His cheeks were moist. His right sleeve was wet and rolled high on his thin arm. He held a bloody rag wrapped around his right hand. Red drops fell to the floor.

The Russian bodyguard nodded and Alexander entered the room. He paused by the door to adjust his eyes to the low light that came through the slats of the window blinds. He looked about the room and enjoyed the scent that rose from a bronze brazier in one corner.

Large fish tanks rested on a pair of red lacquer tables set against the walls. A rim of thin green scum edged both tanks. Many small fish with long snake-like heads swam about actively in one tank as if recently aroused. They moved through the pink-filmed water in a swarm like a single creature. In the other tank he saw a larger tube-like fish, perhaps three feet long, resting with the dormant menacing solidity of a constrictor recently nourished. Evidently a fully grown version of the others, the big fish opened its long mouth and revealed a fence of thin pointed teeth extending from narrow lip to hinged jaw. A round bowl of goldfish rested on a third smaller table beside a woven bamboo cage that was rocking to and fro. Frogs, Alexander realized as he stared. Each of them appeared to have a broken right hind leg. A bit like me, he thought. Several crickets were chirping and leaping against the roof of the frog cage, seeking to avoid the widemouthed amphibians. A steep-sided bamboo sieve hung from a hook above the small table.

"Welcome to you, young Count," said Hak Lee. An open round tin of Pickwick Virginia Cigarettes was set on the low table before his carved blackwood chair. Noticing Alexander's interest, he gestured towards the fish tanks with both hands, without moving his eyes from his guest.

"These are my debt collectors," said the Chinaman, pleased to instruct. "Snakeheads, we call them. Prepared with watercress, the small ones make such fine soup, very restoring for an old man. I prefer the older ones smoked or dried. The Englishmen call them Frankenfish after their heads and habits. They eat everything, especially their own young. Even waterbirds and creatures bigger than themsleves. They mate only with ones of equal size. If they find a smaller partner, they will eat her. When hungry, after they have emptied their own ponds of life, they will leave their water and slither overland two or three miles in search of food."

Hak Lee sighed with a suggestion of humor. "You would not wish to be sleeping in their path, or to be introduced to them if you are in my debt."

"I see." Alexander recalled the man leaving with the bleeding hand.

"Would you care to feed them? They have enjoyed only a few small bites today. It disturbs them if they do not eat more once they begin." Hak Lee gestured towards the frog cage. "It would save me having to rise."

"Of course," said Alexander without hesitation. The snakeheads would be fed anyway and he knew better than to reveal a squeamish weakness to his host. Thinking of the bleeding debtor at the door, he took the sieve and lifted one fat frog from the cage. A cricket was caught between the creature's lips. Before the amphibian could try to leap, Alexander dropped it into the first tank near the tail of the moving mass of the smaller fish. Like a meteor reversing, the snakeheads turned on the swimming frog. In an instant only a pink bubble remained where the crippled frog had made its final breaststroke.

Alexander wondered what Jessica would think of this Chinese peculiarity. He tapped the dripping sieve on the edge of the tank, then hung it on its hook before taking the chair opposite Mr. Hak Lee. His host nodded as he picked at his ear. Alexander looked away and sniffed the gently rising incense.

"I see you notice my old burner," said Hak Lee after a moment. "It has been kept warm since it was cast three hundred years ago. It is like an old man's heart. If it once grows cold, the bronze loses its luster forever."

"Doesn't it go out at night?"

"Never. A piece of glowing charcoal is buried in the ashes of old incense, so it has just enough air to smolder on slowly for several days. A fragment of sandalwood is set on the hot ashes until it shrivels up and smokes away. I have four such burners, one in each place where I do my work. They remind my people to look after my interests even when I am not present."

"Have you had them long?" asked Alexander.

"No. Eleven years. They came to me in payment for a special debt," said Big Ear. "But we must speak of something else. Thanks to you, at last I am beginning to enjoy the steeplechases."

"We have been lucky, sir," said Alexander. "Especially in the Prince of Wales's Stakes. There were only six starters. But I cannot be certain about the Hardoon Handicap tomorrow, or the Boston Plate with those sub-griffins over seven furlongs." He looked to one side when Hak Lee clawed away a dark scab on his inflamed ear.

"The Derby is in a few days," said Hak Lee as if with little interest. "It may be a race that you will not wish to win."

"I will have to do my best, sir," said Alexander, recalling his promise to his father.

"You may find you will wish to come in second or third, I think, rather than first. But it is not a matter for today," said the tall Chinese. "Instead, I have a new proposal for you," said the quiet windy voice. "An offer I trust you will honor me by accepting."

Alexander felt his stomach tighten as he looked back into the black eyes without blinking.

"I wish to be your partner, rather than your vise," said Hak Lee, using the term for an aggressive creditor, well known by now to Alexander.

"The stable is doing better," said Alexander. Advised by Mei-lan never to make arrangements in fragments, he wished to hear everything that Hak Lee had in mind before responding. "There is a waiting list for the Pony Club. We have been very busy."

"So I understand. The boxing, the choir competitions, puppet shows, the pony sales." The Chinese nodded repeatedly. "They tell me your Hall of Arms is now crowded day and night, like the Great World Amusement Palace."

"That is the idea," said Alexander. "Last night we had my new favorite. A knife-throwing contest, with martial artists and throwers from nine countries."

"Congratulations!" said Hak Lee with rare excitement and a new brightness in his eyes. "Knife throwing! When I was young, I myself was rather gifted with a knife. They said I was fast." Big Ear lowered his eyes.

"Yes, sir, so I understand," said Alexander. "Our competitors threw into archery targets at one end of the riding ring while the touts and shills took bets at the other end and everyone ate and drank in the center."

"I wish I had been there," sighed Hak Lee. "Who won, one of those Japanese monkeys from their Bushido club?"

"Actually not, though a Japanese beat the Gurkha and the Cossack. A gypsy from the Portuguese circus won. He beat a Korean master in the finals. The gypsy put three knives inside a horseshoe in less than ten seconds."

"If I were you, young man, this is a skill I would learn myself. One day you will find it useful."

"I am trying," said Alexander. "I'm taking lessons with the Korean master. The gypsy's gone back to Macao with the circus."

"You have done the one thing I thought was impossible in Shanghai, young Karlov. You have brought new gambling opportunities to our city, and you will find me grateful." Hak Lee lifted the tin of cigarettes while he continued.

"New business keeps me young. Now I am investing in the cinema, both the theatres and the films we are making in Shanghai." He held the tin to his nostrils and inhaled noisily. It reminded Alexander of how the Chinese expectorated enthusiastically and cleared their noses freely in the streets and picked their teeth at the dinner table.

"What magic can Hollywood, California, possess that we do not?" Hak Lee reached inside his robe and drew out a card. "Here is a pass for our theatres, the Isis and the Carlton."

"Thank you, sir," said Alexander, accepting the card. He was still amazed at the turnout for last week's competition at the Salle between the Welsh, American and Russian choirs. Shop assistants in borrowed clothes, hungry officers in epaulettes, two patriarchs in long beards and gowns, the thirty Russians had made people cry when they sang. The French judge had decided rightly for the Russians, but the Americans had complained that the French were never fair and that the competition was "fixed." Now that he understood Hak Lee had been wagering on these events, Alexander was no longer certain that this was so unlikely.

"Tomorrow evening we have the Yenisei Cossack Riders and Dancers," said Alexander. "Twenty-four of them, standing on their saddles as they canter, and a Russian Buffet afterwards."

"Of course," said the Master of the Mountain. "I know. But before then I wish you to be free of all your debts. All will be settled and forgotten, every sou and tael, if you take me as your secret partner in the Salle d'Armes."

"What sort of partner, sir?" asked Alexander, hoping to learn more from Hak Lee's propensity to talk, but doubting that he himself would have much choice when the offer was presented.

"Your equal partner. One half."

"One fourth?" asked Alexander. How could one be an equal partner with this man?

"One third," said Hak Lee, coughing, apparently amused by the exchange.

"Done, sir," said Alexander, knowing better than to extend his hand. Not only would he be free of debt, but he knew that now every resource of Chinese Shanghai would be behind him, even the French police.

There were two taps at the door, no doubt somehow signalled by Hak Lee.

"I would be honored if you were to visit the Salle," Alexander said as he rose. He feared he was already late to meet Jessica at the Methodist Mission on Avenue Haig. "But there is one more thing, sir. Our other bargain."

"Ah, of course. The head of Mr. Polyak in exchange for your special services. Your Red friend continues now in Shanghai, though I hear reports of him in Harbin and Nanking not so long ago. Stirring much mischief for us all. Dropping stones into China's deepest pools. We almost caught him here two days ago. But someone warned him. He moved just in time, from a tenement in Chapei, off Kung Woo Road."

Alexander respectfully excused himself. As he hurried to meet Jessica, he began to think that too much time was passing, that Polyak might escape Shanghai and leave him unavenged and without his sister. Could he really entrust his greatest responsibility to another man, even to Hak Lee?

He arrived late at the Mission, but not late enough. The women were still there, the tireless American missionaries and their prizes, a few Chinese victims of the accursed practise.

An elderly Chinese woman, her tiny warped feet unbound, sat hunched like a sick bird on a tall stool in the center of the low stage. The platform normally served as the setting for the Mother Goose Tableaux, Bible lectures and the Young Christian Nativity Pageant. Her eyes lowered, the woman spoke quietly to the American interpreter who stood beside her, Jessica James.

Alexander sat down in the back row and stretched his left leg in the aisle. He took out his pipe, then saw the sign. Two American women with wicker offering baskets came and sat near him, waiting to solicit donations to carry on the work. One pointed at his pipe and shook her head. He set the cold pipe between his teeth.

"When I was six my mother began to bind my feet," translated Jessica as several women in the audience took notes. "Each day she wound the bandages more tightly, stitching the bindings together with needle and thread. My big toes were forced upward, like sprouts of young ginger, the heels bent down." A photographer began setting up his tripod and box camera close to the stage.

"Once a week they soaked my feet in urine to soften the bones, and sometimes, if it was not going well, in a nice monkey broth."

The audience gasped, thrilled, Alexander guessed, at these new horrors. He thought of what Mei-lan had told him. The urine was said to come from young boys. It always worked, she said.

"They made me walk on them each day though the pain was so terrible I could not eat or sleep. If in the night I removed my sleeping shoes and tried to loosen the bindings, I was punished in the morning and they were bound more tightly than before. Every two weeks they forced me into smaller shoes. When I cried, my mother said no rich man would marry me unless I had tiny golden lotus feet that he could hold and squeeze in his palm, like a water chestnut."

Jessica continued to recite as the woman whispered and swung her left leg from side to side. It struck him that the two had done this before. Sometimes he sensed that the translation was running ahead of the speaker. He watched Jessica closely. While admiring her competence and proud of her compassion, he wondered what it was that made her so annoying, apart from her sympathy for revolution? Somehow, it all seemed to be about her, more than about these victims, as if Jesse needed them still more than they needed her. It was as if she were playing a role, perhaps some extension of her parents' patronizing philanthropy. Was she trying to outdo them, to use these causes to make her point?

"Soon the flesh began to rot and on my seventh birthday I lost two toes on my left foot."

Alexander sensed Jessica hardening herself against her own tears as she spoke the other woman's words.

"When I ate fresh meat or fish my feet would swell and drip pus and blood. I used alum powder to stop the bleeding."

Alexander rose quietly, dropped a coin into one of the baskets and stepped from the building.

Young Chinese girls were performing a gymnasium drill in the open courtyard between the Mission and the Methodist Girls' School. Perhaps ten years old, the girls stood on one leg in rows of four or five. Their crisp blue uniforms were belted with white sashes. Each girl gazed up to the sky between her raised hands that met above her head in a graceful arch of pointed fingers.

Relieved to be outside, Alexander sat on a low wooden bench and bought a green tea from a street vendor. He turned and read the small brass plaque screwed into the bench beside him:

A GIFT TO THE CHILDREN OF CHINA,
FROM THE GIRLS AND BOYS
OF THE FIRST METHODIST CHURCH
PALO ALTO, CALIFORNIA.

What must life be like at a place called Palo Alto? He noticed that the heads of the screws had been filed flat so that the small brass fasteners could not be stolen. He wondered what made all these Americans such connoisseurs of misery. What would they do if there were not people less fortunate?

Jessica finally came out and sat beside him on the bench. Her face was flushed.

"Why were you in such a hurry to leave our lecture?" she said.

"I didn't like seeing you so upset," he said, "and I was embarrassed for the old lady."

"It's really all right," said Jessica. "She does it somewhere nearly every day, like a job. We need her to help us get support to make a real end to all this. Some peasants are still doing it in the villages, hoping to increase the sale price of their daughters as wives or prostitutes or household servants."

"I thought it was even more painful once they unbind their feet and try to walk," he said, aware he was provoking her. He restrained himself from adding that to make herself feel better, Jessica was making the old victims feel worse.

"It can be more painful, but we teach them to do it slowly. Then it's not so bad, they say. The Japanese are doing a fantastic job in stamping out binding in Formosa."

"You mean they're punishing any old woman they catch still trying to hobble about the old way?"

"Alex . . ."

He tapped the brass plaque between them on the bench.

"Wasn't California part of Russia once?" he asked with innocence. "Like Alaska? Perhaps you're really Russian. Maybe that's where you get your taste for misery."

"No, Alexander." She shook her head. Why was he always so irritating? "California is not Russian. All you ever had there were a few old trading forts up north."

From the open school windows behind them, they heard girls begin to sing "Onward Christian Soldiers" in Shanghainese. A banging piano encouraged the clear voices, "marching as to war."

"These girls are so lucky," Jessica said. "In the afternoons they go to the Singer Sewing Machine School to learn a trade. They ..."

"How about dinner?" he interrupted. If only he could have Jesse without the politics. "Why don't you choose a restaurant? Or would you rather see a photoplay? There's a new Lionel Barrymore film at the Isis."

"What's it called?"

"*Enemies of Women*, with Barrymore and Alma Rubens. It's all about the Revolution in Russia."

Jessica looked at him, trying to see if he was being provocative. "I'd rather see one of the new Chinese films made right here," she said. "They're mostly about poor young farm girls who come to work in Shanghai. But let's just go to dinner."

Alexander raised his hand at a passing rickshaw.

She rose and waved off the rickshaw. "But we'll take two bikes. You can borrow one from the rack." All but hers were girls' bicycles. Smiling ruefully, Alexander whistled and clapped his hands. The rickshaw came back.

"One thing I can't do, Jesse," he said with more humor than irritation in his voice, "is ride a bicycle. Please think of my rickshaw as an ambulance. We'll follow you."

Annoyed more than chastened, sensing he was pleased to be using his infirmity to irritate her with the rickshaw, Jessica led the way down Jessfield Road to Frenchtown.

They started with tea. Their worlds grew a bit closer as they relaxed. He was learning to wait more patiently for the Jessica he enjoyed.

As she complained about the suppression of women's education in the countryside, Alexander thought of tomorrow's Handicap and prayed that he had got it right. Ever since this morning he had been worrying about what his father would think of the arrangement he had made for the future of the Salle d'Armes. Would he have put survival first, or gambled deeper on the side of independence? Alexander knew the answer. You could tell such things from the way a man rode a horse, his father used to say. But at least Alexander had not turned their business over to Pavel Krupotkin. Then it would all have been for nothing and his father would have cursed him.

"Am I losing you again, Alex?" said Jessica, friendly now, tossing her head and running her hands through her hair to loosen her curls. She reached out and touched his hand. "You've been so busy I've hardly seen you, and we didn't have the chance for a proper hello at the Mission." She leaned across the table to kiss him.

He touched the fingers of one hand to her cheek and kissed her on the lips, fully, then suddenly sat back, his mind exploding.

He knew that taste. There was only one like it.

"Jessica," he said in a new urgent voice. "Where have you been? Who have you been with?"

"What do you mean? You saw me, at the Mission."

"There is tobacco on your breath, pipe tobacco." He sat up straight and stared hard at her, like an executioner. "Telkhis. Who else smokes it except for me?"

She stared back and could not speak. A shadowy fear she had been suppressing was growing in her mind.

"Only one man I know of," he rushed on, his voice strong and loud. "A killer. The Commissar who murdered my father and mother, Viktor Polyak. And I know he's in Shanghai."

Alexander put his hands over Jessica's ears and drew her face towards him across the table, his nose almost touching her mouth. Twice he sniffed and breathed out as she resisted.

"Let me go!" She felt the horror as the two sides of her life closed in on each other.

"How could this be on your breath?" He released Jessica's head and seized her by both wrists. "You have been with him, haven't you? You must have kissed him to smell like that." Half rising, he squeezed her arms as the nearby diners stared, their chopsticks and forks and knives suspended.

"Of course! It's Polyak! It's all part of your damned revolution, isn't it? Isn't it, Jessica?"

"You're hurting me," Jessica said at last. As she tried to free her arms, she knew she had to choose at once. "I don't know anyone called Polyak."

He released her and pulled a flyer from his pocket.

"That's him, isn't it?" He unfolded the picture and flattened it between them on the table with both hands. He turned its face to her. "Where is he?"

Jessica stared down at the picture. She could not touch it. Only the hair was different. Viktor had killed Alexander's father?

"I can't ... It's not possible. Viktor wouldn't kill anyone," she protested, though she knew he would. For his work Viktor would kill even her. To him, her rape was nothing.

"Jessica, please. Tell me. Where is he? He killed my mother and my father. He is the only man who knows where my sister is. If you help him escape, I will never find Katia."

She faltered. Everything was coming together in one horrific union.

"What makes you think he knows where Katia is?"

"We found her picture in his codebook."

Jessica blanched with instant recognition. She recalled helping Viktor create his new codebook, transposing numbers and letters in Shanghainese, to replace the one he had lost. All this time Alexander and his father had been talking about the man that she wanted to follow until China was free.

Alexander rose.

"If you protect him, you are killing my sister as well."

Horrified by Jessica's hesitation, Alexander looked down at her and felt his eyes narrow and the blood pound in his ears. He fought to make his words and his tone measured.

"You help everyone else, Jessica. You help people you don't even know or truly care about. Why won't you help me?"

"Sit down, Alex." Her voice softened. She no longer had a choice. "Please."

He sat, white-faced. His hands trembled.

She could not accept her own complicity.

"I will tell you, Alex. But God help me."

-31-

"This could be our chance to get him, Ivan," whispered Alexander to the Cossack. He recalled the pledge he had made to his father on the boat to Shanghai, to avenge his mother if his father were not alive to do it.

They stood at the entrance to a pork shop at the corner of the alley. They stared out between the swinging hams and ducks suspended from the proprietor's bamboo racks. The long turned-back necks of the ducks served as hooks to hang the birds. The smell of the glossy glazed hams, shining red with vegetable and sesame oil, made Alexander's stomach growl as they waited. Live ducks struggled together in a crowded pen behind them, waiting to be strangled and plucked by an old man with a sagging goiter who sat on a stool surrounded by soft piles of feathers.

The hetman and Alexander watched two Chinese approach with a wheelbarrow. Enormous sacks of rags were bound on either side of the tall creaking wheel.

Alexander knew that two more members of the Gang were waiting in a sampan on the other side of the tenement in case Polyak sought to escape by Soochow Creek. Others were positioned along the alley.

Alexander's stomach tightened as he watched the barrow pull up outside the ragman's shop so that it almost blocked the entrance. One man began to unbind the bulky bags while the other set them on the ground in front of the doorway. Then the two men drew weapons and rushed into the narrow building.

Alexander heard the pop of a single muffled shot. He hurried towards the tenement with Semyonov. Two heavier explosions greeted them as they charged up the stairs. Slower on the steps, Alexander could not prevent Ivan from shouldering his way into the room first with his pistol.

A young Chinese lay dying in the far corner of the crowded space. His twitching body was surrounded by bundles of the Peking Communist magazine *New Youth* and recruiting flyers of the Dyers Union. The man's blood leaked onto the leaflets from wounds in his chest and neck.

The small room smelled of fish and tobacco and gunsmoke.

"Why did you kill him?" asked Alexander, his short sword in hand. "Now he can't tell us what happened to Polyak."

"He shot first." One of the gangsters shrugged and wiped his revolver on a white garment hanging from the door. "He is an old enemy. It was time."

"Mr. Hak Lee would not understand if we found him and did not do something useful," said the other, collecting the dead man's small black pistol. He emptied the bullets into his hand.

Furious at himself and at them, bitter about the near miss, Alexander turned and plunged down the stair without replying. He knew Viktor Polyak would not give him many opportunities.

"I understand your business is doing well," said Madame Wong, offering Alexander a madeleine with his tea.

"Better," he said. "But sometimes I think I am working for your friend."

"Who does not?" Mei-lan swept the air with her ivory fan.

"Yesterday Mr. Hak Lee asked to become my partner at the Salle d'Armes. And he wants me to run a very fast gallop in the early morning ride tomorrow at the track, but then on race day, Saturday, to lose the Derby. He wants me to come in second or third."

"Why not? What does this race really matter?"

"I promised my father Taiga would win the Shanghai Derby." As yet, Alexander had not decided what to do. Whether to do it Hak Lee's way, or his father's, riding and fighting like a Russian officer, no matter where that took him.

"Very dutiful, but your honorable father would understand. There are many ways to win. If you use the Derby to save your business and catch your enemy and avenge your family, how have you lost?"

"I might lose the race without doing any of those things." Alexander helped himself to another small oval ribbed pastry. He always enjoyed the dense almond flavor. "And all of our poor friends will be betting on Taiga to win. Anyway, we don't even know where Polyak is." Alexander had felt a new sense of urgency ever since Hak Lee had mentioned that the Commissar might leave Shanghai.

"If you chase him, you will always be behind him."

"How can I catch him if I don't chase him?" The moment he spoke, Alexander regretted the irritation in his voice. But he had been taught that one must always pursue the wolf at dawn before fresh snow covered its tracks.

"You must hunt him like a woman, not like a man," Mei-lan said gently, slipping in under his anger. "Make him come to you. The next time you learn where this killer is, or how to get a message to him, find a way to lure him to you."

Alexander nodded, thinking of Jessica. He was uncertain how much he could ask of her, and still unclear about her relationship with the

Commissar. Was it just Jesse's infatuation with revolution, or had there been something more?

"Thank you." He rose.

"And when you find this dangerous man," added Mei-lan, "remember to use your weapons, not his. Remember the turtles. Be in your element." Alexander winced as he recalled the powerful hands that had gripped his throat in the train. He considered what weapon he himself must use.

As he rode home, he thought of the Derby, now only three days away. The race would determine his future in Shanghai, for it embodied the dilemma he now faced: choosing between how he wanted to live and what he had to do.

Honor was the heart of it. Should he cheat, or should he ride like a gentleman? Should he continue the compromises necessary to avenge his family, or abandon that obligation and pursue a decent new life, perhaps with Jessica? If he continued to seek vengeance, he would never be able to extricate himself from the dirty involvements it required. Should he choose an old world of revenge or a new life of opportunity? He knew his sense of responsibility towards his family's past could ruin his future. Is that what they would want for him? Of course Katerina made it even harder. She was still an open wound.

"You two are looking rather grave tonight," said Hudson in a loud cheery voice. He rose from the table with another Jessica, the sturdy rosy-faced daughter of an English shipowner visiting from Singapore. "Is it love or war?"

"Hard to tell," said Alexander, glancing at Jessica. He was still shocked that she had known Polyak all this time. Even if he accepted the explanation of her foolish politics, the smell on her lips was an added horror. "I did not kiss him," she had insisted. "I just lit his pipe sometimes." Still, that was an intimacy she had never offered Alexander. But now that she was helping, he was trying to see things differently.

"A bit of each, Billie," said Jessica James, replying at the same time as Alexander and kicking him hard beneath the table.

"Wrong leg," said Alexander.

The jazz band started "Nagasaki," and Hudson and his Jessica left them for the oval dance floor of the enormous second-floor ballroom at the Cercle Sportif.

"Hot ginger and dynamite, there's nothing but that at night," crooned the singer. "Back in Nagasaki where the fellers chew tobaccy and the women wicky wack woo."

An elegant party of Chinese was drinking champagne at the next table. They were smart and at home in English dinner jackets and in hairdos and gowns copied after Hollywood and Paris. The Kungs, Alexander realized, stepping over briefly to pay his respects to his father's friends. Captain Ricard and his family were seated with the French consul at one of the favored corner tables away from the door. Alexander knew François would be annoyed to see him with Jessica. That itself would be worth a bottle of champagne.

"How could Billie find another girl with my name?" said Jessica irritably after he rejoined her. "Do you think he did it on purpose?"

"Perhaps he named her after you." Alexander tried not to smile, but his eyes gave him away. "Maybe Jessicas come here to save China."

Jessica James looked at him and shook her head.

"Maybe I should find another Alexander."

All around them more couples left their tables as the orchestra changed. Smart in wing collars and black tie, their black oiled hair center-parted above soft oval faces, the eleven members of the Filipino band took their places and began the featured American fox-trot, "Blue Skies."

"Carlo!" Alexander raised one hand and called over Shanghai's most celebrated sommelier, said to have come to the port long ago while on the run from a gambling crime in the town for which he was named.

"Count Karlov," bowed the steward, a discerning judge of social distinctions. "Beychevelle, sir?"

"Not tonight. Send two bottles of Heidsieck to Captain Ricard's table with my compliments, Carlo, if you please." He handed the sommelier one of his father's old calling cards.

"Don't you ever forget your obligations?" said Jessica, surprised at the gesture, but remembering the flawed party prize at the Salle d'Armes so many months earlier.

"I wish I could." Alexander smiled without humor in his eyes, then placed both hands flat on the table, thinking of one of the reasons he wanted to see Jessica this evening.

"I need your help again, Jesse, with Polyak."

Jessica shook her head. "I've already done all I can. I gave you the last address I know of." In a way she was relieved for both men that Alex had missed Viktor. She noticed the lines of concentration in Alexander's face. They made him look like a much older man. She feared this pursuit of vengeance was corrupting his youth and perpetuating the horrors of his father's generation. "I thought you asked me here to dance."

"I did, but I need your help once more. You may not have the Commissar's new address, but you know some of his message stops and names. Help me work out which place to send him a message, and what to say to draw him out." He took her hand. "Please, Jesse. Think of my kidnapped sister. What if you were in her place?"

"I understand," said Jessica, hating the idea of betrayal but knowing what she had to do. She wondered if Viktor had raped Katerina as well. She felt she knew the answer. "I promise I'll do my best."

"Thank you." He squeezed her hand. "I'm sorry, but I have to catch Polyak now before he leaves Shanghai. I cannot wait."

Disturbed by his fervor, wishing to smooth out his lines of worry, Jessica stood up. "They're playing 'Tea for Two.'" She held out both hands. "May I have this dance, Count Karlov?"

Alexander's face seemed to clear. "Jesse James can have them all."

They danced until the music stopped. It had to be three o'clock. Their cheeks parted and Jessica stood still, holding Alexander's hand and looking into his eyes. Her cheeks were flushed. Despite his leg, Alexander danced like one of Shanghai's celebrated Russian gigolos, for a time making her feel as if she were the only woman in the world. Perhaps the dance floor of the Cercle Sportif helped. To make it less tiring, so the guests could dance till dawn, it had been built on springs. Jessica was glad that for once she had been careful not to try to lead. She reached up and adjusted the small white rose in the lapel of his dinner jacket.

Alexander was aware that François Ricard was staring at them as the young Frenchman left the dance floor with his portly mother. Carlo and the ice bucket were waiting at their corner table.

"There is one man Viktor always wanted to hear from, but never did," Jessica said. She hesitated to give the name, certain it would work if she did.

"Wouldn't Polyak also want to hear from you?"

"I'm not sure." She shook her head. "I don't think Viktor trusts me anymore, and I haven't heard from him since he moved. But he sent this man a copy of his new code book."

"Who is he, Jesse? Tell me."

She still did not want to give away the name. For her, it represented hope for China. As Alexander waited for her to answer, they stood alone while the dance floor cleared. Jessica thought of the powerful speaker she had seen at the cotton factory before the fighting started.

"Mikhail Borodin," she said. "Lenin's man in China."

"Good morning to you, sir," said Alexander. To his astonishment, he was beginning to enjoy these meetings at the Dragon.

Mr. Hak Lee held two cigarettes in his left palm. The round tin, almost empty, lay on the table before him. With peculiar dexterity he sliced both Pickwicks from end to end with the pointed tip of the nail of his right forefinger. He crushed the tobacco in his fist as if exterminating some insect, then rolled it between both palms while the small flakes fell to the floor. Alexander glanced at the swimming snakeheads while the Master of the Mountain cupped his hands against his nose and breathed deeply until he began to wheeze and cough.

"Good morning, young Count," the lean Chinese said at last. "I understand you ran very fast in today's early morning gallop." He nodded as if pleased. "Your pony's times are the talk of the track boys."

"Are they?"

Hak Lee nodded. "One boy carries my clock."

"Taiga is running well," Alexander said. Too well, he thought.

"You will not forget how she must run in the Derby," said the Chinese, not making it a question. "Second or third."

Alexander held Hak Lee's eye, then drew a sheet of paper from his pocket and unfolded it. With Big Ear he was learning to advance his concerns at the beginning of the conversation.

"I have here, sir, a list of six places where Viktor Polyak is known to collect his messages. A noodle shop, a pharmacy, two fish mongers, one tailor and a teahouse. The Commissar likes fish, and he changes disguises." Alexander handed it over and hoped that Jessica's list had not grown too old.

"These men, and their families," sighed Hak Lee, taking the list without examining it, "will learn to regret providing such a foolish service to an enemy of China."

"But not yet, please. I need your help, sir, to have these places watched until Polyak appears at one of them. If my friends and I tried to do this, they would be onto us at once." He recalled standing at the pork shop with Semyonov. They must have been obvious as two white camels.

"Of course," said the Master of the Mountain. "This is what my people do every day. It is what I used to do, hunting for my debtors. But what will you do after he appears?"

"I will send a message to him there, one that he is not likely to ignore."

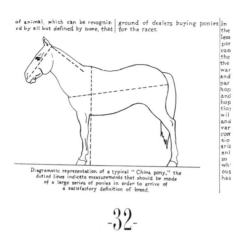

Diagramatic representation of a typical " China pony," the dutied lines indicate measurements that should be made of a large series of ponies in order to arrive of a satisfactory definition of breed.

-32-

"This is harder than I thought, Alex." Jessica looked up from the table and shook her head. She put down her pencil and took a bite of dense Russian cheesecake. Before her lay the sheets on which they were trying to replicate the simple code book that she had helped create and had copied twice for Viktor Polyak. "I can't remember all of it, but I think most of this is right."

"We'll put it aside," said Alexander, pleased with what she had done, impressed with her memory for detail, "and take a fresh look later." He unfolded a different sheet and pushed it towards her. Their hands touched comfortably. "In the meantime, let's work on the message. Here's what I suggest." Jessica looked tired, he thought, distressed, lacking her usual fresh spirit. He wondered again about her relationship with the Commissar.

Then he felt something fussing at his feet. He looked down and saw baby Lu scratching his boot. He stretched one arm and rubbed her silky head. The girl's round face rose slowly above the edge of the table like a sunrise on the horizon. Alexander gave her a messy bit of cheesecake in his fingers and Lu resumed her work.

"You're crazy." Jessica looked up white-faced and dropped the sheet of paper. "If Viktor believes this comes from Borodin, he'll do what it orders him to do, murder more of Shanghai's leading White Russians." She remembered Viktor's voice and eyes when he spoke of his mission in China, his work as a disciple for that man Dzerzhinsky. "He'll try to kill you first, because of your family, then perhaps one or two of your friends."

"Good." Alexander recalled Madame Wong's advice: make Polyak come to him. Jessica's concern confirmed Mei-lan had been correct.

"Please, Alex." She took his hand and squeezed it. "He'll kill you. I know Viktor. He hates the old Russian families."

"I agree." Alexander nodded. He darkened with renewed rage as he remembered the disfigurement of his father's body and the sound of his mother's neck cracking. "He will try. But at least this way Polyak won't leave Shanghai without my having a chance at him."

Jessica shook her head. Biting her pencil, she went back to work and checked the code sheets.

"And in the meantime," said Alexander, rising to attend to his horse, "Taiga has a race to run tomorrow."

A strange odor caught his attention over the fresh smell of the straw and dung. It could only be Krupotkin. Alexander turned as the aggressive voice spoke with unusual softness, with almost a touch of hushed conspiracy.

In the background, Alexander felt the clamor building all around them: the bustle of the stable boys and trainers, the stamping of horses, the cries of hawkers and tipsters, and the rumble of the excited growing crowd as Shanghai gathered at the Race Club. He did not need Pavel Krupotkin to add to the rising pressure of the Derby.

"I have laid a fortune on you today, cousin. Too much money," said Krupotkin, sweating from his stroll around the racing stalls. "More than I have ever wagered on a race before."

He paused and stared at Alexander expectantly, apparently anticipating some assurance of victory. His mouth was slightly open. A touch of what seemed like white foam clouded his lower lip, as if an egg had cracked when dropped too hard into boiling water, releasing stringy traces of partly hardened albumen. "How will this mare of yours run today?"

Alexander looked at Cornelia Litchfield in her revealing ruffled garden-party frock. "Good afternoon to you both," he said, recalling what Cornelia, tipsy, had whispered to him at a party the week before. "I'll be leaving the prince as soon as I've saved enough. Unfortunately my tastes keep getting more expensive."

"Good afternoon, Count," she said now. Leaning across the low stable door, Cornelia kissed Alexander on the cheek. For a moment the jasmine of her perfume protected him. No wonder she used so much. "And good luck." She touched his other cheek with one hand. "You are so handsome in your colors." Then she turned and looked at her companion.

"Here, Pavel." She handed him a fresh white handkerchief.

"Is it true?" said Krupotkin eagerly, snatching the linen as if annoyed by her assistance. "Has your Tiga run the fastest morning gallops they have ever clocked here?"

"Taiga," corrected Alexander sharply. Consumed by his dilemma, he had not much patience for the prince.

"It's Taiga, dear," joined Cornelia.

"Don't talk to me about horses, Corny," Krupotkin sputtered without looking at her. He wiped his mouth and continued hurriedly, before others could arrive and interrupt him. "Should I lay on some more money, cousin? Are you certain you are going to win?"

"Taiga's never been so fast," said Alexander truthfully. "She's in her prime, top condition. Just take a look at her, decide for yourself." This was the only Russian bettor who did not concern him. "And she's running stronger every day." Taiga still had the heart and the go of a steppe pony, but now with the benefit of proper food and care.

"Well then," said Krupotkin, "on your word, I'm going to bet the Casino on her. Most of the money is on Desert Gold." He dropped his handkerchief amidst the stable litter that the *mafoo*, the Chinese horse boy, was busily sweeping together.

Krupotkin leaned his face close to Alexander. When he opened his mouth to speak, it was like the lid coming off a sewer.

"But see you don't disappoint me, cousin." He led Cornelia away to the betting counters as the noise of the crowd grew.

Alexander stroked Taiga's nose. He still did not know what he was going to do: win for his promise to his father, and for the way he wanted to live, or lose to help avenge his family and retain a powerful friend through all the struggles that still mattered. If he chose to lose, he thought, it must be not because he feared Big Ear, but rather because of what he owed his family.

As the mafoo led Taiga from her stall, Jessica James walked up.

"I know you're going to make us all proud today." She took his hand. "Especially your father." Behind her, the din of the assembling crowd grew louder every moment.

"Thank you, Jesse." Alexander kissed her, grateful for everything she was doing to help him find the Commissar, and loving her for it.

Alexander checked the uneven stirrup lengths, then handed her his cane and swung up on his own. He remembered the last time he had done this, with his father giving him a boot up before the Griffin Handicap.

"Please try to stay on this time." Jessica smiled. "Good luck."

Now Alexander could feel the tension in Taiga. He spoke to her and leaned forward and stroked her neck.

The mafoo walked them to the starting line. Alexander felt his own excitement build. The Derby was the season's biggest race. But he was still tormented by the decision he had to make. All his instincts told him to ride like the devil for the win, but he knew that if he denied Hak Lee and made Big Ear lose his bets, the man would be bound by his code to punish Alexander. He would break the Salle d'Armes and upset the scheme to catch Viktor Polyak. It would not be the loss of the money that turned the Master of the Mountain against him. It would be the insult, the lack of respect.

As Alexander lined up with the other eleven starters, his stomach tightened until he could hardly breathe. The stands were full. The center of the track was thronged. The din rolled over him. The noisy moving crowd in the aisles and stands seemed like some huge beast stirring in its lair. The course itself was slick from last night's rain. He glanced along the line of nervous, barely controlled, tight-prancing ponies. He recognized several animals and half a dozen riders: Hideo Tanaka, François Ricard, Billie Hudson, Captain Sassoon among them. All were too busy to acknowledge one another.

What should he do? Perhaps he could win the race and still find a way to make everything else come right.

The flag dropped and the horses bolted forward. Alexander's last thought as Taiga burst from the start was that his father was riding with him.

Almost at once Taiga shared the lead with two others, Sassoon's famous Desert Gold and another pony he did not know. Alexander gave his mare a little restraint, as he would even if racing to win. But she could never win, he thought, if he let her run her own frantic pace over every furlong.

As they approached the first turn, with Tanaka coming up, pressing to join the leaders on the inside, Alexander gave Taiga her free head. If he were wrong and if she could win it her way, maybe he should let her do it.

He felt Taiga's chest expand between his legs. Her energy reached him through the reins as she strained forward and gave all the muscle of her heart. Taiga ran as if she were free again and wild and on the steppe, with the biting sandy wind gusting in her mane. She lost almost no momentum on the turn. Soon he pulled away. Only Desert Gold could hold this early pace beside him. Captain Sassoon rode full forward, high above his pony's shoulders, his legs bent double at the knee, his body parallel to the ground, his head low, his hands half-way along the animal's neck, the way Alexander wished he could ride.

Taiga moved closer to the rail, keeping away from Desert Gold, now a nose ahead on the outside. Alexander was aware of a patch of wet track ahead, a shiny pool gleaming in the grass. Then he saw a whip raised in the air inside by the rail. Hideo Tanaka pressed forward. The slight young Japanese crouched like a goblin over his pony's whithers. His chestnut, shorter than Taiga but with heavy shoulders and chest, seemed to be flying. Dirt and damp sod were thrown up by its pounding hooves. Soon Tanaka, squeezing forward on the rail, was half a stride past them, his pony shouldering slightly into Taiga's path.

Then the chestnut slipped in the wet grass. Its right shoulder dropped and Tanaka's pony fell in front of Taiga.

Faster than Alexander could react, Taiga struck the falling animal. She plunged forward, almost jumping but striking the chestnut with all four hooves before crashing down on top of the other pony. Alexander was flung clear. Thrown into the rail, he broke the wooden fence with his shoulder and fell through it into the screaming crowd.

With a spectator helping him on either side, he scrambled to his feet and leaned on a fence post. His head seemed clear.

"Are you all right, sir?" said a senior British police officer, hurrying to him and taking Alexander by one arm.

"Thank you, yes, I think so," said Alexander slowly. He looked onto the track.

Taiga lay on her side, struggling to rise, kicking violently, snorting. Her thick tail flayed the grass. Farther down the track, the chestnut was already up, still agitated as it high-stepped from side to side. Hideo Tanaka, covered in dirt and grass, was trying to hold his straining pony by the head.

Alexander limped towards Taiga as the officer kept the crowd from the track. The remaining ponies thundered around in the distance. He could feel their pounding hooves through the infield grass.

Taiga was throwing her head violently from side to side and slamming her jaw against the ground. Then she snorted and lunged with her shoulders and rose with a rocking plunging motion when Alexander came to her.

As she struggled to her feet, he saw a jagged bone pierce through the skin of her lower right foreleg. For an instant the hoof touched the grass. Immediately she lifted her broken limb and whinnied, screaming shrilly as he had never heard her.

"No, Taiga!" Alexander cried. He put both arms around her neck. Behind him he was aware of the race finishing distantly to muted cheers. Taiga's nose pressed into his side. He felt her tremble against him.

The police officer walked towards him.

"Would you like me to do it, sir?" the Englishman asked gently, holding a revolver in one hand.

Alexander shook his head. He hugged Taiga and cupped her soft mouth. He put his face against her twitching cheek and closed his eyes before stepping back and taking the revolver from the officer.

Taiga turned her head towards him, as if appealing. He cocked the weapon and aimed for the mid-point between her eyes and ears. He was careful to press the tip of the barrel squarely against her forehead lest the bullet be deflected. He fired. Taiga seemed to turn her head away. Then it swung back towards him and she fell at his feet. Her mane rested over the toes of his boots. At least he had let her run freely once more.

Alexander felt the man take back his pistol. He heard screams from the crowd. But he could not see for the tears that flooded from him. He was aware of Billie cantering to him and leaping down, hugging him as Alexander sobbed. It was the end of so much. His proud start in Shanghai, his adventure in Mongolia, even his first Taiga at home on the estate, all seemed to die with her.

-33-

"I did it," said Jessica, short of breath. She stepped off her bicycle, her words quick and her eyes wide. "I did it. I had a coolie leave the letter with Viktor's favorite fishmonger, in the alley off Changan Road."

Alexander put one hand on her cheek and kissed her, then took the handlebars and walked the bicycle inside the riding hall.

"Bless you, Jesse." He set the bicycle against a wall and turned and hugged her. "You deserve a drink." He was happy she seemed pleased, even excited, by what she had been doing. Now she was part of it. Perhaps she did possess the active courage of the Decembrist women.

They sat in the yard and sipped vodka and lime juice from Russian tea glasses. Steam curled from a teapot that sat atop the old samovar on a side table. Alex seemed to be getting more Slavic every day, she thought. She knew he would appreciate her more if she could cook, but Jessica was not going to spend the rest of her life in a Russian kitchen.

"Now you have to be careful, Alex. I mean it. Viktor will come after you, sooner than you think." She glanced back through the hall. "Where's Ivan? You have to keep him and several of the others with you until this is over."

"Too much of that and Polyak will never come for me." Alexander shook his head. "Your friend hasn't survived the czar's police, the civil war, the Triads, the warlords and the Sûreté by being careless."

"He is not my friend anymore. He never really was," said Jessica, stiffening, but more comfortable now that she was committed to her choice. "You know I am only trying to help you." She tossed her blue cap on the table and shook out her curls.

"Excuse me, Jesse. I didn't mean it that way." He touched up their drinks. He knew she was right. If Polyak were still in Shanghai, he would not delay. The question was which prominent Whites he would hunt down first. It would be Alexander's fault if he started with someone else and killed them. But Alexander guessed he himself might be the first. That would clean up the Karlovs and destroy one of the centers of Little Russia.

"I promise, Jesse, I'll be careful." He covered her hand with his. "Remember," he said, "I saw him break my mother's neck."

She drank and did not reply.

"And you must be careful, too," he added. "He probably knows we're friends."

"I'll be fine," she said. "My parents are back. They want me to go to Hong Kong with them for a week. Some missionary conference on Christian education. It could mean so much to China." It seemed to Alexander that her expression said she would rather stay with him.

"Mr. Hak Lee is waiting to see you in the other room," said Madame Wong. A sketch of a girl, round-faced and without breasts, perhaps ten or eleven years old, rested on the table before her. "He asked me many questions. He has taken such an interest in you."

"He certainly has," Alexander said. A one-third interest, he thought. "I hope he is not too upset about the Derby."

"You need not worry about his losses. Only about his attitude towards you. Mr. Hak Lee believes in one thing: what we call *guanxi*, direct personal loyalty."

There was a knock at the door. The Russian bodyguard opened it from the outside and showed himself and nodded. Alexander rose and kissed Mei-lan gently on the cheek.

"Were you injured in the race, my young Count?" asked Hak Lee after Alexander sat down next door.

"No, sir. Only my horse."

"I hope you will find one more like her in Mongolia next spring."

"I will try," said Alexander, the thought very much in mind. Somewhere in those grasslands, there was another pony like Taiga.

"If you do, you will purchase her with my compliments." Hak Lee inclined himself forward. "And next year we will win or lose the Shanghai Derby together."

Alexander's jaw tightened. He could see there was no end to this involvement.

"I'm sorry about the losses," he said.

"Such things happen." Big Ear shrugged. "Until we became partners, I was accustomed to losing at the track. Others lost on the Derby as well, and in that there is always opportunity and profit."

"Opportunity?"

"I speak of your cousin, Pavel Krupotkin. The prince is a new man. Now he is a debtor rather than a creditor." Hak Lee paused and breathed several slow deep sighs. "I have purchased the notes for the prince's losses, as I have from time to time, and the Belle Aurore itself has now passed into different hands." Big Ear held up his own, the shiny backs of his long yellow nails towards Alexander. "Perhaps you would like to take a share with me in this casino?"

"That might be interesting," said Alexander, tempted but hesitant.

What would he be expected to give up for this? "Now I am waiting for Viktor Polyak to pay me a visit."

"I understand, Count Karlov. If I learn more, you will hear from me," said the Master of the Mountain. "Must I warn you to be careful? Should I provide you with some assistance? I have men who understand these matters."

"No, thank you, sir," said Alexander. "I think this is a matter for us Russians."

-34-

The engine of a parked motorcar growled outside the shadowy entrance to the Salle d'Armes. Alexander felt his stomach harden. Standing beside Osetra in a darkened corner of the hall, he cupped the nose of the big grey. For a moment he saw nothing. In his pocket was the message from Hak Lee: "He comes tonight."

Suddenly a big figure darkened the entrance, then took several slow steps into the gloom of the vast interior. The dark shadow reminded Alexander of a bear padding through the forest at night. The intruder stopped. He squinted towards the dim lamp that glowed like the narrow beam of a distant lighthouse from the yard at the other end of the riding hall. He walked forward, before pausing and turning to his right.

Alexander heard the stairs creak as the man climbed towards what had been his father's bedroom. A door opened. The footsteps became still more quiet. Alexander felt a chill on his throat. There was a brief flare of light as a match was struck in the entrance to the room.

Alexander took the moment to swing his good leg over the tall Mongolian saddle and mount up. He held the horse motionless. A pony snorted and pawed in the stable yard behind him.

He heard fresh footsteps entering what had been his old room. Another match was struck, then burned down to darkness. Alexander had the impression that the intruder was standing at the head of the stairs and staring around the riding hall as if his eyes were becoming accustomed to the gloom.

In the far dark corner of the ring, leaning forward in the saddle, his cheek on the horse's mane, Alexander calmed Osetra with gentle strokes on the shoulder. He heard heavy steps descending the stair, as if the man now felt confident that he was alone. The right moment should come after the visitor left the bottom step.

Alexander gripped the brass hilt of his father's heavy sabre in his right hand. The dark figure advanced towards the center of the ring. Alexander reminded himself to wound, to disable, but not yet to kill. Tonight he must find out what had happened to Katia.

"Ura!" yelled Alexander, standing in his stirrups and digging in his heels. The battle cry of his father's regiment echoed across the hall as Osetra sprang forward. Alexander drew the sabre and charged like a Hussar.

A pistol flashed in the darkness as Alexander's blade reached its target. He thought he felt something punch Osetra. Then he twisted his wrist and turned the blade downward. He felt the curved sword penetrate as the gun cracked a second time. Viktor Polyak screamed a curse. Splinters flew from the metal-trimmed wooden saddle.

Osetra reared and bucked before bolting forward and crashing into the side wall. Alexander fell to the floor, his bad leg jammed against the wall, his weapon lost. Gasping for breath, he raised himself. He peered into the shadowy darkness and made out the running figure as it paused at the entrance, then turned and fired twice.

Bullets struck the wall beside Alexander as he remounted Osetra.

When he arrived at the entrance, he heard the two words the man yelled at the driver before a car door slammed.

"Shanghai Station!"

The vehicle pulled away, accelerating rapidly down the Chemin St. Bernard. Alexander gave chase on horseback. But after crossing a few streets he pulled up at the corner of the Avenue Molière, Osetra agitated and skittish beneath him. He would never beat the car to the station through the darkened empty streets, or once there be able to limp after the running man and catch him before he boarded. And if he did, he had no weapon, except for his short pocket knife, whereas Polyak, wounded as he must be, still had his pistol.

Alexander knew it could be only one train: the Night Express for Nanking.

He turned to his left and trotted Osetra through the deserted streets towards the edge of the city as the half-moon rose.

Soon he was in open Paper Hunt country, "Rubicon Country," the farmland northwest of the city where he had ridden across the railroad tracks so often in the past. He kicked Osetra and began to canter in the moonlight. As they approached the sharp curve near the creek where every train slowed, he pulled in the horse and looked back towards Shanghai. The great city sparkled in the distance, a low dome of brightness that gave way to the moon. He felt entirely alone, like a single Russian warrior on the steppe.

After a time a round bright light emerged from Shanghai and grew larger as it moved along the track towards him. A line of black smoke followed across the more pale blue-black sky.

He walked Osetra back to the stretch of track just before the curve. He paced the horse up and down along the gently raised embankment as the train approached. He stroked the gelding's neck and thought of his father on horseback. He had always looked so graceful, not like that mutilated body at the end. Alexander felt a slick patch of blood where a bullet had nicked Osetra's neck. He was angered by the injury. He wondered if the tall saddle had saved him from a belly wound.

When the train began to slow for the curve, Alexander began to trot. As it approached him, he pressed Osetra into a canter and finally into a full gallop while the black locomotive roared past like an angry demon in the night. Alexander squinted into the smoke that gusted around him. The cars of the passenger train swept alongside. Osetra, unafraid, accustomed to battle and cannon fire and excitement, stayed with the train along the embankment.

As the baggage car passed them, Alexander turned Osetra's nose towards the train until the rapidly revolving wheels seemed to be beneath them. He freed his left foot from the stirrup and reached out with his right arm like a polo player swinging for a wide ball. He seized the passing handle of the rear platform and felt it jerk him forward. He hung on with both hands as the horse pulled away. His right leg found the metal step but his left banged painfully against the side of the car. Unable to bend it at the knee, so numb that he could not move or feel his foot, he feared his left leg might swing against the steel wheels.

Alexander pulled desperately with both arms. He hauled himself up onto the top step and swung open the upper panel of the split door. He climbed over the lower half and fell into the blackness of the baggage car.

For a long moment he lay on his back in the darkness. If he were right, he was once again on a train with Viktor Polyak. This time the outcome must be different.

Alexander sat up and leaned against a wooden chest before striking a match. Steamer trunks and metal footlockers, belted suitcases and leather hatboxes and a lone golf bag were piled around him. He was disappointed to see no gun cases. He considered breaking some locks and rummaging through the luggage for a weapon, perhaps a revolver or large knife if he were lucky. Wounded though Polyak was, and although Alexander was far stronger than when they last met, he knew that the Commissar would probably still outmatch him in a fight.

He started to stand, then collapsed as pain from his leg over-whelmed him.

For a time he sat quietly in the darkness, as if collecting himself before a fencing match, concentrating only on what was immediately before him. It was still a long run to Nanking. He prayed that his leg was not damaged much worse, and that he could carry out what he must do. He recalled Mei-lan telling him to use his advantages in times of conflict and adversity, rather than struggling to overcome his weakness. He had tried to do this, by attacking on horseback with a sword, but he had not succeeded.

"If you were a hawk, would you walk across the fields to catch a rat?" Mei-lan had asked. "No. You would dive like a knife from heaven. If a serpent, you would slide quietly and strangle it."

He considered what he would do afterwards if Polyak were on the train and if he himself managed to survive. Back in Shanghai, he promised himself that he would do better at combining honor and success, by making the stable the beginning of much more, and perhaps by building a life with Jesse. He would have to discover a way to free himself of Hak Lee. And in due course he would find his sister.

Alexander rose, able to see by a patch of moonlight entering through the top half of the door. He cut open the locked golf bag with his pocket knife. Only the English, he thought. He shook his head and remembered Billie Hudson sipping from his flask between shots while he practiced high chips over a field of spring millet. Using the heavy brass head of the putter like the handle of a cane, Alexander hobbled slowly to the front of the baggage car, dragging his left foot, his lower leg numb and the knee on fire.

The door at the end of the car seemed to be secured from the outside. He unbolted the top half, swung it inside and climbed painfully out onto the narrow platform. The next car was a second-class coach. The heads of the passengers stood out in the dim light above the tops of the seats like figures in a light show. Alexander brushed off his filthy jacket and torn trousers, then opened the heavy door and entered the carriage.

Astonished, a party of Chinese merchants looked up at him from a game of mah-jongg that was spread on a case across their knees. They whispered busily to each other as he hobbled by, leaning on the putter.

The following car was a first-class coach with separate compartments and opposing upholstered seats, some already converted to sleepers by busy porters in blue trousers and white jackets. Limping slowly down the windowed side aisle, Alexander checked each compartment as he passed. Had he lost Polyak once again? Torn between mortal tension and a fear of disappointment, he proceeded through the next car and the next, his senses taut like a wolf hunting in the moonlight.

He entered the restaurant car and paused outside the lavatory at the near end of the coach. He sniffed. Over the smells of beef Wellington and Peking duck he detected a familiar odor: Telkhis Mixture.

Alexander edged closer to the dining room and looked carefully along its length. Shaded sconces cast a pink light over the diners. The windows were black against the Chinese night. Waiters were carrying food from the kitchen at the far end of the car. Most tables were occupied by European guests and a few by Chinese. Many were smoking as they took a cocktail and considered the menu. One man was lighting a cigar over an early pot of coffee. But no one was smoking a pipe, and Viktor Polyak was not there. Alexander stepped back into the entrance corridor and sniffed again. The dense smell of the Turkish tobacco was coming from the lavatory, he realized, not the dining room.

He backed against the door to the car and reached up. He loosened the lightbulb until it no longer illuminated the narrow passage before the dining room. Then he opened the heavy entrance door behind him. He prevented it from closing by jamming the golf club into the hinge. Finally he walked past the lavatory door, turned around and waited with his back to the dining room. He opened his pocket knife.

He heard the water running, then a deep cough. The bathroom door opened.

Viktor Polyak stepped into the dim corridor with a pipe burning in his mouth. His right arm was underneath his jacket, his right hand tucked into his blood-soaked shirt between two open buttons. He seemed to fill the narrow passage.

Alexander hurled himself against the man.

Polyak grunted and staggered backward. The door crashed open behind him. With Alexander on top of him, knife in hand, the Commissar fell on his back onto the steel platform outside the car.

Alexander raised his knife above Polyak's throat.

"Where is my sister?" he demanded. "What have you done with Katia?"

"Karlov! You stupid little bastard!" Polyak seized Alexander's right wrist and smashed his hand against the steel post at the edge of the platform. The small knife fell into the darkness between the tracks.

Alexander's right hand felt paralyzed. He must keep Polyak pinned down so his enemy could not use his superior strength.

But he could not stop the man. Polyak heaved up, braced one leg against the end of the car and rolled until he was on top of Alexander. Feeling helpless, Alexander struggled violently but could not free himself. He was desperate to kill the man, but he himself could hardly move.

Alexander's head hung over the end of the platform. He was deafened by the wheels rattling directly beneath him. Astride Alexander, the big man seized his head between both hands. Warm blood flowed down Polyak's right arm onto Alexander's face and into his mouth.

"Little Count Karlov, are you?" said the Commissar, breathing hard. "Katia? Katia? Your sister loves me. She is in a party training school in Moscow. She is one of us."

He began to twist Alexander's head to the left, but Polyak's right arm did not have its full strength and his hand was slick with blood. "If I was not going to kill you now, one day Katerina Krassilnikov probably would."

Feeling the muscles straining on both sides of his neck, Alexander gasped and tried to bend Polyak's fingers back with his left hand.

Ignoring Alexander's effort, his teeth bared, his mouth open wide and snarling, Polyak shook Alexander's head from side to side as he twisted it.

Unable to see clearly, Alexander blinked and squinted. Polyak's blood filmed in his eyes. Alexander's left hand fell against the metal deck. Desperate, spitting Polyak's blood, he braced himself and managed to get his right knee under the Commissar's heavy belly. Then he felt something hot burning under his hand: Polyak's pipe.

Alexander clutched the glowing pipe. He felt that his neck was about to snap. He lifted the pipe by the stem like the handle of a dagger and jammed the hot bowl into Polyak's mouth. Instantly he released the stem and punched Polyak in the jaw with all his strength. The Commissar's mouth snapped shut around the burning pipe.

Polyak released Alexander's head and leaped to his feet. He opened his mouth and screamed above the clamor of the running train. He spat out the pipe and several broken teeth as Alexander kicked him violently between the legs.

Viktor Polyak fell backward over the edge of the platform. Alexander heard his body hit the tracks between the cars. The Commissar screamed once more and was gone.

-35-

Two sedan chairs hesitated at the wide entrance to the Salle d'Armes. A big man in a chalk-striped suit strode forward and looked about the great riding hall. He squinted into each dark corner like an exterminator hunting rats. After a moment he nodded at the bearers and led the canopied chairs across the dirt and sawdust that covered the floor.

Alexander rose from the long table in the yard. He advanced to the doorway and watched the small procession approach his other guests. Behind him, dressed more smartly than he ever had been in Shanghai, Ivan Semyonov got up from his seat in full Cossack kit. His stained red mustache was freshly trimmed. His soiled apron hung from a nearby nail.

Seated between Hideo Tanaka and Billie Hudson, Jessica James watched Alexander walk away and noted how much he was favoring his bad leg. She admired his glossy black boots and his crisp Russian shirt. His shoulders seemed broader. She was happy she had been to the hairdresser and that she was wearing her first French dress, copied from a fashion magazine by a seamstress on the Avenue Foch. It made her feel different. She hoped Alexander would take her upstairs after lunch. Jessica was proud of the success he was making, but she felt guilty for not regretting the death of Viktor, and she was disturbed by the loss of his work for China.

For the first time, as his father had always intended, Alexander was hosting a lunch party in the full Russian country style, as his mother might have done at the estate at Voskrenoye. He had done his best to make it a credit to them both. He hoped he would never have to lose this home as well.

The embroidered linen tablecloth, the cut glasses and the silver all came from the back room of the Siberian Fur Shop on the Avenue Joffre. Ivory chopsticks with silver caps were set beside the knives. Magnums of Beychevelle stood in two silver coasters that covered patches in the linen. Yellow roses filled three vases. Bowls of thick sour cream rested nearby. Small white name cards engraved with a double bear's head were centered on the napkins at the seven places. Only one place was not set. One person was missing. His sister, Katia. Alexander recalled the new name that Polyak had said was now hers: Katerina Krassilnikov.

Gregori stood by the table with a second bottle of champagne and reviewed the arrangements. He, too, was thinking of long summer afternoons at Voskrenoye. Gregori was pleased that the early guests had enjoyed the first zakuskis. The thirsty Britisher and the young Jap had devoured the pelmeny and the tiny pickled tomatoes like well-mannered wolves, gobbling each morsel as if it were their first. Vodka waited in an ice bucket near the head of the table. Often the Major had liked to pour for his guests himself.

Behind Gregori in the open kitchen, Li, obedient for once, or at least cooperative, was preparing Russian dishes with Chinese implements and pots. Strogonoff and marinated short ribs simmered in the woks, releasing the steamy odor of chili, mustard and garlic cooking together.

Asparagus in egg sauce and crisp orange ducklings waited at the edge of the fire, the fat birds already stuffed by the hetman with dark bread crumbs, walnuts and raisins. Apricot meringue tarts and cold zabaglione were hidden under cloth covers on the side table.

Gregori glanced to one side, nodding when he saw Chung pumping up the samovar with an old boot.

Alexander limped to the first sedan chair and pulled back the curtain.

Madame Wong took his hand and descended slowly. He had never realized quite how slight she was. Behind them Mr. Hak Lee emerged and peered about with dark darting eyes, like an immense raven, or some tall blue-black bird hunting insects.

Hak Lee was pleased with his young partner. Upon hearing Alexander's report, Hak Lee had sent two experienced men to dispose of Polyak's body. They had found much dried blood but had returned with only a severed left hand discovered between the tracks. Big Ear had served this remnant to his hungry debt collectors. The clean bones of the large hand now rested in the bottom of one fish tank as an inspiration to his debtors. Either the body had been dragged for miles by the train or the local farmers had disposed of it, no doubt not wishing trouble with the police after they had robbed and stripped the corpse. Meticulous, his men had found two other souvenirs farther down the track: a pipe, and a small German knife, useful perhaps, now that the young count was learning to throw knives like a master. These things Hak Lee had given to his Russian partner, together with the large grey horse his men had recovered from a nearby farmer.

"Welcome to the Salle d'Armes," said Alexander, bowing first to Mei-lan, then to the Master of the Mountain.

Mei-lan smiled and released Alexander's hand. She waited for Hak Lee to precede her and dipped her head as he passed. Then she glided towards the table with short steps, her body bent slightly forward, swaying gracefully like a slender willow in a breeze.

"Good lord," said Billie Hudson under his breath as he watched the two Chinese approach. Noting their feet, he compared Mei-lan's tiny red silk shoes with the black boots of the tall gaunt Chinese. Was this Gilbert and Sullivan, or an American gangster film? Hudson emptied his glass and sought to catch Gregori's eye.

"Madame Wong," said Alexander, "may I present Miss Jessica James." He was excited that Jesse was looking so lovely. For the first time, she was also elegant.

And so he introduced his friends before holding Mei-lan's chair at the place to his right. He noticed the slight stiffness with which his Japanese guest and Hak Lee acknowledged one another, perhaps due to the recent Chinese boycott of all things Japanese. That morning Japanese warships had arrived in the harbor. Already there were nearly as many Japanese living in Shanghai's Little Tokyo as there were Russians in Frenchtown.

"Tanaka," said Hideo to Hak Lee. The Japanese youth bowed from the waist, his body rigid as the two parts of an iron hinge, his hands at his sides, his small face flat and clear as a glass door. Neither man had the wish to touch the other.

But towards Alexander, young Tanaka was showing extreme courtesy, and more than that. Following Taiga's death in the Derby, Hideo had sent a message to Alexander by the consular courier. "Forgive me for this sad accident," read the letter under the crest of the Rising Sun. "Please call on me if I may be of service to you in the future."

"Rice is ready," announced Li to Alexander with a bow.

Only at the races, thought Hudson, had he ever seen such an agglomeration. At least today there were no Frenchmen. He was annoyed that this Cossack across the table seemed to be swilling more than his share. Bullet loops on one's coat at lunch? Just looking at the hairy red-faced villain reminded one of dripping bloody steel and lathered horses galloping about a smoky field with empty saddles.

Gregori poured, then approached carrying a silver platter with a mass of shiny black caviar and thin round blini, lightly buttered. He filled the vodka glasses while the guests finished their champagne.

"Excuse me, if you please," said Alexander, rising at the head of the table. Before continuing, he reached across and turned a wine bottle until he could see the sailboat on the Gironde.

He caught Jesse's eye and she smiled into his with private promise. He noticed the small jade bear swinging from her neck by a fine gold chain. He prayed she would reserve her politics for another afternoon. He knew she was shocked to be lunching with a woman in Madame Wong's sort of business. With an even more trained eye than most of her sex, Mei-lan, of course, had assessed Jessica in an instant and noticed where the green bear hung. And just when Lily had become free at last, thought Mei-lan, with her protector having returned with his wife to Edinburgh. Still, this Russian boy, prosperous now, would not be the first young man to accommodate more than one entertainment while adventuring in Shanghai. He had better hurry, however. Lily had met a film producer, one financed by Mr. Hak Lee. Soon she would become one of the new *vedettes* of the Shanghai cinema.

"May I welcome you all to the first Russian country lunch at the Salle d'Armes," said Alexander. He lifted his champagne glass. A breeze came through the yard, carrying the fresh strong smell of horses, another touch of Voskrenoye.

"And may I welcome you all to Shanghai," sighed Mr. Hak Lee in the brief silence that followed Alexander's words. "And to China," he added quietly, lest they all forget. His black eyes slid slowly over the lean hard Japanese boy, self-contained as an egg. Then he gazed at the other guests and wondered how long Shanghai would be like this. Big Ear considered whether his own world would survive theirs. Perhaps he should make plans for Hong Kong.

Hudson banged his enamel caviar spoon against his empty glass.

"Let us drink to our host, Alexander Karlov," said the young Englishman with spirit. He smiled at his friend. His champagne long finished, Hudson lifted his vodka in toast. "To Count Karlov!"

"Hear, hear," said Jessica, proud of Alexander. Then she glanced down and winked at the Chinese baby playing on the ground next to Alex's chair.

"Thank you," said Alexander. He looked at Ivan Semyonov and the Cossack nodded. His eyes were red. Without speaking, the two Russians emptied their vodkas to a different Count Karlov.

"To Shanghai!" said Alexander Karlov.

A Note About *Shanghai Station*

The golden days of old Shanghai probably lasted from the collapse of the Manchu dynasty in 1911 until the first Japanese attack on the city in 1932. During those 20 years, Shanghai was the most cosmopolitan, romantic and adventurous city in the world. I first became fascinated by Shanghai when I worked in Hong Kong for a British trading house in the 1960s, and studying Shanghai since then has brought together many old Chinese connections and interests spanning the last seventy years.

My parents visited Shanghai during their year-long around-the-world honeymoon in 1932. They stayed in Victor Sassoon's Cathay Hotel in the celebrated harbor-view apartment with its own dining room and panelled library in which Noel Coward later stayed while he was writing *Private Lives*. Thanks to the birthday generosity of Anthony and Susan Hardy, I stayed in the same apartment in 2002 when I was in Shanghai continuing my research. The silver spigots were gone, but one could still watch the shipping on the Whangpu River (now known as the Huangpu River) from the raised marble bathtub. Once the grandest hotel in all of Asia, the Cathay is now called the Peace Hotel. The Hardys came from Hong Kong to join me there on my birthday, as did William and Caroline Courtauld, also old China hands long resident in Hong Kong and Singapore. Caroline Courtauld, the author of magnificent books on Burma and Beijing's Forbidden City, generously shared with me in Shanghai and elsewhere her expertise and her friendships.

Through her friend Diane T. Woo in New York, Caroline Courtauld introduced me to Michael Kan, whose father, Robert, had been the first Chinese to attend Eton. There at school in England, Robert Kan had known my own father and his three younger brothers. The second of these, Michael Bull, had been stricken with polio one summer, leaving his right leg paralyzed in a heavy steel brace. The headmaster wired my grandfather that Michael could not return to school as sports were so important and the school was very spread out. My grandfather cabled back that his four sons would continue to attend school together, wherever that might be. At the time my father was captain of three sports and president of the Eton Society. The four brothers continued at Eton. There Robert Kan arrived one fall day in 1919 and saw my father carrying his crippled younger brother Michael on his back around the school. Bobby Kan became their friend, and never forgot that sight. In due course, he named his own son Michael after my uncle, to whom this book is dedicated.

At school, my uncle Michael replaced my father with a motor-cycle, and, despite his brace, took up fencing, an extremely popular sport at the time. Since his right leg was rigid, he was obliged to lead with his left leg and therefore to fence left-handed, dragging his bad leg as he advanced. Like Alexander Karlov, Uncle Michael was unable to retreat. He won the Eton foils championship in 1923, 1924 and 1925, and the epée championship in 1925, and was runner-up in the inter-school sabre championship in 1924. While at Magdalen College, Oxford, he fenced all weapons and won the University Foils Championship in 1928, when he was Captain of the Oxford University Fencing Club. Many years later, when I visited London as a young man, Uncle Michael would take me around and introduce me to the city. He was still a strikingly attractive, modest and unusually charming man with a limp and a heavy steel brace. Alexander Karlov is fencing for him.

Karlov's instructor Achille Angelo draws his name from two great fencing masters, Achille Marozzo of the 16th century and Domenico Angelo of the 18th century. Most of the fencing quotations and principles attributed to Alexander Karlov's maestro are taken from the writings and life of reputedly the greatest swordsman in history, Aldo Nadi, "the human sword." At six feet and 135 pounds, his body had the whip and strength of a rapier. He and his brother, Nedo Nadi, won eight gold medals in the 1920 Olympics in Antwerp. Aldo Nadi was never defeated as World Professional Champion. His hand truly was quicker than the eye. He combined cerebral and physical brilliance; courtesy with ferocity. Devoted to the Italian foil with its cross-bar handle and leather martingale, Nadi wrote in his book *On Fencing* that he could always disarm any man who faced him with a French foil. I must also thank my old instructor Ido Marion, the fencing coach during my days at Harvard, and St. Clair Clement, the gifted fencing master at St. Bernard's School in New York City, a school named after a small street in Brussels. The Chemin St. Bernard, the address of the Karlov Salle d'Armes, takes its name from that. I am indebted to Mark Hardy a spirited fencing champion and old China hand, for his editorial assistance.

In Russia itself, the Soviets killed many old fencing teachers following the revolution of 1917. In later years, according to the prominent fencing writer Nick Evangelista, they "reinvented" fencing in order to compete in the Olympics, but favored power and athleticism over technique, contrary to the ethic of Aldo Nadi.

I have taken a few liberties in writing *Shanghai Station*, but I hope never disrespectfully, and generally with a view to distilling much of the essence of old Shanghai within the short time-frame of this novel. In 1919, there were two railroad stations in the city, North and South. North Station was the principal station, connecting to Soochow, Nanking and Peking. That is the "Shanghai Station" of this book. In 2002 I walked across Soochow Creek and what had been Chapei to North Station, which I found was being torn down and replaced, an undiscriminating process that sadly is destroying most of old Shanghai. Both traditional Chinese neighborhoods and the elegant tile-roofed houses and tree-lined streets of the French Concession are today being demolished and replaced by high-rise sterility on an inhuman scale. Only the Bund and a few blocks have been saved.

The First National Congress of the Communist Party of China took place in the French Concession of Shanghai in 1921, not in 1919. Mao Tse-tung and two representatives of the Communist International attended. Mikhail Borodin actually arrived in China in 1923. One of his two Soviet military aides in China was called Vladimir Polyak. A Cossack leader named Semenov did fight in Siberia. The Cercle Sportif Français was not completed until 1926. Its main building and handsome ballroom still survive, attached to a modern hotel, the Okura Garden. In addition to the Cathay, the other old grand hotel that survives today is the Jin Jiang, where I enjoyed splendid hospitality. Captain R. E. Sassoon rode Desert Gold in the races and in the Paper Hunts in 1924. The Canidrome did not open until 1928. The Green Dragon Teahouse that I describe on the Rue Lafayette is much like the actual Treasure Teahouse on the Rue du Consulat, as noted in Lynn Pan's interesting book, *Old Shanghai—Gangsters in Paradise*. My description of the Great World Amusement Palace owes much to Josef von Sternberg's presentation of it in *Fun in a Chinese Laundry*. Sternberg himself directed the 1932 film *Shanghai Express*. Harry Warren's song "Nagasaki" was not written until 1928. My Mr. Hak Lee is a combined homage to the legendary Triad gangsters Pockmarked Huang and Du Yuesheng, so well described in Martin Booth's *The Global Phenomenon of the Triads* and in Harriet Sargeant's important history, *Shanghai*. The night of the long knives when the Triads, supported by the Kuomintang and the French police, went after Shanghai's Communists and killed five to ten thousand people, did not take place until April 1927. That was the "Shanghai Massacre" that in 1934 Andre Malraux featured, with brilliant bias, in *La Condition Humaine (Man's Fate)*, a book so well written that its prose is magical even in translation.

As always with works involving research, much is owed by this book to the writings of others, most notably here to the old journalists of the China coast, who produced in Shanghai *The North-China Daily News*, which I read on microfilm for each day of the years 1918 through 1925. Barbara Baker, Fox Butterfield, Stella Dong, Chris Elder, John King Fairbank, Orlando Figes, Tess Johnston, Bruce Lincoln, Evan Mawdsley, Pan Ling, Priscilla Roosevelt, Harrison Salisbury, Edgar Snow, Theodore H. White, Frances Wood, and many others also helped to educate me. C.W. Campbell's *Travels in Mongolia* (1902), Arthur Ransome's *Russia in 1919*, Carl Crow's *Handbook for China* (1921), and Harry Franck's *Wandering in Northern China* (1923) assisted the travels of Alexander Karlov. Howard S. Levy's *Chinese Footbinding* is the indispensable source for most writers on that subject. Most rare and precious was *A History of the Shanghai Paper Hunt Club 1863–1930*, a volume given to me by a lovely special friend who had a bottle of champagne and a birthday cake with a chocolate bull on it waiting for me at the old Cathay Hotel in Shanghai on May 15, 2002.

Specific expertise was generously provided on Russian matters by: Tanya Chebotarev, Curator of the Bakhmeteff Archive of Russian History and Culture at Columbia University; Steve de Angelis, who is presently translating the diaries of Czar Nicholas II; Professor Mikhail Gokhberg of the Russian Academy of Sciences; Victoria Wohlsen of the Tolstoy Foundation; Baroness Garnett Stackelberg, who lived for ten years in old Shanghai; the learned Marilyn Swezey; and by that extraordinary scholar and repository of old Russia, Marvin Lyons. Often, too, I recalled that devoted admirer of my grandmother, the late Sergei Sheremetev, himself a remarkable scholar and splendid representative of much that was best in czarist Russia. His family had owned several of the great estates totalling over two million acres, including Kuskovo, where thousands of guests would arrive in columns of carriages that stretched across miles of countryside. There artists, musicians, English gardeners and troupes of actors were a permanent part of the household. Up to 50,000 guests watched sea battles staged on Kuskovo's man-made lake.

As a young man in need of education, I was privileged to be taken around New York's museums by Sergei Sheremetev, a linguist and scholar of the arts with a complex worldly taste and erudition virtually unknown today.

Thanks to Caroline Courtauld and to my late uncle Michael, while researching this book and attempting to understand what Shanghai was truly like, I have had the privilege of getting to know some of the remarkable survivors of another China. Most of them are highly intelligent, elderly ladies who have survived war and revolution, dislocation and deprivation, but who have retained their dignity and humor while being the custodians of a vanished life. Instead of being shrouded by grief and cynicism and wallowing in a sense of loss, they are uniformly optimistic and appreciative.

Lily Yen, who died this year after celebrating her 100th birthday, was one such lady. Long before the Communists took over China in 1949, she had studied chemistry at university and taught school in districts of severe rural poverty. At that time, she has written, "When girls were born, they were often dumped in the road." During the murderous and barbaric "Cultural Revolution" of 1966-1976, ten families were moved into her magnificent house and she herself was obliged to live for four years in a closet under a staircase. Over lunch at her apartment in Shanghai in 2002, Lily Yen told me how much she had enjoyed the children of those invading families, and how she had learned to relish the arts of survival, especially sewing clothes from old scraps of cloth. During the period of this novel, Lily Yen herself had been a young girl of extraordinary privilege in Shanghai, and she was generous to me with her insights and experiences of the time.

For many Chinese and Shanghainese details I am also indebted to the intelligent assistance of Michael Kan, Mrs. Wellington Koo, Diane T. Woo, Genevieve Young and others. Gene Young's step-father, Dr. V. K. Wellington Koo, one of the great gentlemen of the last century, was acting Prime Minister of China during the 1920's and served as ambassador to France, Great Britain and the United States. Dr. Koo was the only individual to represent his nation at both the 1919 Versailles Treaty that ended World War I and the United Nations founding conference in 1945 in San Francisco, where he signed the U.N. Charter on behalf of China. Dr. Koo had refused to sign the Versailles Treaty due to its transfer of a German "treaty port" in Shantung to the Japanese. During the 1960's he was Vice President of the International Court of Justice at the Hague. His widow, Mrs. Koo, thoughtfully recommended a number of corrections to my manuscript. Lily Yen was the sister of Mrs. Koo. Mrs. Koo's 98th birthday was recently celebrated at a dance at the Waldorf Astoria in New York. Twenty-four of her favorite dishes were served at her birthday dinner, including Longevity Noodles with Preserved Ham and Heart of Shanghai Cabbage.

With regard to racing and horsemanship, I was fortunate to be advised and edited by my friend Preston Madden of Lexington, Kentucky. Presto is the master of Hamburg Place, the breeding farm of seven Kentucky Derby winners. He instructed me on the saddest aspect of working with horses: how to shoot one properly. Arthur Kreizel helped me use his equine library when I was visiting him in the mountains of Mexico, where I survived a jarring fall from his best horse. Details about Mongolia and Mongolian horsemanship were drawn largely from *Around the Sacred Sea*, my son's splendid book about his two-thousand-mile 1993 horseback expedition around Mongolia and Siberia. Christopher B. Ross, a distinguished collector and scholar of military history, assisted me with various military details. Bobby Short, who knows Shanghai himself and relishes its former spirit, kindly advised me on appropriate period music. Dimitri Sevastopoulo and Donald E. Zilkha assisted me with elusive sources. Two restaurants patiently provided me with congenial refuges where I spent many hours working on this book: the Morning Star Café in Manhattan and the Café 1931 in Shanghai.

Both my former agent Carl Brandt, and my present agent Eric

Simonoff of Janklow & Nesbit, contributed a great deal. One of the pleasures of completing *Shanghai Station* was the opportunity to work with that extraordinary young Chinese artist Pan Xing Lei, who drew the map and chapter illustrations from material that I provided for him. Lei was introduced to me by Ethan Cohen, who has displayed Pan's original work at his distinguished gallery on Walker Street in downtown New York. I must also thank my patient readers, although they too often confused friendship with criticism: Paula Carleton, Anthony J. Hardy, Winfield P. Jones, Constance Roosevelt, Dimitri Sevastopoulo, Baroness Stackelburg, Genevieve Young and, most ruthlessly critical and insightful of all, my son Bartle.

—Bartle Bull
November, 2003